THE FAE CHRONICLES
Unraveling Destiny

AMELIA HUTCHINS

Unraveling Destiny
The Fae Chronicles Book Five
Copyright © September 26, 2017 by Amelia Hutchins

ISBN-13: 978-0-9970055-7-8   ISBN-10: 0-9970055-7-2

Cover Art Design: Vera DC Digital Art & Photography
Cover Art Illustrations: Vera DC Digital Art & Photography
Edited by: E & F Indie Services
Copy Editor: Gina Tobin

Copyright © September 26, 2017 Amelia Hutchins
Published by: Amelia Hutchins
Published in (United States of America)

10 9 8 7 6 5 4 3 2 1

Dedication

This book is to all those who lost loved ones over the last year. To the fans who didn't survive to read it. And to all of you badass women out there going through a rough patch, you got this girl. You show me every day how strong women are.

Tammie, you show me what being strong is all about. God received an angel when he took Kimball, but he lives on through you and those beautiful girls. You are my rock star. Don't let anyone kill that beautiful sparkle.

To Gina, Mari, Tasha, my street team, and the role players who spend countless hours helping and loving these characters as much as me, thank you. Without you these books wouldn't have what they do, a home in each heart they live in.

For Sasha Sweet, Danielle Martin who both lost a piece of themselves this year, you are stronger than any of us could ever hope to be, even if it doesn't feel like it yet. Don't lose your sparkle.

To the fans who have remained with since the beginning, and the new ones I've picked up along the way, you rock my socks off!

To my family who don't mind me disappearing for countless hours to write, I love you monsters the most!

Zoey, I love you more than you will ever know.

ALSO BY
Amelia Hutchins

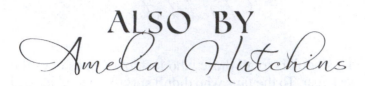

The Fae Chronicles

Fighting Destiny
Taunting Destiny
Escaping Destiny
Seducing Destiny
Unraveling Destiny
Book 6 - TBA

The Elite Guards

A Demon's Dark Embrace
Book 2 - TBA

A Guardian's Diary

Darkest Before Dawn
Death Before Dawn
Final Part, Book 3 - TBA

MONSTERS SERIES

Playing with Monsters
Sleeping With Monsters - Late 2017/Early 2018

WARNING

This book contains sexually explicit scenes and adult language, and may be considered offensive to some readers. It is intended for sale to adults ONLY, as defined by the laws of the country in which you made your purchase. Please store your files wisely, where they cannot be accessed by under-aged readers.

This book is not intended for anyone under the age of 18, or anyone who doesn't like lip biting, throw your ass on the bed, tear your clothes off and leave you panting dominant alpha male characters. It's dark, dangerous, intense, gritty and raw book. Scenes are dark, disturbing and scorching HOT. This read is soul crushing, tear jerking, leave you hanging on the edge of your seat, fast paced read.   Side Effects may include, but are not limited to: Drooling, lip biting, wet panties, crying and screaming at the author. If any of these things happen, do not seek medical attention—get the next book in the series and enjoy the ride!

~~*~*~*~*~*~*~*~*~*

THE FAE CHRONICLES

Unraveling Destiny

Chapter ONE

I felt my hair being pulled, and pain ripped through my stomach as something hit it. A pained groan slipped from my lips. Something warm and wet dripped down my face and I cried out even louder than before. We were under attack! I mumbled for Ryder to call for the Elite Guard, and to let loose the beast on whoever had invaded our room and was attacking.

"Synthia," a deep rumble of laughter sounded; that laugh mixed with gurgling noises, forced me to pry one eye open. It felt as if each lid was held in place by lead weights. "I don't think we need the Elite Guard or the beast to deal with the babies."

"The hell you say, those are not babies; they're monsters. What the hell do they have against sleep?" I mumbled as I watched as Kahleena gurgled and continued to drool on my face and neck as she looked down at me with a cherubic smile. "Minions of darkness—that's what they are. Ones sent by the Mages to slowly torture us through lack of sleep and cuteness."

Zander head butted my stomach while Kahleena yanked at a handful of hair to better support herself.

Cade continually kicked the other side of my stomach while he sucked greedily on his tiny fist. I was seriously rethinking the entire idea of lessening the handmaidens' duties to give us more time as a family.

"They wanted their mother," he said, his golden eyes aglow with laughter. "I doubt they are sent by the Mages, Pet. They've been hanging out with Ristan too much, and I think they thrive on mischief," he laughed huskily. The sound washed over me and I smiled, unable to resist the sound of his husky timbre. He made his way back to the bed and sat beside us, lifting Kahleena as he untangled my hair from her tiny hand. He carefully moved Zander, and gave me enough room so that I could sit up.

Once I managed to sit up, I smiled down at the little monsters, who watched me back. I leaned over, kissing Kahleena on her cheek, and watched as her golden eyes, which were so much like her father's, glowed, as if they were lit from within. My little one had begun to thrive, and was by far the naughtiest of the three. She was also the leader, and I suspected she was the smartest of the trio. While Cade seemed to be the muscle, Zander would happily watch the chaos the other two wrought on us, which Zahruk speculated would make him the lethal one as they grew older. I was pretty sure Kahleena got her brains from me, even though Ryder was quick to take credit for it.

"My little monsters," I whispered softly. My throat tightened as I considered just how blessed we were. I picked Cade up and cuddled him to my chest. Zander watched, his little lips quivering until Ryder picked him up in his free arm and rested on the bed beside me.

"They have to sleep sooner or later, right? I'm

beginning to understand why my father kept his brood of children locked in the pavilion."

I hit his arm and smirked. "Maybe we should lock ourselves in the pavilion?" I laughed, and watched as he frowned.

"We could, but we're planning a wedding, remember?" he murmured, leaning over to place a gentle kiss on my temple.

"We could always elope. Las Vegas is still a viable option," I offered. "Besides, I totally have a thing for Elvis and all his bling. Those sequins," I sighed heavily, and added a little growling noise deep in my throat. "It's sexy as fuck."

"The entire realm is anticipating this wedding, Synthia. The Mages have been quiet for a while, and I intend to marry you properly. Tell me, who is this Elvis and where can I find him so I can kill him?"

"He's dead already, and you and I are freaking exhausted. I can't even keep my eyes open. If the Mages showed up, they could literally push me over and I'd be a goner. I'm getting a little worried that Danu has been so quiet. She's been constant since the last time the Mages tried something, and now it's just silence. It's not like her. I know she was keeping her distance because of whatever happened between her and Ristan, but she has never gone completely dark before. It makes me curious to know what really transpired between those two, and how it could be so bad," I mused out loud as my fingers absently stroked Cade's soft curls, hugging him a little tighter as the thought of war played in my mind. "And I'm also worried about their future and what it will hold."

"They have a Goddess for a mother—their future

will be whatever they wish it to be. They will be loved, and raised to be strong and fair to others. We will win this war and heal this world. I won't allow anything less. Our children will have the world, whichever they choose, at their fingertips, and we will be right behind them, building them up." He glanced up at me with a smirk of fond amusement. "Things are changing quickly for all of us. I seem to remember that it wasn't long ago that you thought that the Horde King pranced around wearing high heels and lipstick, Pet. We have come a long way since then."

"I said that, didn't I?" I frowned, and he nodded.

"You were perceptive and guarded back then. Now, I just wiggle my eyebrows and your clothes just fall off," he laughed.

"That's not how that works. You take them off with magic; I have very little to do with it," I groaned. "Gods save me, but I love you. Even though you drive me batshit crazy, Fairy," I smiled. "But you can't know what the future will hold. Everything can change in a blink of an eye around here. Let's just try to focus on today," I whispered as I leaned over to kiss him, only to hear all three babies begin to snuffle and cry. They had something against Mommy and Daddy kissing. It was both cute and annoying at the same time. Zander grabbed his father's hair, and Kahleena wailed while shedding big fat alligator tears as she tried to push me away from him. Cade…well, Cade growled like a puppy, a trait he'd inherited from his father.

"Maybe they *were* sent by the Mages," he groaned and pulled away.

"Told you," I laughed, as a knock at the door disrupted the bliss inside the bedroom. I watched as

Ryder looked in my direction, quickly glamouring me into a pair of jeans and a black T-shirt. Once he was satisfied that I was dressed properly, he quickly kissed my cheek, much to the dismay of the babies, if the disgruntled looks on their faces were anything to go by.

"Enter," he called out, his eyes twinkling as Kahleena made a growling noise while she watched him, her lip puckered out.

"It's about time you got the fuck up," Ristan quipped as he peered around the door at us, his eyes filled with laughter. He leaned against the doorjamb, much to the delight of Kahleena, who gurgled and held her arms up, ignoring her father for her favorite uncle. He returned her smile, wiggling his fingers at her in hello. "We've got a huge problem. One that can't wait for you to eye-fuck each other or for you to cuddle the little beasties," he said softly.

"What is it?" I asked, curious to know why his mood had shifted so quickly from playful to cautious.

"I think I know why you keep feeling pain, and why we are feeling a disturbance in Faery. I've taken the liberty of calling in the handmaidens. They'll take the babies to the nursery; the Elite Guard is waiting downstairs for you to join us. What we just discovered is something that is hard to explain without showing you."

The pain that had been randomly coursing through my body had been worsening over the last few days, which was also contributing to the lack of sleep. Danu had connected me to Faery so that I'd be able to protect it, but unlike her, if the land died, I wouldn't.

I watched as Darynda gracefully floated into the

room with a steaming cup of coffee, which she set on the nightstand. She was careful to keep it away from little hands as she straightened and smiled down softly at Cade, who placed his head against my breasts and looked at her carefully. Cade was a momma's boy to his core; he loved to cuddle and would spend countless hours listening to my heartbeat, unlike Kahleena who preferred her father, or Zander who had a tendency of watching us with a frown on his cute little brow. Mere months old, and they'd been hitting milestones that terrified me.

It bothered me that we had no idea how long they'd remain little. Fae children aged faster than human children, while Gods could mature from infancy to adults in mere days. With their mixed genetics, we were left guessing and waiting to see how fast they'd mature. Eliran had done all sorts of tests, but each one came back inconclusive, and it left us drawing straws at what the answer would be.

It was part of the reason I'd dismissed the handmaidens from the nursery at nighttime, much to their dismay, and done the mothering myself. I wanted to experience what time they had as children to the fullest. The thought of missing out, well, it fucking terrified me to the very fiber of my being. Not even Danu could tell us if they'd age rapidly or slowly.

I handed a fussy Cade to Darynda and watched while she cradled him as if he'd shatter. Then, she nodded to the other girls, who awaited permission from Ryder.

"What is it?" Ryder asked, his golden eyes filling with black as he turned and nodded to Darynda, who in turn nodded to the nearest of the handmaidens to retrieve the babes.

"My guess? It's the beginning of a huge clusterfuck, which again, you have to see to believe," Ristan stated as he leaned over and kissed Kahleena on her way out of the room. She frowned and waved her arms for him to pick her up, and his brow creased with a hint of worry as he turned back to his King.

I felt my stomach drop, knowing that it had to be something huge for him to be in such a strained mood that he wouldn't take a few moments to indulge my daughter's every whim. I accepted Ryder's hand and stood up, ignoring the coffee that was calling me its bitch from the nightstand.

"How bad?" I whispered and swallowed hard as I contemplated burying my head beneath the pillows.

"At first we assumed it was Lucian's shit going awry, but I'm not so sure it is anymore," Ristan supplied.

"Wait, Lucian's shit was huge. Like, break down walls, world-changing shit," I groaned. We couldn't catch a break. "It's not that big, right?" My eyes held his silver ones as he swallowed and didn't do anything to stop the direction my thoughts were moving in. I swallowed hard again. The knot in my throat lodged there firmly and refused to budge. "Let's go."

"Agreed," Ryder stated. His hand brushed against mine, his fingers threaded with mine and he brought my hand to his lips and kissed my knuckles. "Day by day, Witch," he reminded me as we exited the bedroom.

The Elite Guard waited in the Great Hall, probably having grown impatient for us to make our way to them. Ryder pulled me closer and nodded to the men, probably using the mental link with his brothers that

I'd lost the ability to use over the last couple of weeks. Something had blocked me from being able to channel it, which we blamed on whatever was going wonky in Faery. That or it was because my new powers were playing hide and seek with me as I tried to learn how to use them correctly.

"You go ahead; let me know when it's safe to bring Synthia," Ryder ordered.

Once the men sifted out, I turned and glared at him. "I'm not made of glass, and I don't break easily."

"I know, but we don't have babies around right now who will cry when I do this," he murmured, pushing me against the wall and brushing his lips against mine. Gentle at first, yet that heat grew, as if it was connected to everything inside of me that made me a woman. I growled against his lips as I deepened the kiss, missing the feel of him against me without the babies' radar going crazy and the inevitable fussing that would break out. His hands cupped my ass, and he lifted me as his mouth made my inner hussy scream for more. Loud coughing behind us forced me to release his lips, a saucy smile and muffled laughter bubbling in my throat as Ristan watched.

"By all means, continue. I'll just stand here, watching," Ristan commented. "If need be, I'll be happy to give some pointers as well."

"I bet you would too, pervert," I groaned.

"Most definitely, Flower," he laughed. "If you two are done fucking around, the area is clear and we are ready for you."

"Indeed," Ryder growled, pressing a kiss to my forehead. "The babies can remain with the handmaidens tonight."

"Let's see what is happening with whatever the hell is wrong. Afterwards, we can take a long stroll at the Fairy Pools."

I let my legs slowly drop to the floor before I curled into Ryder's protective embrace as we sifted and the landscape of our new location materialized in front of me. My eyes took in the disturbance; my stomach dropped and tears burned my eyes. This was worse than I could have ever imagined. My hands trembled as what I was seeing came fully into focus.

"That is Spokane," I whispered. "How is Spokane in Faery?" I demanded, unable to compute what the hell my eyes were seeing.

"Step back and look again," Ristan said grimly, his usual cockiness absent from his tone.

I stepped back and exhaled as the magnitude of it hit me. The portal looked new, and it was huge. There was nothing stopping the Fae from leaving Faery, or the humans from entering this beautiful but deadly world.

"What about the other portals?" I asked, trying to wrap my mind around what this meant for both races.

"There is one more like this one; the permanent ones seem to be unaffected," he informed us carefully. "The one near the Pavilion seems stable. This one and the other are behaving like something triggered them to open and grow; nothing we do is working to stop it from happening. We've tried combining magic, and it only makes them grow more rapidly. Without knowing what the catalyst or spell was that triggered this, it's hard to prevent more from opening and growing. Besides magic, we're at a loss for how to stop it. At the rate they are growing now, we won't be able to effectively guard them for much longer," Zahruk interjected, his luminous blue eyes probing mine for a moment before turning to gaze intensely at Ryder.

Ryder looked at the portal for a few moments and raised both hands towards it. He closed his eyes and cocked his head to the side, as if he was concentrating. A small crease appeared on his forehead as the edges of the portal took on a golden tinge that glowed brightly for a few moments, then faded away as his hands seemed to lose their grip and slid to either side of the portal he must have been envisioning in his mind. Ryder shook his head in disbelief and tried again, only to have the same result.

"Portals tend to feel much the way that fabric feels; I can tear one open or seal one with little disruption. I can feel this portal, but it won't allow me to manipulate or pull it in either direction," he said warily.

"Ristan and Cailean said the same thing when they tried. The portals you open are far larger than the ones they create, so we were hoping that you could close this one." Zahruk tore his eyes away from Ryder and looked at me. "Synthia, perhaps you might be able to stop it from growing. Your magic seems to work differently than ours does."

"I blow shit up, Zahruk, or did my last mishap slip your mind so easily?" I snapped in frustration. "I can't use my powers properly, and what happens if I try and I make it worse?"

"It doesn't hurt to try," he countered. "We lose nothing by trying, and right now I'm not sure it could get any worse than it already is. There's a damn open door that leads in and out of Faery—it can't get much worse than that."

I looked at the portal and nodded. He was right: what could it hurt to try? I was connected to the land, and I could feel it—something larger than I could explain was working to open these portals. I closed my eyes, drew power from Faery to me, and sent out feelers. I whispered the spell I'd learned from the Guild for strength.

Old habits, but with the gaping hole between worlds, I needed every trick in my bag to be strong enough to heal the damage. I called on Danu, on Hecate, and whoever else I could remember for strength and courage, and I prayed to the Gods of old for any added blessing with the spell.

Nothing fucking happened.

I opened my eyes and shook my head, only to find myself glowing with an iridescent blue hue that I'd seen once before—on Danu, when she'd been pissed.

"Shit," I yipped as I felt the intense power flowing through me. "Not sure I'm in control here. You guys… should probably back up," I whispered. I turned, aimed my hand at the portal, and power shot from my hand and through the portal, hitting a building that began to crumble as the beam of power hit it. "Not good," I groaned, pulling the magic back to me, watching as the world seemed to hit rewind and the building went back to the way it was, stone by stone, until it was in the condition it was in before I'd screwed it up.

"Gods," Ryder whispered, "did you see that?" he asked of no one in particular, and I turned to look at him.

"Yeah, I saw it, but I'm not sure I believe it," Zahruk replied.

"Flower, aim your hands at the edges of the portal and try it again," Ristan directed.

I turned and aimed my hands at the portal and let the power loose from my fingertips, and sound echoed through me, right before we were all thrown backwards by an invisible power shift. I turned and glared at the portal, gasping as it grew in size. As we watched it almost tripled in size until it was the length of a football field.

"Just great," I mumbled. "I broke Faery."

"You didn't break it," Zahruk offered in my defense, trying to ease my guilt. "If the Horde discovers there's a way out…"

"They already know," I interrupted. "They have to; it's the only thing that explains the reports we have been getting of Horde creatures wreaking havoc in Tèrra. I just don't understand why the portals would be continuing to grow. What if they found a spell or way to eradicate the very fiber of Faery and take away the thin veil between the worlds? Ristan told us he'd seen a new portal that wasn't a part of this world before; what if more than the two you know of are opening up and spreading like this one?"

"If they are, we haven't found them yet," Zahruk gritted out. "Last week we did a portal check to see if any had been opened by magic not linked to Faery; there was nothing. When we did our weekly check this morning, we found this one and the other one both wide open—and yet there was no trace of magic or taint of the Mages. We tried a few things to close them but nothing worked. The more we tried to close them, the larger they grew. We wanted to exhaust all options before we brought it to you, but with the rate they're growing, we couldn't wait any longer." Zahruk frowned, worried as much as I was about what these portals could mean to both worlds.

"You were aware of this hours ago and yet you're just telling me now?" Ryder demanded.

"We wanted you to have at least a little time together before we brought another problem to you. We exhausted every idea we could think of before dragging you out to see this." Zahruk shrugged his shoulders and exhaled a helpless sigh of frustration.

"We can cancel the wedding; at least until we can figure this out," I mumbled. "Faery comes first."

"We're not cancelling the wedding," Ryder growled. "That is not an option. It gives the people hope. We can manage this. Don't argue with me," he added quickly when I opened my mouth to do just that.

"We could do it right now. We could gather everyone today and just say our vows," I offered. I knew he wouldn't do it. Madisyn had been looking forward to it, and Ryder wanted me to have the big wedding that would make a statement to all of the Fae Castes. I also wondered if some of the pressure for this whole lavish wedding thing was what he was raised with. Normally, in their world, royal weddings were never for love; typically, they were for political gain and had to be grand affairs. Oh, he said all the appropriate things, like he wanted to give me a wedding that I always wanted—or what he thought I wanted—and I loved him for it, but this was our world. I didn't need some big ceremony to know he was mine, or to prove that I loved him. I just did, and it was as simple as that. I'd be fine saying our vows barefoot in a meadow, as long as he was beside me.

"I'm giving you a wedding, one to rival the history books. I promised both of your mothers that I would do this properly, and we are doing it. We've been through worse shit together," he whispered. He leaned down and kissed my cheek. "I'm marrying you properly, and I am getting that honeymoon. When the wedding is over, no one will question your position, or which world you belong to anymore."

I raised a brow and frowned. "Someone has?"

"A lot have; most don't think you're truly a Goddess. A few have already been dealt with," Ryder announced.

"You killed them for questioning me?"

"I've killed for a hell of a lot less, Pet," he smirked. "Besides, if I let them live after bad mouthing my queen, others would do so as well. I can't show weakness—this is the Horde. The Horde is ruled by strength and fear."

"You know if you kill them, more will just come forward with a worse theory or opinion," I stated, and he smiled coldly.

"Let them," he grinned.

"Fine, we will do the damn wedding. We have too much to do, and all at the same time. We need to start rebuilding the Guild. We need to get teachers in place and a strong group inside of it to protect it from anyone who challenges our right to lead it. We fix this mess with the portals—and once we do all that, we hunt Faolán down like a fucking dog, agreed?" My eyes locked with his in silent battle; a subtle nod was the only agreement he gave.

"Fucking bloodthirsty wench," he whispered as he narrowed his eyes on my lips. "I love it when you talk like that. Reminds me of the saucy little Witch who walked into the Dark Fortress and shook my fucking world like a snow globe."

"You know what a snow globe is, but you don't know who Elvis is?" I laughed.

"We need to get back to the Castle and figure out what to do about posting more guards at the portals. If any humans get in, this world would consume them before we were even aware they were here," he affirmed as he watched me, ignoring my Elvis dig.

"I'll try seeing if Danu will answer my call," I said, turning to look at Spokane through the portal that continued to widen as I watched it. "We're going to need a lot of help if it continues to grow like this."

"If it continues at the rate it is, Faery and Tèrra will be one world before we even have a chance to stop it."

Chapter
TWO

I paced the length of the bedroom as Ryder leaned against the wall. It was tense between the two of us, and my hands continually balled into fists as I tried to formulate a plan inside my head. The portal was now roughly the length of North Spokane and too big to guard, not that we could even spare the manpower. Doing so would leave the Horde's castle unprotected, and we were already at war.

"You think this is the best option?" His golden eyes tensed and a slight frown line graced his forehead.

"No, but do you see another way?" I asked as I held my hands up helplessly. "How long before the Horde creatures that chose not to follow you leave Faery, or the people your father pissed off notice that there's a fucking hole they can sneak through that is open and unguarded?" My voice was off, filled with pain and uncertainty of what I'd asked him to accept.

"Synthia, we have time to wait for Danu," he offered.

"No, we don't. She's vanished, and that scares me, and now there are ginormous holes in Faery and we have no idea of how to fix said holes. We can't let them stay here. You told me many times that the Horde will seek out a weakness and use it against you. They have three now. I won't stand around and watch the Mages—or any of our other enemies—come in to take them from us, because by now you and I know that they're aware of the huge ass holes in our world. Everyone expects us to send them to Danu, so we won't. We will switch tactics—we'll send them to the Blood Kingdom, and they will remain there until the wedding. No one can know except those who absolutely need to know, and that list only includes those with direct access to the babies. Only your brothers—and out of them, only the few who you trust knowing where we have sent the babies. Madisyn and my father will guard them with their lives, we know that. It's the last place in the world anyone would expect us to send them."

"And if they grow and we miss it?" His voice filled with pain as he considered losing whatever we had of their precious childhood.

"Then we miss it," I whispered through a lump in my throat. "I don't know what Destiny has planned, but I do know that, as their parents, we can't allow them to remain where they are—in danger. They know we love them more than anything else in this world, but so do our enemies. I think we should send Cailean—and probably Sinjinn—with them to hide and protect them. I need to get the Guild up and running. You have an entire kingdom to run. If too many get out of Faery, the entire world is going to know Faery is weak and unprotected. You told me once that ruling has to be your priority, and that shouldn't change. I get that now, Fairy. I get that you gave me away because you loved this world enough to sacrifice your own happiness for it. I can't ask you to change that now, not when Faery needs you the most, nor do I expect you to ignore your duties. I've already called for Madisyn and my father; they'll be here within the hour. I need to ready the babies to travel, and you need to ready Cailean and Sinjinn and keep everyone else away from these rooms."

"I love you." He moved closer and wrapped his arms around me. "I hate the idea of being away from them, but you're right. They're the one thing that can be used against us and we can't chance it. Not with those portals growing by the hour. If they made me choose between you and the babies, and this world, it would be my family every time."

"Pray to the Gods that they're merciful, and that they allow them to remain babies a little while longer. Madisyn will bring them home for the wedding, and for now, we pretend they're still here. We lock down the floor and keep only those who need to know aware of what is happening. Makayla will go with the babies and Darynda will remain here. They would realize something was amiss if Darynda left, but Makayla is new. For this plan to work, we will have to come to their room and stay inside for the times we normally visit them. We pretend everything is the same, and hope our enemies think it is."

It seemed like we always had enemies crawling out of the woodwork, ever since Ryder had ascended to the throne. It had been a tense few months, with only minimal attempts on his life, and no one had been bold enough to make a move for his children, but sacrifices were about to be made to protect this world, and I wasn't stupid enough to assume that I would make it through unscathed. I was sending the babies away to protect them, but also to protect myself from doing the unthinkable. If they ended up in the hands of the enemy, I'd do anything to get them back. I'd destroy worlds to keep them safe, and the thought terrified me to my very soul. They were more than a weakness, they were everything to us.

"I'll get Sinjinn and have him bring Cailean. I'll also call for a war counsel with only the Elite Guard, which won't seem amiss considering what's happening," he whispered as his fingers threaded through mine, and he tugged me closer. "You prepare our children to go visit their grandparents, and we will figure this out. I promise you, they'll only be gone for a few days."

~~*

"Here." I glamoured another baby outfit for Darynda to pack as I mentally screamed for Danu to reply. "Kahleena can't sleep without her bear. Ristan got it from some boutique in France, and she adores it. Please make sure it's packed as well."

"I'll grab it, my lady," Makayla whispered, a frown pulling at her full lips as she wiped at a tear that was making its way down her cheek.

"Stop, all of you. Look at me," I demanded. "I'm barely holding my shit together, so you have to be strong. This isn't forever; it's only until after the wedding festivities have ended."

"We just worry for you," Darynda offered as her green eyes watched me. "You're their mother, and sending them away can't be easy on you."

"No, it isn't, but it will keep them safe," I whispered as I swallowed the lump that seemed permanently wedged in my throat. "In the end, keeping them safe and protected is all that matters."

Our hands froze and our heads snapped to the door as it opened. Olivia tentatively stepped inside and wiggled her fingers in silent greeting.

"Ristan sent me up." She tentatively made her way to me and the stacks of folded clothes on the bed. "He said you could probably use a friend and maybe an extra pair of hands?"

Olivia and I had started out pretty rocky. I hadn't liked her for what had happened to Ristan, yet she'd grown on me once I'd let my defenses down and let her through. She was Ristan's better half now, and they were in love. I understood where she'd assumed the worst with him, and how she'd been played so easily by the Guild Elder, since I'd been raised the same way.

"Help is very welcome, Olivia. You cannot even begin to imagine how much stuff three babies need to go anywhere. It's insane. I need diaper bags filled with clothing and the essentials. My mother and father will be here soon to take them to safety," I chatted happily, as if my entire world wasn't crumbling apart. "Hey, has Alden talked to you yet about the new Guild?" I needed to change the subject, fast. My eyes watched as she absently searched the room. "Olivia?" I called as I stopped what I was doing to look at her.

"Sorry, what?" she whispered timidly, her eyes filling with unshed tears.

I needed to gut something, tear it apart with my bare hands to get away from the crying shit, because I was about to join her and become a blubbering idiot.

"What is it?" I asked pointedly, watching her for any sign of something being off. Her hands trembled as she picked up and started folding a small shirt that had a multitude of tiny blue Dragons splayed across the fabric. "Spit it out."

"Do you know if Ristan wants to have children?" She lowered her voice and bit her lip nervously as she looked at the others in the room. "I mean, I know he's really good with your babies and that he absolutely adores them, but does he want children of his own? His father was an abusive piece of shit who was brutal to him. I wouldn't blame him if he never wanted to have children of his own, but we're together, and I sort of want and need to know."

I gawked a little, watching as her hands absently touched upon her midriff before she swallowed and looked back up at me.

"You're pregnant," I guessed. I watched as the color drained from her face as she looked at the others in the room. "They'll keep your secret; they're bound to me."

"I'm late, really late." She wrung her hands. "I always wanted kids, lots and lots of them. But now that it might be real, I'm terrified. I don't even know if I am ready for this. I mean, thinking you want it and really doing it aren't the same thing. I'm not even sure if I'd be a good mother; I never had one of my own. I don't really know anything about babies; kids, sure. I'm great with kids, but they don't come out talking. I loved teaching, but when the bell rang I sent them back to their dormitories. I've never really even held a baby, much less taken care of one. I don't know if

I can do it. I'm freaking out, aren't I?" she babbled, closing her eyes with an exhale.

"Darynda, bring me Cade, please." I didn't take my eyes off of Olivia as she tried to fight the tears that threatened to spill over. Once Darynda had Mr. Cuddle Monkey in her arms and was walking in my direction, I shook my head. "Hand him to Olivia—she needs to practice."

"I…Uh…I can't actually hold a baby," Olivia squeaked with wide eyes as Cade was thrust into her arms and cooed happily. Panic consumed her features and she started to hold him away from her body. I raised a brow pointedly at her when he started to fuss. "What's wrong with him?"

"Hold him closer to your body, and watch his head. He likes to head-butt sometimes. Randomly, without warning." I waited until she did as I told her to before I went back to glamouring and folding clothes. "Babies aren't tricky. I understand you're freaking out, but they're pretty damn easy unless you're running on no sleep and they don't want to go back to bed. They're also partial to waking you up in the middle of the night for no other reason than to see if you open your eyes." I laughed as she grimaced.

"I'm just a librarian, though, and I won't be able to send a baby to a dorm for the night," she mumbled.

"I was an assassin who killed people. I was pretty damn deadly, and good at what I did. You were a teacher and a librarian. You taught children, and I was kept away from them. If I can do this, you can. Holding them is half the battle, but when it's your own child, it just comes to you. I was terrified I'd hurt them or drop them, but I've done neither of those things. My point is, if a trained assassin can be domesticated and figure out how to swaddle a baby, you're going to be fine," I finished with a friendly smile as she began to bounce Cade gently in her arms. "Cade is pretty easy; he enjoys boobs and getting his stomach filled with pretty much anything the handmaidens come up with. Cade looked up at Olivia and offered her a toothless grin before he rested his head against her breasts.

"How do you do it?" She took a seat on one of the many rockers in the room. "How do you face the Fae every day, knowing you killed a staggering amount of them in our world?" she questioned as she looked down at Cade nervously and back at me. "I know you did it. I filed the paperwork; every report from every mission you went on was archived. Now you have to live among them knowing exactly what they are capable of. You make it look easy, as if you were never on the other side, against them."

I frowned and chose my words carefully, as she was trying to adapt to a world and lifestyle I had barely gotten a handle on myself. "I wasn't just good at it, Olivia. I was the best licensed killer in the Spokane Guild. That part of my life, and yours, it's a part of the past. They've killed ours, and we've killed theirs. Well, not ours per se, but you know what I mean. Humans and the Fae have been at war long before we were even born. I live among them, yeah, but they know exactly who I am. I don't hide my past from them; instead, I'm very open about it. It's who I am, and just because we're here now doesn't change what we are or how we got here. If you can take the blinders off and look beyond the hate that both sides have for each other, you can see the good in them too. It's a choice, like everything else in life. You choose what you do, and how you do it. I choose to be happy and love Ryder, and anything else beyond that, for me, is trivial." I watched as a little line creased her brow and a small frown played on her mouth. "Does it bother you, living among creatures we blindly hated, were taught to hate?"

"No, well, sometimes. I guess it does," Olivia swallowed nervously. "Occasionally I see one of them, and I know exactly how it kills and what they do to humans, and I can't help but hate it. I have every archive and word I've ever written about them stuck in my head. I can't turn it off, and I know a lot of it was nothing but lies, but some of it was fact, and some of the creatures here are horrible."

"Yes, they are," I agreed. "Here, though, they're not the same. Out there, in our world, it's a different playground for them. They need rules, like everyone else. Like most children, when left to their own devices, they create chaos. Ryder kills those who kill the humans maliciously. He enforces his rules and laws. He protects the humans because I ask it of him. That's what I choose to focus on. Look at humans—I mean, some are vicious, hateful creatures created in the bowels of hell. Not all are good, and not all are evil. Satan was an angel who was cast from heaven. He was God's favorite son. It is proof that anyone can fall, and anyone can choose to be good or bad. It is not just one race, or one kind of creature who is bad."

"I think he likes me," she said, smiling sheepishly down at Cade, who watched her with keen interest as he sucked on his fingers.

"Have you told Ristan that you're late?" I smirked distractedly at the way Cade's fingers that weren't stuffed in his mouth wrapped around Olivia's.

"No, I needed someone else to talk to since I was

freaking out. At first, I thought it might just be all the changes I went through, and all the drama of what was going on around us. Elijah would know more about my physiology, but I don't feel comfortable talking to him about this. Ristan's worried about you guys and the portal fiasco, so I didn't think it was the right time to add to his stress." She looked away nervously and began making little cooing noises at Cade.

"He's pretty easygoing—and you could always offer him a heart to chew on while you told him."

"What?" she asked with a deep frown. "The baby chews on hearts?" she gasped.

"Ristan, but never mind, it's probably not a good idea anyway," I laughed.

"Do you regret not being able to feed your children naturally?" She looked away, shy at asking such a personal question.

I winced and then shrugged. "I died. It wasn't really like I had another choice. I can't complain about it considering I'm still here to enjoy them. In the end, nothing else matters. I do intend to find the ones who tried to kill me and my children. I intend to rip their heads off while they're still alive, but that's a story for another time."

"You just seriously said you planned to murder someone with a smile on your face," she laughed nervously.

"Olivia, let's get real for a moment. Do you really think I changed who I was, just because what I am changed?" I took a break from folding the babies' clothes to talk. The babies had a lot of shit they needed to have packed, and we'd barely scratched the surface.

Sure, my parents could glamour anything the babies needed, but I liked that they got the pampering and the mundane things done naturally. It made bonding easier, and I was hanging onto that. "I changed, but I am the same girl you read about. I'm the girl who was raised in the Guild to kill. My brother murdered my adoptive parents because he believed he had some magical way to siphon my powers for himself and become the Blood Heir in my place. He raped my foster mother, leaving her hanging between a mindless drone and a sex addict while my father watched. I had to be quiet behind a hidden panel in the wall as I watched everything that he and his asshole friends did. They were both killed in front of me, and my mother didn't care because she had lost her mind. Alden and Marie saved me, but what happened became a huge part of me. It drove me to be the best. That psycho tried to rape me when I was in labor, and if someone else hadn't stopped it from happening, he would have. Faolán will never stop until one of us is dead. I don't intend to die, which means I'm going to have to kill him. I have to win. Winning will mean that I will never have to look over my shoulder for him again. He's the kind of person this world is safer without."

"I didn't know about your parents," she murmured. "I mean, I knew a little bit about your parents, but they didn't archive the details. If they did, someone removed them because we were all curious about you, and we peeked a time or two. I actually can't fault you for wanting him dead." I nodded absently in acknowledgement of her genuine sadness for my parents and what Faolán had put me and my foster parents through.

"So," I began, redirecting the subject back to her, since she was deflecting. "Are you afraid Ristan will leave you if you tell him you're pregnant?" Without meaning to, I had read her emotions. It had been a challenge to put a lid on my powers lately; one of the more uncomfortable side effects was randomly popping into the thoughts going on in other people's heads. I sensed her discomfort, her inability to tell him for fear he'd react badly and that what they had would crumble. She was also still scared shitless of motherhood and the unknown territory it brought with it. Having just experienced that myself, I could relate.

"Terrified of it," she exhaled. "I want kids, but the thought that it might be happening so fast scares the shit out of me. I didn't have a mom, and I know next to nothing about having babies, or what happens when you do have one."

"Ristan would never leave you. He's loyal, and yes, he can be stubborn as hell, but he loves you, Olivia. He loves children. It's true, and it's no secret that his own childhood was utter shit, but so was Ryder's. Ryder is a pushover when it comes to our babies. He was terrified of them at first, of the fact that we were having a baby, then two babies. He's the best father I could ask for my children, though. He's their protector, and their calm, their comfort. He only has to hold Kahleena and he melts. The entire Elite Guard is made up of the fiercest warriors of the Horde, and each and every one of them turns into a giant man-child when they enter the nursery."

"That's reassuring, but I'd like to keep this between us for now? At least until I know for sure that I am, and I can figure out how to break the news. He has so much on his plate already, and I don't want to add to it."

I studied her and nodded. I didn't want to keep it

from Ristan, but it was her place to tell him when she was ready. Girls had to stick together in this place, since the numbers weren't exactly on our side.

"Fine, but Cade is asleep and I need help packing," I laughed. "Set him in his crib and help me pack these bags. My parents will be here soon, and I need to at least get their favorite blankets and toys packed. Adam and Ristan keep bringing more and they keep getting spoiled rotten," I explained and watched as she smiled and nodded, red curls bouncing as she agreed. "I'm going to the Guild tomorrow to see what is needed for the rebuild; would you like to come with me?"

"Last time I was there, the upper levels were all rubble." She grimaced as her cheeks flushed with unwarranted guilt.

"Pretty much, but the main level is stable and the catacombs are still secure," I clarified. "We have to get it up and running as fast as possible. With the problems with the portals, it's going to be needed now more than ever."

"Mmm, beautiful girls with beautiful babies… so domesticated." Masculine laughter accompanied a smooth, even baritone. It made me smile. I lifted my eyes to the familiar voice and found silver eyes watching me as Vlad leaned against the doorframe lazily. "I never pegged you for a domesticated creature, Synthia. However, it does look good on you."

"Dracula, this is Olivia," I introduced. "She's Ristan's better half."

"We've had the pleasure of meeting already," he countered dryly, and winked at Olivia as she left the room. "Ryder said you planned to go to the Guild. Soon?"

"Very soon," I agreed.

"He explained the situation; are you sure it's wise?"

"No, it's probably not wise but what other choice do we have? I won't allow the Horde to slaughter my hometown. Right about now, I'm guessing it's total chaos out there."

"You'd be correct." He sat in the rocking chair that Olivia had just vacated. "Bedlam and total chaos," he mused as he folded his hands in his lap and stared at me. "Lucian is using ancient magic to keep the hell gates closed, but it won't last forever. The Witches in Metaline Falls have no idea what is happening around them either. Smart, but then again, he seems more than capable of managing chaos than most people. However, the Guild is in shambles, and it's being watched by a small group of Seattle Enforcers. It looks like they've been sitting on it since we paid them that last visit. My guess is that they're waiting for you."

"And?"

"And you're going anyway," he grumbled.

"Yes, I am. Tell Lucian I expect him to pay us a visit and that I am in need of Alden for a few hours tomorrow. He can see that my uncle is escorted and safely delivered. I will make sure he's returned later, when we finish with the new layout and name the new Guild."

"You expect me to tell Lucian what you want him to do?" Vlad raised an eyebrow skeptically. "He won't just do as we ask, Synthia. He's dealing with his own mess, and from what I've seen, he isn't enjoying it.

I'm only aware of what is going on because I've had people watching him and reporting back, which I'm sure he's aware of. Not much passes his notice."

"He's got his hands full, I'm sure. I can't imagine he's enjoying keeping his distance from Lena. It doesn't change anything, though. I need Alden with me tomorrow. I promised him that I would keep him updated on anything that pertains to the new Guild. I'm not afraid of Lucian, and I respect that one single mistake could bring down everything he's worked on since we left them. On second thought, you keep Ryder busy, and I'll go," I said, with a wicked smile on my lips while Vlad swore violently, then swore again as Zander giggled at his words as I vanished.

Chapter
THREE

I entered the lavish nightclub, my eyes seeking out any hidden threat as I made my way to the bar. Behind the bar was a silver fox; his green eyes watched me carefully as I approached him. His jaw was covered in a five o'clock shadow, and the first few buttons of his freshly starched white shirt were left undone. I wanted to order a drink, but the elusive owner was already aware of my presence in his establishment.

"What would the lady like?" The bartender moved in front of me and set his hands on the polished bar. His eyes slowly slid down my body until he found the pulsing brands I'd glamoured. "Fae?" he smirked. "We don't get a lot of Fae in here, not before the downstairs club is open for business."

"I'm not here for that," I purred, smirking on cue, and letting him assume I wasn't a threat.

"Synthia, Lucian will see you in his office," one of Lucian's men interrupted as he placed a hand on my bare shoulder. "Now," he growled when I failed to turn around fast enough.

I turned, smiled brightly, and placed my hands on

his massive chest. "Calm your tits, Man-Bun, before you rip your shirt on accident," I laughed. His eyes narrowed as he let loose a tendril of his power. I followed suit, pretending to ignore the way his lips opened in surprise, or the way those inside the club turned to look as I let out a little too much power. "I'm not here to cause problems. I simply came to speak to your boss. So lead the way," I directed, watching as he closed his lips and jerked his head once to acknowledge that I'd spoken.

"This way, Goddess." He walked towards the back of the club without looking back to see if I was following his lead.

"He's redone this place since we were here last," I acknowledged.

"We're going to be here longer than he intended," he shrugged. "Might as well enjoy the time we're fucking stuck here."

"Fair enough—and you've invited other creatures inside the barrier?" I curiously noted that some of the creatures scattered around the nightclub weren't human, but without looking closer, I couldn't make out what they were.

"Keep your friends close, and your enemies closer," he mumbled, not sounding happy about it.

"Or slaughter them and be done with it." I smirked as his shoulders shook in silent laughter.

"Smart and pretty; deadly combination, from my experience," he chuckled.

"And you have a lot of experience?" I made my way up the stairs and moved deeper into the darkened hallway. Most of the walls were glass, giving the elusive owner a glimpse of his club and any who entered it.

"Not as much as Lucian, but then again, I don't chase tail; it chases me," he murmured before turning and walking backwards easily. "Why run if you don't have to? Make the women work for it."

"Nothing worth having ever comes easily," I noted.

"Nothing worth having comes easily and yet here you are, beautiful," he smirked.

"I'm involved," I countered without skipping a beat.

"Shit happens," he smiled roguishly.

"It does, but should shit happen, nothing and no one will stop me from bringing him back," I warned.

"Sometimes the world doesn't need another hero, sometimes it needs a monster." He stopped in front of the huge doors to Lucian's office. "Heroes care if people are hurt, but sometimes you can't save them; better to have someone who doesn't care about collateral damage," he muttered. His eyes narrowed as if he was trying to get me to understand his point.

"I understand," I agreed. "And sometimes the world needs a hero and villain to balance it out and save both the innocent and the guilty. Sometimes, the monster can be both." The door opened and I turned, giving the owner of the club a seductive grin.

"Lucian," I greeted with a gentle nod of my head in acknowledgment. "It's good to see that you've decided to stick around here." We both knew he wasn't going anywhere anytime soon. Not with Lena still under his spell.

"Synthia, to what do I owe this unexpected visit?" His keen eyes moved to the glamoured brands and back to mine in amusement. "Your fiancé is well?" Slowly those midnight eyes moved to the man beside me in silent dismissal before moving back to mine.

"The Horde King is well," I answered.

"And he let you come here alone?" He gave me an assessing glance.

"I didn't ask permission." I sauntered into his office and his wards sizzled at my presence. "I am my own keeper, and I'm not in danger here. Killing me wouldn't serve a purpose. You are a wealth of knowledge and I simply need to run a few things by you. Answer them or don't—the choice is yours. You can lower the wards, though; I didn't come to start a war with you."

He didn't respond, and yet I felt the wards as he neutralized them. He hadn't moved a single finger, which meant he was more powerful than we'd initially thought him to be. His eyes watched me, and I wondered if he thought I was here for the pleasure that his club below offered, or if he was already aware of my reason for being here.

My eyes skimmed the office for any sign of hidden threats, and stopped at a painting that appeared to be several centuries old. The woman in the painting looked a lot like Magdalena, but certain things were off, such as the slant of her lips and the color of her eyes.

"Has she figured out that she's been reborn?" I glanced over my shoulder. I sensed Lucian was a little too close for comfort, but I also felt his unease as I examined the portrait. I was fishing here, and I knew it, but we had no idea what Lena really was, besides powerful—and dangerous, if she decided to be.

"There's been no proof that she has been," he evaded. "They do look similar, but nothing is certain, nor do I suspect she's Katarina's reborn soul. Lucifer didn't take Lena, he took Kendra."

"I can see some similarities in the two women, which means you can too. You protect her, which says a lot. You could have killed her, and yet you hesitated. I watched you; if you're not in love with the girl, you're in the process of falling in love with her. Then there is the portrait, which has familiar bone structure, so she has at least been born into Katarina's family tree—then again, that doesn't mean much either."

"You're fishing," he growled. I could feel him trying to push past the walls in my mind.

"And you need to stay the fuck out of my head. I am fishing because you don't like to ask for help, but you have it from us should you need it. Lena may not be the one who holds the seal, but she is very powerful, yet she's pure from what I saw of her. She's innocent of any past sins, or at least her soul has been absolved of any. Do you think the seal would allow it to remain so if she held it?"

"Time will reveal the truth," he said smoothly, and then changed the subject, closing it off to discussion. "You're changing." His eyes watched me as mine had just done to him. "Witch, Fae, and now a Goddess. It's quite the upgrade, isn't it? You had to have someone pretty high up the food chain helping you to get where you are."

"That wasn't a question."

"No, it wasn't. It was an observation. The Guild has been leveled?" His tone was innocently curious, but his eyes gave him away.

"Don't play with me. I know you've watched the news, or read a paper. You are, after all, a businessman. You know it was leveled, and you used that destruction to your advantage when you had Ristan take Olivia inside to get you a few things that you or your men couldn't seem to get to," I said carefully. "I've also been aware of your men slinking outside the rubble of the Guild, which tells me you need something else that's hiding inside there. Something that is deep in the catacombs, which are still heavily warded, would be my guess."

"That's not really your business."

"I beg to differ," I countered. "I'm about to rebuild it, and if there's something you need….well, I can be reasonable."

"You don't strike me as one who begs for much, Synthia. You expect me to barter for my own property?" Although the tone of his voice seemed calm and even, the power inside the room was becoming uncomfortable, and I wasn't sure he meant for it to be that way. Whatever the Guild had, he wanted it back.

"Can you get inside?" I tipped my head to the side as I watched him. "No, didn't think so. Whatever it is, it's been heavily warded directly against you or your kind. You'd need someone that the wards wouldn't attack, and you don't have anyone, or you'd already have it. If I am guessing correctly, you were checking to see if perhaps Ristan or Olivia could access it when you sent them in the last time. Like I said, I can be reasonable, but in exchange, I'd ask something from you."

"Indeed, and here I thought you were different from the others," he sneered.

"I have questions, you have knowledge. It's not like I'm asking for your soul, Lucian. I need answers, it's simple."

He turned and moved to his desk, his posture stiff as he rounded the wooden desk and sat behind it, leaning back as if he wasn't at all worried about what I intended to ask him. I ignored his invitation as he waved his hand at the seat in front of his desk. Instead, I made my way to an open bottle of aged Scotch and chilled glasses that waited on a nearby credenza. Had he been expecting company? Was I intruding on plans, or did he always keep chilled glasses on standby? I shrugged off the questions and grabbed both glasses and the bottle of Scotch before I walked to his desk. I moved around it until I was on the same side as he was, then set the glasses down before sitting down on the surface of his desk, letting my legs dangle as I poured the Scotch for both of us.

"What could the Guild have taken that you want bad enough to give me answers?" I mused, more to myself than to him, knowing he wasn't enjoying this line of questioning. "It wouldn't be a file, or you'd have added that to your bargain with Vlad, so it has to be something you didn't want us to know was there. And of course, you took all the files from Lena's house that Kendra copied from the Guild. So my guess is it's something you'd kill for to possess. All I'm asking for in return is for you to answer my questions."

"So, rather than barter, you expect me to answer your questions in order to get my property back?" he growled, remaining still as he watched me.

"I do," I grinned. "Do you really think I would be here if it wasn't important? Ryder doesn't know I'm here right now, and he's not going to be happy when he figures out where I am. I've risked a lot by coming here, so that should tell you exactly where I stand."

"He doesn't know you came to me," he mused with a wolfish grin. "I could take you prisoner and exchange you for what I want, and he'd hand it over just as easily as you would. Only I wouldn't have to answer dick."

"I'm not asking for dick, Lucian," I wiggled my brows, knowing he wouldn't risk making new enemies while he had a house of cards that could tumble at any moment. "I promise that none of my questions are about you, or anything that involves you. It's not about your Witch, nor will it hurt anyone for you to answer them."

"Does it have to do with the failing portals?" he questioned as I handed him a glass.

"It could," I answered carefully.

"Fine, but here's the deal, Synthia. I'm not going to tell you what it is that I need, not until I am prepared to retrieve it. At that time, you'll give me what I want with no questions asked. I will, in return, answer any questions you ask of me right now, as long as you don't ask any that pertain to who or what I am, or why I am here."

"Deal, but you'll answer them truthfully, or to the best of your knowledge."

"Fine, I promise not to lie to you. We can seal the deal with a kiss." His mouth curled into a soft, sly smirk.

"We can seal the deal with a handshake." I held out my hand to shake as his lips tugged up at the corners as he fought off a smile.

"Deal; can't blame a fellow for trying to steal a kiss from the future Queen of the Horde, can you?"

"Actually, I could, but I'd be lying if I said I wasn't the least bit intrigued by what it is you do to the Witches around here to make them oblivious to what you really are. My guess is you bat those pretty midnight blue eyes and they go weak in the knees."

"I do a lot more than that," he murmured.

"No, you don't. You only have an interest in one Witch in this world, and at the moment, she doesn't even know it, does she?"

He growled and shook his head. "Don't go there, not when I'm feeling generous."

"First question," I began, allowing him a respite from his girl troubles. "What do you know about the portals of Faery?"

"Not much, other than someone found a way to open a few and that they have grown to enormous proportions. Even now, the wild Fae are slipping through and causing panic with the humans."

"Do you know if your problems could have triggered it?"

"If my problems had triggered it, Synthia, it wouldn't be portals opening; it would be the veils between worlds coming down. The entire rift that protects Faery would disappear and it would become a part of earth. If that does happen, hell and earth will also become one."

"Do you know how to fix it?" My heart shriveled a little at the thought of what he was describing.

"No. I'm not sure it can be fixed. Much like the hell gates, once they are fractured you either have to close them for good or seal all access to this world from Faery. You'd also no longer be able to open portals to come back. It wouldn't be possible to leave any open or make new ones."

I swallowed the lump that stuck in my throat as his words hit home. I wouldn't be able to come back here, ever. I'd lose Alden and Adrian. We'd be unable to watch over the Fae who were in this world, or the ones we'd sanctioned to be here.

"The Seattle Guild—I know you have people watching it. Have they sent anyone to Spokane?"

"They have, but we've intervened and kept it free of any of their Enforcers. For the most part to protect my interests," he replied carefully.

"You've killed them?" I felt a little sick at the thought of more Guild deaths.

"Yes; however, they would have killed you, so consider it a favor. I knew you would be the one to rebuild the Guild here; Alden told me as much when I approached him about a few other artifacts that the Guild had possession of."

"The Seattle Guild sent them to kill me?"

"They had iron bullets. They had pictures of you and a man with long, dark hair and green eyes, which I assume is the real Dark Prince. The Guild doesn't like to let those who know its secrets live. You know that, so your surprise piques my own curiosity. You thought they'd leave you alone?"

"No, I am not that naïve. I knew they'd come, but I figured they would send Mages, since that's who really wants me dead. Back to the portal thing; I've seen Ryder create some pretty big portals and I know of a few others that can open and close them as well. Do you know of anyone else who could be strong enough to mess with the portals, like opening these giant ass ones that can't be closed by anyone else?"

"I know many who are strong enough. It would require knowledge, and a vast understanding of how the portals function. You're probably looking for someone who lives inside Faery and wants to be freed, not an outside threat. The Guild wants the Fae gone. The Mages are anarchists who want to destroy the Fae, but they lack the knowledge needed to pull something like this off. They've lived outside of Faery and had no idea how to fracture portals. Your threat is, more than likely, inside Faery, doing it beneath your nose. Something inside that world wants out."

"Freaking awesome," I huffed as I leaned my head back and closed my eyes. "Do you have any idea how many creatures reside in that world?" I asked, not expecting an answer.

"Of course, I do. But you're not looking for a needle in a haystack. You're looking for one race that has the ability to move without being seen, and is a part of the land itself. There are not a lot of races that have the power and knowledge to do something on that scale. My question is: How do you intend to keep the Fae inside when so many want out?"

"That's easy, we fucking destroy them if they try to leave." I gave him a wicked smile. "We just allow the beast to rattle his cage and go free long enough to make sure they know we're not fucking around."

"You don't think that would turn the Horde against their newly crowned King?" He sipped his drink and observed me with a gleam of speculation in his eyes.

"I think that he needs to show them he's a fair King, but that in times of need, he can be a fucking monster. It's the Horde. They need to follow their King and kneel before him; if they refuse to kneel, then he'll need to remind them that he's the scariest fucking monster in that world."

"Sometimes it takes a monster to rule," he agreed.

"And sometimes the monster becomes the hero," I mused, and saw his eyes tear away from the glass to grudgingly hold mine.

"Are we done?" he grumbled.

"Do you love her enough to let her go if she doesn't want to become Lena again?" I cringed inwardly as he tensed.

"I killed Katarina to free her." His voice was soft, thoughtful. "Lena is different; she's so much more than Katarina ever was, and she's strong. If there's a chance she is who I am looking for, there's no way to free her from what will awaken. Lucifer thinks Kendra holds it, and I hope he's right. There's been no sign of him; however, the veils are still holding up—and trust me, we'd know if they came down."

"So Lucifer could be wrong in assuming it was Kendra who held the soul and seal?"

"He took Kendra because his lackeys thought she was Lena; he wasn't aware that they were identical twins. He had no idea if she held the seal, and neither do we. It would explain why the veils are still holding. Or he just hasn't crawled out of the between and made his way to hell yet. He has no clue what he's looking for; but here's the punch in the teeth: Neither do we."

"So it could potentially be anyone in the coven." I worried my lower lip for a moment before completing my line of thought. "Even Lena," I whispered with a twinge of regret.

"I almost want to pray that it is anyone else— almost."

"Because you have feelings for Lena," I mused. "I don't envy your situation, and while you could easily kill them all and be done with it, you have found a way to give them mercy. I admire that. But this is a seriously fucked up house of cards, and no matter how you stack it, eventually it's going to fall. I pray for your sake and the sake of the worlds, that when it comes to it, you're not forced to make that choice. It's fucking morbid, but I'll be honest, I always did love a good romance story. You're a good man, even if you don't want to be. You are not as evil as you want everyone to believe, and that should count for something, Lucian. But don't worry; I won't whisper a word of it to anyone else, not even Ryder. War is coming to Faery. I hope that when the time comes, you'll help us. We can use some powerful allies, and we'd gladly owe you for it."

"I will be in contact with you, Synthia. When I am ready, you will give me what I ask for." He brushed me aside with a flick of his hand, purposely ignoring my request.

"Actually, we didn't shake on it." I hopped off his desk and looked at him as he rose to his full height. I watched his eyes burn red as he considered ripping my head off. "It's a good thing I'm honorable," I smirked as I held out my hand and watched him frown. "Not every asshole is out to get you, Lucian. Not everyone expects something from you, and some of us may even wish to consider you an ally. Sometimes you have to trust people to stand beside you," I said as I reached for his hand and slipped my fingers against his. "I'll also need my uncle tomorrow, and I'd prefer not to be the one who interferes with what you have going on here. I'll be here around one or so; please have him here and I'll make sure he leaves without an incident, and is returned the moment I am finished with him. If I don't come, it means I've decided it isn't safe enough for him to be there."

"You could have sifted with the wards down; why didn't you?" He made his way around the desk.

"Because I made a deal, and you answered my questions. There's also the fact that you have Alden. You promised me he wouldn't be harmed, and I intend to hold you to that. And, again, some of us aren't out to fuck you over. You now know that if we make a deal, I will always honor it. Remember that, because I may need your help soon. This one I'd almost sell my soul to accomplish. Almost," I whispered as I shook his hand, kissed his cheek, and vanished.

I materialized into the chambers that Ryder and I shared, to a growling Ryder, who didn't look the least bit impressed. I moved towards him slowly and frowned.

"Yes, I know you didn't want me to meet with Lucian, but someone had to go—and if you went, he would have asked for more than he did."

"And just what the fuck could he have said that was worth trading him anything for?" he snapped.

"I think I know how to narrow down the list of who could be opening new portals." I tried to keep my tone bright and positive.

His golden eyes glowed with barely suppressed anger. "What did you promise him, Pet?"

"He hasn't told me yet, but I'm pretty sure it's going to be something from inside the Spokane Guild's catacombs," I muttered and looked away from his eyes. Negotiating with Lucian was a huge risk.

He relaxed and pulled me into his arms. "Don't do that again," he murmured against my ear.

"Lucian isn't as horrible as everyone makes him out to be. He's got a heart beneath that armor, one that beats for Lena. He knows we know his weakness, and he also knows he can trust us now."

"Ever consider that maybe he wants us to underestimate him?" he kissed my forehead and the side of my neck, making my pulse tick wildly. "Your parents are in the war room with the babies. It's time to say goodbye."

Chapter FOUR

I sat between Madisyn and Darynda as bags were handed to the small entourage who had come to retrieve the babies. Liam frowned as he picked up yet another bag and hefted it over his shoulder.

"We do know how to glamour in the Blood Kingdom, sister," he grunted as he was weighed down with another heavy bag. The familiarity with which he called me sister tugged on my heart.

"I didn't say you couldn't," I retorted as I moved to sit on the floor with the babies.

"She wants to be the one who creates their wardrobe. It's perfectly normal, and not an easy thing when you know your child is leaving you." Madisyn squeezed my shoulder in encouragement. She probably did the exact same thing when she sent me off for my own safety. "We will protect them with our lives, and the nursery we set up is in the far wing of the palace, protected by wards—and no one will be allowed in unless they are sanctioned by you and Ryder."

"They don't sleep a lot, and they don't like to be

separated, and if you try to walk with Kahleena out of their sight, they tend to scream," I advised, fighting the emotions that tugged inside of me. My stomach twisted and my eyes burned. I wanted to hold them close and never let them go, but there was too much that required Ryder's and my attention right now, and I knew in my heart that this was the right thing to do for the children. "Cade likes to cuddle and Zander always wants to feed first." I swallowed. "Zander doesn't like to be held too long. If his brother and sister are picked up and he isn't, he gets jealous and then he'll allow it."

"Kahleena likes to be between them when she sleeps," Ryder added. He could sense that I was about to lose it, and he knelt beside me. "Cade doesn't like baths, but he doesn't mind them so much if he isn't alone in it. We wash them together to prevent him from screaming."

"Synthia." Liam laid his hand over his heart. "They'll be loved, but more than that, they'll be safe. I have my fiercest protectors with me, and we will die before we allow anyone to hurt them. They are blood of my blood, and I vow that we will never allow them to come to harm."

"I know, and I'm sending Cailean with you too. He will protect my children and watch over them. He did it for me." I looked up at the silent man who stood beside me, observing my pain. "I know you want to remain here, but I need you with my children, Cailean."

Cailean's dark brown and spring green eyes turned to me, and he frowned. "I wish to stay with you and protect you."

"I know, but I don't need to be protected; Ryder and his brothers have that protection thing handled." I smiled weakly. "My children need you, and you vowed to protect them—I'm calling that vow in. You will go with them to the Blood Kingdom and you will protect them with your last dying breath, should the need arise. No one knows Faolán as you do, and he would be the one to come after them. You will not fail me twice; we both know it. You asked me to forgive you for failing to protect me. Here is where you show me your worth."

"As you wish, my princess," he said, nodding his head in acknowledgement, which caused his light blonde hair to move in front of his face. "I will protect them for you, I vow it."

It took over an hour before I was willing to finally say goodbye to the babies, and even then, it took longer to get me out of the war room and into the throne room, where we heard the grievances of the people for the rest of the day.

Everyone pretended it was all normal. Darynda and the rest of the handmaidens were going to take shifts in the nursery, and the Elite Guard placed heavy wards, sealing the entry points with magical barriers to prevent anyone unauthorized from entering the living quarter floors. New wards were placed in plain view of the people inside the castle, and to them, it looked as if we were simply adding to the existing ones to protect the triplets.

Everything was normal, except Ryder wasn't listening to the people who came in and complained about mundane shit—my heart wasn't in it either.

"My King?" a low Fae asked, his muted brown

hair and eyes searching my face before moving back to Ryder's.

"Tell us again." I tried to redirect my attention to the situation at hand.

"My village was invaded by shape shifters. The village and surrounding farms were completely sacked and ruined. They took our food, set fire to our houses and they stole a few of our females," the lower caste Fae explained.

"How do you know it was shape shifters that did this?" I raised an eyebrow speculatively.

"Because they took the form of Dragons and they no longer walk the lands or fly the skies. They were all slaughtered at Alazander's orders," he stammered, and lowered himself to the floor as he got on his knees. He shook his head as if he'd done a great wrong to his King. "I mean no disrespect my King—only that it is the truth of what happened." I sensed Ryder tense at the mention of Dragons, or maybe it was the mention of his father, but it got my attention.

"Speak freely," Ryder said softly. "I am aware of my father's deeds."

"Wait, Dragons are real?" I interrupted, my eyes bulging a little.

"Thousands of years ago, they roamed the skies of these lands," Ryder acknowledged. "Eventually their numbers dwindled, and a few hundred years ago my father ordered the slaughter of what remained of their people."

"He killed an entire race?" I wasn't sure I was hearing him right. Here I thought Hitler was the worst killer in our history, but Alazander was probably in hell having coffee with him about now.

"Alazander ordered that every Dragon in Faery be slaughtered, even the females and their young. No one was spared, and afterwards, the castle of the Dragon Lord was burned to nothing more than a blackened reminder that Alazander had no mercy in his soul. I can personally vouch to the fact that there are no Dragons left in Faery, since I was present when the last Dragon fell," Ryder rumbled.

"I swear it, my King. I saw it with my own eyes. It was a Dragon," the Fae argued.

"Okay, so you saw a Dragon." I waved my hand a little bit to try and get the angry Fae in front of me to calm down. "How can you be sure it wasn't a different kind of shape shifter?"

"Because the kind of shifters that can imitate a Dragon cannot hold the form for very long...minutes at best," the lesser Fae disclosed.

"Did you have eyes on it the entire time?" I narrowed my eyes at him as my mind jumped from scenario to scenario. "Or could it have changed forms several times when you saw it? Since you are alive and your wife is missing, I'm assuming you weren't close to the village when it happened." Or he was the world's biggest asshole.

"I wasn't close, but I was close enough to know what I saw, and I saw Dragons," he mumbled nervously.

"And where did the Dragons take your wife to...?" Ryder observed him carefully. Ok, so it seemed as if Ryder was getting the same vibe I was getting from this guy.

"Haggis, Sire." He bowed again. "My name is Haggis. I followed them to the mortal world, to the portal. They went through it. I found pieces of her dress, and other things…and blood, so much blood."

"What are the chances that it was a true Dragon?" I glanced at Ryder, who turned and considered my question. "What if your father didn't kill them all?"

"Pray to your God that he did, because if they've hidden for hundreds of years and have been breeding this entire time, we'd most likely face a war with them. We have enough to deal with as is; Dragons aren't something I want to add to it." He paused, looked at Haggis, and exhaled. "I will send men out to investigate this claim and we will let you know of our findings. One last question: Are you sure they passed through into the mortal realm, or could they have led you there to make you assume they had passed through it?"

"I guess they may have doubled back, but it is forbidden to pass through the portal. I turned around and came directly here, my King," he mumbled as he wrung his hands together with worry.

"Thank you for your honesty; we will look into this matter immediately." Ryder stood, turned to the guards who watched him, and spoke loudly. "Court will resume tomorrow; any other grievances will wait until then to be heard."

I stood to follow him when the wards began to glow around us. I paused, and turned to watch as the Elite Guard surrounded us. The lesser Fae were rushed from the room and more guards moved in to guard the doors as Ryder turned and moved me towards the war room situated behind the throne.

"Someone has breached the living quarters," Ryder growled, and my stomach did a somersault. I stopped walking and looked at him, my heart stuck in my throat as I growled as well.

"Go; find out who it is and show them no mercy. No one comes into our house and tries to harm our children. Their bodies can hang from the battlements of the castle as a warning to anyone who tries to harm the babies."

"Damn," Ristan sighed. "Bloodthirsty vixen suits you, Flower."

"I know you won't go if I do, so go, Ryder, I'll wait here with Ristan," I said firmly, watching as his clothes disappeared and the beast stood before me in all his winged glory. "Go destroy them. Leave enough of their bodies to serve as a warning to any other who dares mess with our little beasties."

I was followed into the war room by Ristan, Olivia, and a few guards. I didn't sit as Ristan suggested. Instead, I paced the length of the room until I noticed Ristan tilting his head to the side, as if he were listening to someone speaking to him. I tilted mine, but it was silent. The wards inside the room continued to pulse in silent alarm, and my powers had fizzled the ability to hear the men when they spoke on their channel in each other's heads, and yet I held out hope that eventually I'd be able to hear them again.

"What is it?" I leaned closer, as if I could magically pick up what was being said along the mental pathway.

"Darynda is hurt, but she'll live. Zahruk is taking her to Eliran, but Ciara is gone. They can't find her, and Darynda says she was taken. We can't reach her on the mental link, and Ryder can't feel her presence inside the castle. The bracelet he gave her that had a tracking charm on it was torn from her wrist. There are also signs of a struggle, and a lot of blood."

"Why would someone take Ciara? I thought she was in the Pavilion?" I probed.

"She wanted to help with the new wards and she was part of the rotation with the handmaidens on pretend nursery duties; there was no reason not to allow it. Not with the amount of guards protecting the living quarters."

"They got away?" I wondered how the crap it was possible with an entire army in the residence. "How is that possible?"

"I'm not sure, but Ryder and Zahruk are heading out to search the grounds with the rest of the Elite Guard, with the exception of me. I'm stuck babysitting until…Ow," he groaned and I raised my eyes to find Olivia shaking her hand after punching Ristan's shoulder, while giving him *the* look. He held his hands up at her innocently. "Hey, I'm here protecting you two until they return."

"How does someone get inside the castle without being seen?" I pondered. "Unless they were already inside, just waiting for their chance to strike," I mumbled. Mentally, I started going through every scenario I could think of, knowing that Ristan would chime in if I made any damn sense.

"They could have been inside, that's possible. We were allowing more of the lesser Fae into the castle since Ryder took the throne, and Ciara was just allowed outside the Pavilion about the same time.

She's the only acknowledged daughter of Alazander, and once the rest of the women were released from the Pavilion, there was no keeping her there anymore, even though she would have been a target for our enemies. News of the triplets hasn't yet reached the Farlands, and we have enemies aplenty there."

"Would the people of the Farlands know how to open portals?" I tested and observed his expression as he considered it.

"Anything is possible; however they're mostly farm people, and peaceful. It's why they live away from the Horde castle. We seem to cause mayhem no matter how hard we try not to. Over the past fifty years or so, there have been increasing reports of our enemies hiding among the peaceful farmers."

"Where are the Farlands located?" I made my way over to Ryder's chair and sat in it, since I knew he'd sense I was there; it would give him my strength as he searched for his baby sister.

Ristan cracked a lopsided grin and shook his head. "Far. It's kinda why it's named the *Farlands*."

"Smartass," I groaned as I rubbed my temples. "Where did the Dragons live?"

"Closer to here, in a castle on the farthest end of the north-eastern side of the Horde lands. They were Horde, or at least they were until father destroyed them."

"How would we know if any survived?" I dropped my hands to the table as I ran my finger over Ryder's crest and name.

"They couldn't have. He hunted them down, the

ones who ran were ferreted out, and he didn't stop until every Dragon was removed from this world," Ristan's voice was soft and his shoulders slumped as he took his seat and pulled Olivia down to sit on his lap. "I think it was almost six hundred years ago when it happened. The Dragon Lord refused to send his daughter to be one of Alazander's concubines. They were a proud people, and of course, they'd heard the rumors of the horrors Father did to his wives and concubines. Fury wanted no part of sending his only daughter to the Horde King. In an effort to hide her, he sent her to the Light King, who promised to protect her. Only, he had no intention of hiding her; instead he handed her over to our father in front of the Dragon Lord, and Alazander tore her apart as his Elite Guard held Fury down. Once she was dead, Alazander tortured Fury slowly before eventually killing him." He closed his eyes and something that looked like regret passed over his features as he sighed heavily. "Every once in a while, as sleep takes me, I can hear her screams mingling with the wrath of the Dragon Lord as he fought to escape us; I can still hear the cries of the children as they were slaughtered when we marched on their keep." Olivia shivered in his arms as he opened his strange silvery eyes and looked at me sadly. "Without their lord, the Dragons fell easily and, eventually, became little more than a myth of our history."

"Well then," I grimaced as I imagined the horrors of what they'd done to an entire race. "That tells me he assumed he got them all, but I still think we should check out that castle. Because if they're not all dead, they sure as hell have a reason to want us all dead, and I for one can't really fault them."

"Neither do I, but it isn't Alazander they want now. Ryder led the raids. If he hadn't, Alazander would have tried to kill him, or at the very least retaliated against him. Remember, Ryder was the Heir at the time." Ristan looked at me meaningfully.

"Ryder killed them?" I whispered, and felt the chair warm beneath me. "Damn, that explains why he said they were *all* dead."

"We didn't have a choice back then; we don't even know for sure if he would have killed Ryder or made him watch as Alazander killed one of us that he was close to. Zahruk and I had several other brothers by that time, ones who we were rather fond of; Aodhan was just a child then."

I chewed my lip as I considered Ryder back then, having to follow orders of a murderous asshole. It was hard to understand how he was honorable, and hadn't been tainted by the evil that was his father. People still assumed he was because Alazander forced him to dish out horrible shit, and if he didn't, those he loved would have paid the price.

"I think we should pay that castle a visit, just to be sure," I said firmly, watching as Ristan squirmed in his chair. "We have to know if any survived, and if they did, we need to explain Ryder's side of it. We will wait for the men, of course, but what other lead do we have? Ciara is out there, and she could be hurt since there was that much blood," I exhaled, and mentally chided myself for even thinking that we may already be too late to save her.

Chapter FIVE

"No fucking way," Ryder growled, his hands fisted at his sides as he prowled the room. He continued until I stood in his path.

"We can't just stand around not doing anything, Ryder!" I argued, my eyes narrowing as his glared. "Don't look at me like that."

"I have scouts out scouring the skies and searching every inch of Faery for her," he snapped.

I hugged him, wrapping my arms around his waist and holding him tightly. "I'm afraid too, but Haggis said he saw a Dragon. Other shifters can't take that form, and only a few creatures can hold it for more than a few minutes. What will it hurt to go look and make sure? We can reach it by nightfall, and if anyone catches a trace of her before then, you'll know about it, right?" I asked.

"I razed the castle, Synthia. It's nothing but a burned-out husk."

"I've seen homeless people sleep in cardboard boxes."

His lips tugged into a confused frown as he thought through my words. "Why would anyone live in a box?"

"Because they couldn't afford rent." I shrugged, not really wanting to discuss the details of how humans ended up homeless. He continued to stare. "When people can't afford to pay for a place to sleep and the shelters fill up, they end up outside. Sometimes people prefer to be outside. So they just sleep in whatever they can find—listen, that's not the point. I'm saying that if any survived, it would make sense that they would go home. It's familiar, and no matter how bad the place was wrecked, it's still their home."

"If you go, you'll see what *I* did to them." His voice was soft, almost pained as he watched my face intently. "That's not something I wanted you to see— ever."

"No, I'll see what your asshole father forced you to do to them. Being coerced with the life of another in the balance isn't fair, and I know you, Ryder; I know you'd do whatever it took to protect your family."

"Remember that," he muttered. "Fine, we'll go, but you will be wearing the armor of the Elite Guard, and seeing that you are insisting on this insanity, the full Guard will go with us, to be safe."

"Fine," I agreed, watching as he frowned. "Oh, for Pete's sake, I'm not going to argue it. We could be facing Dragons!"

"Who the hell is Pete?" he demanded, and I burst out laughing.

"It's just a saying," I whispered as I stood on tiptoes to kiss him.

"When we get back, we need to discuss wedding plans," he muttered. "The timing is bad, and with Ciara gone, we should probably postpone it, but I can't. I want to marry you and the people need to see us continuing on even through the chaos. They need to know that we are going to be alright."

"We will be alright, Fairy. Even if Faery is wide open, we'll be okay. It's us; we've been through too much now to not be okay."

~~*

Once I'd glamoured the armor of the Elite Guard on, Ryder slid a lightweight, almost transparent cloak around my shoulders and fastened it at the base of my throat. It was a cloak that could act as camouflage, taking on the characteristics of my surroundings with a mere thought—and it held a spell in it so that those in the Elite Guard could easily track where I was. Ryder wore a similar one, and told me that it was a way to stay hidden from the enemy while being easily found and protected by the men.

We'd left the Horde castle with our minds on the unknown enemy who had infiltrated it. Darynda was still recovering in the infirmary with Eliran, and even though he hadn't admitted it, I could tell that Zahruk was worried about her. I'd found him pacing outside her room. He'd left the moment I'd discovered him, so I had yet to speak with him about it, but the point seemed moot since the man was a concrete slab when it came to emotions, or discussing them.

My eyes wandered to Ryder, who seemed tense,

and with good cause. The entire group seemed somber and tense; I guess it was because they'd either heard of the horrors of what had happened here under Alazander's orders, or were participants to the carnage that must have transpired in this place. Ristan had explained a little more about what had happened on the day of the battle, and it had turned my stomach. The coffee I'd sipped turned bland and tasteless as I'd listened quietly to his words. Even when I thought that Dragons were mythical creatures, I never once thought they were weak and, logically, a Fae army VS a Dragon army defending their home should have lost. They didn't lose because those shifters, who took their Dragon form, were no match for the man that was currently hidden by the magnificent wrapping of the Fae male who rode on the other side of me.

Because it had been centuries since any of these men had been here, we had taken huge war horses, and Ryder's had red eyes. Zahruk, Dristan, and Aodhan were in wolf form, sniffing ahead to be sure no enemies lay in wait to attack us.

"After we crest the next hill, the castle should be visible," Ryder announced grimly.

"It's in a strategic location." I wondered how anyone made it out this far on foot.

Once we crested the next hill, the charred remains of a once proud castle lay ahead on the horizon, positioned between the two moons of Faery. A statue of a Dragon in mid-flight stood forlornly in the courtyard, abandoned, covered in moss from centuries of neglect, yet the form was still visible.

The ride down the hill was tense. Skeletal remains that looked both Dragon as well as human-ish littered the fields where the start of the battle had occurred. Swords rested with the warriors that had once proudly wielded them, covered with debris from a battle that happened so long ago it was almost forgotten. I hadn't expected this, to see the fallen that still lay upon the battlefield, never claimed for burial. It showed exactly the viciousness with which Ryder had carried out the assault under Alazander's orders. No one had been left alive to bury their dead; no one had survived.

The wall of the castle was also covered in thick moss and plants that creeped up through the cracks to reach for the heat of the sun. Vibrant flowers sprouted from the greenery along the castle's high walls. It looked as if it had been plucked from the pages of a historian's book from the middle ages. Beautiful, yet abandoned and forgotten.

The place was eerily silent. As silent as the dead who littered the ground and had become part of the land. It was green, as if the ground tried to conceal the horrors that had occurred with signs of life. Nothing moved, and the sound of the hooves of the horses was the only noise we could hear.

We dismounted in the courtyard, surrounded by walls that had been built to keep enemies out. But they never stood a chance against Ryder, a creature who'd fight the monsters of hell to protect his brothers. I knew the Horde King could only be killed by the Heir to the Horde, but what about the Heir? Could Ryder have been killed by another before he became King? What if Ryder had fallen in battle to the Dragons? Would his father have even cared? Probably not. Alazander probably would have gone to the next son or Heir to conquer or destroy anyone who fought against him or denied him his way.

We had yet to break the silence of the eerie courtyard, and I didn't dare make a sound as I followed Ryder up the stairs to the castle. He pushed the doors open; his shoulders slumped as if he was ashamed of what had happened here.

"Alazander didn't give you a choice," I murmured, breaking the silence as his brothers circled us protectively.

"I was strong enough then to dethrone him. I chose not to," Ryder replied, stepping over the threshold and into the entrance of the castle.

Bones scattered across the stone floors. Some of the remains still had weapons buried in their torsos, and others appeared to have died holding theirs. They were so old that they appeared to become part of the floors they'd died on. It was a massacre, and no matter what I said, Ryder carried the heavy guilt of it on his shoulders. It wasn't until we reached the main hall that I flinched. Tiny bones covered the floor, crunching beneath our feet. You couldn't step around them. There were just too many to avoid them.

"The Dragons rounded their children up and slaughtered them here when we breached the courtyard," he mumbled distractedly. His hand reached for mine and I slipped my fingers through his as we continued deeper into the darkened interior. Light filtered in through the decaying drapes, exposing the horror of the charred walls and remains of the next room.

"What was in here?" I turned to get a better look at the little charred silhouettes on the floor.

"The young. Children; about a quarter of the dead children were mere infants. They slaughtered them with Dragon fire. They figured death by fire was better, anything would have been better than allowing us to be the ones to take them."

"This wasn't your fault," I protested softly, and spread out my arms at the destruction. "This is really why you took me to the ruins, wasn't it? You said that that place was a reminder of what could happen if we strayed from *her* designs for this world. You were also talking about what happened here." I sucked in a huge lungful of air as pieces fell into place. "Gods, you told me that when you inherited the Heir brands that the Dragons formed. That was centuries before you were forced to do this—you were forced to wipe out a people that you shared kinship with." My words became softer at the pain in his eyes. "The drawing in the sand of the two larger Dragons and the three baby Dragons…that was you, trying to pass something of what happened to them on to me and our children. It was guilt—your guilt, to be exact. Don't you realize that those who are real monsters—like you think you are—don't return to shrines of those they wronged? Monsters don't care about the deaths they leave behind, and they sure as shit don't return to honor them long after they are dead."

"Look at the ashes, Synthia, and tell me a monster didn't decide their fate. That a monster didn't force their hand," he demanded.

My eyes took in the ashes that still lingered upon the floor. I fought the sourness in my throat, and flinched as I ripped my hand away from Ryder to cover my mouth. I swallowed and shook my head. They'd killed their own babies to protect them.

"I told you I was a monster." I could barely hear his words as he looked away.

"You didn't have a choice. A monster chose their fate, for sure, but you're not that monster. Your father did this, and you were his weapon of choice," I bit out once I could speak without throwing up. "I'm not blaming you, so stop trying to make me, Fairy. In my world, at a place called Okinawa during World War II, something very similar happened. War is messy, and in all wars, the innocent suffer the most. The fault lies with the one at the top who gave the order to attack, not with the soldiers who were forced to follow the orders."

"*I* blame me," he mumbled. "They sure as fuck blame me."

"They're dead, the dead don't hate. They don't blame, they're indifferent to it. I'm sure they made the best choice they could, and chose to take their children out of this life on their own terms. Who knows what your father would have done to them, or demanded you do to them?" I asked. "No one knows, so maybe they were right to do as they did. They wouldn't have lived, so at least they didn't suffer."

"They burned them to death, Synthia," Ristan murmured from where he stood across the room.

"Yes, but isn't that better than being hurt repeatedly, or made to do horrendous shit at the bidding of some crazed lunatic with a power kick who won't let you die? There's always something worse that can happen. Always," I growled. "You don't know that he wouldn't have kept them as pets, and yes, I know he'd done it to his prisoners before. I know what he did to my brother. I know what Ryder was forced to do to protect you and the others. Ryder is nothing like your father—he'll never be like him."

"The next room was where most of their females were killed." Ryder's voice was hollow, and he shuddered as if he'd gone back to when this had happened. "Some died more horrifically than the others."

I didn't want to see what had been done to the women. The soldiers' bones had revealed how they'd fallen, and I could imagine the atrocities done to innocent women. Bones could tell a story, one that the living could try to piece together and understand. I felt horrible for the people who had once lived and died in this fashion. Ryder had been a pawn, one used by a monster that held his weaknesses over him in threat. He'd had no more power than the dead, who now lay long forgotten on the moss-and dust-covered floors we now stood on.

Ryder pushed the door open and dust particles filled the air. We held our breath, preparing to see what horrors the wooden doors hid from the world. I stepped into the room and paused. The room was clean, and lit candles sputtered with the rush of fresh air, melted wax pooling onto the freshly polished surface of a piano.

"What in the fucking Goonies," Ristan whispered, his hand slipping into mine.

"What are you doing?" I whispered.

"I'm scared. Hold me, Flower," he frowned at me as his lips struggled not to turn into a smile.

"This room wasn't like this, during or after the siege," Ryder growled, his eyes searching the room and turned to me.

"It doesn't necessarily mean the Dragons survived.

I told you about the homeless people; maybe someone or something else moved in. Something could have decided it was a safe place to stay," I offered.

Ristan picked up a medallion from a freshly polished side table and held it up to the candlelight; it had a double-headed Dragon molded into it. I swallowed and somehow managed to swallow the groan that tried to bubble up.

"They could have thought it looked cool," I offered. I was the master of Could-Have. "There's no proof, remember what you told me? This is Faery, anything can happen. Never believe it until you actually see it. Haggis probably didn't see a Dragon; he ran like a bitch to save his own ass. If it was my wife, I would have run after them, and I wouldn't have stopped trailing them until I knew for damn sure what had taken her."

"Kinky, Flower," Ristan mused with a devilish grin.

"Stuff it, Demon," I warned as I began examining the walls to figure out how whoever it was had gotten out, other than the door we came through. "There's another way into this room. Someone was here recently, and no one could have gotten out through that door without being seen," I explained when the men looked at me questioningly. "No one came in the way we did; nothing was disturbed until we disturbed it. They have to have another way into this room."

"She has a point," Aodhan agreed. "Someone is really into weaponry and High Fae battle tactics," he mused, picking up the heavy tomes that were stacked on the floor beside a dingy mattress.

"Someone may have been researching how to try

and destroy High Fae for revenge," Ryder said, his eyes on me. "We need to get you back to the castle."

"I'm not going anywhere," I growled. "Listen, I get that you have a shady as shit past—I know what I'm signing up for. I'm not some weak-ass girl who needs to be protected, Fairy. Whatever fucks with you will need protection from me, because Goddess be warned, I will fuck up anything and anyone who seeks to harm my future husband. Understand?"

"Where do I sign up for one like her?" Aodhan winked.

I had just started to search for a secret passageway when a noise sounded across the room. The entire Elite Guard, who'd followed us into the room, sprang into action. I was shoved back, my body hugged against the back of Ryder's hard body. His weapon was drawn, and we waited to see who entered.

Clicking noises continued, and then the sound of rock sliding against rock echoed through the room. No one breathed or made a noise until fresh air filled the room. Ryder relaxed and I peeked around his wide back to find a shirtless Zahruk staring at us from a hidden doorway.

"I followed a fresh scent from the woods to a tunnel by the shores. There's a cave beneath the castle that leads into the dungeons of this place," he announced as everyone returned their weapons into their scabbards. "Probably an escape route, should the castle ever be besieged," he mused. "Too bad they didn't use it when we came." His eyes held Ryder's in solidarity.

"They couldn't use it; we flanked them and sent soldiers to the beach in case they had one. It was searched as well, to be sure no one survived," Ryder explained.

"Someone else has been here, or someone survived and is plotting revenge," Zahruk growled, ignoring the tinge of guilt in Ryder's tone. They were connected in ways that I'd never be able to understand, but I knew enough about it to know that if Ryder felt something, his brothers knew exactly what it was. "There's something you need to see."

We followed him down a winding path, one that led into a room in the bowels of the castle. Sword blades reflected the candlelight. I picked one up; it was light despite the blade being forged from iron.

"Dragons were Fae, right?" I pressed.

"Aye," Aodhan agreed.

"Why would Fae have iron blades made?"

"They wouldn't, but Mages or our other enemies might," Ryder growled.

"I think we just stumbled upon a store of weapons for the upcoming war." I smiled grimly. "Let's destroy them, shall we?"

"No; replace them with a similar-weighted metal," Ryder ordered. "Let them come to us with weapons that won't harm us as easily as iron can. Let them think they are safe here. At least we can monitor it now that we are aware of it. Let's figure out where this tunnel leads to and go from there."

Chapter SIX

Days had gone by, and with every passing moment, I missed my children more and more. I couldn't place them in danger, and with war looming closer every day, I didn't dare sneak away to see them. I feared for the Fae, and for the humans who had become their victims.

Vlad had brought us news of human murders that he and Adrian had investigated and believed had been killed by Fae. The instances of humans becoming FIZ were increasing at alarming rates. Likewise, the clubs had been packed with Fae who'd sauntered out of Faery into a new world, where they'd have unlimited food and entertainment at their fingertips.

It had gotten out of hand rather quickly, which was why I stood with half of the Elite Guard in front of the Spokane Guild. I'd sent a message to Lucian through Vlad, cancelling the meeting I'd requested with Alden. I didn't want him out here, exposed. I could feel the eyes of the Enforcers on us, and knew they wouldn't attack us here and now, but that didn't mean I wouldn't if they threatened us. Alden would have been thrown into the middle of it, and he didn't need to be.

"How many?" I asked, not bothering to turn my head as Adrian returned.

"Five or more, but they don't seem to be making a move yet," Adrian confirmed as he moved back to my side. "None are familiar to me. Not that I was around when the last group graduated to Enforcer ranks from this Guild. I've been gone longer than you have."

"They won't make a move against us, not here. They would be exposed, and we have the advantage. There are also too many unknowns. Right now, the only thing they're sure of is that we can kill them. We outnumber them. We also hold the wild card on power and they can feel it. I made sure to tap the Leyline so that it would be felt by any close enough to get in our way. It will give them pause with the amount of power I used to do so."

"Sending a message?" he asked, his turquoise eyes watching me with a sideways glance.

"Go big or go home, right? We're moving in, and they need to know we won't allow them to interfere. They can choose to get out of our way, or be put in the ground. Either works for me." I blinked, startled as Ryder materialized in front of me. "Still protected?"

"It's stable, but a fucking mess. Lucian wasn't the only one trying to get in. From the look of it, I'd say we had a few interested parties trying to get past the wards," he replied, his eyes looking past me, over my shoulder to where the Guild Enforcers probably hid.

"Ignore them; they're just curious little monkeys, come to see what we're all about," I smiled.

"They're an unknown, and I don't like unknowns—or surprises," he growled as he stepped closer, his eyes moving from me to Adrian and back with annoyance.

"Play nice, Fairy, we're on their turf. It can't be easy to watch us take it from right beneath their noses."

"They're coming," he warned, and I turned, looking over my shoulder.

"Sure as shit, they've got balls. I'm impressed." I gave them a cheeky grin, hoping they behaved, since Ryder could wipe them from existence with a single thought. I turned, crossed my arms, and waited.

"You need to leave here; the Fae have no right to be inside our Guild," the leader shouted, even though I was close enough to hear him just fine. He was a thirty-something, blonde and blue-eyed little thing, but he held enough power to do damage; just not to us.

"No?" I countered.

"No, now turn around and get out of our world," he sneered.

I moved without hesitation, grabbing his arm and bending it behind his back, and forced his head to the side as I held a knife to his throat with my other hand. Then, I looked at the others with a determined grin. "I don't recognize any of you, so you aren't from this Guild and have no right to be proprietary here. I am Synthia, born of the Fae but raised in *this* Guild. I may not have a right according to the Guild laws, but this Guild? This one is mine. If you think to take it from me, you better bring more than this little group of Enforcers, because I have the Horde and Faery in its entirety standing with me." I looked at each of the startled Enforcers meaningfully. "It's united, and while we don't want war, I will fight to keep this Guild. I will personally tear down every fucking Guild in this world to keep this one safe, so I hope when you return to your Elders, you make it known that we are Faery. We don't want war, but if you try to stop us, we will wage it—and make no mistake, we will win. We are here to take down the Fae who feed upon the humans against their will and to their detriment. However, we will no longer allow you to publicly assassinate them on the stairs of your Guilds to breed hostility and hate among The Guild or with the humans. After what the Seattle Guild pulled, you're lucky I haven't demanded blood. You get a pass today, but there won't be a second one. The Guild has an infestation it needs to work on eradicating. Any attempts to interfere here will be considered an act of war, and we won't hesitate to retaliate. Now leave, and if I were you, I'd start running," I growled as I pushed the Enforcer away from myself, and watched him swing around at me. I didn't flinch.

"You won't get away with this," he sneered, and I smiled coldly.

I let my power wrap around him, feeling the moment the Fae behind me followed my lead. The air crackled around us until Ryder released his and the lights around us shattered. Street lamps blew out, car alarms went off, and the air around us was thick with the rich scent of ozone. I'd missed his unique power; the shit was addicting. It slithered around me; the hair on my arms rose in awareness of the raw electricity that sizzled from him. I pushed more, seeing if I could match his, and windows of the cars and buildings around us exploded outwards and rained down on everyone in a glittery, prismatic display.

"Too much?" I asked Ryder, feigning innocence

and ignoring the sheet-white faces of the Guild Enforcers.

"Yeah, just a little bit; dial it back a notch and try again," Adrian laughed, his eyes smiling as he turned to me and winked.

"Do we have to pay for the car windows?" I winced.

"We could leave notes," he offered.

"Yeah, let's tell people to bill it to the Guild—you know, their Guild, not ours. I would hate to start off in debt—and they kinda owe us."

"What the fuck are you?" the Enforcer demanded, which forced me to stop joking around with Adrian.

"Something that you couldn't even imagine in your worst nightmares," I growled. Adrian laughed. "Too much again? Damn, I always wanted to say that." Okay, so I was a dork, but I could live with that. "Seriously, though, we're the Horde. You know, the ones whispered about in the Guild history lessons. The ones you know nothing about because the King was thought to be on a walkabout? Well, I found him, and he'll be helping me run this Guild, so make sure that when you tell the Guild you got your ass whooped by Synthia McKenna, you tell them I brought friends to restore this Guild that we are claiming for Faery. Now, run."

I watched as they stood still, watching us as they considered what the best option was. I tapped my foot, wondering where the hell they'd found this group at. "Adrian, how many of them do we need to let live to deliver a message to the Guild?"

"One." He smiled coldly, and we watched as they turned and tucked tail as they ran for their lives.

"They'll be back soon, Pet." Ryder nodded after the retreating Enforcers.

"I'm planning on it." I smiled and then grimaced as I looked at the silent Guild. "Now, let's go check out the damage."

"Troublemaker," Ryder smiled. His head tilted and his eyes narrowed as I watched him. When he righted his head, he looked torn.

"What is it?" I asked.

"We have a lead on Ciara," he replied softly, his eyes searching mine as he frowned.

"Go," I said as I stood on my tiptoes to kiss his lips. "Go find her. Bring her home to her family. I'll stay and take care of this."

"I'm not leaving you," he argued.

"I'm not alone, Fairy. I have Adam, Adrian, and Vlad with me. I'll be perfectly fine. You take Ristan and Zahruk with you," I replied confidently. "Your men have already made sure that it's safe for me, and they've been scouring every inch of the catacombs for any threats. I can do this; you go and find your sister," I purred as I stood on tiptoes to kiss him again. "No one said it would be easy, but then again, nothing worth it ever is. Two worlds need us," I smiled as I placed my hands on his chest. "Yours and mine, remember? We can't be locked at the hip every moment of the day. I can handle the rebuild while you search for Ciara."

"You better sift if there is any sign of trouble,

woman," he growled as he placed a soft kiss on my forehead. "I want you home tonight; we've no babies in our bed, and I plan to ravish you."

"Ravish me? That almost sounds like a threat?" I teased.

"Jesus," Adam grumbled in mock disgust, his eyes smiling at me.

"Vlad." Ryder gave the man in question a pointed look. "She doesn't leave your side," he warned as his fingers softly threaded through mine as he brought my fingers to his lips. "Under no circumstances does she leave your sight."

"I don't need a babysitter," I mumbled as I pulled my hand away and placed them on my hips. "I'm a grown ass woman."

"I just got you back, Witch. I'm not taking chances with you," he laughed as he winked and sifted out before I could argue further.

Chapter SEVEN

The inside of the Guild appeared to be in the same condition it was in the last time we were here cleaning it up. Piles of debris still littered the floors and a fine sheen of dust covered everything. It wrenched my stomach and tugged at my heartstrings to see it in such disarray. What had once been a proud, strong fortress and sanctuary for misfits and orphans had become nothing more than a sad pile of rubble. I'd spent most of my life here within these walls, thinking I was part of something. This Guild was a part of me, and seeing it like this, well, it broke my heart.

"Hard to see it like this." Adam's voice was soft as he looked around at the debris. His thick black hair clung to his forehead from Spokane's unusually hot spring. Tri-colored eyes in shades of emerald and lime green looked at me with a shared loss. It mattered little what we had become; this place was a part of us and always would be. "Not sure why you want to even bother with this."

"This was our home, Adam. We can't leave it like this," I muttered. He'd been here since it had been leveled, we all had. Walking through it now, I saw what he saw. It would take a lot to get this place up and running, but now more than ever, it was needed. "Vlad reported that the Seattle Guild turned away two orphans last week. I fear it's because of us, because we were orphans who turned out to be Fae instead of Witches. It's our fault they're being turned away. The two orphans are in human foster homes for the time being, and you know that won't work out well, so I want this place up and running, at least well enough that we can take the ones that the Guild rejects as soon as possible. This world is also about to be invaded. With the portals opening randomly and widening, someone has to stand between the humans and the Fae. We can save people again," I whispered with excitement. "Don't you miss it?" *I* did. I missed the thrill that came from the hunt, from the missions that came with saving the innocents.

"I miss it," he agreed with a firm shake of his dark head. "I also have other shit going on, Syn. Never in my wildest imaginings did I ever think I would have the kinds of responsibilities I have now. I have duties to an entire race of people. Oh, and not to mention, I still have to find the Light Heir."

"And what do you plan to do with her once you've found her?" Now that he was bringing her up, I was curious to know his feelings on the matter at hand.

"Fuck her," he grumbled dejectedly. "Put an heir in her belly."

"Come again?" I coughed to hide the shock I felt at his jaded words.

"You heard me," he muttered softly.

"Is that all she'll be? A womb to house the child of prophecy?" I returned, watching him carefully.

"That's all she'll ever be to me, yes. I'll do what is needed to secure an heir, but don't expect me to love her. I had the love of my life and I lost her," he snapped, his eyes glowing a luminescent green as he stared at me in open challenge. He wanted me to argue, but it wasn't because he was mad; he was still hurting.

This wasn't the Adam I knew as well as I knew myself. That Adam was carefree—always smiling and joking around Adam. That man was my familiar, or had been until my body had died and I had come back as a Goddess. Adam post-Larissa's death, post-Transition, post-losing everything that he knew and understood, was someone that made me constantly feel like I needed to walk on eggshells when I was around him.

A troubling thought flicked across my mind. Was the reason Adam was so complacent to marry me when he thought I was the Light Heir because it was a way for him to be able to fulfill what was expected of him? It was a way for him to fulfill his duties without being forced to try and love someone and feel like he was betraying Larissa. At the time, we were comfortable with each other, but there wouldn't have been that soul-crushing type of love between the two of us, and he knew I didn't expect it of him.

"We both lost her, Adam. We both loved her," I whispered as I tilted my head and frowned as I watched his throat bob with emotion. "It's okay to love again; you know she'd want you to. Larissa was never selfish, nor would she want you to live without love. She expected us to let her go; she even asked for us to let her go, and we haven't yet."

"I can't, end of discussion."

I watched as he walked ahead of me, his hands fisted tightly. He was mourning, but instead of hitting the final stages, he was stuck in anger. Keir had reported to us that Adam was feeding gluttonously, without care for who he fed from. The Fae who preferred to feed from pain tended to gravitate towards Adam, some had taken to following him around, which spoke volumes to how much pain he was in. I wanted to grab hold of him and shake him, but grief was tricky. Everyone processed it differently.

"He's hurting," Vlad murmured from beside me, my silent bodyguard.

"I know, but eventually he has to let her go." I turned to look at Vlad, noting how carefully he was watching me, so I swiftly changed the subject. "The builder is here?"

"You have to let her go too," he said softly, refusing to let me off the hook. "The builder is here, and while you won't be happy with what it is, you will be happy with what he can create."

I side-eyed Vlad and frowned at his cryptic meaning as we progressed deeper into the rubble of the Guild. He nodded to the broken staircase that led into the library area of the Guild, and I suppressed a groan as the entourage slowly moved towards it. Once there, Vlad sifted us without waiting to see if I would do it myself. Always the gentlemen, he cleared us from the debris and released my hand as we stepped through the wards the Fae had placed the last time we were here.

"I can hear your heart hammering, Syn," Vlad mused with a smirk.

"Nosferatu," I hissed with a seductive smile on

my lips.

"Indeed, beautiful girl." He smiled genially as he held out his elbow in silent invitation. I accepted, slipping my arm through his as he sidestepped debris that littered the floor. The Fae had done their part, fortifying the ceilings the last time we'd been here. We made sure it was safe enough for us to enter it without fear of it collapsing on our heads.

I was lost in my thoughts of what we'd have to face by rebuilding it when we turned the last corner and the monstrosity came into sight. I stiffened at Vlad's side; my stomach flopped as nausea and hate churned in my belly.

Adrian and Adam tensed beside me; each reached for weapons, and only hesitated because Vlad waved his hand in greeting to the monster, who watched us with wariness etched in his grotesque features.

"It's okay," Vlad assured us. "He's on our side. For now."

The monstrosity turned his gaze from Vlad to me. It had grayish skin that clung loosely to its bones, and clumps of greasy hair were plastered against its skull while some areas of its head had no hair at all. It smiled, revealing rows of razor sharp teeth that were brown and yellow; some still had tidbits of a recent kill stuck in them. Hollow eyes watched me with amusement as I swallowed furiously to prevent my lunch from coming back up.

Adam and Adrian looked to me for guidance as we slowly, carefully moved closer to it. Their instincts mirrored mine, and Adam closed the distance between us until his hand was a hairbreadth from mine, ever vigilant and protective of me, as we'd been before we'd become Fae. We'd spent years hunting monsters like this one down. We'd slaughtered many of them over the years, ridding the humans of the threat these creatures posed to them.

"Jesus," Adam growled as his other hand touched his sword; other colorful cuss words seemed to flow freely from his lips. The entire room was tense, strained with the silent need to kill the monster lurking within our reach. Vlad rolled his neck and watched me with unease. He knew nothing was okay inside this room; the tension rolling off of us was thick enough to cut with a knife.

Adam had been with me when I'd cut down the first one of these assholes. In Faery, these things were called *Fiacla an éadóchais*, but we had our own name for them in the Guild. We called them Rotting Corpses because, to a human, it would smell like rain and roses to disguise the smell of rotting flesh and, unless it fed from flesh frequently, it withered until its own death loomed. The teeth he licked as he watched us could shred flesh from bone with almost surgical precision, while numbing its victim to the pain. To a human, they would see a beautiful creature and feel nothing but the intense pleasure that was delivered from the thousands of needlelike fronds in its fingers while their flesh and muscle was peeled away. This was a tactic used by these creatures so they wouldn't attract unwanted attention while they were feeding. Most of the ones we had come across, however, enjoyed the sound of its victims screaming and fed on the terror that rolled off of them as they realized their fate. The last time we killed one, it was in the process of killing a child that couldn't have been more than five years old. It was one of the many reasons why we were rather eager to put this thing down and keep a few more people safe.

"This is Foul; he's the builder," Vlad introduced with a firm tone in his voice. His eyes moved from mine to the creature's.

"Foul, indeed," I growled as I struggled against the urge to jump across the table that stood between us and kill the monster. These things didn't belong anywhere in our world.

"He can build what we need in days instead of years, Synthia. He can have the Guild up and functioning this week if we asked it of him," Vlad explained. "Foul is on a very short leash from the Horde King—one misstep and Ryder will end him."

"She's beautiful, need to taste it," it sneered as it started to move around the table, only to stop as everyone reached for a weapon. I flinched as its naked, flaccid body came into full view. Its cock hung limply between legs that had loose flesh sagging from its bones.

"Foul, if you want to remain breathing, I suggest you don't touch the Horde King's fiancée. Now, put on something proper before I remove that useless cock from your body," Vlad warned in a hiss laced with the promise of death.

"Pity, such smooth flesh would taste of heaven," Foul whined with an earsplitting shrill. "I change deal, her instead." It nodded, causing flesh to jiggle before it remolded to its body and once again clung loosely from the bones. It stood well over seven feet, towering over us as it watched me with keen interest. I didn't move or dare show an ounce of weakness, because this thing could lunge with lightning speed and I had no doubts in my mind that it would ever make it to me alive. I was standing with trained killers, though.

He wouldn't get within an inch of me before they dispatched him to hell.

"Foul, I can find another builder who will rebuild this place, and not be as much trouble," Vlad warned, his eyes sharp with anger as he watched Foul's every move.

"I live," it hissed. "I get Layla," he crooned and smiled, revealing more rows of serrated teeth.

"Layla?" I questioned, turning to look at Vlad. No way in hell was I bartering with this creature with someone else's life.

"Layla is seventeen and dying from a rare blood disorder that can't be cured. It's incredibly painful for her, and this is one way for her to at least have a relatively painless death," Vlad explained. "She wants to leave this world on her terms, and I brokered the deal for the new Guild."

"She wants what he can do?" I swallowed the urge to throw up. Some people couldn't be saved from their own desires, or stupidity. It was a lesson I'd learned long ago.

"She's dying; she approached us, wanting to be taken by the Fae," Vlad said as he watched me. "The Fae can't help what is wrong with her; she could go to Faery, but she would still be in agony and eventually die. We tried to change her over, but she almost killed the vampire who chose to sire her; her blood is that deadly. Foul craves the taste of human flesh and knows the risk her blood poses to us and potentially poses to him. He also knows what the Guild will do to him if they catch him in the act of enjoying another Snack Pack of the human variety, and he is willing to take the risk. Synthia, believe it or not, this was the most palatable option we had to get this Guild up and running in the shortest amount of time possible."

My eyes moved to Adrian, who nodded, but it wasn't for what Vlad assumed. He probably figured I was checking my facts with Adrian; in reality I was letting Adrian know I intended to kill this monster the moment the Guild was finished. There was no way I was taking the chance that the girl's blood might not do the deed for me, nor would I let Foul have her. If death was what she wanted, I would see if Eliran could find a more humane way to help her meet her end. I met Adam's eyes briefly, sensing his own thoughts mirrored mine as the scent of roses grew overpowering in the room. When my eyes moved back to the *Fiacla an éadóchais*, I wanted to throw up.

"Foul, put your cock away and behave like you want to live," Adrian hissed, the warning in his tone absolute as he pulled out a dagger and placed it on the table. "You'll get no other warning."

Something that looked nasty oozed from the creature's lips as he smiled at Adrian and then glamoured on clothing. Once it had, the room began to stink once again of mold and mildew, which was welcoming, considering the alternative.

I placed my palms flat on the table and leveled the monster with a chilling look. My power blanketed the room, causing its thin hair to stand on end with the static electricity that pulsed from my side of the table. I was flanked by Adam and Vlad, both silent as I gave a show of power to stop the monster's rude antics.

"Show me the plans, or I have no use for you," I said softly, without a single ounce of the hate I was feeling in my tone. I watched him stare at me with those dead eyes as my power filled the air until the room was electrified with it.

"Is no fun, this one," it sneered as it pushed papers aside and splayed its fingers apart as a neon blue 3D replica of a building took shape between his fingers. The replica grew as Foul spread his arms wide, as if it was stretching taffy. "Is strategically built as the King asked it to be so," he hissed. "The lines here; it is enough magic to feed the spells that will guard the walls and doors." The 3D Guild pulsed with magic that showed up as neon green beams. Each exit held a spell barrier, or so I assumed. The more I stared at it, the more I saw the old Guild's floorplans had been used, but had been redone to be more functional. "The doors will alert those inside to hostilities from the ones who enter. The wards above it will change to different colors based off of intent to those who enter. Instead of having just the guards in main entrance, we placed a wall here." It pointed out a divider wall. "Last one had vulnerabilities there. Now it doesn't. Building is protected from attack by magical barriers as well." Foul pinched his fingers together and then widened them, giving an exploded view of the entire 3D building, to show the plan for each floor in far greater detail. "This part of building, people will be able to monitor what each creature is that comes in." Foul pointed out a few rooms that were closed off. "Each wall opens into floors below for exit, should the wards fail. The King said safety was biggest concern to protect those who run it, as well as students and those who reside inside of it."

"And the magic, how will it be delivered to the wards directly?" I questioned and watched as he moved his fingers in an arch to reveal a line of purple color that flowed from the catacombs below us. "The wards that would be needed to filter out or stop those who shouldn't have access to the Guild are usually placed by a strong spell-master, but they can fail unless there is a reliable source of power."

"Raw power lies below," he stated, watching me carefully. "Building built on the Leylines. Leylines has enough power to run entire city, should the need arise."

I swallowed as I watched the *Fiacla an éadóchais*. It knew the building was built on the Leylines, which meant Foul could feel the power that pulsed through the walls as it flowed up through the ruins of the Guild. Not many creatures could feel the lines, which told me this one could draw power from them. Creatures who could tap the lines always knew where they were. It could be the difference between life and death. I'd been unaware that his kind could draw from them. I tucked the info into my brain for later.

"Continue," I said softly, even though I didn't want to stomach another second with the monster.

"Lines can be manipulated with magic to flow through the building to give enough power to run anything you wish it to. Should the city go dark, Guild would stand like a beacon against it. Entrance to catacombs was challenge. We decide to make it a maze of rooms, ones which move accordingly to a timer. Only those with upper clearance will be able to access the rooms or open the doors to them. It will take a little while to learn each day's pattern, but it will keep your enemies from reaching what the Guild hides inside it. The living quarters will be biggest challenge; it will be up to you as how they are accessed. Vlad say it important to protect those who live there the most. I build it to read marks, much like tattoos. It alerts you to any who enter it without clearance to be in them.

Can make them nullify enemy who enters without proper right to be there as well."

"Nullify?" I questioned, watching as his sunken eyes rose from the 3D map.

"Make them unable to move or to harm anyone until someone could get inside and secure them. It takes some Fae seconds to kill their prey, which is why it would nullify anything out of place inside the living area. That way, those inside could run to protection until someone with upper clearance could remove threat."

"This room, what is its purpose?" I pointed at a floor that looked empty but was divided by a glass wall.

"Training area, with cameras to monitor progress of students and tools to teach them," he said, using his fingers to push away the other floors. He threw his arms wide, which caused everyone but me to draw weapons. "Calm, is only map," he snickered as the map grew to reveal miniature people training inside the fully equipped gyms. Two gyms, one for children and the other for older kids who were more advanced. There was a room where kids moved their fingers as glowing lines moved around the room, revealing it was protected as they practiced magic.

Memories moved through my mind as I watched a set of kids sparring, trying to knock each other down as they tried to impress the others, who watched them from the side of the gymnasium.

"Vlad and King say you would have need to train, the room would be spelled in case of accidents. I made entire floor for train because the King say you'd want room. He say make it magical, impenetrable from the outside. I made it so. It will be connected to lines that flow beneath. Every side guarded, every entrance will be warded to keep out any who seek to do harm. Is this not what you wanted?"

"It is, but why wasn't anything built down here?" I pointed to the lower floors that had yet to be shown to us, and watched as his sullen eyes narrowed.

"Nothing good down there. Reeks of death and many bad things," he snickered, or he tried to. "Long after the kill, death continues to linger unlike above. Is slaughterhouse, this place of horror. Is warded to keep things like me out. Down there, is not my kills, not my problem to clean up. Wasn't in deal," he hissed coldly.

"What is that supposed to mean?" I crossed my arms over my chest as I watched him.

"Someone took those lives for reason. Best to let the dead linger down there, instead of up here. Tied to the sanctuary for which they lay, sacrificed for a purpose. No fun there," he replied, and at my pointed glare, he began anew. "They were here first, they serve a purpose. This was no temple of magic, no sacred place of peace. It was used to hide secrets; lives were sacrificed for those secrets to remain in the shadows. Is not sacred land, but a house of horror that Witches created. What lies beneath is your problem, not mine."

"You can't get in down there, can you?" I guessed.

"I say it warded, you not hear me," he growled. "Evil lies below, more so than I am. Souls it takes, but true death not come. What sleeps will rise, and when rises, there will be no place safe enough for any of us to hide."

"What the hell does that mean?" I huffed, waiting to see how much he knew about what was hidden below, but when he didn't answer and it appeared he was done speaking about it, I relented and changed the subject. "How long to build the new Guild?" I wanted a timeframe, because the moment he finished it, he was leaving this world.

"Few hours, possibly a day. Magical wards take longer but those are your King's problem. I build, he will fine-tune it."

"A few *hours*?" I blurted, and as he nodded I turned to confirm it with a look from Vlad.

"Adrian, Adam?" I asked, waiting to see what they said.

"It works, and it would be protected," Adrian agreed.

"We need Alden to look it over and agree," Adam mused. "This kind of magic is a little beyond our scope of knowledge, don't you think?" Adam frowned as he watched the kids wield the magic on the replica. "He should be included in this, and his knowledge is valuable and needed in this rebuild."

"I'll talk him through the details later," I sighed as I lifted my eyes to hold the monster's gaze. "We'll be in touch, Foul."

We waited for it to leave before I turned on Vlad and glared at him. "Next time, a head's up would be nice."

"You would have killed him had I told you what he was. You personally hunted them down for fun before you met us."

"Because they kill children since they make easy victims! The first one I killed had taken children from a school and kept them inside his home, which was nothing more than an abandoned warehouse. When it was ready to feed from their flesh, he'd let them think they had a chance to live and escape him. It let them run for days inside his home, a glamoured illusion of endless hallways and rooms. Once they saw what they thought was to be their freedom, he'd kill them. By the time my coven breached the warehouse and killed it, only three children remained. I think that even with all the therapy in the world, they will never live functional lives. So yes, I hunted them down and I killed every single one of them that I could find. I'd do it again if it meant a child got to grow into an adult without worrying if their flesh was creamy enough to catch the eye of a Rotting Corpse. No one deserves to die that way."

"No wonder you hated the Fae; you only saw the bad," Vlad muttered as he turned and looked around the room. "We need to get you home."

"No, I need to go down into the temple and see what the fuck he was talking about," I mumbled as I worried my bottom lip with my teeth. "Alden used to go down there once a week and we were never allowed down there. I need to see what it is that he and the other Elders were going down there for. I have to do this right, and I'm not sure he'd tell us what was down there even if we asked, so best we go have a look-see and figure it out for ourselves."

"Just like old times," Adam mused with a wolfish grin. "Breaking the rules and sneaking around in the tombs."

"Well, this time we can't actually get in trouble,"

I pointed out as we made our way down the passages until we came across one of the ceremonial rooms. "Blood," I whispered with a deep frown. It wasn't here the last time we had passed through. It wasn't fresh, but I could see the reddish-brown stains on the floor.

"Balls," Adrian sniggered. "Didn't you tell us about that one before?" He patted my shoulder to get my attention. "Plus, I remember some other blood that was spilled down here, but it wasn't so innocent," Adrian said silkily and my cheeks bloomed with heat. "This place has got a lot of history."

"Focus," I laughed nervously and pushed against his shoulder as his eyes heated. He'd taken my virginity in one of these ceremonial rooms. "I'm not that little girl anymore, vampire."

"You were never a little girl," he mused and then nodded as Vlad gave him a silent warning.

"We have history," I told Vlad. "That history is ours. It can't be washed away, no matter who we are with now."

"Be that as it may, Ryder will have my balls should the kid slip up and try to seduce you."

"That's why it is called *history*, Vlad. It's in the past. That's where it will stay," I smiled coyly and winked at Vlad. "Now, let us go to the bowels of this place and see what wicked shit lies in the history of the Guild, shall we?"

Chapter
EIGHT

We stood in front of a large door that held the mark of a pentagram and stared at the intricate wards protecting it. I knew them like I knew the back of my hand. I'd watched countless times as the Elders had woven spells for the wards. As a teenager, I'd been curious as to what was down there, and now, I wasn't so sure I wanted to know.

"It's heavily warded," Vlad broke the silence. "I'm not sure we should go down there."

"So don't; you wait up here and we'll go down."

Vlad looked at me and shook his head. "I'm at your side. However, I'm not sure Ryder would approve of this."

"So don't tell him," I offered. I brought my fingers up and started tracing the intricate pattern to undo the wards; one by one they came down, until the door was the only thing blocking our path. My hand touched the wood and a shiver raced down my spine.

I pushed the door open and everyone tensed as power rushed from the doorway and into the chamber.

I exhaled and stepped closer, only to feel Vlad pull me back as a feminine shape of a ghost appeared and smiled as she looked through us. We stepped back as she moved from the top of the staircase and floated to an altar towards the back of the chamber.

"What the hell," Adrian whispered, which made the ghost turn towards us and tilt its head. It exposed the neck, which looked as if it had been slit to the bone.

"Well, didn't see that coming," Adam whispered.

"It's just one ghost," I murmured, hoping it was all that was down here. "It must be tied to this location."

"She may have been sacrificed," Vlad pointed out. "She does have her throat slit, which is common in sacrifices."

All three of us stared at Vlad with worried looks. "Just how old *are* you?" I peered at him after he snorted at our faces.

"Old enough to have witnessed a few back in the day," he mused as he moved in front of me to block my path.

"Vlad," I warned.

"I'll go first," he said quickly. "Who knows what other crazy shit lies in wait down there."

"Fine," I conceded, knowing he wouldn't let me go first since he'd made a promise to Ryder and I was already pushing my luck. "What was it like, watching someone be killed as a sacrifice?" I cringed at my awkward attempt at making small talk.

"The first one I watched, well, it was horrible. She

went willingly to spare the others in her village from the monster in the castle," he muttered.

"Monster?"

"Me," he growled. "Her name was Vatina; she was beautiful and yet so naïve. Her people believed that if a virgin was sacrificed to appease the monster, no more bloodless corpses would turn up."

"You were feeding from her village?" I guessed, and he pointed at me and nodded in the affirmative, as if I had won some sort of prize.

"I was young in the terms of being a vampire; she was much younger. Wallachia was a turbulent place with the Turks raiding it and, well, usually it was easy enough to blame them for my actions. Eventually, a mystic discovered a few corpses had been bled dry. They were actually spies that I had dispatched to protect my land, but the bodies were enough to scare the villagers witless," Vlad recounted, lost in his memories from another time, another place. "So they offered a sacrifice to cleanse the earth of my darkness. She volunteered, to bring honor to her family who had done some wrong generations before. I was in the crowd as she walked so proudly to the altar, so beautiful," he explained with a faraway look in his eyes. "She wasn't even a woman yet, as far as I was concerned, barely fourteen—but in those days, she was old enough to take a husband and breed. She had on a sheer gown that exposed every curve," he whispered and swallowed loudly. "She looked me right in the eyes as I stood there among them, and begged for the darkness to leave their lands. She knew who and what I was, as I had fed from her before; she knew she had nothing to fear from me, yet she gave her life to clean the stain from her family name.

They slit her throat. It took her seconds to bleed out. I considered intervening, but it was what she wanted. Vatina had no idea that she had been sacrificed with my blood running through her veins. After they buried her, I returned to retrieve her."

"That is twisted," Adrian said from behind me.

"Back then it was life," Vlad explained. "She was too beautiful to die so young, and for something so pointless. To this day, she hates me for what I did."

"Not that, those," Adrian mumbled as he pointed to the walls surrounding us, which had skulls embedded in it, all with a hexagram carved in their foreheads. Each was marked with a roman numeral in the center of the hexagram.

"Wow," I whispered as I lifted my finger to trace the line of one, only to watch as it began to glow from my touch. The others that lined the wall began to glow as well. I swallowed down the urge to tuck tail and go back up, but I had to know what was down here. "They're filled with power, but it's protection power."

"It is meant to protect this place," Vlad announced. "There's something down here that they offered sacrifices to protect. Judging by the skulls, each one was a young woman."

"How can you tell?" My eyes moved over several of the closer ones as I tried to see what he had. Maybe it was a vampire superpower.

"Men tend to have thicker skulls than women," he explained as I snorted and tried to hold back a nervous giggle. "Women's skulls are usually smaller than men's in size, and the mandible on the jaw is shorter. There's also the orbit cavity. Women have a sharper edge than males, and there's also the glaring fact that there is a group of female spirits at the bottom of these stairs."

I looked over his shoulder and groaned. It had been a while since I'd dealt with ghosts. I hadn't gone back to the cemetery since I had been there with Larissa, because it hurt to know she'd sacrificed whatever power she had to help us. She wouldn't be there, and Adrian wasn't buried there, obviously. Eventually, though, I'd have to go see the spirits there. I owed them that much.

"They can't seem to communicate," Adrian said softly, but I doubted that was the case.

"Or they don't want to," I replied. "Ghosts are picky with who they choose to communicate, and normally it takes a Necromancer to speak or communicate with them properly. I can do it, and they know it. They're choosing not to speak. The one above is newer than these ones. She hasn't adapted, which would explain why she looked through us. These ones, they can see us."

"Friend or foe?" Adam enquired.

"I have no idea," I muttered as I watched one who looked oddly familiar. She stood in the back, watching us as we slowly, carefully moved down the steps. Once we got closer to the large room at the bottom of the steps, the steps turned into skulls. "There are more skulls than spirits," I whispered as I tried to figure out what was off about this place.

I'd never seen them bring girls down here, and yet some wore fashions from this century. My heart hammered against my ribs as I tried to deduce what the fuck had happened. Alden had insisted we stay away from here, but I'd assumed it was because of the wards.

"Synthia, she's wearing a concert tee from a *Nirvana* concert," Vlad pointed out as a ghostly girl walked through the others and turned her head to look through us as the others watched us, seeing us.

"She's newer," I whispered. "What the hell is the Guild hiding that they'd need human sacrifices for?"

"The line, maybe?" Adam asked.

"The Leylines were here before the Guild was built. They don't require a sacrifice to stay powered, just the rites of Samhain and a few other traditional days of the year. Human sacrifice is reserved for dark magic or ancient spells that the Guild wouldn't have the balls to use without a Changeling to cast it."

"You mean a Mage," Adrian muttered helpfully.

"No," I shook my head. "Quickie update: it seems a lot of what the Guild taught us was bullshit. Ryder told me that what the Guild was calling Druids were really Changelings. Well, at least they were before they separated into two groups. Some became Mages and others became Witches. The strength of the magic that was cast here had to have been the work of one of those old ones."

The moment our feet touched the ground, flames leapt from candles to light the room we stood in. Glyphs glowed from the walls down winding tunnels, which led away from where we stood. My heart pounded as something flittered through my mind, like butterfly wings searching my memories.

"Stop that," I growled as one of the older ghosts

watched me. I sensed that she was probably the first of the group to be sacrificed. "Stay out of my head."

"It's dark in there," she said softly. "So much darkness for one so young," she continued as she floated towards me.

"Don't worry; I made friends with my demons a long time ago. Occasionally I can even talk one of them into painting my nails if I ask real nice," I assured her as I felt her skimming my memories. I should have stopped her, but I sensed if I did, she'd stop talking. "What is this place?"

I sensed the other ghosts digging through my companions' minds but, as if they were all connected, they latched onto mine and I swallowed hard as the ghosts dug at my memories. They were looking for something, but what? I exhaled as pain lanced through my mind as they dug through the important memories, moving each one away when they decided it wasn't needed. It wasn't until they found the one of Ristan screaming to remove the babies from my womb as I lay dying that they paused and withdrew.

"You have given birth, you're a mother," one whispered as she watched me carefully.

"I have," I admitted.

"But not in this body," another said softly, her eyes filled with wonder. "You are dead, but alive. Like *she* is," she whispered.

"Like who?" I inquired, watching as they grew excited. "Who here is like me?"

I watched as the ghosts moved to one of the largest tunnels and floated down it, forcing us to almost jog to keep up with them. When they stopped, I paused. I could feel the power pulsing from whatever lay beyond the door we stood in front of. They watched us, and looked at me expectantly.

"Who is behind that door?" I asked carefully.

"She who can never die, yet is not allowed to live, either," one answered cryptically.

"Is she evil?" I asked, wondering if they'd answer, or if they would even know the answer since, to them, whoever it was probably wouldn't seem evil to them.

"She is neither good nor evil, and she neither lives nor dies," another one said as she tilted her head, revealing her neckline, which, like the others, was sliced to the bone.

"Why were you sacrificed?" I countered, hoping it would throw them off enough to answer.

"To feed her," one whispered. "To keep her from living or dying," the young girl said with a soft smile. "We bleed so that she remains as she is."

"What happens if she wakes up?" I asked, wondering what the hell we'd just stepped into. None of them answered me, and one by one, they started to vanish. "Stay," I cried, but it was as if they feared whoever lay behind the door, and they evaporated to nothing more than mist.

"That isn't good," Adam muttered, and Adrian agreed. "Maybe we shouldn't open it?"

"And what, rebuild the Guild without knowing if we are living on top of a freaking monster?"

"You have a point, but dark magic, blood magic,

and ancient magic are tricky. What if we open the door and it wakes *up* that monster?" Adrian's turquoise eyes bored into mine with worry.

"I can't reopen the Guild without knowing everything about it. I can't bring kids here if I don't know all the facts. Some of those ghosts are from this decade, which means they died while we were living here. Someone or something made sacrifices in this Guild without us knowing it, and that, well that scares the shit out of me," I admitted as I used my magic to push the door open.

Inside the room was a woman eternally young and beautiful, who lay in a glass box that was etched in ancient glyphs, curses maybe. Like the sacrifices, her hair was the color of a raven's wing and she had ice blue eyes that seemed to be staring at something on the ceiling. Her hands were clasped together, and she looked as if she was merely sleeping. Eerie blue lights burned along the walls, which I somehow knew were linked to the Leylines that ran right below her glass box.

"Fucking hell, is that who I think it is?" Adrian whispered, and my eyes turned to him.

"It's not Hecate," I whispered as I worried my lip with my teeth. "If it's who I think it is, we need to back out of here, and fast. No one can speak a word of this outside of this crypt."

"Synthia," Vlad warned.

"Vlad, I don't want to lie to Ryder either," I said. "If she is who I think she is, if she wakes, war will be the least of our worries. Portals popping up randomly will be kid's play. I have to get to Alden and ask him what he knows. Until then, the Guild being rebuilt is on hold. No one comes down here, and no one speaks of what is down here either. Gods save us if she wakes," I whispered as I moved out the door, waiting until they'd followed me out before I started replacing wards.

"Synthia," Vlad started again, watching me as I placed ward after ward until I began to tire from it. I sagged once I was sure no one would try to touch the door or the wards.

"Let's get out of here, now," I urged, ignoring him as I moved past him and rushed towards the stairs as if the hounds of hell were nipping at my heels.

Chapter
NINE

My mind raced with the complications of what we'd discovered, but also over the problems we already had. We couldn't catch our breath before more problems arose for us. How Ryder expected to have a wedding in the middle of the chaos just boggled me.

The building plans Foul had drafted would work, but I had to have a sit-down with Alden and discuss them—and the body in the glass box beneath the Guild. There were stories about the Leylines, hundreds of them, but not one that could be proven as true. Most had been told to us by the Guild librarians. Those had been of mythical creatures, like Gods who gave us magic so that Witches continued to exist. Fables and bedtime stories told to make the minds of children flourish with hope. As an adult, living in the world I was now, I could see how kernels of truth could flourish into those fanciful tales.

My eyes moved to the door. Every passing moment Ryder was gone, I worried more. I hated being apart, but my day hadn't been normal either. I'd been tossed one curveball after another, with the worst being the end of the day. I hated not being able to just tell him what it was, but whispering it out loud scared me. It made me paranoid that something in the universe was listening, and would alert our enemies to the ticking time bomb beneath the Guild.

I was dressed in a white Grecian style nightie, which had an empire bodice and spaghetti straps with tiny bows on the shoulders. It flowed to my ankles with a satin softness that floated with every step I took, until I stopped in front of the bed and bowed my head.

Where the hell was he? I exhaled and brought my hand up to my shoulder as I tried to rub the tension from it. I closed my eyes as I felt him enter the room behind me. Relief washed through me. One of his hands slid onto my shoulder and he rubbed it where mine had been as his other slid around my waist. He said nothing, but the spice of his unique scent filled my senses, comforting me. We didn't need words. Ryder and I could communicate through touch or a simple look that said more than words ever could.

"Hard day, Witch," he murmured as his lips touched the top of my spine, brushing soft kisses over it, sending sensual rivulets of heat to my core.

"I hate not being able to speak to find you and talk to you whenever I want. I miss the connection," I murmured, not bothering to turn around. His mouth was heaven against my flesh. "Any sign of Ciara?"

"We found a few things out, but nothing is certain yet." He pushed my hair away from my neck and softly caressed my flesh with his lips. My body clenched in reply and a soft moan tore from my lips. "I can smell you," he purred as he continued to wreck my system with his skilled lips. "Gods, I've missed seeing you this vulnerable," he murmured.

"I'm never vulnerable," I smiled as I felt the strap of the nightgown slip from my shoulder, exposing the globe of my breasts. His hand cupped it, testing the weight as he caressed it.

"You're wrong," he growled as he squeezed, and I gasped in response. "I know you are, because when I'm away from you, I'm vulnerable. I find myself looking for you. Over my shoulder, that empty void at my side. I feel like a crazed beast searching for you when you're not with me." His voice dropped to a whisper and he kissed my shoulder, his hands tightening on both my breast and my hair.

I smiled as tears filled my eyes. We were each other's weakness. He was right; when he wasn't near, I searched for him. Every tick of the clock reminded me that he wasn't beside me, and I hated it, and yet I wouldn't change it for anything.

"We'll just have to live with that then, won't we?" I mused as his fingers rolled my nipple between them, which made my stomach flip in excitement. He had skill with those sinful lips. He was the only man who could kiss you into an orgasm without touching below the waist. He slowly moved his lips over my shoulder, nipping at the sensitive flesh. His hand moved from my breast to cup my chin; he lifted it, and his mouth moved over my ear, the sound of his husky growl setting every nerve in my body on fire.

He pulled my hair harder, and I moaned in response. His hand released my chin and moved to the other strap, slipping it down from my body to leave me bared before him. His other hand freed my hair as his fingers traced my spine with feather soft touches. He took his time, drawing little circles on my flesh as he kissed his way slowly down my spine.

"I've missed this," he murmured in a throaty tone that made me want to turn around and kiss him. His mouth kissed the curve of my hip as he slowly sent my body into a startling state of need. Slowly he kissed the back of my thighs; his hot breath fanned my ass and pussy as he leisurely worked my flesh with his lips.

"Ryder, I'm hanging by a thread," I whimpered as I felt him standing up behind me. He pushed my legs apart with slight pressure from his knees, allowing his fingers to slip through the slick mess, slowly parting my flesh as he ran them lengthwise through it. He didn't enter me, instead, he teased until my knees threatened to give out.

"Let me know when it breaks," he laughed huskily against my ear. "I have no intention of letting you come yet," he growled as his fingers found my clitoris and slowly moved in a circular pattern. "Close your eyes," he ordered, and I did, even as the sensation of falling took root. I leaned against him as he continued to work my sex.

One minute we'd been in our bedroom inside the castle, and the next we were standing naked in a beautiful meadow. Glowing flowers illuminated the ground while tiny fireflies danced around them. The breeze rustled my hair as I leaned my head against him, taking in the exquisite scenery around us. We made the only sounds; his touch continued to pull moans from my lips as he brought me to the edge of sanity and dangled me over the ledge.

He released me and turned me towards him, slowly finding my hands as he pulled me closer, until his cock was flush against my belly. I looked up into glowing golden eyes that sparkled with a million tiny stars captured in their depths.

"I've wanted to bring you here since you came back to me," he admitted. "It's the flowering fields, where the fairies pull a special magic from here that makes the stones of the Fairy Pools glow. This is what I think of when I think of you. You light up my world, Pet; no matter how dark it gets, you mirror this field in my soul," he whispered as he lifted me up and I wrapped my legs around him.

Ryder didn't do sweet talk a lot, but when he did, it laid me bare. It turned me inside out and fucked with my head like nothing else could. I kissed him, claiming his lips in a gentle kiss as my hands raked through his hair. He groaned and I exhaled as I captured his tongue, claiming it in a dance as old as time. This man, this creature, he was my soul.

"I love you," I whispered. I wanted him buried inside my warmth; I was soaking wet with need for him. I could feel that throb pulsing inside of me, one that danced to a beat only he could use to make my body sing.

"You want me buried inside of you, don't you, Pet? This pussy wants me deep," he growled as he grabbed my hair and pulled it back, exposing my neck to his greedy lips. He kissed and sucked on my pulse. "How deep do you want me?" he asked, his voice rough as he slowly continued to kiss my neck, chin and lips.

"Soul deep," I whimpered as I felt his silken flesh rubbing against mine. I was so fucking close, and still so far away. He loved control, and very seldom would he give it up. In this department, he could have it, but he damn well had to earn it first.

"Who owns it?" he mused, his golden eyes lit

from within as he watched me carefully.

"I do," I growled as his thickness slid through my silken folds without entering them.

"Who does?" he asked, his brow rising as he watched me. I slid my hands through his soft tresses of hair and yanked on it as I claimed his mouth hungrily. "I love it when you play hard to get, because it ends with you sore and me fed," he laughed huskily.

"Is that so?" I whispered as I rubbed my core along his rigid length. I was so close to coming without his help.

"Naughty little Witch," he growled hungrily as he set me on the ground and pulled me with him. I was so close, that my mind had hit the haze. I numbly followed behind him, obedient as he pulled me into a pond I hadn't even noticed. The water glowed green from the glow stones that also heated the pools. "You don't own that pussy. You can make it come, Pet, but I make it wet, take it to the edge and have it trembling for more, and when I'm finished with you, you'll be absolutely sure who owns it."

"It is part of *my* body," I teased as he turned and wrapped his fingers around my waist and lifted me onto a rock in the middle of the water. It was smooth, perfect for sunbathing on.

"Spread your legs," he ordered, and my eyes swung back to his as he smiled. Liquid amber watched me as I leaned back and spread my legs apart. I tried to focus on him, but the multitude of lights made my eyes search the meadows. He watched me, never demanding I stop taking in the beauty around us. This world was as untamed and beautiful as he was. It was also as dangerous as he was.

He kept his eyes on me as I looked around the meadow, taking in the beauty he'd wanted to share with me. Two moons glowed high in the midnight sky, adding their light to the beauty of the lush fields. The scent of Jasmine and other fragrant flowers filled the air, floating on the breeze.

"This is breathtaking," I whispered, afraid to ruin the serenity that the meadows offered.

"This is our reality," he said softly. "The magic here can kill mortals." He smiled wolfishly. "The flowers like to feed from flesh, but normally they tend to remain dormant while adding their beauty to the lands."

"If this is our reality, a land of deadly beauty, I'll take it if you are beside me." I swallowed as my eyes settled on him.

"This world as well as yours will try to tear us apart, Synthia."

"Let them try to," I growled as I slipped my legs into the heated water. "I refuse to live in a reality where we don't have this. Us. This." I motioned between us with my finger. "We're more than we've ever been, and the world can continue to try to rip us apart, because it only makes us closer and stronger. So yes, I'm yours. Every part of me belongs to you, Fairy. I've always been yours. I was blind before, but I can see you now, all of you. You're the other piece of me. You're what I was missing all this time. Now that I've found you and this love between us, I'd kill to keep it. I'd destroy worlds to be with you."

"I fall in love with you a little more every time I look at you." He swallowed. "Every time you laugh, something unfurls inside of me and I have to pinch myself to know you're real. That you chose me, even though I know I don't deserve you," he growled as he cupped my face between his hands and moved his lips inches from mine. "Sometimes I watch these lips move and I'm not sure what I want more. To kiss them, or fuck them." He laughed wickedly.

"You always say the sweetest shit, Fairy," I laughed as I lifted my head and inched forward to claim his mouth in a hungry kiss that ended with a fervent need to never let him go.

He wiggled his fingers and a blindfold appeared in his hands. He smiled and watched me as I grinned. He really did love control. I could give an inch, because I knew I'd be screaming his name and he'd own me by the time we finished here. I leaned up, expecting him to wrap the blindfold around my head; instead, he continued to watch me.

I was about to ask what his game was, when a masculine hand reached around from beside me and my eyes moved to a second Ryder. I started to sit up, confused as to what was happening, when the first one placed his hand on my thighs and stopped me from bolting.

"It's just me, Pet," he promised, as his clone touched my breast, testing the weight with the exact same roguish grin on his lips. "My powers are growing the more I feed from you," he murmured as the other one took the blindfold and moved to the other side of the smooth rock. He caressed my neck, kissing it gently as he drew the blindfold across my eyes and tied it at the back of my head. My heart accelerated as the world was shut out. "I want you to feel me; I'm both. I can be more," he laughed throatily. "I can be whatever you need me to be."

"Ryder, this is....new," I admitted with a swallow, as my breasts were grabbed roughly and something hot fanned against my pussy at the same time. "I've never done this before," I admitted, the fear spiking as sweat trickled down my spine.

"I know," he laughed as he sucked on my clit abruptly, pulling a cry from my lips. "Don't worry; I plan to go easy on you the first time. Come to me, put your arms out," he commanded, and I did, feeling him pulling me off the rock and into the water as splashing sounded from the other side. "I'm both, so when he's inside of you, it will also be me. He is an extension of me."

"So you can clone?" I whimpered as his hands gripped my ass hard.

"I can multiply; I think it has something to do with me fucking a Goddess. You feed me power, so it's the only reason I can think of as to why my power is growing. So it's the least I can do to test its limits on your sweet flesh," he said huskily as he handed me up to the other Ryder.

I was freaking out. I felt the other one lifting me to him as he sat on the rock. He turned my back against his chest, pulling me into a sitting pose on his lap and positioning his cock against my flesh, and before I could say anything, I was sliding down his thick, rigid cock. His hands used my hips to propel me down until he was buried in my pussy until it ached. I felt something hot fanning my flesh and then Ryder was working circles against my clitoris with his mouth as his clone brought me slowly up his length.

The Ryder sucking my clit moaned as I was pushed down until there was nothing more to take of his twin's cock. His hungry mouth sucked, kissed, and licked my flesh wildly, as if he was ravenous and I was his dinner. The sound of his moans alone was enough to send me sailing over the edge, but the moment I thought I'd fall, he pulled me off his cock and pushed me flat on my stomach on the rock.

Hands moved me; my legs were spread as something soft and salty pressed against my lips, rubbing against them until I opened to accept what was being offered. I felt the other Ryder burying fingers deep in my wet pussy as I struggled to accommodate the cock in my mouth.

"Now this is something to see," he growled as he pressed hard on the base of my spine as I tried to arch my ass for his cock. "Such a greedy thing; you need more, don't you?" he crooned as he removed his fingers and slid the wet tip of his cock over my welcoming flesh. I felt him entering me, and tried to remind myself it was just like his magic when he used to fill me full. Only, I'd never felt this full.

They rocked my body in perfect rhythm, proof that it was one man taking control and taking me over the edge of no return. The gentle breeze was the only reminder that we were outside, exposed and in an erotic position for any voyeur to see. Hands cupped my breasts, and then pinched my nipples as the other worked my clitoris until I was screaming around the massive cock in my mouth as I shattered.

Hands moved me the moment my body started to fall back to earth. I was set in the water as one moved to stand behind me, lifting me as the other moved around in front of me. I was spread wide, my legs held apart from behind as the other stepped up to my exposed pussy. His cock slapped my sensitive flesh and I cried out, knowing he'd soon enter me. I felt his cock rubbing against my pussy, enjoying the wetness it offered him. He pushed inside, and I moaned explosively as he and the other one moved. One leaned against the rock as the other helped hold me open and exposed to both cocks.

The other didn't enter me; instead, he held me while Ryder fucked me without mercy. His cock moved with inhuman speed as it pounded my flesh until I felt myself falling. I was yanked off a cock, spun around until my ass was high in the air, and then I was entered as the other kissed my mouth hungrily. It was overwhelming, and yet I wanted it all.

"More," I groaned against the lips that kissed me, and I heard throaty laughter from behind me. "I want it all."

"Mine," was growled, and I whimpered as I felt rough hands gripping my ass as the cock inside me grew until I was struggling to get off of it. Wild thrusts took control as my body was ravished and pushed to its limits. Ryder crooned in my ear, begging me to stay with him as whatever was behind me went crazy with lust. The beast had taken control of one of the clones, and teeth skimmed my shoulder. "So sweet," it purred and I spread wider, taking more than I ever thought possible. I felt a cock touching my lips, and then the blindfold was removed as amber eyes watched the beast over my shoulder.

"Gods," he whispered as he looked down to find me watching him with the tip of his glorious cock in my mouth. He'd never glimpsed his own beast. His eyes were wild with wonder, and I wasn't sure if it was because I was taking his beast while he watched, or because he'd come face to face with his own inner demon. I was ripped backwards away from Ryder's cock. My instinct was to fight, because Ryder wouldn't save me if the beast had control of one of his clones while he controlled the other. "Synthia," he warned, even as his hand stroked his cock to the beat of his monster that rocked my body as if I was a rag doll. I was being fucked while he was helpless to anything but watch us. Claws fondled my breasts, and I knew without having to turn around that the beast was watching Ryder as he fucked me in open challenge.

"Watch me," I whimpered as my hand moved to my flesh and started to stroke it. I wasn't sure what the hell was going on with them, only that Ryder couldn't fight his beast because it was a part of him. A part of himself that he probably never expected to see. His golden eyes lowered to my flesh, and then he stepped closer. I whimpered as I was yanked off of a thick cock and pushed back to the rock as the beast stared at Ryder.

I turned over, spread my legs, and slapped my own flesh, forcing the monster and Ryder to watch me instead of each other. I whimpered as the sensitive flesh protested in pain, but then the beast was there, sucking on my flesh with ravenous hunger as he sent me sailing over the edge, pushing his fingers deep into my pussy and then withdrawing them as he stood up and bared his fangs territorially at Ryder. Wings unfurled from his back as he shoved his cock to the hilt inside of me, which caused my body to spasm as wave after wave of orgasm rushed through me.

Ryder growled, his eyes glowing brighter than I'd ever seen them glow before as I exploded in ecstasy. One minute I'd been with the beast, and the next, it was Ryder between my legs, driving into the welcoming wetness of my body's multitude of releases. When he finally came, I was little more than a boneless, crying mess. He bent over and whispered sweet words as he apologized. I wasn't crying from the pain, because let's be honest, I wasn't going to be walking tomorrow without wincing, but because he saw his beast and he'd taken control back.

"You won," I moaned as he pulled out and rained kisses over my flesh.

"What?" he asked as he sat me up and looked at my bruised flesh. "Gods, Synthia…"

"Don't you Gods me, I fucking loved it," I laughed as I grabbed his cock, stroking him to readiness again.

"Synthia, he's a fucking monster. He was hurting you," he growled. "I watched him," he said with a disgusted look that took me back. "He grew until he hurt you. He could have ripped you apart."

"He won't hurt me," I assured him. "He knows my limits, and yeah, watching it was probably different from getting the view you are used to, but he loves me. He's never given me more than I can handle, and neither have you. When he starts to hurt me, he pulls back and you take control. You think he wouldn't fight you for it?" I asked, watching him.

"I love you," he whispered as he pulled me into his arms and kissed me deeply.

"I love you too, all of you. He's mine too, Ryder. You have nothing to fear from him where I'm concerned. There have been many times where he could have hurt me and didn't, and I'm sure watching us together wasn't part of your plans tonight. I'm glad you got to meet him, though, face to face."

"I'm not sure how you didn't run screaming the first time he showed himself to you," he groaned as he hugged me even tighter.

"You can't see him when he's in control, can you?" I murmured.

"No; I sense and can see what he sees." He shrugged. "I've only ever caught a glimpse of him through your eyes, and that wasn't near enough to prepare me for today."

"I'm glad you brought me here, and more than that, Fairy, I'm glad you met your demon. He's a part of you, and I accept everything you are and will be. You and me, Fairy. Forever and ever," I murmured as I smiled at the man I was going to marry. If someone had told me this would be my world, I'd have laughed at them and called them crazy. Now, now I couldn't imagine a life without him in it.

Chapter TEN

"Are you strutting?" Ristan mocked as Ryder grinned at me as we walked into the main hall, where a select few of the Elite Guard were gathering so that we could strategize about what to do about the fractured portals.

"I am," he purred as he smiled and winked at me.

"Leave him alone," I laughed. "I love that smile."

"You would. You put it there, Flower. He never smiles like that for us," Ristan mocked with a wink and nod, as he led the way to the large, elegant room.

"You don't do what she does for me," Ryder countered, and a blush bloomed across my cheeks.

"You're damn right I don't, and I'm not about to try either!" He chuckled, his eyes smiling as he watched me fidget under his knowing gaze. Kinky fuckery was something Ristan was all too good with. "Anything from Danu on the portals yet?" He reached back at an awkward angle to scratch at something on his back that seemed to be irritating him as he switched to a much safer topic.

"No, she's been quiet for too long. I tried calling for her again last night when we got back, but she hasn't answered me. I'm getting rather worried; it's out of character for her. She's usually rather fond of being a nuisance, so this silence worries me."

"Maybe she found someone else to torment," Ristan muttered under his breath, which made me wonder just what the fuck had gone on between them. Danu had been absent more and more since the turmoil in this world began escalating—which coincided with when Olivia and Ristan had begun to spend more time here in Faery.

"She promised to train me, and so far, I'm pretty sure I'm playing havoc with the sheep in Faery. The other day, the entire herd tried escaping from the pen as soon as I got near it." I could see the corners of their mouths twitching as they struggled not to laugh at me.

I'd blown up one sheep, one! Gah, they acted like I'd meant to do it.

"Poor sheep," Ryder chuckled.

"It was one sheep, one!" I huffed. "It's not like I have the same powers as I used to. I can literally move my fingers and shit explodes. She needs to get her ass back here and teach me how to use it before the Mages are here and it's too damn late to learn how to use it."

We'd just entered the main hall when Olivia approached Ristan. Out of the corner of my eye, I noticed she was wringing her hands nervously; her eyes were red and puffy and my heart flipped a little as I wondered what the cause of her upset was.

"Ristan," she whispered, as if it was for his ears alone. "I need to talk to you." She worried her lip with her teeth.

"Olivia," he smiled and kissed her, not caring one little bit that everyone was watching their exchange. "You look beautiful, what's wrong?" He gently grasped both of her shoulders and peered at her face when his eyes finally noted the puffiness of hers.

"I need to speak to you in private," she murmured in a rush as she bounced nervously from one foot to the other.

"Olivia, I'm rather busy right now," Ristan replied uncomfortably as he looked around the room at the small assembly gathered. "Can we speak about whatever it is later?"

"This can't wait anymore," she whispered impatiently. "I need to talk to you right now."

"Olivia," he said carefully. His eyes took in her nervous energy.

I crossed my arms over my chest and watched it unfold. I could tell that he was sensing something was wrong, but it didn't look like he was getting a sense of her overwhelming panic yet. She was upset, and she'd probably gone to see Eliran as I'd instructed her to. He could normally read her, but we had a ton of shit going on at the moment, and his worry for Ciara was taking a lot out of him.

"I can't leave right now," Ristan clarified patiently when she didn't answer him; his eyes watched her with confusion. They slowly lowered to her hands that were clutching the front of the waistband of the skirt she was wearing, as if she was trying to hold onto that small piece of fabric for support. Her feet shuffled as he slowly brought his eyes back to hers, a worried look in their beautiful depths.

"I'm late!" she exploded as if the secret could no longer be concealed. Oh, Gods. Her hands slapped over her mouth in mortification and she wildly looked around the room for help. I swallowed and struggled with how to help her. She squared her shoulders and I exhaled as she soldiered on. "I'm late and it's *your* fault," she growled meaningfully as she poked her finger at his chest.

"You're not late, we just started," Ristan said slowly with a comical look on his face. It faltered as her words started to sink in, and he frowned for a moment, as if he was confused about what was his fault. Hesitantly he tried again. "Olivia, I glamoured you clean and I tried to dress you so you wouldn't have to spend so much time figuring out what to wear, but you wouldn't let me, so it really isn't my fault you were almost late for the meeting. It hasn't started yet, so no reason to be upset, love."

I laughed silently at his triumphant deduction, only to see his grin wilt as he watched her, waiting for her response. Was that the only thing he could come up with, or was he only saying that because he didn't want to understand what she was trying to tell him? I stifled a groan as her eyes zoomed in on mine with a silent plea for help. I should offer her a lifeline, but I wanted to give her a chance to be the one to tell him he was going to be a father.

"I'm *late*," she hissed.

"We've only just…" he paused as I injected myself into the conversation.

"She's late, as in she didn't get her period. She hasn't been cursed by Mother Nature in a while, and won't be for some time," I explained, and swirling silver eyes turned on me, the look of pain took me by surprise as his eyes moved between me and her. The Demon was great with kinky shit; any sexual position you couldn't name, he could. Jokes? The Demon had endless supplies of them on hand, and he was an encyclopedia on the world's best movies, but apparently, he had a thick skull. This topic seemed to sail right over his head.

I watched as the color of his skin seemed to fluctuate between red and back to his usual alabaster coloring. I wondered if I should fetch him or Olivia a bucket to toss their cookies in. Both looked uncomfortable, and the men snickering around us weren't helping the situation. When Ristan failed to say anything else, I continued.

"Congratulations, you're going to be a father," I announced, enjoying being able to finally fuck with him. After all, he'd cut me open and I wanted a little payback, even though I loved him for saving my babies. He, however, didn't look happy. As a matter of fact; he looked like he was angry and sort of hurt. My eyes moved between him and Olivia, who was watching Ristan's reaction with a mixture of horror and panic. "So, do we call a Demon and Angel mix a Dangel? Or, what will it actually be?" I asked, playing for the best-sounding combo to lighten the mood.

"We won't call it anything. I can't have children," Ristan rasped out angrily, the swirl in his silver and black eyes was frenzied as they locked on Olivia's with a look of betrayal and hurt. The hair on my nape stood up and I swallowed. *Uh-oh.*

"Well, she's having a baby, your baby. You guys should probably do this in private, come to think of it," I offered as my stomach flipped with unease. Olivia didn't strike me as the kind to sleep around. She loved Ristan. That much I would bet my life on. "Maybe you should speak with Eliran, maybe he can help you guys?"

"She's not having my child. I can't breed. Alazander made damn sure of it when he sterilized me so I wouldn't be able to create life. He didn't want me adding to the Horde gene pool. So he made sure I wouldn't be able to procreate when he took everything else from me," Ristan spat out furiously.

"Shit," Ryder cursed as his eyes changed from gold to black, his anger for his father pulsing from deep within.

"Balls," I whispered with a frown.

"That makes no sense," Olivia cried as her frown mirrored mine as tears slid from her eyes.

"It's true," Ristan growled, and I knew without needing to read his mind that he was about to put the word 'ass' in assumption. "I can't have children, so if you're expecting…"

"Don't finish that thought, Demon," I offered, and angry, swirling eyes turned on me.

"Stay the fuck out of it," he hissed, and I could feel his pain radiating from deep inside of him. This beautiful creature wanted babies. He loved mine with a fierceness that only made me love the crazy bastard more.

"Ristan," Ryder warned, but I stayed him with a

wave of my hand. There was an awkward silence that filled the hall as everyone waited to see what happened next. Ristan glared at me and then Olivia, as Ryder glared at me. Ristan moved to Olivia and placed his mouth close to her ear as they whispered so that no one else could hear them. Something caught my eye as we waited for what Olivia or Ristan would do next.

Danu was watching me from the other side of the great hall, near the unlit fireplace. Her image shimmered, faded, and disappeared. Startled, I blinked, trying to find her again in the sparsely populated hall. I spun around, searching for her. A gentle touch on my shoulder turned me towards where she stood, fading in and out of sight.

"What's wrong with you?" I blurted, but it took her a moment to register my words.

"I made it so." Her voice was so faint, I could barely hear her.

"Made *what* so?" I asked carefully.

"I did this for him, Synthia," she explained as her image continued to shimmer and appeared to grow weaker with every passing second. "He adores your children, especially Kahleena, and he deserves to be happy with children of his own. I owed him that much. It's my gift to him, the ability to be able to breed again; considering all he's lost, it isn't much."

"What exactly did you do to him?" I asked, feeling the tension rise behind me as everyone figured out I was speaking to Danu, who had apparently played some part in undoing what Alazander had done to Ristan so long ago. I was hoping it wasn't as weird as replacing eggs or his little swimmers with someone else's.

"What occurred between me and Ristan is not your business, daughter mine. You have bigger problems to worry about. Fixing the Tree didn't repair Faery as we'd hoped it would. I've lost the power to be seen in this world except by those of my own blood. I am weakening. Something much bigger is happening, and you have to figure it out. Faery is in trouble, and so am I; if the damage cannot be fixed, I will cease to exist."

"You're dying?" I asked as my throat constricted and tears pricked at my eyes.

"I am connected to Faery, and it's damaged. You have seen the portals that cannot be closed. If this world connects to Tèrra, I will fade away to nothing. I'm tied to it, Synthia. You are not. While you can feel what is happening to Faery, you're not connected on the same level. I couldn't chance it, not with you."

"That's why you brought me back," I whispered. "Because if you die, someone else has to take your place," I exhaled. "You tied me to the Fae and not Faery so that if the world dies, I'm still tied to the Fae. You knew this might happen," I accused. "You should have told me so we could have stopped it from getting this far. You didn't bring me back to save Faery at all, because you were already dying, which meant you knew Faery was, didn't you?"

"Did I? Or did I selfishly save my child the only way I could? You are blood of my blood, and the only daughter who hasn't betrayed me. You may not think it, but I do love you very much, Synthia," she whispered. "I couldn't save this world *and* you. I had to make a choice. I chose you. By choosing you over this place, the others have noticed. This world may die, and you may have to abandon it at some point, but you won't abandon our people. I knew this scenario may come to light, but I had no questions about your loyalty in the grand scheme of the bigger picture. If you can't save this world, it will be all right. I've lived a good life; I'm tired."

"No, not okay, Danu!" I growled. "If we can't save this one, you die, correct? You tied yourself to that damn tree and it can't live outside of Faery because it is the heart of this world. You tell me what to do, you tell me how to fix it now," I cried. My hands fisted as my eyes burned with unshed tears. I struggled to remain calm; struggled to keep breathing without breaking down. "No, you tell me what I need to do and I will do it."

"It's not that simple. There are other things happening in the human world, and this world is not the only one that is crumbling. Something is upsetting the balance, and that isn't something we can control. This is bigger than us, daughter. I will do what I can to protect your children for as long as I can. Find the Stag; he may know more about the portals than I do. He can train you, Synthia; he can help where I can't."

"I don't want the Stag to train me, I want you. I want my mother," I argued, knowing she couldn't do it. I felt like I was losing her, and that she was fine with it happening. Why wasn't she fighting? Why wasn't she pissed?

"Because I chose you and, given the chance to do it again, I'd choose you every time. I interfered, and if this is the cost, I'll gladly pay it. Tell Ristan that I am sorry. Sorry for all that was done to him by his father that I couldn't stop or change because I am not supposed to interfere directly. I am already paying the price for defying *them* by interfering with you. So there isn't anything else they can do to me if I interfere for him now. This is why I can return that which was taken from him physically, when I couldn't help him before. For centuries, he has faithfully served me; he deserves at least this much. I only hope it is enough to restore everything that was lost. My powers, however, are not at their fullest." Her voice was soft and full of regret as her form shimmered and dimmed as she began to fade from my sight. "I love you, daughter, more than you could ever know."

"Danu!" I screamed when she vanished. "You get back here!" I spun in a wide circle as I searched for her. I stopped as my eyes latched onto Ryder like a lifeline and I rushed into his arms, burying my face against his chest. Danu's words had drained the warmth from my world, but Ryder refilled it as his arms wrapped me as he sensed my pain.

"What the fuck did Danu do now?" Ristan snapped angrily. I didn't blame him, but I was in pain too.

"She chose me," I whispered as I ignored Ristan and looked up into the amber eyes that centered my world and kept it from teetering over the edge. He anchored me. "By bringing me back she chose me, and her own life is now hanging in the balance as the price for mine. She's dying." I swallowed a sob as Ryder's arms held me and kept me from falling when my legs refused to support me due to the pain that lanced through me as I said the words out loud. Once I found my balance, I turned and looked at Ristan, who was frozen in place, a look of uncertainty on his face. Tears burned and threatened to fall. "I don't know what happened between you two, but since you both have chosen to leave us in the dark about it, so be it. Whatever happened, it's in the past, so leave it there. Danu is dying. Whatever occurred, it no longer matters because we've got a lot bigger problem than

the portals being fractured. Faery is dying. We have
to work together to figure out how to save it. She did
say that she fixed whatever Alazander broke and that
your boys," my eyes moved to his dick and back up
to him with meaning, "can make swimmers again.
She made it sound like you may eventually get other
things back, but she didn't say when. It sounds like it
was her parting gift for whatever transpired between
you, even though she didn't quite say that. Just that
she wasn't supposed to interfere and it wasn't until
she broke the rules with me that she was able to do
this. Without Faery, there is no Danu. So right now
we need to fix this world and then you can go back to
hating her."

"Danu can't die," Ristan argued softly. His eyes
spoke of his fears, but it wasn't for him or Olivia.
There wasn't any gratitude for whatever it was
that he was going to get back, only fear for Danu. I
swallowed my anger and shook my head. Whatever
had happened between the two, he'd loved her once
upon a time. Deeply.

"She can die, she's tied to Faery. I'm tied to the
people; until the last Fae draws breath, I'll exist.
She's told me several times that she couldn't directly
interfere in our matters, but when I died, she brought
me back. She gave her life for mine, and I don't accept
that. We have to fix whatever is wrong with Faery."

"We will, Synthia," Ryder assured me. His
hand slipped in mine and he pulled me close to his
welcoming heat. "We'll save it, because it's our
world."

"I'm going to be a father," Ristan whispered, and
I turned, watching as he kissed Olivia deeply with a
look of wonder I'd never forget. For whatever shit

Danu had done to him, it looked like she'd tried to make it right. I just wasn't sure if it was a reward for a lifetime of service, atonement, or both.

"What about Ciara? She's still out there and could be hurt," Dristan wondered out loud.

"Ciara is strong. She's smart; she'll buy time until we can get to her," Ryder murmured as he kissed the top of my head. "We'll find her. It may not be today or tomorrow. We will find her, though, I am sure of it. And whoever took her will understand what pain truly is."

Chapter ELEVEN

I walked around in the nursery, slowly taking in the toys and empty cribs. My heart felt like it was splitting apart; my duty to the realm and my children were supposed to be one and the same, and yet to save one, I had to send other away.

"Synthia." Liam's voice startled me as he materialized inside the room.

"How did you sift in here?" I demanded, my hand covering my wildly beating heart.

"Ryder gave us specific marks to be able to do it; he wanted to surprise you today since Madisyn is coming to help with the wedding plans."

Oh yeah, today I was being fitted for the dress. The one I would walk down the aisle in, and pledge my life to my King and Kingdom.

"I'm surprised." I frowned, trying not to sound disappointed that he hadn't brought my children with him.

"No, I'm not the surprise," he laughed, his tri-colored eyes smiling as I frowned deeper. "It's in here." He turned the knob to the other door that opened up into the nursery playroom.

I watched as it opened and the beautiful sound of babies playing greeted me. I moved inside, finding Ryder already on the floor with our daughter in his lap. He looked up at me and grinned. I exhaled and slowly sank to the floor in front of him as I accepted Cade from Sinjinn, who beamed with a knowing smile.

"I thought you could use a reminder of why we are fighting so hard to save this world," Ryder murmured as he kissed Kahleena's platinum curls. They'd grown, and as I watched, Kahleena stood and took a wobbly step towards me with her hands extended.

"She can walk?" I swallowed.

"She's starting to," Ryder remarked as he turned to watch Zander crawling to us. "They've grown a little since they've been away."

"We missed her first steps, their first steps?" I asked as I felt my throat tighten. "What else did we miss?" I looked at Liam as he sat beside me, the scar on his face tightening as he smiled. I watched as his smile faded as tears misted in my eyes.

"They say a few words now, mostly 'momma' when we glamour your image for them. They say 'Fairy' when we show them Ryder's, which I assume is because you call him that," Liam said proudly. "They're smart. Mother says they are smarter than most of the babies she's ever seen, and I'm pretty sure they can sift already. Kahleena is making the most progress. She's very smart and determined. She seems to be in charge and the others follow her lead."

I grinned; I'd warned them that my daughter

would be in charge of her brothers. Her tiny fingers touched my face and I smiled as shining amber eyes searched my face and she made a soft cooing noise that tugged at my heart. I'd known they may grow a little, but we'd missed so much in the short time they'd been away from us.

"Momma," she cooed and then laughed excitedly.

"You're so big now," I whispered as I leaned over and kissed her nose and forehead. "I've missed you all so much."

"She's just like you," Ryder snorted as he held his hand out for Zander, who tried to show off his mad skills with walking and ended up falling on his butt after a moment. His little lip stuck out as he pouted, but Ryder held out his finger for Zander's tiny hand to grasp, and helped him up so he could walk the short distance to his father. "Hey, Zander," Ryder whispered as he pulled him close and kissed his dark head.

"Gods save us if they're anything like you, Fairy," I laughed as I smiled at him over the top of Kahleena's head.

"Fairy," Cade said in a tiny voice that made me throw back my head and bark with laughter.

"You're incorrigible," he growled as he leveled his gaze with Cade's and said 'daddy' several times.

"Da-da," he said watching Ryder, his purplish-blue eyes lighting with accomplishment as he repeated it.

There was a knock at the door and scuffling as Ristan and Olivia entered, the others close on their heels. One by one the Elite Guard piled in and moved close to the walls, until we were all sitting together with the children in the middle.

"We're going to need more room soon," Ryder grumbled playfully. Children weren't exactly plentiful in Faery, so each child was considered a joy and a blessing. Even with this understanding, I knew in my heart that his brothers adored our children above and beyond what the average Fae felt for the young of this world, and we'd never stop them from visiting with the children, since we knew they missed them as much as we did.

"Yes, we are," I agreed with a grin. I watched as Kahleena homed in on Ristan and stood up, causing him to let out a soft curse as she started her clumsy trek towards him.

"She walks?" he whispered, probably to keep from startling her as she wobbled towards him. "She couldn't even really crawl when she left." He gasped when she almost fell. I watched Olivia as she watched Ristan; every time Kahleena almost fell, he'd lurch a little closer. I could see the effort for which it took him not to move to her, to actually allow my daughter to make it to him.

"Ristan," she cooed as she finally reached him. His jaw dropped and I grinned; yeah, she was pretty badass for a toddler. She leaned against him and rested her head on his chest as she plugged her thumb into her mouth and watched me.

"She just said my name," he laughed nervously. "It's only been a few days."

"They have grown a lot," Liam explained as Sinjinn nodded his agreement.

"They have begun to display magic, which is very

rare at this age. We have seen them bring objects to themselves when they want something. Two days ago, Zander's teddy bear seemed to come to life and was talking," Sinjinn added. "They're busy, but when they sense it becoming overwhelming for us to handle, they reel it in and calm down. It's as if they can feel our emotions. There have been some signs that they have been sifting, but no one has actually caught them doing it and I am not sure if I have ever heard of any Fae that has ever sifted as an infant."

"They're not infants," I pointed out and watched as Ryder absorbed what was being said. "Besides, I pulled Adam to me. He was my familiar and I remember my foster mother telling me about the magic I did as an infant."

"You are a true child of Danu and you have her blood, Pet. You were also half Fae, so it stands to reason that you would be more powerful," he reasoned as he tried to cradle Zander, who was having no part of it. I watched as he settled in his father's lap and grinned at me.

"Your mother is downstairs," Olivia spoke softly. "You have cake to taste and dresses to look at today. We'll stay with the babies until you are finished," she offered sheepishly as her cheeks pinked with embarrassment. "I think I need the practice."

"They just got here," I frowned. "Can't it wait?"

"Madisyn is excited for your big day." Liam laughed as he stood and held his arms out to take Cade. "I hear that the handfasting celebration Kier and Mari hosted for you will pale in comparison to the grandeur of the celebration our mother has planned for you."

"Not sure why she is planning on such a huge

celebration. The last few didn't seem to go very well…" Ristan groused softly as Olivia gave him a curious glance. "The last one was almost the death of me."

I gave Ristan a sour look as I hugged Cade and kissed his chubby cheek before handing him to my brother.

"We will make sure to give you some time with them before we go home," Liam assured me.

I stood and dusted off my butt as I watched Ryder hand off Zander and turn to face me. I didn't want to plan my wedding; I wanted to cuddle with the babies and sleep to the sound of their sweet noises.

"Come on, Pet," Ryder said as he reached for my hand and sifted us out of the nursery rooms.

Chapter
TWELVE

I was seated at a table with Ryder, and it seemed like we must have taste-tested every type of cake ever made. There was decadent chocolate, red velvet, and so many more that we lost track. Madisyn had brought the chef here from Tèrra to make the wedding cake and the accompanying secondary cakes for the Horde (literally and figuratively) of Fae that would be coming to the wedding. Ryder told me proudly that the chef was part of the whole 'human fairytale wedding' he was trying to give me.

"This is good," Ryder commented as he spooned dark chocolate cake with buttercream frosting into my mouth.

"Mmm," I moaned around the mouthful. "That is really good."

"There's several more to try," Madisyn said as she spooned her own mouthful of cake and hummed as she shook her head. "That *is* really good. Maybe we should have him make small samples of each type of cake for the guests. You know, like those petit fours?"

The chef looked panicked for a moment as I

smiled and shook my head. "I don't think that will be necessary, and just for the record, I can't eat anymore cake today." I wiped my mouth and placed the napkin on the table. "I like the dark chocolate with the buttercream icing for the main cake, you?" I glanced over at Ryder as he licked frosting from his lips.

"It's your choice," he smiled and I couldn't help but smile back.

"It's *our* day," I answered. "That means you get to pick too, and since you don't get to see my dress or pick it, you have to choose the cake."

"Dark chocolate with buttercream icing," Ryder's tone was commanding even though he watched me with a wicked grin that tugged at my heart.

"We need a design," Madisyn said as she pulled out the catalog and started thumbing through it. She pointed out several ideas that were all over-the-top and extravagant. "This one is my favorite," she said as she pointed to a cake that had more layers than anyone could possibly need. I swallowed a groan when she and Ryder began discussing colors to celebrate each caste, as well as the representatives of the other creatures who inhabited Faery—that he'd invited to be present during the celebration. This meant that creatures such as Goblins, Dearg Due, Red Caps, and Púcas would be in attendance, as well as the Sluagh host. Just what every fairytale wedding needed.

"Red, black, white, and gold," Madisyn agreed as she gave detailed instructions to the chef, who looked a little flustered by their detailed designs.

I pulled the catalogue towards myself and started to look through it, finding smaller cakes with less detailed designs. I still wasn't sold on having a huge wedding. Something smaller and intimate would be fine, yet I didn't want to hurt Madisyn's feelings—or Ryder's, since he too was also pushing for some big, elaborate wedding that would make a statement to all of Faery.

"Synthia?" Ryder called, and I looked up. The cake they'd designed took up the entire table. "This?"

"That's enough cake to feed China," I whispered with a frown.

"There are a lot of people coming to the wedding," he explained. "We'll need fifty or more cakes to feed the crowd."

I swallowed and forced a smile. "It looks great." Being Fae, neither of them noticed I'd lied. I waited for them to go back to planning and continued to peruse the catalogue. My eyes skimmed over a cake that was made to look like a tree trunk, and on the light brown frosting of the trunk were initials carved into the center of a heart. I smiled, turning the page to see the other side which said, 'And they lived happily ever after,' on it. I pulled the page from the book while the others were discussing plans for the order that had enough chocolate to kill twenty grown men. Then, I listened as Madisyn and Ryder issued orders for the monster cake. The poor chef looked like he was going to have a heart attack until Ryder told him that he was only going to have to make the main ginormous cake and several smaller cakes, and the Fae would be able to replicate his work for the crowd.

"Dress time?" Madisyn asked and I shook my head.

"Venue, where are we getting married?" I inquired, and she looked confused.

"Here, of course. You are marrying into the Horde, so it is proper for it to be done here. Unless you'd like to marry in a chapel or a church like the humans do." She frowned and I guess I couldn't blame her, as a castle had more of a fairytale feel to it than a chapel did. Of course, based on the scale that Madisyn and Ryder were talking about, we wouldn't be able to fit everyone in a chapel unless someone had a hell of an extendable room spell that they could cast on it!

By the time we got through with this planning, we were all going to have some serious frown lines. I nodded and agreed that it was fine to do it here, and watched them wink at each other as I was escorted by Ryder into the great hall, which had been decorated in crimson, red, and gold. Tiny fireflies lit the tables and as I got closer, I realized they were fairies. Bright red rose petals had been mixed with white ones to cover the floor of the entire room. It was a sight to see, but it felt off, and the more I looked around, the more I felt overwhelmed by the proceedings.

Madisyn wanted this, Ryder was agreeing because it's what he thought I wanted, and I was agreeing because I didn't want to hurt anyone's feelings. I'd marry Ryder naked in the Fairy Pools if it was up to me. Ryder's hand tightened in mine and I looked up, finding his golden eyes searching my face.

"You don't like it?" he guessed, and I swallowed hard.

"It's beautiful," I replied easily, because it really was; it just wasn't me.

"It's perfect!" Madisyn squealed, and I smiled genially at her excitement. "It's our colors mixed with his; of course, the Horde and Blood Fae have never been united, so the scale of the event will be huge. The actual ceremonial version will be like this." She waved her hands. Flames erupted from the candles as she moved things around to reveal sitting rows that extended farther then the room allowed. The room swam in amber hues with red carpets that had only white petals covering them. "This is what it will look like to begin with."

"It's pretty," I assured her as she watched me.

"Is it too much?" She looked from me to Ryder uncertainly.

"Not at all—dresses?" I tried not to cringe as she clapped happily.

"I need a list of who you have for bridesmaids." She was busy looking at her list as her offhand request hit me like a punch in the stomach.

I paused, my stomach dropped, and I shook my head.

"I don't really have anyone," I replied softly. The lump in my throat stuck, my hands sweat, and my eyes misted as I swallowed the pain. Larissa was supposed to be here; she was supposed to be my best bitch. We'd planned this shit out and now she was gone. "I don't need any."

"You have to have some friends?" Confusion played across her beautiful features, and I laughed.

"I can ask Adam," I answered. "He'll be my bridesmaid, or maybe he can be the man of honor. Pretty sure he won't need a dress, though," I whispered hoarsely. "We should go try the wedding dresses on. I want to get back to the babies as soon as possible."

"Of course," she murmured softly, as if something caught in her throat.

Three hours later, I stood in front of the mirror in what had to have been the fiftieth dress Madisyn had me try on. It had a jeweled bodice, which she'd informed me were genuine diamonds. Thin gold chains crisscrossed over the back to attach to the bodice. The skirt was huge, and had flowing yards of fabric that a dressmaker held in her arms, or tried to. It was heavy and while it was beautiful, it was too much.

"This is it!" Madisyn clapped.

I closed my eyes as I turned to look at her and shook my head. It was so not my dress.

"Can you make one in red?" I asked, watching as the dressmaker frowned and nodded.

"It isn't traditional," she offered.

"Tell that to all of the Hindu or Chinese brides," I grumbled as Madisyn helped me out of the heavy dress, and I smiled as the dressmaker walked to the wardrobe and glamoured a lovely creation of red.

"Red?" Madisyn asked as she bit her lip and tried to figure out what I was doing.

"Blood Fae," I replied as I accepted the dress and carefully slipped into it. The design was simple: a high waist and a strapless bodice that had crimson lace sewn into the design. The crimson skirt fell in graceful folds to the floor. Not what I would have chosen if the wedding was up to me, yet it was lovely.

"You look beautiful," Madisyn whispered as she wiped away tears. "This is the one."

"It is," I smiled. "Now, I want to see my babies," I grumbled as I changed with a simple thought and enjoyed the soft fabric that covered my body.

"Let's go see them then; you deserve it," she replied as she slipped her fingers through mine and we sifted into the nursery.

The men were watching the babies when I sifted in. Each one smiled and went on playing with the babes. Ryder smiled and watched me as I made my way towards him and lowered myself to sit between his legs.

"You found the dress?" he murmured against my ear.

"I did."

"Don't get too attached to it, because I make no promises that it will be in one piece after you utter the words, 'I do.'"

"Is that so?" I mocked as Cade turned, looked at me, and giggled.

"It is absolutely so," he laughed as he wrapped his arms around me and we watched the children playing with his brothers.

We had to find Ciara, because if we didn't, she'd miss out on their entire childhood.

Chapter
THIRTEEN

I spent an hour with the wedding planner, who gasped at each of my requests and shook her head. I knew that it was outlandish, but there were a few touches of my own that I wanted to add to my wedding. I wasn't sure why we needed a wedding planner; Madisyn was like a wedding planner on steroids and a case of Red Bull. Once I'd finished, I met Ryder in the main hall and explained why I had to go meet up with Lucian. I stopped his grumpy response with a hand as I tilted my head and glared at him.

"You're leaving to search for your sister. Our children are back where they are safe, and I have to speak with Alden. I won't be the one to topple that freaky house of cards Lucian's building, and you have to look for Ciara. If you can't find her by wedding time, Adam will be my man of honor."

"You can't call for me if you need help," he growled.

"I said I'd take Ristan and Adam with me," I argued. "I'm taking an entire babysitting detail because I can't take an entire armed guard detail with me, and you know it. It draws more attention than anything else. Ristan will call for you if anything goes wrong. I will meet you back here tonight, and then you can spank me for misbehaving."

"See if Lucian's learned anything else about the portals—and Syn, I don't need you to be bad to spank that ass," he smiled wolfishly.

"Watch it or I might tie you up and spank your ass," I warned.

"You can try; it might be interesting to watch," he laughed as he kissed me. "Be good, Witch, and don't be brave or try to save anyone when I'm not with you."

"Fine, no being Superwoman, got it," I joked as I kissed him again and glamoured on leather pants with a white camisole that said, *'Witches do it better,'* across the chest. "I promise to not save any stray animals either; lesson learned with that one."

"Wait, did you just admit to learning something?" he laughed as I glowered at him.

"Watch it," I warned as I pulled away. "I'm off to find my bodyguards, O' Ancient One," I laughed.

"That age gives me the ability to know things, like how to make you scream my name all night long, so don't knock it, little girl."

"Ooh, he's got skills," I winked as I sifted, getting the last word in since he couldn't speak in my mind. I entered the library and peered over Ristan's shoulder as he thumbed through a paperback of *Parenting for Dummies*. I laughed, and silver and black eyes turned on me. "That's not going to help. You know what to do—plus I heard that book has some pretty impractical advice in it."

"I was only curious, and some of the tips in here seem pretty good. Not that there is very much that a human with a doctorate can give tips about that will apply too much to a child that will have a mix of parentage that mine will. Demon and Fae children have their own quirks that are different from human, then we have to factor in Olivia's unique parentage, and no, I am not about to hunt down Elijah for a little chit-chat about the tendencies of angelic children," he said as he shook his head.

"Look at me, Demon," I demanded softly as I clasped his face between my hands once he'd turned. "You got this, and you know you do. You held my babies; you helped me with my babies. You are going to do just fine."

"I can't believe she can walk and talk," he huffed as his forehead wrinkled slightly, as if he was more upset that he missed out on her baby time. "Kahleena wasn't supposed to grow; I wanted her to stay little for, well, forever," he chuckled.

"Agreed," I mumbled. "My kids are pretty badass, but it terrifies me that they can do so much magic already. What scares me, though, is, if they can already do as much as they can, what happens when they're older?"

"They'll have us," he answered, and I frowned.

"Actually, I need your help on a few things. Secret things," I teased with a mischievous smile. "I need the wedding news to hit every corner of this world and mine. I want it screamed from the rooftops."

"Flower, if you scream it from the rooftops,

everyone will know when it is happening."

"Pretty much everyone already knows," I grumbled. "There is a certain person I *need* to hear it. I *need* him here; I can't wait for him any longer."

"And by him you mean…?" He hesitated, eyes narrowing as he watched me.

"Don't ask questions you don't want to hear the answer to," I mumbled as I turned and watched Adam enter the room.

"Is there a reason Dristan just told me that I'll look great in a dress?" he asked, green eyes probing mine.

"I need you to be my maid of honor," I whispered so low that I knew he hadn't heard me. I had to do a test run, because it sounded ridiculous sliding off my tongue.

"Excuse me?" he stammered, stopping dead in his tracks as he stared at me.

"I don't have anyone to be my maid of honor, or bridesmaids, for that matter," I replied meaningfully. "Larissa was supposed to be my maid of honor, but she can't be. Ciara is missing, and if I ask Darynda, a whole bunch of handmaidens will get pissy—plus if I ask them, Madisyn will get upset because of this whole shitty Caste hierarchy. Outside of those two, I don't know the women here well enough for them to be my maid of honor, so it has to be you, Adam. You're my best friend. There will be no dresses for you, though," I laughed nervously.

"Synthia," he grumbled as he watched me. "Fine, but I'm not holding anyone's hand as I walk down the aisle, and I will be addressed as the man of honor. I'll punch the first asshole that tries to call me the maid of honor."

"Deal," I laughed.

"You haven't heard the rest," he warned.

"No?" That couldn't be good.

"No; Keir wants me to marry the Light Heir when we find her, so I'll need a best man. You're it." He winked as he made his way to the table and looked at the book Ristan was reading. "Damn, do you even know which breed it will be?"

"No idea, and no idea what we will call it," I admitted.

"It won't be called a Dangel," Ristan grumbled.

"That just sounds wrong." I smiled, watching as he shrugged. "I wonder if it will have wings and a tail, and prove us all wrong by being perfectly flawed, just like his daddy."

"Pray to the Gods she doesn't," he grated. "Demon bits and pieces have a tendency to kill easily."

"She?" I smirked.

"Kahleena needs help; she's outnumbered," he replied as he stood up. "Shall we? We're wasting daylight." My eyes skimmed the other books he was reading. *Dragon Rites by Fire, Dragon's Territory Maps*, and *The Art of Kama Sutra During Pregnancy*.

"*Kama Sutra During Pregnancy*, hmm?" I grinned and he smirked as he pushed the books into a neat pile on the thick wood table.

"Women are hornier when pregnant, and I never stop looking for ways to enhance the sexual experience of my partner."

"Wow, look at you, honing those skills," I giggled as he held his hand out. "Let us go invade a sex club, because there's nothing like a little reading material before going to a pay-to-play sex club, am I right?" I snorted as he laughed.

"I have all the sex I need now, thanks."

Ristan opened a portal for us, which opened only a few steps from the doors of the club. We made our way past the portal and it closed with a weird chuff of air behind Ristan. I smiled at the bouncer as his eyes read the words printed across my breasts.

"Do they really?" he pondered as he raised his eyes to mine.

"Of course, they do everything better," I smirked as he nodded towards the club.

"It's a fuck-fest in there. Might want to put this on," he said, extending his arm to hand me a necklace.

I smirked as I remembered the fit I'd thrown when Ryder had tried to put a collar on me. "Bane, are you trying to collar me, boy?" I laughed.

"I wouldn't dream of it, Witch," he answered softly. "Lucian is inside; he had a feeling you would be stopping by. He already sent a car for Alden. He should arrive shortly."

"He's intuitive, isn't he?" I asked, smirking as I followed Ristan through the door as I examined the necklace with my powers. Once I determined that there was nothing magical about it, I went ahead and fastened it around my neck. Lucian ran a sex club, one where mostly otherworld type creatures and some humans came to find release from the everyday boring charade they lived.

"Lucian tries to anticipate and know what might be needed before it is needed," he smirked, nodding his head towards the door. "Enter, but I must warn you, it's anything goes tonight."

"Just the way we like it," I replied wickedly as I wiggled my brows at him.

Chapter
FOURTEEN

We made our way through the packed nightclub, knowing that the moment we'd entered, all eyes had turned in our direction. Once I reached the bar, I took a seat and scanned the rowdy crowd. Humans watched the creatures, some with fear while others looked for a release that only the immortals could offer. I took in the different castes of Fae, dancing and necking with humans in the open. Lena—or should I say *Kendra*—was also out there, dancing to a sultry beat with a few familiar Witches from her coven. No men dared get close to her, but it could have also had something to do with Lucian watching her closely.

My eyes slowly looked over the outfit she was wearing, taking in the short skirt and fuck-me heels. Each move she made was calculated; each curve swayed to the sultry song as her hands slowly trailed over her hips. She stared at something in the corner— or someone. Every beat of the song increased the frenzy on the dance floor. My ear picked up the subtle compulsion in the tone, and I smirked.

"What can I get you?" a bartender from behind the bar shouted, forcing me to move my attention to him. He was younger than I'd expected, not a day over twenty-one, judging by the barely-there fuzz he was trying to grow. Glyphs pulsed beneath the skin on his arms, and looked a lot like the ones the Fae had. He wasn't Fae, though, and I'd bet my soul that those were created from magic to imitate the Fae's. Blue eyes held mine as I narrowed my gaze on his. He wasn't human, but he wasn't something I could put my finger on either. I smirked as his eyes widened as my brands appeared, pulsing beneath the surface.

"Gin and tonic," I said, watching as his eyes remained on the brands, as if he was entranced. "Like them?" I heard Adam and Ristan's snickers as they watched this wannabe take in real Fae royalty. Adam's brands slithered to life; his hand touched the bar and the kid was enthralled, but the moment Adam's eyes began to glow, the kid lost color as he figured out exactly what he was looking at.

"You're so beautiful," he swallowed hard and his hands shook slightly. "Take me with you."

"Excuse me?" I sputtered.

"That escalated rather quickly," Ristan snickered. "And what exactly would she take you with her to do?"

"I don't care what she does. Fuck me, use me, or kill me. Make me unable to feel this pain anymore. I can't watch her anymore. I know I deserve it, but I can't do it anymore. She doesn't even remember me," he cried, wiping away a tear as we tried to figure out what his damage was.

"That's enough, Brandon. They're not here to save your sorry soul," Lucian's deep timbre pulled my gaze to where he stood behind us.

"I can't do this for eternity!" Brandon shouted, moving away from where Lucian took a seat at the bar. "Not a moment longer," he sobbed, and I watched as Lucian nodded and his men moved, pulling the young bartender out from behind the bar as the silver fox took his place.

"Sorry about that." Lucian nodded to the new bartender as he poured the gin and tonic I'd asked for. "Brandon owes me his soul, so until I decide otherwise, he has to watch his former fiancée every night. She, however, doesn't even know who he is."

"And why does he owe you his soul?"

"Brandon sold his soul to become Fae." Lucian's eyes held mine as his lips curved into a smile. "Of course, I did explain that no one can become Fae unless they are born as such, but he cared little about the details, as long as he appeared to be what he wanted. High Fae—to land the girl. His girlfriend, on the other hand, sold hers to forget the pain she'd endured as a child at the hands of her father. Neither specified any details. So, here they are, in my debt. Brandon, however, broke the rules and tried to find a loophole in the deal, so he will now spend eternity watching the love of his life as she waits tables without a fucking clue as to who he is."

"Well, okay then." I turned and took a deep drink. "I see Kendra is here, watching you," I smirked as I dropped the matter of the soul and glanced back at Lucian. My eyes flickered to the dance floor and then back to him. "She also doesn't like that you're sitting close to me."

Midnight eyes watched me with cold detachment. This creature was dark, and yet I knew he wasn't frozen to his core. There was something about him that made me want to hug him, and yet I knew it wouldn't be welcomed.

"You look like heaven tonight." His eyes moved from me to the dance floor.

"You look like hell, on the other hand," I replied, watching as those eyes turned on me. "I'm not your friend. I won't lie to you just to kick it," I offered when he raised a brow to me.

"Blunt," he laughed, drinking the aged Scotch without a thought. "American slang from a soon-to-be-Fae-Queen?"

I rolled my eyes and brought the conversation back to him. "It can't be easy, watching her dance," I murmured, knowing he'd hear it. "She's watching you back, though, that's a good sign.

"You know that how?" he smirked.

"I have tits." I grinned. "It makes me a better judge of those who also have tits. I think she's actually pissed that you're so close to me."

"You can't know that," he dismissed my comment with a slight flick of his hand as he turned and peered over his shoulder.

"Want to bet?" I challenged, and at his nod, I smiled. "Want to know how I know she's watching you? That she's not happy with my being this close to you? I'll show you. Don't kiss or touch me at all. Just watch her reaction as I get a little too close to you." I slid from the chair and stood in front of him. "Spread your legs," I whispered, watching as his piercing blue eyes observed me as if I was a snake, ready to strike.

"There's no trick here, Lucian. Nothing but showing you she's interested in you," I assured him. Once he'd opened his legs, I slid between them, placing my hands on his thighs as I smiled and tilted my head. He smelled divine, freshly showered, with a touch of something pure uniquely male. My lips tipped upward to a smile as I bit my lip and stared into his eyes. My hand lifted to brush his soft hair away from his ear as I placed my lips close to it. "Touch my shoulder, and watch her eyes. They'll narrow ever so slightly as her pupils dilate with anger. Right now, her heart is racing with anger that I'm bold and that you're allowing me to be so. Next, she'll signal to the girls she came with to leave the dance floor so you won't notice that she's stopped moving." I backed up and grinned. "She's here to seduce and conquer; those heels are all fuck-me. That skirt is short on purpose. You may know women, but you don't know what it's like to love someone and not know why. Lena's in there, and she probably doesn't even know why it's pissing her off."

"She's been here three nights in a row," he grumbled as he turned back to the bar.

"Three nights in row…in a similar outfit?" I took another sip of my drink.

"Fuck-me heels, skirt short enough that a stiff wind would show me that perfect ass of hers," he saluted me with his glass to emphasize his point.

"Witches do it better," I mused and when he turned and looked at me, I frowned. "Are you sure she hasn't set you as a target? Three nights in fuck-me heels is serious business, Lucian." I laughed. "She's being trained by Alden, so if I were you, I'd expect the unexpected." I considered what Alden may be up to here.

"She comes in with her coven and tries to blend in with the others. Well, she tries to, but I don't let the males get too close to her. You think she is here because of your uncle's meddling in their coven?" His eyes narrowed as he watched Kendra sway to the slow song that filtered through the club.

"I think she has the same teacher I had, and I think she's marked you. You, or someone else inside this club," I shrugged. "I'd be careful of her, at least. Alden was the best teacher at the Guild; he would feel compelled to help her, considering everything that's happened here."

"You're not what I expected you to be." His lips tightened with a hint of a frown and he shook his head slightly. "None of you assholes are."

"Sorry to shatter your illusion that everyone is an asshole and wants something from you," I laughed. My eyes moved to the door as Alden entered. I exhaled and stood. "I need a quiet place to talk with my uncle, please."

"Take my table," he offered, and made a gesture towards a booth in the back. "It's warded, and no one will bother you there."

"Thank you." I stood up and sensed Ristan and Adam moving in closer to follow me to the booth Lucian had directed me to. Once I was close to the table, I paused, turning to look at Ristan, who nodded and pulled Adam with him to stand guard as I slid into the booth.

Once Alden approached and slid into the booth beside me, I turned and looked at him closely. He was happy here, and he looked younger, if that was possible. No frown lines marred his face, and the smile on his face was genuine.

"We need to talk, old man," I stated bluntly. "About what lies in a warded and sealed chamber in the deepest part of the Guild," I informed him. His head jerked up and his expression blanched almost as white as the table cloth on the table. He swallowed hard as one of the waitresses approached the table and placed Scotch in front of Alden, and a fresh gin and tonic in front of me before moving on.

"You saw the souls?" He lifted the drink up and didn't bother sniffing it first. He downed the glass's contents and shook his head.

"Quite a few of them," I confirmed as I leaned towards him and lowered my voice. "And something else, something that scared the shit out of me, Alden. Tell me she isn't who I think she is."

"You saw her?" He winced as pain flashed across his face.

"Who is she?" There was no way he was going to deflect or get away from this conversation. "No skipping around the subject; I need to know before we start bringing kids into that Guild again."

He tipped his head up to the ceiling, as if he was warring with how much to tell me. "She's everything. You have no idea what you've done by taking control of this Guild, do you?" He dropped his head in his hands.

"No, which is why you're going to explain to me exactly who she is," I growled softly. "And then you're going to explain why girls have been sacrificed to keep her in stasis. I now know why the Seattle Guild is willing to fight to obtain control of the Spokane

Guild. Whatever she is, she's powerful."

"When I was a child at the Guild, we were taught about the Original Witches. It was a small coven that was born of Hecate's direct line. Even now, it's believed that their few descendants are among the most powerful Witches alive. The Original Witches, however, were dangerous alone, but together they could destroy towns, or even entire cities if they wanted to. No one bothered them, and they were among the most powerful creatures of this world that chose to live in the shadows. They were content to remain there, until news of the Witch trials made it to their ears. At first it was a whisper, and then as time moved on, they got louder. As the torture and killings became worse, the Original Witches came out of the shadows and slaughtered entire villages and towns as they made their way to Salem to find the people responsible for putting their children to death. They drove the Witch Hunters to commit suicide and created plagues that swept across the lands, killing thousands.

"There was fear for what it would mean for those of the Witches who had escaped the trials and were hiding. The Americas and England were on the brink of war already, but to add Witches to it, with their numbers dwindling, was not something they could endure. It was around this time that Lena's coven split from the others, and the Guilds were formed. The Original Witches continued killing, and the Guild feared that they would annihilate any chance of monitoring and policing those of the Otherworld— actually Faery—so they set to making bargains with some of the heads of the other covens, who would eventually join them in creating the other Guilds. They put their case before the Paladins, and made powerful allies to help them capture and imprison the

Original Witches. At first, the Guild captured them, but even in a magical prison, they continued to cause havoc. Being locked up together made them stronger. It made them angrier, and soon covens started falling to strange illnesses. Some lost their magic, while others went mad from the voices inside their heads. There were many that called for the death of these Witches, but everyone was fearful that killing so many of Hecate's direct line could bring her wrath on us all. Now the Paladins have their own magic, magic that isn't of this world. The Guild and covens agreed to their idea to place the Witches in stasis and use the Leylines beneath the Guilds to leach power from the Witches to weaken them. This was a happy way of neutralizing the Witches, but not killing them. Once the Paladins put the Witches in stasis, they were moved to the depths of thirteen different covens. As Guilds were founded in the Midwest and on the Pacific seaboard, three of those Witches were moved—and one of them was interred under the Spokane Guild. They have been asleep for a very long time, and now that you have taken control of the Spokane Guild, the National Guild will not stop fighting you until she is back in their care, Synthia. If any of them wake, they will go after those they consider to be their enemies."

"They'll go after the Guild," I whispered as I considered what I'd just stepped into.

"Or us, for being in the Guild," he corrected. "We know they are connected, but not how or why they are. Some speculate that if one was to wake, the others would follow her, but it's speculation, of course. However, if it happens, God save our souls because they will have no mercy."

"And the souls?" I really didn't want to know more about the Witch. I got it, end of days shit. Why was it always worst-case scenario? Why couldn't we find one situation that wasn't tied to some kind of end of the world shit?

"Sacrifices to keep them in stasis," he replied quietly, and swallowed hard. "Paladin magic comes with a blood cost, and we paid it. Thirteen souls a year to contain thirteen Witches."

"And Hecate didn't interfere? She just allowed this to happen to her daughters?"

"She hasn't been seen or heard of since just before her direct line began their slaughter of the humans. We never knew how she felt about it; all we know is that she didn't intervene to save them. Spells were done at the beginning of all that chaos, to call Hecate forth to save the covens from what her daughters were doing, and she never came. Either she is no longer among us, or she's chosen to forsake us. We have no idea which one it is. The Guild continues to teach of her, but they have little real knowledge of her. To us, she's our God. There is no proof she exists anymore, and yet we still do her bidding and follow her rules."

I swallowed the information and observed him carefully as I asked my next question. "Have *you* killed to keep that Witch in stasis?"

"Yes. And I would do it again, and probably will. Only Elders are aware of what is sleeping beneath the Guilds. It is our duty to keep them there, asleep. Another thing to consider—because the Witches Guild draws on those same Leylines used to keep them weak and in stasis—is that those thirteen Witches now know every Witch alive. Imagine if they woke up knowing what the Guild has done to them?"

"They could potentially wipe out every Witch

on the continent," I groaned as I rubbed my temples. "Any creature who taps those Leylines has allowed the Original Witches inside of them, haven't they?"

"They have, including you," he replied as he closed his eyes briefly and tipped his glass back, finishing it.

"We have Pandora's box sleeping beneath the Guild, which we are supposed to be breaking ground on now and building a new future. How can we bring innocent children into it knowing that?"

"Because this world needs those children safe and trained right, and we need them now more than ever before," he replied confidently. "I'm aware of the Fae flooding this world. I know you and those entrusted with the guardianship of the permanent portals wouldn't allow that if you had a way to guard them. Which means something has gone horribly wrong with the portals," he said pointedly.

I was afraid to answer him for a moment as I tried to absorb everything that Alden had told me. Then I thought of what Ryder, Ristan, and Dristan had explained to me of the history of Faery and how it related to the Witches and the Guilds, and more pieces of the puzzle began to fill in.

"Ok, I'm going to call bullshit on some of this, old man. You and I both know that the Guild has been spoon feeding us a distorted history of where we come from and who did what. Hecate is a Goddess like Danu is. They aren't supposed to interfere directly, and if they do, there are serious consequences. But consequences from who?" I spoke slowly as I worked it out with Alden as my sounding board. "The first Witches, even before the Druids, were Changelings from what Ryder told me, so that means that Hecate had to have been playing the horizontal mambo with Changelings to have created this line, which explains why they are so strong. They're not just Witches, they are Demi-Gods." Alden blinked slowly and nodded his agreement that this could be true. "And if this is the case, then perhaps Hecate or some other high God helped nudge along the relationship between the covens and the Paladins as an indirect way of neutralizing her children. That way, they got around killing them and being accused of interfering." I peered at Alden as another thought occurred to me.

"Alden, Paladins aren't exactly plentiful, and the Guild normally calls them in when all hell breaks loose. When everything first went down, you were guarded by twelve of them. Larissa told me she didn't know who sent them; do you?" If this was going where I thought it was, then there was more in play than any of us realized.

"No." Alden shook his head. "I assumed it was someone from the Washington Guilds. They were only with me for a short while, and then the Guild sent their own people in; I didn't question it and I haven't seen one since." He scowled as he began to see the same picture that was forming in my mind. I didn't know much about the Paladins, other than they were from outside of our world and their magic was different. They weren't Fae and they weren't human; who were they, and who did they really report to?

"So to wake one up, we'd probably need an actual Paladin?"

"That, or possibly a Druid; they hadn't died out when the Witches were put in stasis, and I know they were part of the allies recruited to put them there. It's been a long time since one of those was seen around the States, though."

"The Changelings became the Druids, who split apart and became the Mages and the Witches Guild," I recited. "Could one of them have decided not to choose a side, and hid? Do you think they are still alive?"

"It's possible. If they were a half-blood, the chances of immortality are higher. And if that history is the case, then my blood is so weakened, it just helps me look good." Alden chuckled.

"Ok, then try this on. If the Mages are taking over the Guilds and they are causing an imbalance because of their war with the Fae; is it possible that someone else is involved in this? Someone who sent Paladins in to guard you? Paladins who might have been reporting to whoever controls them about what was going on with the Guilds," I mused as I worked it out with him.

"It's possible," Alden admitted. "If that is the case, you have to ask yourself; are they friendly with the Fae, or against the Fae?"

"That's a really good question." I finished my drink as Alden made a motion to a waitress to get us another round of drinks, then gave me a thoughtful look and sighed.

"We'll figure this out; in the meantime, show me the floor plans."

Chapter FIFTEEN

We spent the next few days going over every detail of the new Guild with the men that Ryder trusted the most. When we weren't in planning sessions for the Guild, our time was spent between searching for any trace or sign of Ciara and planning the upcoming wedding. Ryder and his brothers were terrified of what may have happened, and with every passing day, any hope of finding her alive was fading.

I hated being unable to devote additional manpower or time to finding her, but with the portals growing and the Horde already being spread thin, it just wasn't an option. It would leave the Horde's stronghold more exposed than it already was.

The world around us seemed calm, serene. Like we weren't standing at the edge of the war we knew was coming. Like there wasn't a hole into this world, one we couldn't close no matter how many experts we brought in to try. Nothing seemed to stop them from slowly expanding.

I spent my mornings planning the wedding, then missing my children by the afternoon. By midnight, I tired myself out, training until I fell into bed, exhausted to the point of tears, but knowing how important it was to prepare my body and mind for any battle I might face.

This fragile peace wouldn't last for long, and we all waited with bated breath for the one thing that would be the breaking point and take us into full-scale war. The Mages had been quiet. Quiet usually meant that they were plotting and planning and at their most dangerous, so no one allowed our readiness to slip; no one grew lax with their inactivity. We'd taken a huge part of their weapon arsenal when we'd taken the God they thought would make them invincible, and they were probably licking their wounded pride. Even with that knowledge, we knew they wouldn't wait long before they made their next move, and we'd be ready for them when the time came.

Faolán was yet another problem I knew was lurking, just waiting to stab me in the back when I least expected it. He wouldn't stop hunting me until one of us was dead, and it wouldn't be me who fell. I plotted and planned, and hated the fact that when I did end his life, Madisyn would be hurt by it. I couldn't find a way around it, not with his evil taint threatening the very lives of my children. He'd crossed a line with what he'd done, and he had to be stopped.

"Ryder agreed that we should have feasting areas in the courtyard, as well as around the outside of the castle during the wedding reception, so that anyone who wants to share in the revelry of your wedding can. After all, I understand that a few centuries ago in the human world, it was customary for feasting to take place for several days when royalty would wed. I think this would be a nice homage to that tradition!" Madisyn chirped, pulling me from the troubles playing in my mind.

"What?" I turned away from the window to look in her direction, where she sat perched in a dainty chair as she picked at the assortment of cupcakes Darynda had brought earlier with our tea.

"You've not heard anything I've said all morning, Synthia," she fussed, pursing her lips into a tight frown. "Should I come back later?"

"No, it sounds fine. Set it up wherever you like." I shrugged tiredly. "I'm sorry, my mind is elsewhere."

"Obviously, but we need to finish planning this wedding." Without a hint of irritation, she patted the empty spot on the sofa next to herself. "Come, sit with me and I will show you what I have planned."

I ignored her hint and moved to the chair opposite of her in the lounge we had decided to use for planning the wedding. She had pictures spread out with additional options of bridesmaids' dresses, cakes, and layouts of what the great hall would look like once she'd had her people set it up. I thought we had already decided what was going to be done, but by the look of determination in Madisyn's eye, she had some very different ideas in mind than I did for the wedding.

"This is your dress, because while I appreciate that you wanted to wear red for the Blood Kingdom, it's unheard of to wear red to your wedding. Ryder was very clear about what we were allowed to do with your wedding, since he wanted a traditional one, like that of the humans'."

He'd changed my dress? I stared at the creation and frowned. It was beautiful, with a bell-shaped skirt, and a lace bodice with a train and a veil. In fact, it looked like one I'd been admiring when I was about five years old, but that was because it looked like every cliché out of every Disney Princess movie ever made.

"What do you think?" she asked excitedly, and I raised my eyes to hers and gave her a soft smile.

"It's beautiful." It was, but it wasn't me. My stomach flipped and nerves came up without warning. I was doing this; but it was frustrating, as nothing I said or did stopped Madisyn or Ryder from making this wedding huge. "It's a lot of fabric," I forced out, trying to be polite, and watched as she grinned.

"It's perfect, and I think that out of all the dresses I saw, this will flatter your figure the best. I also think you should wear your hair up, in curls like this." She fluttered her fingers and I could feel my hair being pulled back and twisted, and soft curling ringlets framed my face. "See!" she crowed excitedly and glamoured a hand mirror for me and I looked at the elaborate hairstyle she had created. "It will flatter your features, and everyone will be able to see the diamonds better."

"Diamonds?" I asked woodenly. I wasn't shocked with anything the Fae could create. I was just surprised she'd mentioned diamonds, because I'd planned on wearing pearls.

"This." she pointed at a catalogue of jewelry. The diamonds were the size of an infant's fist and gaudy. They were set in a platinum setting with smaller diamonds that created a waterfall effect all the way around the neckline. "It will make your eyes pop and it will also draw attention to your crown. Ryder has been looking at different concepts all week!"

"A crown?" I parroted, wondering when the

hell these two had so much time to plan this shit. I had barely seen him unless he was falling into bed, too tired to do anything else but sleep. Not that the Fae really needed to sleep much, but they needed to detach from the world or they'd go insane. Yet the man was planning our wedding in every minute detail with Madisyn. It was at this point I had the sneaking suspicion that a lot of this drama was more of Madisyn's agenda than Ryder's or mine. Ryder knew me better than this, and while Madisyn wasn't necessarily lying, I knew she was being very clever with what words she was choosing each time I asked her if a change was Ryder's idea. I had a feeling that both Ryder and I were being manipulated because neither of us had the heart to hurt her feelings, and she was, for all intents and purposes, becoming momzilla of the bride, disguised as a beautiful Fairy Queen.

"You are a princess. You cannot marry into the Horde without your status changing, and so when you walk down the aisle, you will have a tiara, and when he sets the crown on your head, you will be raised from Blood Princess to the Queen of the Horde."

"Of course," I whispered as she passed me drawings that ranged from those of the tiara that had a blood ruby in it, to a golden crown that was embedded with hundreds of diamonds and looked heavy as hell. I was going to have to work on my neck muscles if they expected me to wear it daily.

"You'll get used to it," Madisyn assured me as she took in my frown. "It is a reminder of your station here, and the people will need to see you with it on. The Horde thrives on power, and if they forget it for a moment, you will need to remind them of who you are."

"I know." I nodded. "How many days before the wedding?" I sipped the tea Darynda had made—chamomile, to calm my nerves as I waited for the men to return from searching for Ciara.

"Two days," she frowned. "You couldn't have possibly forgotten already. You helped me send the invitations out."

"How could I forget?" I grumbled. I couldn't remember who we had invited because there had been so many that I'd stopped asking who was who. I didn't really care because I wasn't into this *big* wedding, and I was secretly more impressed with the army of tiny winged Fae that were charged with the delivery of all the ostentatious envelopes.

"So, we will be doing a rehearsal tomorrow, and I think you should consider changing your mind and allow the babies to be here for the ceremony. They should be here with you."

"Absolutely not," I replied, much harsher than I had intended to. "Madisyn, I'd like nothing more than for them to be present, but until Faolán is captured and dealt with, I won't risk them being where he could use them against us. I'm sorry, but I won't chance it."

"I understand," she said softly. Her eyes watered as she turned away from me. I knew it was difficult for her to grasp, but her son was a monster. I'd left out a lot of the things he'd done to me, but I wouldn't place my children into the precarious position of being used against me. They were defenseless, and innocent in this.

"Anything else that needs my attention?" I sighed.

"Shoes; you have yet to pick out the ones you

want to wear." She shuffled through the papers until she found what she was looking for. She handed me a page full of what looked to be different styles of glittering, almost transparent shoes. "Ryder said he had seen you admiring some shoes that you said a story character wore. What was she called…Cinderella? He described the story, so we found some designs for similar ones."

I grinned as I looked through the delicate looking shoes, and settled on a pair that had small heels and didn't look like they'd break if I walked in them. Once we'd finished with a few more details, she left, reminding me of the rehearsal wedding tomorrow so that I wouldn't be lost when the time came to walk down the aisle to Ryder.

Once she'd sifted, I moved to the study and pulled out the maps I'd been poring over before she'd arrived. There was a patch of rough terrain and mountains that the men had immediately scratched off the search grid and, while they dismissed it, my instincts were drawn to it. If I was hiding from the Horde, I would go to the last place in this world that they'd think to look. But hey, that was just me. Ryder had explained to me that no one would look there because it wasn't habitable— even the plant life there was carnivorous. He'd told me in vivid detail about it and the monstrous creatures that were part of the land itself.

I paused and tilted my head, my finger moved over the map as I glamoured on my form-fitting armor, swept the ridiculous curls into a ponytail, and glamoured a few cleverly concealed sheaths for daggers at the wrist grieves, hips, and boots. I moved towards the window and looked down at the men, who were just returning from the search, and considered waiting for Ryder, but as I watched him dismount from his horse with slumped shoulders, I knew what I had to do.

I hated that every time they returned, they grew a little more defeated at the prospect that she may not be out there to be saved. There had been a lot of blood on the floor and furnishings when she'd been taken, and it had been hers. She'd fought her attacker with everything she had, but just how much had it cost her?

Her life?

I watched as amber eyes rose to mine as if he sensed my presence in the window, and he shook his dark head. Defeat was new to him, but he wasn't ready to admit it yet, and neither was I.

Chapter
SIXTEEN

I'd sifted into the area that I had chosen to call the Monstrous Mountains. Ryder, locked himself in the war room with his men to pore over more charts. He'd scour this entire world to find her; she was the only acknowledged daughter born to Alazander, and Ryder's only sister. One he'd vowed to protect. Being unable to find her was hurting them all. They all loved her.

I moved through the trails slowly for hours, looking for any hidden threat, anything that would prove that Dragons or anyone else had been present here. I made it through a group of trees and stopped cold as the sight in the clearing came into view.

The smell of meat cooking lingered in the air as the mist parted momentarily and revealed a camp. Genius, hiding among the mist, which was normally too thick to see through, even from the skies above.

I could hear the voices of men and women moving around, and the sound of children playing erupted as squeals came from somewhere deeper in the camp. I made my way to the edge of the camp as my eyes adjusted to the dense mist as it parted and swirled. I noticed that tents had been erected around the outer perimeter, and wards had been carved into large stones around the tents to keep up the magic of the mist and disguise these people from intruders, which was probably why no one knew they were here.

I pulled an invisibility glamour around myself, then worked my way around the edge of camp to watch as men congregated in groups that were either sparring or gaming, and women tended to cooking fires or cared for the children. Some of them were carrying heavy baskets of clothing or other things. The fog shifted, and I realized there were not just several tents; there were *hundreds* of them set up in this clearing. It wasn't just a camp that had been set up overnight; it was a very well-established one that must have been here for years. I could make out rocks with runes carved into them littering the border of the camp, and the more I looked, the more wards I saw.

My instinct was to back away and go grab Ryder, but if these were the Dragons, I needed more proof than just my suspicions. I exhaled and scanned the camp, looking for the biggest tent. I hadn't come this far to go home without proof, or without looking for Ciara.

I watched the men, noting they had Dragon tattoos or glyphs that matched Ryder's. Ryder had mentioned that the Dragon brands had developed shortly after he had received the Heir brands. These ones moved on their skin—proof of what they were. Glyphs couldn't be faked; they remained true to the breed, and these were mother-freaking Dragons. Holy farting Fairy buckets. Dragons!

I backed up until I was hidden in the line of trees that I'd originally come from as I figured out my next move. I should have left, should have run to Ryder and told him immediately of this discovery, but I wasn't going to do it and I knew that. These men looked almost human.

Some men and women stood around large campfires and shared drinks as they talked within their small groups. Small boys played with wooden swords, and I swallowed past a lump as I realized what this was.

Displaced people who had banded together to survive.

If I returned and told Ryder what I had found, he'd need to neutralize the threat. He'd have to, and I hated knowing that it was probably what I needed to do. On the other hand, we needed to know more about them, what they were doing and planning. I doubted they could forgive him easily, even if he'd only been following orders. However, they'd survived it; he hadn't wiped out an entire race after all. I watched as a man moved into an empty space and shifted, taking the form of a huge, glittering green Dragon, and with a sweep of his gigantic wings, he took to the air. A scout? They'd remained hidden this long because they'd been smart. They'd moved into a place that was thought of as uninhabitable, and yet here they were—motherfucking Dragons.

My eyes moved back to the camp and settled on the largest tent, which had guards surrounding it. Either someone important was in there, or they had someone that they didn't want to escape from there. I'd have to search the other tents, but my money was on the tent that looked like it belonged to whoever was in charge of this place.

I slowly made my way to where a warded post was set into the ground. My fingers extended, pushing, testing the wards, and when they didn't go off, I stepped through them. I paused, expecting them to sound a siren of alarm, but they didn't. Once I knew I was safe, I walked deeper into the camp, past the playing children to where a couple of the men were playing a game with dice that looked like crystals as they cheered and clapped each other on the back.

"Damn! You have to be cheating, Aiden, no one is that lucky!" the man who sat opposite of the table shouted as he slammed his palms on the table and glared in open challenge.

"It is dice; you cannot cheat at it, Syphon. Look at them! Then watch your tongue before you accuse me of cheating you," the other growled, death peering from his eyes as he watched his opponent.

"No one is that bloody lucky," Syphon snapped and removed his hands from the table. I moved away from them, watchful of those around me so that no one ran into me. I made my way to the closest tent and stood in front of it for a few moments, listening for anyone who might be inside before moving on to the next.

Tent after tent revealed no sound, no noise. Everyone seemed to be outside, working or playing in different groups. There was a gap in the tents where a group of women were baking different types of bread in stone-like ovens, talking briskly in excited tones; I paused when I heard reference to the Horde whore.

"He'll show her how our people felt as they raped innocent women," one commented while she stirred something in a large wooden bowl.

"If you ask me, he should just take her head and return it to the King on a pike. He'd be done with it, and we could wash our hands of her. Her presence here places us all in danger."

"If he did that, they'd be sure to come. Right now they search for her everywhere, but they'll never look here. Not when so many other monsters hide in these mountains. I, for one, am sick of being here, hiding like rats. These mountains are freezing my tits off."

"Faye dearie, you barely have teats," an older woman teased as she stifled a laugh behind her hand as the other woman peered down at her tits. "Not even big enough to feed a bairn, girl. Now all of you shush your slander. The Lord knows his business; whatever he decides to do with her is his business. It's not chatter for the baking oven. Now get to work; this food doesn't cook itself, you know. Plus, we have washing to do or we will all be wearing our undergarments soon."

I swallowed and moved past them, heading directly towards the biggest tent here. Once I was there, I noted the guards I'd seen earlier and stopped as I considered something that I hadn't thought of before I'd entered the camp: I couldn't get into a tent without them noticing the flap move. I held my breath as I heard a whimper from the other side. The flap opened without warning and I slipped inside as a large, burly man pushed his way out.

My heart stopped beating as my eyes adjusted to the dimness of the tent and I got a good look at Ciara. She was wearing only a thin, torn, and ragged dress, and was chained in a standing position to one of the tent supports. Her hair hung in unkempt waves, and her cheeks were bright red as she glared at a man who was lounging atop a bed piled with furs. His hair was light brown, reaching a few inches below his shoulders. Twin Dragons in midflight had been tattooed on his sinewy back. His ass was firm, and his cock was limp but even so—it was impressive.

"Blushing from the Horde princess?" he taunted, crystal blue eyes watching her every move. He sat up and I eyed his naked perfection, but more so, Ciara's blush intensified as he stood and moved closer to where she was chained. His hand cupped her chin and lifted it until she was forced to make eye contact with him. "You have nothing to fear from me, Ciara. I don't force myself upon unwilling women as your kind is known for doing. I don't slaughter the innocent. No, you needn't ever fear that I'd lower myself to fucking you, no matter how much I'd enjoy this beautiful flesh." He swallowed hard, and I could tell it was taking everything he had not to do exactly what he'd just vowed he wouldn't do. She flinched, and it took effort not to pull my blades and end his life right then and there.

"Do what you will to me, Blane, but I will never be used to lure my brothers here to their deaths. You forget, I *am* Horde," she hissed as her eyes slowly moved from his face to his other features with a hungry look. "You'll have to feed me sooner or later, or watch me wither away. I need to feed regularly, and I'm ravenous. Tell me, Dragon, which will it be? Watch me wither and lose your only tool for revenge, or feed me?" she taunted in a throaty tone that left little to wonder what her game was: seduction.

I grinned. Here we'd been worried about her, and she was holding her own. I was so proud. She'd survived, and she wasn't afraid of him. At least, she wasn't showing that she was. She moved her hips and the thin belt cinched around her waist that gave a hint of her curves chimed like an alarm. She was a fucking trap. My eyes slowly moved to a gold chain that rested on her hips, and I noticed it had thin metal slivers that dug into her flesh as she moved. I blanched, but kept my temper under control as blood appeared where the slivers had dug into her exposed skin.

Blane's eyes hadn't missed it either; he swallowed as small trickles of blood trailed down her waist and onto the remains of the dress, which had dried blood covering a large section of it. He swallowed as she wiggled her hips a tiny bit more, watching his reaction. His hand slowly rubbed down his face as he turned and moved so quickly that I had no warning to move. Luckily, he passed without bumping into me as he exited the tent. I grinned at Ciara, knowing she had rattled him so badly that he'd left without even bothering to grab a pair of pants.

I watched as Ciara's features crumpled and her eyes watered. I slowly moved to the other side of her, noting the markings on the inside of the tent were indeed wards to keep her and any other creature of the Horde inside this tent, should they enter it. Yep, definitely a trap.

"Ciara," I whispered.

"Syn?" she called out, and I hushed her.

"Quiet or the guards will hear you," I hissed. "Are you hurt?" I murmured softly, and when she shook her head, I released the breath I'd been holding. "Dragons, who knew?" I slowly lowered myself to be eye level with the chain and belt she wore, so as not to create more pain than she was already experiencing.

"My brothers?" she whispered.

"Going crazy looking for you," I murmured, focusing on the weird links.

"They can't find me here, Syn," she rushed out, flinching as one of the tiny slivers jabbed her a little too deeply as I touched the chain. "It's a trap, and the moment anyone from the Horde enters, they won't be able to escape. The entire camp is rigged to capture them should they try to sneak in."

"I know; I'm aware of the wards and this…" I paused and waved at the tent, listening as Blane approached.

"You need to go, now," she hissed.

The flap was thrown open and Blane strode in, still naked and holding a pail of water that he placed at her feet. He watched her speculatively for a few moments.

"Talking to yourself?" he mocked, his fingers slowly trailing over her breasts as he watched her body react. I could take him, but her reaction to him gave me pause. Her pupils dilated, and her back arched as if his touch excited her.

Shock me, Ciara, the naughty little imp. She liked him.

"I don't talk to myself, I talk to Gods," she sneered and kicked the bucket over, sending suds over the tarp that covered the ground beneath her feet.

"That was stupid," he growled, and two of the guards opened the flap to see what the disturbance had been about. Their swords were drawn, ready to cut Ciara to ribbons if she'd escaped. "You could just use glamour, and then you wouldn't stink or need me to wash your flesh, woman."

I almost snickered. She was smart; magic left a taint in the air. Had she used it to clean herself up, her brothers could have traced it. She knew they were tearing this world apart to find her, and all she would have had to do was use her magic to bring them right to her, to this well-laid trap they'd created with her as the bait.

I watched as he gripped a handful of her hair and twisted her head back. His lips inched towards her ear as his body closed the distance between them. He wasn't as unaffected as he pretended to be either.

My hand slowly moved to the dagger at my hip but as I watched, he struggled against his emotions. I didn't dare try to read his mind, because he might feel it. I could feel his power, intense, raw, and hot. The more turned on he got, the hotter the temperature in the tent was. It put a whole new meaning to the phrase 'hot damn'.

His lips grazed hers and she moaned as she opened her mouth in a slanted smile, then closed her eyes as she felt him fight a battle between what he wanted to do and what he intended to do.

"Feed me or free me," she murmured against his lips. "One or the other, Dragon—or, kill me, and send my remains to my brother. You'll have to choose soon, because time isn't something I have."

"You think I'd fall for your shit?" he snapped coldly as he backed away from her, glaring murderously at her. "Seductress of the Horde, do you feed from many men? Part these thighs for any cock willing to feed you?"

I almost growled, but her laughter startled me.

"Any who are willing, Dragon," She laughed and wiggled her hips, and more blood seeped from the chain and down the gown. "A girl has to feed, and with my appetite, often is preferred."

"You're not adding me to their numbers," he snarled. His hands moved to his head and his fingers threaded through his hair as he calmed his breathing. His dick throbbed, and yet he held himself composed as he moved to the bed, giving me his back.

I took a step and he paused, turned, and looked at Ciara carefully. His eyes searched the tent speculatively and then he turned, allowing me to breathe as he pulled a pair of pants from the bed and shoved his legs into them.

"Keep testing me and you may not like how I choose to feed you," he warned. "I won't be kept or swayed from my goal by a slick pussy, or a willing whore."

I swallowed and considered gutting him. Fuck the consequences. Screw it if she liked him; that mouth of his needed to be taught a lesson. I watched as his eyes moved to the blood, and the muscle in his jaw ticked with his anger. He didn't like her hurting herself either.

Interesting.

Did she know that? Had she picked up on it and continued to use it? He grabbed a shirt from the same pile his pants had been in, a sword, and a harness, and moved towards her slowly as he smiled with a coldness that sent a shiver racing down my spine.

"He will come for you, even if I have to lure him

with bits and pieces of you, Ciara. After I've killed him and taken his throne, I may just keep you chained to my bed for eternity. I wonder if you'd beg me to feed you then, or would you beg me for a painless death?"

"He has a Goddess at his side; he will not fall to you, Dragon whelp," she countered. "Do you have any idea how powerful Synthia is? She could be in here with us right now and you'd never know it until your blood covered this very floor. You can't ward against her, no one can. You think she'd allow him to walk into your trap alone? She'd spot those wards inside that forest; she'd see them miles before they ever reached them. You're a fool; take your people and leave. Live—he won't care that you are alive, Blane, trust me. Just go. Before it's too late."

"He's the Horde King; he won't walk in, Ciara, he'll sift. By then, it will be too late for him to turn back. He's a cold-blooded killer—I know, I was there when he slaughtered my people. He killed my people; my mother was raped and killed by some of his men as I watched them from where I was hidden by my mother's maid. I won't run from him, not again. Last time I was a mere lad; now, I'm a man who will pay him back for what he did. I won't allow it to happen again."

"He was following orders. He has always regretted what he was forced to do to your people," she whispered softly. "He killed our father not long ago. He made sure that the real killer paid for his deeds."

"He took that monster that drove your father mad into him. It's only a matter of time before he follows his own father's steps and destroys what little remains of this world. He didn't kill him because of his deeds, he killed him because he craved power; we've heard it whispered from the very day he killed his sire. Killing Alazander doesn't absolve him of his crimes. Those who he killed were innocent; they didn't deserve to die like that, or to be left for the carrion birds," he growled, his blue eyes filling with ice that were laced with hate as he watched Ciara swallow against the malice she saw in his beautiful, watery depths.

"My brother's beast is his own, not my father's. I know what he is. I was there the day he killed my father. I saw what happened and why it happened. Ryder isn't what you think he is," she replied carefully, watching the Dragon as he moved even closer to her. "Do you think our monster of a father was any kinder to his children? He used us; he tore my brothers down until they had no choice but to do as he bid them, and if they fought against him, he would kill whoever they were closest to. He tortured them, but Ryder is not our father; they're nothing alike."

"And you'd lie to protect him," he hissed.

"I'm Fae, asshole. One hundred percent High Fae royalty and you know it. I can't lie!" she growled and glared at him. "I'm telling you the truth!"

"Who says the Fae can't lie? The Guild? How do you know that isn't something they fed to the Guild so that they would buy it? If I was the High Fae of old, I'd have told them the same thing. Takes out torture, now doesn't it? They'd buy anything they told them because of course, the Fae *cannot* tell a lie."

"You're the most stubborn asshole in this entire world! Would you listen to me?" She growled as she struggled against the chains that held her.

I frowned. He made sense, because if I was the

Fae, I'd have told them that too, even if it wasn't true.

"The more you fight, the more you drain what little strength you have left, Ciara," he said smoothly as his crystal blue eyes slowly trailed over her breasts where the tattered dress failed to hide her ample cleavage, which moved with every angry breath she took. "If I were you, I'd reserve that energy. I have no plans of feeding you or falling prey to your seduction, temptress."

He wouldn't feed her, but I would. My power left no residue that could be traced, nor would it be felt by anyone in this camp.

I watched as he moved to the flap and turned back around. His eyes narrowed and I could see the muscle in his jaw working as he decided what to say.

"I didn't ask for this, but I won't allow that monster to have another opportunity to harm anyone else. To destroy any other caste of Faery. You are innocent, but so were my people. So were the infants that were killed to prevent them from becoming pets for the Horde King's sick pleasure. The people out there?" He pointed outside of the tent. "All of them are survivors or their children. We have to kill that monster. We have waited, bided our time, and that time is now. Don't move too much, Princess. Your blood gives me no pleasure," he gritted out before he turned and exited the tent.

I waited and watched as Ciara lowered her head and looked at where I had been standing before.

"You have to go, Synthia. You have to keep my brothers away from them. They will fight to the death, and none of them will win. I can't live knowing that it was my actions that bring down these people or the

Horde King. I know he won't stop looking for me, but he has to."

"Did they create the problems with the portals?" My voice was barely above a whisper.

"No. They don't bother themselves with the problems of Faery. They do, however, steal women, as they have only a few of their own. Dragon births are typically male, and since most of their females were lost in the *Battle of Dragons*, they now take them from villages that won't be noticed by the Horde and mate with them. I think it's why there aren't thousands of them here right now. What you saw out there are the ones who were either away when the Horde attacked, were wounded and left for dead after battle, or were just small children that escaped. From what I have overheard, they have a few small encampments now, scattered in rough locations that most wouldn't dare to think to look in. Most are not inhabited by creatures because of the locale. Dragon Aery is what they call their new home, and Blane is their born King. He was there the day Ryder slaughtered the Dragons; he watched him do it."

"The chain, I think I can get it off of you." I kept my voice low as I contemplated what she'd told me. I had been probing it, my eyes catching minute details of the chain, but then it glowed as she hastily interrupted me.

"You can't," she hissed. "It's set to slice me in half should it be tampered with. I'm a trap, made to lure the Horde here to watch me die as they try to free me from it. Blane isn't a bad guy; he's damaged. He's endured a lot, and I think I can reach him, Syn. I just need time. The chain, however, I believe is one of the relics my brother is looking for."

"If that's the case, it's a pretty fucked up relic. Ciara, I'm not leaving you here," I snapped.

"You are because you have to," she whispered frantically as tears slid down her cheeks. "Promise me you won't let my brothers come. Keep them safe. I will get free, I promise."

"If he doesn't feed you, you'll weaken and waste away. There is a lot of emotion in this camp. Anger, pain, resentment, hate; it's not enough to keep you going for long," I growled as I struggled against the emotions warring inside of me. I couldn't get this close and just leave her, but the more I looked at the chain, the more the details of it became apparent. It couldn't be removed from her. Not by anyone except the person who put it there. Worse than that, the thin belt she was wearing had some kind of beacon in it, like a tracker. Probably a fail-safe in case she did manage to escape.

"He will feed me," she replied confidently. "I'm going to break through to him, and I'm going to make him see I'm flesh and blood, just as he is. You have to go now. Please, trust me. My brothers don't; they think I'm weak because I was born female, but I'm not. I can do this, and end this war before it really starts."

I frowned and placed my hand on her shoulder, pumping power into her and feeding her enough to last a while. The wards on the tent started to glow, so I lessened the amount of power I was giving her. Her hair grew fuller, lusher in color as I fed her. The dark circles beneath her eyes vanished and her body filled out a bit, no longer starved for nutrients. Her flesh looked healthier now and, just to screw with his head a little bit, I cleaned her up and glamoured a fresh top and skirt on her body that would leave her midriff and the chain exposed.

I stepped back and watched as the violet glow in her eyes subsided from the feeding. I shook my head, unsure if I could do as she was asking, but I did trust her. I knew her; she was strong and stubborn, as her brother was. If she could end this war before it got to our doorsteps, it may be worth it.

I hugged her briefly and whispered close to her ear, "Ciara, I will come back for you. I will figure out how to remove that chain and I will come to get you. You have a very short window of time; I can't watch your brothers endure failure as they come home without you for much longer. Do what you can, but I will be back. Understood?"

"He comes," she whispered, and I moved to the flap, pushing myself against the tent's side as men rushed in with weapons drawn. As they moved in, I moved out with one last look at Ciara as she smiled as the Dragon King entered with his own guards close at his heels.

"She did it," one of the men cheered from inside the tent. "I told you she was too vain to remain dirty," he snickered as he grabbed her arm and turned it over. "Vanity is a bitch, Ciara."

"Is it?" she purred as her eyes lifted to their King's. "Or was it something else?" she smiled saucily.

"Ready the weapons and have the men prepare to fight the Horde, should they come for her," Blane gritted out coldly.

I swallowed, and prayed to the Gods that Ciara knew what she was doing. I'd kill them all before I let them touch Ryder. Every single last one of them.

Chapter
SEVENTEEN

I was standing on the balcony that was off of our bedroom chambers as I waited for Ryder to come to bed. Guilt washed through me as I considered what I had agreed to. I'd left Ciara in the care of Ryder's enemies, and I hated it, but I understood where she was coming from. She wanted to prove her worth, but at what cost?

She wanted to stop a war, but what if she gave her life to do it, and we still ended up at war with the Dragons? I rested my arms on the wall of the balcony and looked over the magnificent view as I tried to make sense of everything that had happened over the past year, and especially the last few weeks. I was burning up with secrets that I hated keeping from Ryder. I hated lying to him, even if it was to protect him from those who might try and hurt him.

"You're thinking too hard." The deep timbre of his voice made me jump. I turned around and gave him a small look of annoyance. I hated when he sifted in without warning. "Worried about the wedding?" His hands captured mine and pulled me close.

I swallowed and shook my head. "There's

something I need to tell you and I need you to not freak out. I need you to trust me," I murmured, then nibbled my lower lip and peered nervously into his golden eyes.

"Synthia, we have no secrets," he growled. "I keep nothing from you."

"I know we don't, which is why I have to tell you something. I need you to not freak out or go caveman on me, okay? I made some promises, and I don't want to start our marriage with any secrets between us."

"What are you hiding?" he demanded sharply. "What secrets?"

"Do you trust me?" I murmured softly, fighting the tightening of my throat as I watched the war of mistrust play across his features.

"Synthia," he warned.

"Do you trust me?"

"Yes, of course," he snapped.

"There is an Original Witch beneath the Guild. That is why the Seattle Guild isn't backing down, and if other creatures knew she was there, they'd come to try and take her from us."

He nodded. "I knew that," he replied and I blinked. "Synthia, I'm not stupid. I know my enemies and I make it my business to try and figure out what they hide from me. The Seattle Guild sent Enforcers to take me out the first week I entered Tèrra in the guise of the Dark Prince. So, I took them out before they became a problem. I also made a move for the Elders at the Guild who gave the order, and they sang before Ristan used the first blade on them. He has been following Elders around the Seattle and Spokane Guilds for years and found out about her existence quite a while ago." His fingers lightly traced my lips as he tried to gauge how shocked or angry I might be at his tactics. "You know who I am, what I am, so don't get mad that I will retaliate against my enemies; otherwise, some might think I am weak."

"I found her," I blurted after I'd digested the news that he'd murdered not only those who had been sent to kill him, but the ones who gave the orders as well. I couldn't blame him for that. I would have done the same, since the Guild standards are kill or be killed, and that some of the Elders had called some pretty self-serving hits mixed in with legitimate Guild hits over the last century.

"The Original Witch; you just said that," he prompted with an easy smile when he was sure I hadn't been upset that he'd killed Guild members.

"Ryder, I need you to promise me you will trust her, and that you will trust in her. I need for you to not ask me where she is."

He was still for a moment, then he stepped away from me. "You found Ciara," he said stiffly.

"I did." I nodded. "She's alive, and she's safe."

"Where is she?" he growled and when I stepped closer, he took another step away from me. I stopped and snorted as I looked up at him. "You will tell me where my sister is, now."

"No, I won't. Because you will charge in there like some fucking maniac and try to save her, but if you do that, you will watch her die. So no, Ryder, I won't tell you where she is. You can call off the wedding if it's what you want, but I can't tell you where she is just yet. I'm sorry, I love you too much to do that." I turned and left the balcony, listening to his heavy breathing as he struggled with what I'd told him.

I wasn't starting our lives together with other people's lies. I also wasn't sending him into that trap, nor could I bear for him to watch his sister be torn apart by some magic chain the moment he entered that tent, because I wasn't sure he'd come back from something like that as the same man I loved. I had also promised Ciara, and for some reason, I trusted her abilities.

I sifted out our bedroom and into the main hall, and was heading towards the garden when he grabbed my arm and spun me around as Ristan and Zahruk entered the room.

"You will tell me where my sister is!" he demanded. "It's not your fight, and you have no right to keep it from me; I am your King!"

"No, you're not," I mumbled as I struggled with my anger. "I was raised human, and while I admit you are King here, you don't get to order me around, Fairy. I am not telling you where she is!"

"Flower…" Ristan hesitated as Ryder interrupted him.

"Ask her where Ciara is," Ryder growled, his tone raised in anger.

"Yes, ask me where she is, Demon, and I will tell you nothing. Not a word more about her whereabouts than I have already told him! Tell that pompous asshole brother of yours that she's bait. They have her rigged as a fucking trap for him and the rest of you overprotective cavemen; they are hoping you will all march in there like Rambo so they can get all of you. So no, I won't tell him shit until I figure out how to get that belt off of her."

"What belt?" Zahruk interrupted, his calm and calculating demeanor slipping at the mention of Ciara.

"The one that will rip her apart should anyone from the Horde touch her or try to move her. The room where she's being held is warded for the Horde, not just as an alarm, but to immobilize anyone from the Horde as well." I took a deep, calming breath and shook my head slightly, trying to sort my thoughts. "I know where she is, but I don't know how to get her out of there without getting her killed. Until I do, no one is going in. She is surrounded by an army, Fairy. I won't lose you and if you hate me for it, fine. You can hate me, but you will at least be around to do so." I poked at his chest angrily. "They might not be able to kill you, but I am sure there are other things they can do to you that would be equally as awful. I still have nightmares of the Mages stuffing you full of iron. I'll be in the garden keeping my promise to the tree if you need me, because promises are something I try my hardest to keep. I danced on the line of breaking two today," I said with a gentle resolve to my tone. "That's more than I have broken in my entire life. So hate me or don't, hell, cancel the wedding—that's your choice, but I won't lose you to them. That is something I just won't do. So I'm going to figure out how to free her, and when I do, I will tell you where she is. Until then, you all need to have a little faith in her because she pretty much ordered me to leave her there. You raised her, all of you. She isn't defenseless, and she's a lot stronger than you all think she is. Give yourselves and her a little credit, because you trained a warrior while raising her to be a lady. I'm not sorry that I can't tell you where she is right now, because I know she's going to show you what she is made of. She's just like you: stubborn, pigheaded, but loyal and brilliant."

I started walking away as Zahruk turned and followed Ryder as he headed to the war room. I knew instinctively that Ristan trailed behind me as I pushed through the gates that led to the gardens and rushed through the main greenhouse, out into the open night air. I exhaled a shaky breath as I sat on one of the main benches that overlooked the Elder tree saplings.

"Flower, you left her behind," he accused with a hint of frustrated anger lacing his tone. "So explain the rest of it to me."

"You think I wanted to leave her there? If I'd had a choice I would have knocked her stubborn ass out and brought her back with me. I can't get the chain off of her, and if she moves in any way it perceives as a threat, it tears her skin. But, she never flinched or showed an ounce of pain. Ciara thinks it's one of the fucking relics you guys are looking for. I think she's probably right, but I won't know for sure until I hit the libraries and look that thing up. I hated leaving her, but she's stronger than any of us give her credit for; she told me to go so she could stop us from going to war."

"Who has her?" He motioned for me to scoot over and sat on the bench next to me. If anyone understood what I was doing right now, the Demon did, even if it was his sister who was at risk right now.

"The King of the Dragons," I whispered as I closed my eyes. "Ryder's going to leave me, isn't he?"

"No; he's upset, but he's not stupid."

"I can't lose him," I replied as I looked at Ristan and found him observing me as he waited patiently for me to spill the rest of what was running through my mind. I leaned my head against his shoulder and exhaled a long breath. "They blame him, unfairly, but I get it. I understand Blane's reasons. Blane is the Dragon King, and I guess he watched Ryder slaughter his family. I know that need to avenge those who were unjustly killed." I swallowed and looked at him. "He's me, but with a dick."

Ristan laughed, but his smile faltered and he shook his head. "Then you also know we have to kill him before he moves against Ryder."

"I know," I sighed sadly. "I can get back to where she is. The wards surrounding the camp and Ciara didn't detect me, probably because he's only trying to catch Horde Fae, but I don't think his revenge will end with him. I think that if we have to kill them all, history will repeat itself yet again."

"Sometimes I think we are stuck on an endless loop, one we don't have the power to stop," he said thoughtfully, and nodded his head to the side as if listening to something. "Ryder's waiting for you in your room, Flower. Be gentle with him; he isn't used to being one step behind, and you finding her first bent his ego a little, considering you weren't even looking for her as far as he was concerned."

"She's not just your sister anymore, Demon, she's my soon-to-be sister-in-law, and do you really think I wouldn't go looking?" I stood and turned to look at him.

"No, I just figured you'd have tried sooner, but we've had something flying at our heads from every which way for weeks, and you've had to send your own children away to keep them safe." He made a little noise as he stood and took a few steps towards the greenhouse. "You pick your battles, Synthia, you always have. If you say she can't be rescued until we figure out how this chain works, I believe you. I say we, because you aren't alone in this. Dristan and I know the libraries pretty well, and we can help you find what this thing on her is and how to disable it. The question is how long do you think it will be before this Blane figures out we aren't coming and he kills her and sends her home in pieces?"

"She's not who he blames," I shrugged. "He blames Ryder. I don't think he'll harm her. Scare her, yes. But she's smarter than even I thought she was, and I think he and the rest of you have all underestimated her. He left her filthy and in rags, yet she knew if she used her magic you'd find her. She is waging war with her brain; you all should be proud. It's more than I would have figured out, had I been in her place."

"Your *would-be* King grows impatient," he smirked and nodded when I grinned. "Synthia, you told him he wasn't your King in the main hall with the servants present." He laughed when I frowned. "Go to him, tell him how you really feel; the truth this time, eh?"

"Thanks, Demon," I groaned as I watched his image blur as he sifted out.

I sifted into the bedroom and discovered an angry Ryder pacing the floor. Each stride was painful to watch, knowing that I could put a quick end to this, and yet Ciara deserved a chance at trying to prevent bloodshed her way. She knew how much the demise of the Dragons bothered Ryder, and if she could find a way to make peace between the Dragons and her brothers, I was willing to give her that chance, even if they weren't.

I moved towards the bed and paused, considered what I should say, what I *could* say, and found myself at a loss for the right words.

"I made a vow too. A vow to protect her from anyone and anything the moment she was born, Witch. She's my responsibility."

"I respect that." I nodded slightly and turned to look at him. "She's with the Dragon King."

"What?" he snapped and I frowned as the color drained from his face. "He's long dead...you saw, there was nothing left of the Dragons."

"Yeah, well, the Dragons I saw earlier today were pretty convincing, and I'm not talking about shifters that can hold the form for a few minutes. I saw one transform and take to the sky. They survived. The Dragon King's son escaped the day you guys attacked. And let me tell you, he's waited a very long time to pay you back for it." He grabbed my shoulders and I could tell it was taking everything he had not to shake me.

"Synthia, where the hell is he holding her? He will kill her!" The wild look in his eyes was pure fear for his sister.

"No, he won't kill her, because he needs her alive to lure you to her. He won't hurt her if he thinks she's serving a purpose, which gives us time to figure out how to get that belt off of her. She's fed, and she told me to leave. She's not hurt, but she could be if we run in there without a plan. The place she is being held is warded; if you go, you will be caught. Worse than that, you'd get there in time to watch her die. I am not completely sure, but I think that belt is some kind of relic, and if anyone tries to take that thing off, she will be torn in two. So there. Now you know, Fairy. You can't save her by charging in there like you want to, so I need you to trust me, and we will figure this out together. You and your brothers can stop searching, but I would recommend you continue to send out patrols every day that look like they *are* still searching. I also know that the Dragons had nothing to do with the portals, which puts us right back at where we were."

"Synthia, what if he hurts her because I didn't come?" He struggled against the instincts he'd fine-tuned over the past millennia. He wanted to rush in and save the day, but he couldn't.

"He looked like it hurt him when she moved the wrong way and the belt drew blood." I cringed inside as he stiffened. Oh, yeah, he did not like his baby sister being hurt in any way. "He doesn't enjoy causing her pain, but he would if he thought it would hurt you. She thinks she can reach him and prevent him from seeking revenge against you. I don't buy it, but it is possible. People who survive horrible things can forgive the ones who caused them pain," I murmured as I moved closer and stood in front of him. "I blamed you for what happened to my parents. I also forgave you for being Fae. I fell in love with the one creature I hated most in any world."

"You didn't forgive Faolán," he argued.

"I actually had to. Not for him, but for me and also for you. Hate is dark, and it was strangling me. I had to forgive him to love you. I chose you, Ryder, and I'd do it every time. Madisyn also needed me to forgive him. So I did, but I know he has to die; it's about self-defense and survival now. He has to die so that my children are safe."

"You never told me you forgave him." I caught a thoughtful look of wonder on his face as he pulled me close and kissed the top of my head.

"I couldn't; I couldn't admit that I'd forgiven a monster. Not out loud, but for Madisyn I had to try and show her that I did. The moment I actually did, though, I felt like a weight had been lifted from me; like the light was turned back on and that it no longer could touch me. So I have to think that if I can stop hating someone who has done me so much wrong, there is hope for Blane."

"You know his name?" His voice was tight as he loosened his hold and looked down at me.

"Well, I didn't sit down to tea with him, Fairy," I snickered as I slapped his arm playfully. "I observed him because if I had thought he'd hurt her, I wouldn't be here without her, belt or no belt. So I watched him and the way he was interacting with her, and I think if anyone can reach him, it's Ciara."

"You think she will be okay until we figure out how to save her?" He glanced at me, almost fearing to hope that she would be all right without his intervening.

"I do, because she's Ciara, and she's got the stubbornness of you plus your cool head, the quick wit of Ristan, and the fierceness of Zahruk running through her veins. She's a part of all of you because you raised her. Trust her, and I promise to keep an eye on the situation but only if I can be sure that you will stay out of it—just until we can figure out how to get her out alive."

"I trust you, Witch," he muttered as he turned me around and kissed the back of my neck softly. "But I'm still spanking you for being reckless."

"You think you can?" I taunted and backed away from him, the wicked grin playing at the corners of my mouth enough to show him I'd fight to save the pain he intended to inflict on my hind end.

"Indeed, Synthia. I think I can," he grinned.

"Ryder, if you spank me, so help me Gods!" I warned as he began to stalk me slowly, as if I was his prey.

"You kept secrets from me, Pet, there has to be a consequence," he explained calmly. "Now, I had planned to take you slowly for hours, but now I think a little torture is in order, a little pain mixed with pleasure...or a lot," he grinned as he reached for me and I sifted across the room to keep away from him.

"Game on, Fairy," I smiled and sifted again before he could catch me.

Chapter EIGHTEEN

I watched as Madisyn continually wrung her hands. There had been absolute bedlam since the moment I'd awoken this morning. It was our wedding day, and everyone was on edge. Security inside the castle had been beefed up, and I had guards stationed at my door. No one was comfortable because there were too many creatures squeezed into the castle today.

"You look beautiful, Sorcha, doesn't she, Adam?" Madisyn said, forcing my eyes to lift from my trembling hands to meet Adam's. "I meant Synthia, I'm sorry. It's just that today my daughter is truly here."

"She's the most beautiful thing I've seen in a while," he agreed, taking pressure off her mistake, even though he himself was handsome in a morning coat styled tuxedo with a black tie and gray vest, his hair neatly pulled back.

Mine was piled elegantly atop my head. The silver crown that kept it caged had blood red rubies at each raised peak. Silver bracelets that matched the bands around my biceps tinkled musically every time I moved. I had just enough makeup to enhance my

features, and yet it looked natural. The dress wasn't
the one we'd selected together, but a last-minute
surprise that Madisyn glamoured on me—and I could
have sworn the sneaky Fae Queen was going to start
crying if I didn't give in and wear it. This one was a
creamy white taffeta and had an open back with cross
straps and organza ruffles that flowed beautifully to
the floor. The front had a deep V-neckline, and the veil
was sheer and edged with almost transparent lace that
had been used in Madisyn's own wedding so long ago.

I stood up from the small vanity and turned to
Madisyn and Adam, who waited with me as the
guards did a perimeter search before it was time to
walk down the aisle and marry my Fairy. My nerves
were everywhere; my heart hammered against my
chest as I considered what I was doing.

I still wasn't afraid to bind myself to Ryder; I loved
him. It was something I knew to the very fiber of my
being. I wasn't afraid of spending the rest of my very
long life with him; for me, there was no other option.
He was mine. The rest wasn't of importance as long
as we had that. I was nervous and edgy because so
many things could go wrong today. We had so many
creatures set to be inside the castle that, if anyone who
wished us ill wanted in, it would be easy to do.

"Nerves, Syn?" Adam moved closer and handed
me a glass of red wine.

"No, not about marrying him," I replied softly. "I
love him. I'm just worried about everything else that
could go wrong today."

"We all are." He gave me a small smirk as I accepted
the glass and his hand, and he gripped mine with
enough force to reassure me. I pulled my hand back

and set the wine on the table that had refreshments on it. "Larissa would have loved this," he smiled, and his eyes twinkled fondly at me. "She'd have been going crazy that you were going to be a queen."

"She would have; she would have tried on all of the crowns by now. She would have loved it here, probably more than any of us."

Larissa would have planned the entire wedding with Madisyn; she would have loved it. Ever since we'd been kids, she'd always had her shit together, and she had been the one who wanted the kids, the big wedding, and the prince. Not me. I swallowed the lump that formed in my throat as I tried to recall what she looked like. It was as if time was erasing my beloved friend from my mind.

"I don't remember what she looked like," I whispered through trembling lips. "Adam." I turned to look at him with tears in my eyes. "I can't remember what Larissa looked like."

"Big green eyes, the color of the greenest spring grasses in existence." His voice was gentle as he reached out and touched my face. "Chestnut hair that couldn't be tamed," he smirked. "It was so wild that she had to pin it up before she could sleep at night. You remember how much she complained about it? It never did what she wanted it to, and yet every morning it looked perfect, as if she'd spent hours arranging it instead of the few minutes we were allowed to ready for missions. Not a single strand looked out of place, and you use to tease her about it, because she always looked ready to go to war the moment she rolled out of bed."

"She was always so prepared." I tried to pat at

the corners of my eyes to make sure I wasn't tearing up. "Her makeup was never off, nor did she ever look exhausted like the rest of us."

"No, she was always refreshed from what little sleep we'd gotten," he laughed.

"You remember her pink pajamas with the frogs?" I laughed.

"Oh God, they were falling apart," he snorted. "They did hug her ass nicely, though."

"Pervert," I laughed. Tears blurred my vision and I chewed my lip as a sob escaped. "I miss her. I want her here with me today so badly."

"You'll ruin your makeup," he chided as he stepped closer and hugged me tightly. "She would have given anything to be here if she could have."

"I know, but there's not a day that I don't think of her and miss her being a part of this." I swallowed as I pulled away and carefully wiped my eyes.

"We all miss her," he agreed.

"Synthia, it's almost time," Madisyn interrupted as she opened the door and spoke with the guards for a moment. "I need to take my place." She motioned for Adam to follow her. "Adam will wait for you and your father at the doors of the throne room, just like we practiced."

"Okay." I pushed up on my tiptoes to kiss Adam's cheek before hugging Madisyn, who beamed in response.

"You are a sight today. One that the lands will speak of until the end of time," she said roughly before she wiped at her eyes and smiled. "Thank you for allowing me to do this for you."

"I wouldn't have it any other way." I dabbed at the corners of my eyes as I watched them leave. Once the door was closed, I exhaled and moved back to the vanity, staring at the reflection of a stranger.

I watched as my image shimmered to the look I wanted. For a moment, I was me when I'd been no more than an Enforcer, glowing blue glyphs enhanced with the invisible ink, then my image shimmered to the girl I'd been upon first arriving in Faery. The Heir brands swirled upon my flesh, fanning out as they fought each other for dominance upon my flesh. They climbed my arms in thin lines to form a mixed colored Celtic knot of womanhood on my shoulders. The place where the stars for my guardians had once rested as a reminder of what I'd lost. One for each life I'd lost in my childhood. My eyes closed and, when I opened them, they were the brilliant azure and lilac colored ones I'd inherited after Transitioning. Delicate thin black lines surrounded my irises, the tricolor of Fae royalty. I opened my mouth, watching as the delicate fangs extended. This was what I was supposed to look like, this was me.

"There she is," I whispered at the reflection, watching as the brands struggled for dominance. Dark red, gold, black, and silver pulsed along my arms as power radiated from each strand. The white ink of the Guild pulsed as well, glowing strong and sure even against the Fae brands. It had been a long time since I'd seen them or anything that I'd had since before coming to Faery. That girl was still in there, but she wasn't the same.

I reached up and began pulling the veil over my

face as a knock sounded from the door. I moved to it without thought as it opened and Lasair walked in. He looked regal in his suit, but his eyes looked different today. He nodded to the guards and directed them to wait for us in the outer hallway to guard our entry into the main hall.

Once inside, he turned violet and cobalt eyes on me and smiled as he slowly looked me over. His smile, however, gave me pause, and the hair on my nape stood up in awareness that something was wrong.

"Lasair?" I looked at him speculatively, trying to figure out what was off as he smiled a generous smile at me, his brilliant eyes seemed to twinkle.

"Sorcha, my sweet, is something amiss?" he asked, revealing perfect teeth.

"Not at all, Faolán," I growled as I watched him. His eyes narrowed and he grinned, and as I watched him close the door, I swallowed the urge to scream for help. "I knew you'd get the message I sent out." I watched as he locked us into the room.

I wasn't afraid of him. I wouldn't be afraid of him any longer. He'd taken up too much of my life with worrying about where he was, or what he was doing. He was insane, and the only way to protect myself and my babies, was to take him out of the equation.

"Afraid, sister dear?" he smirked as he produced blades and gave up pretending to be our father. His features shimmered back to the ones that had haunted me for most of my life. He was still beautiful; his eyes shone deceivingly, the ethereal beauty of the Fae his only redeeming quality, but it was a lie. What lay beneath that beautiful façade was monstrous. He tilted his head and watched me as he stepped closer, only for me to sidestep, placing more distance between us.

"I am not afraid of you," I replied easily, showing no weakness. He was cold, maniacal, and his kind fed off fear. I glamoured the veil off and stepped out of the Cinderella shoes I'd worn for Ryder. He loved fucking me in heels that looked particularly hot on his shoulders. "I was as a child, when you slaughtered the people who were protecting me. Did you know how close you were to me that day?" I taunted, drawing his attention away from my breasts, which his eyes feasted on. "I was there, brother. I watched you take my adopted mother over and over again before you bashed in my father's head. I was right beneath your nose and you still couldn't find me. So close, Faolán, and yet always just out of your reach."

"You're alone now, sister, and I've brought others with me. Others who want to see the end of your betrothed's line. The Horde will be no more when I finish with them, and when I have, you'll be mine. This time, I will take what is rightfully mine from you. I may even allow you a little pleasure before I end your pathetic life."

"Always with the fucking; Faolán, I'm your sister. You sick fuck," I laughed. "You're not man enough to take me, not now, not ever. Whoever you brought here will be slaughtered, and this will end here and now."

"It ends when I find your twins and slaughter them," he shouted, spittle exploding from his lips.

"Triplets, Faolán, I had three. Three children who are all more worthy of inheriting the Heir brands than you. I pity you; you're a sad little thing." I shook my head in disgust as I glamoured swords and waited for him to strike. "You always lose, and that's because you want it too bad. Too much. You'll never lead any caste of the Fae, because you are not a leader. You ran to the Mages and sought their help because you're too weak to do anything yourself. Here, we call you Faolán the Failure; born to fail anything you set out to do."

"I captured you once, whore; I will do it again and I will force him to watch as I spread your thighs and take you. You will scream for me; whether in pleasure or pain, you will scream!" he shouted as he lunged, and I danced around it, dodging the attack and deflecting it with my blades as I placed my back to the door and watched him.

His blades were iron, the handles were wrapped in swathes of cloth, but to the Fae, they were deadly. He'd been carrying them, slowly draining himself to get to me. I'd been waiting for him, knowing that this wedding wouldn't happen if he showed, but this was more important.

This was everything.

"Iron?" I raised an eyebrow at him, wondering why he was working so hard to kill me if he intended to have me still.

"Iron kills Fae; you think I came here to take prisoners?" he spat.

"No, I think you came here to die," I answered calmly.

He lunged, swinging, and I parried as he advanced. An age-old dance of warriors, each swing was effortless as I deflected his blows with my lighter, thinner blades. I dropped and rolled when he got too close to me, kicking out as I went down, which sent him crashing through the doors he'd entered through.

The moment we entered the halls, the sound of faint screams reached my ears, and I ignored it. Nothing mattered except killing him. I brought my blade up as he lunged, deflecting the blow that had been meant to sever my head from my body.

I stepped backwards, and for a moment I seemed to lose control of my body as a concussive blast of noise and sheer force knocked me off my feet; stone and wood blew around the hallway. The explosion sent both me and Faolán sailing as debris scattered over us and landed everywhere. I was the first up, searching for my blades as my ears continued to ring from the noise. I was covered in a sheen of fine dust from the stone. I didn't stop to look as I found a blade and turned in time to deflect another blow and lunge, and then parried him as he attacked ruthlessly.

My heart skipped a beat as screams erupted from the main hall, the place where Ryder was supposed to be waiting to marry me. I didn't dare run to him, because Faolán would vanish the moment I did. I was down a blade, having lost it in the debris, and I could feel the wards around us humming with the warning of danger.

In my free hand, I brought up an energy ball; fluorescent blue power sailed through the air at Faolán before he could think to block it. It hit him in his chest, sending him careening into the wall behind him. Smoke billowed from the hall, and my heart beat wildly as the screams lingered. Terrified shrieks and moans of pain carried on the billowing smoke that reached into the hallway, filling it with a smoky haze that made it next to impossible to see Faolán.

One after another I continued to slam magical balls of energy in his direction. Unable to see if I hit the mark, I moved closer, only to feel searing pain as one of his hit me. I ducked, not daring to roll with the rocks and other debris that littered the floor. My side was on fire, but I wasn't losing this battle.

I remained still, unmoving. I didn't even dare to breathe as he searched for me in the thick, billowing smoke. The moment he got close, I brought my sword up and slid it through his center, but he pulled away from the pain. His scream told me I'd hit my mark, and once again I was silent as I moved across the room, using the smoke as a screen and a shield.

He fumbled. The sound of feet crushing rock gave his position away and, once again, I gave up my location to swing my blade as I used my other hand to project energy from it; his grunt of pain was satisfying.

"You bitch, you ruined everything!" he shouted, the sound hollow; he must have been choking on the blood that was surely flowing from his lungs. "I should have been the Heir, and then I could have killed our sniveling father and taken his crown! But you, you ruined it all! They threw you away like trash, and you could have stayed away and lived, but you returned to Faery and triggered your destiny. Now, that destiny will kill you!"

"I'm not just the Heir to the Blood throne, Faolán. I'm a Goddess," I snapped angrily. "No one would have let you sit on that throne, no one! You are evil to the very center of your rotten core. Danu and Faery would have fought you so that the heir brands would go to Liam over you. This land fights against those who harm it, or hadn't you noticed that?"

"I would have killed them all—and their children!" he shouted, catching me off guard as he shot another energy ball towards me, hitting the side of my head.

He lunged, trying to use the element of surprise against me. I was ready, and swung my blade as I felt the power in the room shift in the hall, and he collided with my blade. It stuck through his shoulder, but once again he moved away into the thick clouds of smoke.

I went silent, sensing him as he cradled his arm and grunted with pain. I moved soundlessly, gliding over the rubble as I snuck closer to him. The moment I did, I paused, staring at his back. His shoulders drooped in defeat; he was defeated and he knew it.

"You can change," I tried. For Madisyn's sake, I would at least try—but my hope died an ignoble death as he turned with his hands full of energy. In that moment, I knew he'd never change what he was: Evil until his last dying breath.

My sword swung out before he could send the huge glowing balls of magic at me, severing muscle from flesh as his head detached from his body and went rolling across the debris-strewn floor. My eyes followed it as it rolled towards the screams that still filled the hall. Blood dripped from my face, and I vaguely realized it was arterial flow from his decapitation. My dress was ripped, torn from the fight, and yet I didn't stop, I couldn't.

My feet moved, as if pulled by an invisible cord. I walked towards the chaos I heard, and into the room where I'd been about to pledge my life to Ryder's. There was no joy in killing Faolán, only a sense of peace in knowing he'd never touch me or my children ever again.

I waved my hand, clearing the smoke that filled the room, and gasped as bodies were revealed. Bodies with limbs missing and dead corpses littered the floor. Adam was laying on the floor, forcing me to move into action as I made my way through the bodies to get to him.

"No, no, get up," I pleaded as I searched the room for Ryder. "Adam, please," I begged, and when he opened his eyes, I sagged in relief. My magic searched him for injuries, finding several contusions but nothing that would be debilitating. "What happened?"

"Jesus," he gasped, holding onto me as he searched me for injuries. "You're bleeding."

"It's not my blood," I assured him. "Ryder?"

"I don't know; he wasn't here when the room exploded."

"How did it explode?" I asked, looking around, searching for clues. The debris went outwards; rocks were thrown outwards from what had once been a wall. The damage was the worst by the dais, which meant it was the point of the origin of the blast. "It was meant to kill him." I tried to swallow the lump that appeared in my throat at that realization.

"You don't know that," he grunted as I helped him to his feet as we stumbled over the bodies, stone, and debris.

"Look at it, it's gone," I whispered as I swallowed the scream that was lodged in my throat. There was no sign of him or his brothers. My eyes moved to those who were stirring, finding Lasair, Keir, and Madisyn on the far side of the room, covered in dust and blood. "Could they have found a way to kill him? I can't lose him, Adam," I sobbed. I couldn't. He was my world. If he was gone, I'd unravel. I'd come apart. I'd become a monster to avenge him. "We have to help the wounded," I announced resolutely. My voice quivered as I fought to control it. "We have to get them out of here."

I watched as Adam reached down, picking up a child who he had shielded from the explosive blast, and closed his eyes. He opened them, looked at me, and tried to sift again. Nothing happened.

"It's a ward, to nullify Fae magic," I whispered as I sent feelers out to figure out what was blocking him. "This wasn't a hit," I said softly, for Adam's ears alone. "This was the Guild; those are Witch spells and wards." They'd placed a spell to keep the Fae from sifting, to block our power, which meant they'd come here to send a message, to take something.

My stomach dropped as I turned and looked at the dais, where it had been. The attack on the main hall would have been a distraction, which meant whatever they'd come for hadn't been inside the hall yet.

"We need to find Zahruk and Ristan." I fought against the fear that was trying to engulf me.

"And Ryder." Adam looked around the room for my fiancé as I looked at him with cold eyes and nodded.

"And Ryder."

Chapter
NINETEEN

I moved through the hall, numb and oblivious to the crying and screaming that surrounded me. Blood covered my dress, belonged to Faolán as well as others who I had helped as we moved the dead and the debris into the courtyard while we cleared the room to be able to reach the living. Adam was at my side; and hadn't left it in the hours that had followed the explosion.

I'd done my best to take control of the situation, although chaos still reigned inside the main hall as people struggled to get to the dead or the dying. The wards that had prevented the Fae from sifting had been found and disabled.

The worst part of finding them was seeing the runes that I knew like the back of my hand. Guild runes. The smooth rocks with runes etched in them were found scattered against the walls outside the castle, as well as inside. The bomb that had first exploded had been placed beneath the dais of Ryder's throne. Smaller energy bombs had been placed at several other locations throughout the castle, making the number of wounded climb into the hundreds. Explosives didn't have the power to kill or wound Fae; surround the bomb with iron fragments, though, and you have another matter completely. Iron nails, filings, and other small metallic particles were embedded in the walls, support columns and mixed in with the debris from the bombs. This wasn't a normal weapon for the Guild, but the smaller energy bombs were something even a novice at the Guild would know how to use.

I spun in a circle, taking in the severity of the damage. It wasn't until a group of familiar men walked in that my heart stuck in my throat, and the floor seemed to fall from beneath me. Ristan and Zahruk slowly made their way through the mess to where I stood. I unconsciously held my breath and felt Adam's hand at the small of my back for comfort.

"Where is he?" I whispered, barely loud enough for even the Fae to discern.

"We should go somewhere quiet. We need to talk." I had never heard Zahruk speak so softly before, and the set of his jaw told me this wasn't going to be good. His blue eyes searched my face as I sagged against Adam so I wouldn't fall in view of those who needed my strength.

"Where is he?" I repeated shakily, unable to stop the question from leaving my tongue. "I have to know." Once they said the words I had been dreading, I couldn't go back to not knowing.

"They took him," Ristan said carefully.

"Okay." I took a deep breath as I swayed, the reality of it hitting me. "Where the fuck were you guys?" I demanded with accusation lacing my tone.

Zahruk glanced at Ristan and then back at me as if he was weighing his words. "You said you needed to speak with him." His piercing gaze seared mine. "Change of heart, you told him. So he went with you to the council chambers to discuss it." Zahruk waved his hand to where the council chambers that adjoined the throne room were and I saw that the doors were smashed open. "Madisyn joined us a few moments later and said you were ready. That's when we figured out that it wasn't you in the room with him. He was gone before we were able to break the door down," he let out an angry sigh. "We searched for him for hours, but there wasn't a sign of him anywhere. Whoever took him had it planned out to the very last detail because they didn't leave a single clue as to where they have taken him."

"The Guild," I scowled. "It was the Guild. No clues, other than every fucking bomb fragment they left behind, have Guild fingerprints all over them."

"How do you know that?" he asked.

"The energy bombs that were used are common diversion weapons. Adam is a specialist in making those types of bombs and grenades. The runes outside and inside the castle are basic ones, but they hold enough power to keep Fae from sifting," I pointed to Ristan, "he would have seen the runes for those types of wards all over the place when he was in the Spokane Guild. I know the Guild; I know their signs in an attack. If I was going to come into Faery to take the strongest creature, I would have planned something similar. This assault was only a diversion to make us focus on it instead of what was really happening."

"Where do you think they would have taken him?" Ristan grimaced.

"My guess would be the Seattle Guild. It is the

closest and the most fortified one to the portal that is failing." I spoke on autopilot, unable to wrap my mind around what had happened. "We need to get the people out of here, down to Eliran. We've lost a lot of people."

"Damage control can wait; the King is missing," Zahruk hissed.

"The King is with the Guild. We can't just walk in and get him. We need a plan," I stated, watching as he considered what I'd said, and after a moment, nodded his agreement somewhat hesitantly. "Help us move the ones with the most critical injuries; the others can wait."

"Synthia, are you all right?" Ristan murmured as he took in the blood smeared and splattered on my face and dress.

"It's not my blood," I assured him, watching as he looked around the room and gave a firm nod. "Faolán is dead," I blurted. "He showed up just before the bombs went off, and I made sure that he wouldn't ever threaten me or mine again." I moved away from Adam and the men as I walked towards the wounded, desperately trying to keep my mind busy so that I wouldn't give in to the urge to crumble. I wanted to fall to my knees and scream, cry, something. I couldn't. I had eyes on me; they needed to see me behaving like a leader, not cave in to the pain and panic I felt.

"You did what?" Zahruk demanded, and Adam pointed to the body that Madisyn was sitting next to.

"He's gone. That's all that matters."

My eyes slowly went to where Madisyn sat. She'd been hysterical when Adam had carried Faolán's headless body out with the intentions of laying his body with the rest of the dead, when Madisyn had stopped him. I hadn't made eye contact with her yet, nor had I offered comfort, even though I knew the pain she was in had to be eating her alive. He'd turned on his family, on me. It had taken everything I had in me to offer him a chance to change his ways, but his actions had told me everything I needed to know.

"She will want to take him home," Ristan said softly. "He cannot be buried in the Blood Kingdom and can't be honored in death. It's too bad he can't be subjected to the traitor's punishment by having his skin harvested regularly over the next couple of centuries, however, he must be cast to the abyss as the traitor he was."

"She is aware of that. Lasair has stated as much already. She just needs a moment; he was her child, no matter how much of a monster he'd become." I sifted a body to the courtyard and came back, glamouring the blood from my hands as I trembled with uncertainty of what the Guild intended to do with Ryder. The Guild had very limited information on the Horde; it was the one race we'd fumbled blindly against. That would work in our favor for getting him back.

I kept busy until the last of the dead had been removed from the hall, cleaned and shrouded for burial. Adam had suggested that Keir bring in the Shadow Warriors, the Dark Fae's version of the Elite Guard for a few days, since we were spread thin already. It was a welcome show of support on their part. The Crimson Guard also arrived and had taken up position around us in the hall. More and more of the Elite Guard returned; each one gave a report, which Zahruk relayed to me. No one had found a trace of Ryder, and with each one who came back empty-handed, I began to feel sick to my stomach.

Once we'd finished, Zahruk and Ristan walked with me to the chambers I shared with Ryder. Each step closer felt as if it would destroy me.

"We'll find him and bring him back to you, Flower," Ristan assured me when I stopped walking, my arms wrapping around my stomach. Tears burned my eyes, but I refused to allow them to drop.

"Synthia," Zahruk hesitated as he looked around at those who might overhear, then grabbed my arm and pulled me close. Together, we made our way down the corridor to the chambers. He opened the door for me and waited until I was inside. "You can do this." He smiled grimly as if to reassure me.

"I can't," I sniffed as the tears I'd been fighting fell, and my knees gave out as a violent shudder tore through me. I hit the floor before either Zahruk or Ristan expected it and wrapped my arms around my stomach again and cried. "I can't do this without him. I can't breathe without him," I sobbed. I couldn't; my body shook violently, and I wanted to crawl into a ball and stay there, on the floor, in the fetal position.

"Fuck," Zahruk snapped as he reached down and picked me up, then handed me off to Ristan, who moved to the bed, holding me against him. "She can't face them like this," he growled, his fingers threading through his hair as he pushed it out of his face.

"She just needs a moment or two. She can do this," Ristan muttered in an attempt at encouragement.

I cried until I couldn't cry anymore, and once the tears abated, I pulled away from Ristan and looked at him. He and Zahruk both looked exhausted and uncertain, which only made the pain hit home harder. I straightened my spine, wiped away the tears, and spoke with more authority than I felt.

"What's the plan, gentlemen?"

"We need the Horde, we know that. They won't follow you, and they are already aware that Ryder is missing. News spreads like fire in Faery." Zahruk's tone was weary, yet still rang with authority.

"Can't we ask them to help us," I asked.

"It's not that easy. The Horde follows the one who holds the beast, and you don't hold it, Synthia. None of us do. The only other way is to lead them through power and fear of repercussion from not helping. "

"So, we make them fear us," I growled. "We kill any who question our command; if the leaders of the Castes do, we will kill them too." I looked at both of them fiercely. "Call them to us; if they refuse to follow me, I'll have to change their minds."

"And how will you do that?" Zahruk piercing eyes watched me for any sign of weakness.

"By speaking their language," I answered with a hard stare. "He is their King; they will fight with me to get him back."

"If we back her, it might work," Ristan offered. "They no longer consider her an outsider," he explained when we both just stared at him. "Don't look at me like that. It's the Horde—they fucking love power. If the Elite Guard backs her, they will think twice about questioning her when she orders them to follow her."

"It might work," Zahruk agreed as he rubbed his chin, and a calculating gleam entered his eyes. "But even with the numbers that the Horde has, we will still need more people to back us. I don't imagine the Guild hasn't realized that we won't sit by passively and not come for him. It took effort to get him, and I don't think they intend to just hand him back to us."

"They will fight us, and they will die."

Ristan and Zahruk watched me as I swallowed the words. I'd kill for him. I'd wreck worlds for him. He was the air that filled my lungs. Ryder was my world, and if they thought they could walk in here and take that from me, they were insane.

"Call for the Horde. Anyone who doesn't heed the call to arms will need to be dealt with severely and immediately," I ordered as I righted the bloody wedding dress and smoothed the skirt that I'd refused to change out of. I looked at my chipped nails and then back up to Zahruk as he smiled. "I'm prepared to do what is needed to get him back, and more. This can't go unanswered. We have to answer in kind, and if they fight us, they will die. They need to see us standing together, united. They need to know we won't let this kind of thing go without paying them back tenfold. That is the way of the Horde, is it not? You will council me and stand with me as we send out the call to arms." I was proud of myself for not losing it. I wanted to, I needed to. I wanted to walk into the Guild and bring him home, but I knew that the only way for the Guild to take him, was to enlist help from someone strong enough to do it.

A knock at the door drew all eyes to it, and Ristan was the first to move towards it. Adam slipped through, green eyes locked with mine, and he flinched at the sight of the puffiness around my eyes from crying. I moved to him and held his hand as I looked into his eyes, smiling the best I could as I tried to reassure him that I was okay, yet words didn't come. I wasn't okay.

"What do you need from me, Synthia?" Adam asked quietly.

"I need to know that this castle is protected while Ryder and I are gone. If you can have some of the Shadow Warriors remain here a little longer than a few days, I can leave knowing it will be protected when I am gone. I can't leave our people exposed, not when so many of the wounded were Horde. Right now, if the Dragons attacked, they'd take the castle. We can't allow that to happen."

Adam looked at us with confusion. "Dragons? I think I'm missing something, but whatever you need it's yours. I'll guard the castle with my life." His eyes searched mine for any sign that I wasn't okay. He knew me, knew I wasn't okay by a long shot, but he wouldn't point it out, not here.

"Thank you," I murmured softly. "Adam, if I don't come back from this," I started, and then stopped as he shook his head.

"No, I won't lose you too," he snapped. "Don't even think it."

"I need to know that if I go out there and I don't come home, that my children are protected and loved. You are my oldest friend, and I know you'd protect them from anyone who wished them harm, so give me this, Adam. I have no plans of not coming back, but they took Ryder, which means whoever is helping them is very strong. God bolts alone wouldn't stop Ryder from fighting, which tells me they have something else fighting with them against us."

"What the hell could they possibly have that could neutralize Ryder?" he asked as his green eyes searched my face.

"An Original Witch, or possibly twelve of them," I announced as I glanced at Zahruk and Ristan uncomfortably. "We have one beneath the Spokane Guild. Alden confirmed who Sleeping Beauty is, which means the Guild has access to the rest of the coven."

"Shit," he replied as his mouth opened and closed. "I thought they were just myths that the Elders used to scare us into behaving."

"I wish they had been," I replied as I moved away from him with Ristan and Zahruk flanking my sides behind me.

Chapter TWENTY

We moved through the corridors soundlessly, everyone watching our every move. The Horde was already looking for any sign of weakness within our ranks. Any sign of blood, and they'd try to figure out a way to crown a new King before I could get Ryder back here and back on his throne. I'd be damned if I showed them any sign of weakness. The King wasn't dead; he was just misplaced for the moment. Besides, no one held his beast, and that was normally what decided the new King here.

Yes, I wanted to fall down and curl into a ball, but I wouldn't. I would keep my head held high, erect my defenses, and straighten my tilted crown. They may have thrown the first punch, but I'd make sure I got the last hit in and I would watch them fall.

"We will get him back," Ristan murmured gently as he stopped me in the throne room as Zahruk ushered people out of it. I waited for them to clear the room as Ristan watched me carefully. "Remember, you can show no fear in there. Inside that council room we need the Guild Enforcer. You will be Ryder's proxy, his surrogate, and if they smell a single whiff of fear in that room, this thing doesn't work."

"I have no fear of what I have to do, Demon." I turned and gave him a determined glare. "If I have to destroy the Guild to get him back, I won't think twice about it. I will be sure to send a clear, decisive message to them. I will make it so clear that they never even think to try something like this again. If they fight us, or refuse to give him back, they will die." I looked between Ristan and Zahruk and strengthened my resolve. "No one can be allowed to think Faery is weak, or we will have more than just the Mages at our gates. If I have to become the monster they claim us to be, so be it, I will become it. I will do anything it takes to end up with Ryder back here, at my side."

"You're sure you can do that?" Ristan questioned, and when I gave a stiff nod, he continued. "The Horde, they are going to push you, question your ability to lead them."

"I won't give them a chance; should they argue, I will respond in a language they know all too well. The Guild hit us hard. We have to hit back harder. I need the Horde behind us when we do, so they cannot question my right to lead until he is returned to his throne."

"It's the Horde," Zahruk interjected. "They are bipolar at best on a good day. Today they've heard the rumors that the King was taken by our enemies. That he wasn't strong enough to fight off those who invaded, and whatever the people are whispering about is filling their heads with idiotic ideas. They won't be easy to tame alone."

"I won't be alone." I patted his shoulder reassuringly. "I'll have you guys at my side. You will be my eyes and ears, and lead me in the right direction here. I wasn't born of the Horde, but you are the leaders of the Elite Guard. They will at least think twice about fucking with us with you two next to me."

"We need to get on with this," Ristan nodded. "Daylight is wasting."

"Indeed, are you ready, Goddess?" Zahruk extended his elbow to me as his piercing blue eyes held mine with a confidence I wasn't sure I deserved yet. I hadn't pulled it off, and my stomach was tied in knots at the mere idea of facing this war council—and the Horde.

"I'm ready," I affirmed as I slipped my arm through his as Ristan opened the door to reveal a room full of people. I'd sat in on the council before, but at that time it had been at Ryder's side, and only with the Elite Guard present. Now Keir, my father, and the heads of the smaller castes and clans sat around the table with their guards at their backs. I moved into the room, forcing myself to pretend that everything was okay.

Once I reached the chair reserved for Ryder, I paused, which Zahruk was ready for. He pulled out the chair and calmly placed his hand on my shoulder for support. It felt like the floor was crumbling beneath my feet as I stared at the chair reserved for the King. My King, my love, was gone.

"Thank you for coming," I said without a trace of weakness. Adam and Adrian watched me as I pulled strength from them. "We need to finish having people sweep the castle and remove the remaining wards left behind by our enemies. We need to fix the damage to the castle and find stonemasons who can start rebuilding the walls immediately. I'd prefer Fae stonemasons who can rebuild with magic, if possible, as time is of the essence here. The bodies need to be burned, or taken home to be buried, but they cannot remain in the courtyard. Their presence is causing those who live and remain in the castle to be weak, and weakness is not something we need right now. If any do not stand with us during this time, they are to be banned from this kingdom. The Guild has Ryder, therefore we will go in and we will get him back. We will destroy any who stand in our way. Once we have him back, we will level the Guild to the ground and raze the rubble that remains. The message will be clear to anyone who tries to fuck with us: We stand united, and we won't be played with. Is there anyone who would like to voice a concern?" I was proud that I wasn't visibly trembling, and my voice had somehow remained cold and calculated. I was falling apart inside, but on the outside, I was in control.

"What happens if they have killed him?" Liam spoke up; my father laid his hand on Liam's arm in a gentle reminder for caution.

"That's not a possibility," I replied without showing how much that thought frightened me. The Guild didn't know what could kill the Horde King, few did, but it didn't mean they wouldn't try to achieve that goal. My worry was that I knew how resourceful they were, and if there was a way to do it that we didn't know about, they would quickly try to find it. "The Guild does nothing by chance. They took him because they want something. Something only he has."

There was a knock at the door and we all paused as Aodhan opened it. I watched as Alden and Lucian stepped in, followed by a few of Lucian's men. My eyes scanned them as they took in the sight of me, covered in blood, in the King's place at the war council. I hadn't wanted Alden here for this.

"Anything else?" I asked as confidently as I could, while Liam watched me carefully.

"But what if he *is* dead, Synthia. You have to consider that possibility. You can't lead the Horde, and they will expect a King to replace him. If Ryder is dead, there will be challenges for the throne if Danu doesn't choose another as Heir to the Horde right away. The Horde isn't run by blood, it's run by strength."

"He isn't dead, Liam," I growled.

"So, say he isn't, and we go in and slaughter the Guild, and send that message," he continued as my eyes met Alden's and I saw the color draining from his face. "Then we have yet another enemy at our doors."

"They have already proven they are our enemy. Adam, Adrian, and I recognized their calling cards all over the place after the attack, and if we hesitate they will come again. We go in, and if they oppose us, we destroy them all. There is no other option."

"We can't go in there to get him back and then not give them a show of strength they will never forget, because the moment we get there, they will attempt to destroy him, and then they will try and march on the rest of Faery," Ristan added.

"What would they want from him?" I wondered, staring at Alden. "Why come for the Horde King?"

"Because if you're going to show strength, Synthia, you walk in and you take the biggest motherfucker the other side has," Lucian said.

My eyes moved from Alden to Lucian, and back to Alden. "Why him, why take the strongest of the Fae?"

"Because they would want the one thing which could kill Fae, his beast," Alden said. "They used to speak of rumors, ones that said the beast could be removed from the host. The Guild is desperate; they had to be if they came here. Something happened that set them off; we find out what that is, and we will find them."

"They'd need a host, how would they try to find one?" I wondered. It didn't work like that, but then again, they didn't know that. They didn't know dick.

"They'd try to make one," Alden countered.

"Not an easy thing. The beast doesn't separate like that," I advised. "The Heir or host is chosen by Danu, not by power."

"They don't know that. They're blind. Desperation makes them sloppy, and they know very little about the Horde. They assume if they find a powerful enough host, they will control the beast." Alden's voice was tired. These were his peers at one time, and I was sure it wasn't sitting well with him that he would have to help us find a way to defeat the people he had once considered his associates and friends.

"Who would have planned something this big?" I asked.

"Mages who exist among the Elders inside the Guild; somebody formulated a plan, and someone else helped them find the way to carry it out."

"Not enough knowledge to pull this off without

someone on the inside," I stated, chewing my lip before I released it with a frown. "They were here, inside the castle. They had to be cloaked in glamour. Wards take time to place; they would have had to have been here. Who would they go to for help?"

"Some Changelings can use glamour, as can some Paladins. Even Druids were rumored to be able to use glamour," Alden offered. "If I wanted to send a clear message to the Fae, I'd take the one thing they fear. I'd come for the beast and try to make him mine."

"The beast can't be removed; it doesn't work like that," I insisted.

"That may be, but they don't know that. I didn't know that until you told me just now. The Guild knows next to nothing about the Horde, other than that the beast rules them by brutal strength and fear. Control the beast, control the Horde. It's a mindset."

"But not a fact. Who is strong enough to guard the Guild against us?" I asked.

"Witches will guard the Guild, but the Elders will call Paladins in if they feel threatened," he shrugged and frowned. "You go to Seattle, Synthia, and you will have to shed blood to get him back."

"I'd spill enough to fill the oceans, Alden. Vast oceans and endless seas to get him back. They took him from me, and they've taken enough. I won't walk away from this. You won't ask me to, because you, more than anyone else here, knows I can't. I'm done losing those I love to a mindless, faceless, cowardly enemy. This will end here for the Guild. I will take him by force; if they fight, they will fall. It is a choice. They took my man, and I won't hesitate to do what is needed to get him back. Out of everything they could have done, they shouldn't have come here. Not today, not ever."

"You took their Witch and Guild, so they retaliated by taking your King. You started this, kid. You shook their world up, and you expected them to just walk away. It doesn't work like that and you know it. They want your attention and now they have it. You want to get someone's attention, you walk in and you cause a scene, you shake it up in a way that will leave a lasting impression. But if you want to get a point across that you're not afraid, you walk in and you take the biggest one down, point made. Ryder is the strongest of the Fae, and he's yours. The Fae weren't the target here, Synthia. You were."

"I got the message, but they fucked up. They miscalculated, and that's going to cost them," I snapped.

"You can't kill them all. Not all of them are Mages."

"I'm going in there, Alden, and I am getting him back no matter the cost. They killed children at the Spokane Guild and again today. That isn't part of the Guild's mission statement. They are not the same Guild anymore. Not with monsters helping to run it— and there is no way right now for us to separate the wheat from the chaff. They chose to become murderers when they placed a bomb inside that hall, knowing there were innocent lives that would be harmed. They could have done this cleanly, you and I both know that. They chose poorly, and for that, if they fight me, they will fall. The Guild will not take from me. Never again. I didn't start this, or choose to do this. They did this. If you can't back me or this is too hard for you, I understand. Don't think you can stop me, though.

He's the father of my children and the love of my life. I will do anything I have to in order to get him back. I'm not asking for your help because I know this will put you in a difficult position, but my loyalty is no longer to the Guild."

I took a deep breath and leveled my steadfast gaze on every person assembled in the council room. My voice rang out with my determined resolve. "I'm Synthia, Goddess of Faery and the Queen of the Horde. I will reign down blood and fire to get my King back, and if I have to do it without you, so be it. I will not fall. I will not bow. I will become the monster they accuse us of being if they wish it. You can either stand with me in solidarity, or stay the hell out of my way. The choice is yours. I expect a decision and a response from all of you within the next few hours. I suggest you think it over and consider your decision carefully."

Chapter
TWENTY~ONE

I leaned against the wall for support, my eyes closed as I ran my hands slowly along the soft silk of the wedding dress I still wore. It was in tatters, ripped and coated in the blood of the innocents who had died today, along with Faolán's. I'd taken off the heels, and now wore boots that were easier to maneuver in. My hair had been piled atop my head, giving an entirely new meaning to messy bun. It was still sticky with blood that had mixed with the glitter Madisyn had sprinkled in it for the wedding.

I hadn't even stopped to wonder if she was okay, which probably made me the worst daughter in the world. I couldn't. Focusing on the events of today would be debilitating if I allowed myself to do it, so it was best to try and focus on what was happening now. In light of everything that happened, I really wanted to sift into the Blood Kingdom and hold my babies while I cried for their father and what might be happening to him at this moment.

I hadn't come this far to lose him, and I wouldn't lose him, no matter what happened. I was going to get my guy back; I just had to figure out how. I opened my eyes to find Zahruk and Ristan watching me.

"I'm not going to start crying again," I said with enough determination that I almost believed it.

"I know," Zahruk replied casually, as if our world wasn't sitting in the balance or in someone else's hands at the moment. "You're a fighter, we all know it. I have no doubt that you can lead us and get him back. I do, however, think you should retire that gown. It's rather ruined."

"Yeah, just give me a few and I'll get right on that," I sighed as I tried to close my eyes again, only to hear the shuffling of feet as Alden and Lucian made their entrance. I patiently waited as Alden cleared his throat, buying time as he considered what to say to me. I didn't speak, just stared into the eyes of the man who had raised me. I knew he'd come, because this was the man who had raised me. No matter what happened, or how we had changed, he was my family.

I hadn't sent word to him or asked him to come. I was just grateful he did, though. He had vast knowledge and understanding of the Guild, and that was priceless. I also had a feeling that helping us was something he needed to do to absolve himself of the guilt he felt for the part he played in the Guild's plans so long ago, and possibly to try and help those that weren't truly corrupted by the Mages, just being misled.

He exhaled and shook his head as he stared into my eyes. "It's gone, isn't it, kid?" he asked as he took a place against the wall beside me. "That last little shred of humanity you have been holding onto, it was stolen from you today. They took it from you, and the only way to get it back is to get him back, isn't it?"

"I didn't pick this fight. I don't want them dead,

but if that is what it takes to bring him back, so be it. I won't lose him, Alden. I have given up enough of me to the Guild; they don't get to do this to me or anyone else. Not anymore."

"I know you didn't, kid. It isn't our Guild anymore; they're playing by new rules now. They allowed evil within the ranks and we have to come to terms with that. Me more than you, but I'm here. I'm on your side. I have always been on your side, even when it didn't seem like it. If they've woken the Original Witches, we have to assume the Mages have promised them something. There's no way that they would help the Guild without expecting something in return, not when they know it played a huge part in taking them down. My guess is they've been promised more than just their freedom, and if they are still hell-bent on taking out the humans, we can't allow that to happen."

"Do you think they brought one of the Original Witches here, to Faery?" I asked.

"Who else would be able to take Ryder away from you on your wedding day, kid? He wouldn't have been easy to grab. There was no sign of a struggle, so you tell me, who is strong enough to take the Horde King without a fight?"

"Honestly, I have no idea," I groaned.

"Someone with enough power had to be brought here for that purpose," Alden pressed.

"Why wouldn't they just kill the Elders that woke them up outright? The Original Witches are powerful enough to; they're Demi-Gods, like I was. Once they are out of stasis, why not just escape, why help them?"

"Because you have their sister, and the Elders

probably told them as much. Look, I have no idea if the Elders woke one, several or all of the members of the coven that they had access to. I fear I may have spoken hastily about their connection, and what we assumed would happen, should one awaken. Not that it matters now, anyway. At the end of the day, the Elders turned those Witches against you as well as the Fae, so they took from you and Faery to get your attention."

"I didn't take their fucking sister," I snapped. "I got slapped upside the head with that one. I sure as shit don't want their sister, and I also don't want them destroying the humans. I know they are low on the food chain lately, but that isn't right. They don't deserve to be punished for something that happened so long ago. These humans didn't even have anything to do with it, much less know anything about it."

"No, but they won't see it like that. They've been in stasis, so for them, it was yesterday," he countered. "And the Mages that are hiding within the ranks of the Guild don't care about right or wrong or the body count; they only care about winning."

"That's brilliant when you think about it, the assholes. They have an enemy, so they wake up an enemy to attack their other enemy."

"The enemy of my enemy is my friend."

"Damn, why didn't I think of that?" I whispered as I shook my head sadly.

"Back to your humanity, kid," he said after a moment of silence. "I know you have a right to attack by force, and I understand why you would want to, but not all of them deserve to die. I'm not judging you if you decide to destroy them. I'm just asking you not to become the monster they think you are to get him back. Don't let them take that sliver of humanity that's left inside of you."

"I didn't lose it, it's there. It just has to adapt to being in both worlds. I can't abandon this one now, and I won't. I won't abandon that one either. We will fix the portals, and we will rebuild what we have lost, but not until I have him back. I won't rest until he's home."

"Good; you're going to need to keep a level head if you want to get him back," he nodded as if he was satisfied with where my head was at.

Keir, Liam, Elijah, and Lasair approached solemnly. I waited with my breath stuck in my lungs as they looked at me. Lasair bowed almost imperceptibly, and inclined his head towards me.

"We're in, Synthia. You are the key to this world, and without you, it will die faster than it already is. So, we're in. I will send Liam and the Crimson Guard, and Keir will send his son, Adam, who will bring the Light Knights, as well as the Shadow Warriors. We found out this morning about a mess in the Light Kingdom that Princess Shea left behind. Evidently, she left her stewardship of the Light Kingdom a few weeks ago without warning or word. Adam had agreed to take over stewardship of the Light Kingdom after the wedding; however, the events of today have made alterations to our original plan for now." Lasair swallowed; his solemn eyes didn't condemn me, or judge.

"I guess Adam better get busy finding the real Light Heir then," I mused. My eyes slowly found Adam where he stood, ramrod straight at my words.

"But that's a subject for another day. Right now, we have a bigger problem."

"Synthia," Zahruk interrupted. "There are a few leaders of the Horde outside the gates, waiting; they have demanded to speak to the..." He looked at Ristan in askance as the Demon grinned back at him, anticipating my reaction to what Zahruk was going to say next. "...pretender to the throne."

"Then let's not keep them," I said as I glamoured on black leather pants, and a black corset that had daggers of every length inserted into clever sheaths that were reinforced along the boning of the corset. I also glamoured on a slender sword at each hip. The boots were the finishing touch, black to match my outfit, and comfortable enough to move in. Several times a week, Ryder and I had been sneaking away and practicing for this type of situation. Not that he ever dreamed that he would be taken, but he wanted to ensure that if, for any reason, I had to personally fight to get the respect of the Horde, I would be prepared. As for the blood that had been spattered in my hair and on my face, I didn't bother to glamour it clean. I wanted these assholes to see it and hopefully understand that I wasn't someone that they should underestimate.

"I'm ready," I confirmed, and palmed my daggers as Zahruk and Ristan took their positions at my flank, just as they would have done for Ryder. The others fell in behind the captain of the Elite Guard and the Demon, and walked purposefully with us as we made our way through the castle. We walked because I needed the time to prepare mentally, and they knew it. It was also an important show of force and solidarity. The staff stopped and turned, watching as we made our way to the main gates. The four groups of warriors fell into step as we passed them in the hall. Elijah even signaled for the misfits to join us. Together, we walked towards the uncertainty of what awaited us.

There was no way of knowing if this was merely a challenge of my leadership, or if they'd try to overthrow us. It was the Horde—the deadliest, vilest creatures known to this world, as well as Tèrra. They were unpredictable at best and understood two things: power and death. Ryder had been dealing with small uprisings before this shit had happened, and now I had to figure out how to prove to them that I was worthy of sitting on his throne in his absence. I had to prove that I was powerful enough to keep them in check— and strong enough to punish them if they stepped out of line.

"Show no fear," Zahruk whispered.

"Don't let them talk over you, Flower. Don't break eye contact first, no matter what they do. Head up, shoulders back, and show those fangs you've been hiding."

"I plan to."

Chapter
TWENTY-TWO

Outside, the noise from the crowd was deafening. The stench of death lingered with a faint tinge of sulfur and blood as the crowd waiting outside the gates made rude noises. They paid no attention to the shrouded bodies that waited in the courtyard for their kin to take them home for burial, or away for burning if they weren't claimed. The rough group that waited for us and called themselves the leaders of the Horde had very little loyalty among them, not unless you belonged to the caste of the Horde that ruled.

"Who does this bitch think she is?" One of the taller 'leaders' snickered as we approached.

"Your queen," a creature that looked like a Goblin with red eyes snorted. Blood dribbled from the red cap on his head, identifying him As a Dunter or a Powrie. Great; they were blood thirsty and fast little assholes. The only difference between the two types of Red Caps was the amount of kills they had under their bloody caps.

"My queen," the first heckler chortled. "I'd bend her over and show her what queens are good for. She'd know her place and not be leaving us waiting at her gates, pretending her pussy makes her our new King."

I listened to them as I approached, stopping just short of where they stood. I waited in silence, allowing them to continue to talk shit. I didn't look away, didn't back down. I squared my shoulders and waited patiently. They stopped, and as they turned, the eyes of one of the males who'd been talking shit about me widened as he took in the sight of me.

"She doesn't look like much," the male said as his iridescent eyes slid over my body, stopping to watch my breasts rise and fall with each breath I took. Those eyes raised and he snorted. "Not even enough meat on her to keep a man warm at night." I tried to figure out what kind of creature he was and came up blank. He was extremely tall and emaciated, with long, black, lank hair that descended well past his shoulders. His iridescent eyes had shadows around them that gave the appearance of being sunken in. His lips were slightly blue and his skin was so pale that it was almost corpse-like.

The crowd behind him jeered, shouting their agreement as they chimed in with insults of their own. I grinned at his lewd remarks and waited for the noise of the crowd to die down. Once it was at a tolerable level, I spoke.

"Your King needs your help," I called out to the crowd, and watched as the asshole laughed openly.

"He isn't here, sweetheart," he snorted. "I say we take his woman and his Kingdom. I didn't much care for the prick anyway."

"Which caste do you lead?" I asked, and he grinned as if he found my question funny.

"The Sluagh has no leader," he laughed, and again, his posse snorted and chuckled. "But I guess if we had to pick one, it would be me." The creatures behind him nodded.

"Good to know," I snapped as I lunged before he could react. I wrapped my legs around his waist and held on as he tried to dislodge me. Zahruk and Ristan also lunged into fighting positions, getting close until I screamed for them to remain where they were. My hands twisted the neck of the ghoul-like creature and I bit into his carotid, tearing the flesh from his neck as I let my legs drop to the ground and spit it out. "Now pick another leader," I shouted to the onlookers.

No one moved, no one responded. They gasped, as if they couldn't comprehend what had just happened. The asshole dropped to his knees as his arterial vein sprayed blood. Blood dripped from my chin as I brought my hand up and wiped it away with the back of my hand, as the crowd stared at me.

"I suggest you choose wisely," I offered as I turned and walked back to Ristan, who had a stupid grin on his face. I was going to ruin it all by throwing up the vile taste of coppery blood that lingered in my mouth.

"Damn, Flower, savage as fuck," he laughed quietly as his grin widened.

"It's the only thing they understand," I growled.

"You have their attention, now keep it," he encouraged. "Your next challenger will be faster and or stronger than he was. That little maneuver of yours will take a while to heal, but I don't think he is going to be back in the fight anytime soon."

"Good to know," I mused as I turned and stared

down the crowd who watched me for any sign of weakness. "How long do you think it will be for them to regroup and choose a warrior?"

"It won't take them long, and they are probably going to send a few warriors. Lathe was one of their best, and you just tore his neck out with your teeth, which honestly, I couldn't be any prouder if you ripped his heart out and shared it with me. However, they will be ready for that move next time."

"Swords it is." I nodded. "Too bad, I was *so* looking forward to gagging on a bit more blood."

"You two are fucking twisted," Zahruk grumbled beside us.

"Jealous because you haven't ripped anyone apart lately?" I mocked with a grin on my lips.

"Who says I haven't?" Zahruk drawled, turning to grin as I frowned.

"Why do you guys get all the action and I have to stay home?" I pouted as I wondered why Ryder hadn't shared any of that with me.

"Because you will be Queen of the Horde," Zahruk said without any attitude in his tone. "We can't lose both of you, so one must remain in the residence at all times."

"Here they come." Ristan moved in closer to my side. "Chin up, Buttercup, you got this," he muttered as he took my slender, elegant swords and handed me his dual bladed ones. "You can count on rounds two and three being to the death; you'll need iron."

Ristan was one of the few Fae creatures I knew

of who could use or wield iron blades easily. He'd moved so quickly that I wasn't sure anyone else had noted the switch. I moved closer, as several males stepped forward. The ringing sound of steel being drawn brought my hands to the blades at my sides, and I smiled as the biggest one moved in. He had to have been over nine feet tall, with short gray hair all over his body, and his face looked a little like an ape, but I knew from experience that everything they said about the bigger the guy, the harder they fall was true.

I drew my blades the moment the grey man lunged, dropped to my knees and sliced his legs at the knees. His screams tore through the air, and I rolled with the blades as I came back up, swinging in a wide arc, which sent his head sailing into the crowd that watched us.

A gang of Powries came at me all at the same time, forming a circle around me. I grinned and swung, swords cutting through flesh like butter because Ristan's blades were always sharpened correctly and ready to go. Grunts and cries sounded as I spun, not bothering to stop. I sliced, stabbed, and massacred the evil little bastards, until I was standing before the Horde, bathed in the blood of their so-called leaders, victorious.

"Choose again. This time, I suggest you take a few minutes to think about it first," I demanded as I turned and moved back to my allies, glancing at them as they gave me a wide berth. Not even Ristan spoke as blood ran in rivulets from my flesh to the ground, pooling at my feet.

No one came forward; the Horde stared at me, soaked in their leaders' blood. They bickered and pushed each other towards me, but none came forward.

I waited, giving them the chance to choose or follow me. After a few moments passed, I tried again.

"Your King needs your aid, you can give it or you can be hunted down and slaughtered like the faithless dogs you are behaving like. You will follow me into battle, or I will let loose the hounds with your scent." I could sense Zahruk, Dristan and Aodhan moving closer to me, giving credence to my threat. "They will hunt you down; not even hell can save you once the hounds have your scent. I demand an answer within the next ten minutes or we begin hunting. Do you understand me?" I shouted. When no one answered, I growled and let loose an immense amount of power that surprised even me. My hands lifted to the sky and then slammed down.

The entire Horde that had gathered at the main gates was on their knees, bowing in the dirt. I slowly pushed my hands further down and imagined smashing their smug faces into the earth. I heard gasps of pain and surprised cries as joints cracked, and I could hear the ground buckling from the pressure I was exerting on these creatures.

"Yes!" one of the males shouted. "I yield. I'll bow to you, my Queen."

I smiled, allowing him to rise. One by one they begged for mercy and rose, spattered with the dirt and mud of this world. I exhaled and closed my eyes as the crowd continued to pledge themselves to me. I'd done it; I'd brought the Horde to their knees. I'd had to use my power, but hey, it was a win, and we needed one right now.

"Ready your strongest warriors and prepare them for battle," I shouted victoriously. I turned and looked at Zahruk, who wore his usual dour expression, as if this was exactly what he expected to happen. Then I glanced at Ristan, who nodded with something akin to pride in his eyes.

"You were born for this, Synthia," he murmured softly. "I don't think the Horde has ever begged mercy before."

"The Horde has never met me. At least, not in this capacity. They'll know who is to wed their King when I finish here. That much I promise you. Besides, I've faced worse odds before when I was a Witch."

"Yes, but you're not a Witch, Goddess. You are ours now. They will follow you anywhere you or Ryder asks them to go," Zahruk said. "The Horde will once again, follow their King into battle—willingly."

"Zahruk, hate to break the speech, but until I get Ryder back, let's not worry about worlds. I want my fucking Fairy back, and I want him now."

"Tomorrow we ride, Flower. The United Castes of Faery," Ristan grinned. "This should be interesting; someone better make some fucking popcorn to bring along."

"Demon, that sounds like a wrestling league and not at all official-like," I warned as I stared him down, and then blanched from the coppery scent of my new perfume. "Get this shit off me, my magic is tapped."

"I kinda like you in red, Flower. It's kind of a rose hue, and suits you very well."

"Demon…" I growled.

"Fine." He grinned as he waved his hand and I

was finally cleansed of the sins of the day. I'd just killed seven Fae; seven less who could help us. Seven who had families somewhere, maybe even children? It was a win, though, and right now, we needed it.

"Take me back to my chambers," I whispered as I trembled with the need to be close to Ryder. "I need to rest before we head out to pick a fight with the Guild."

Chapter
TWENTY-THREE

The bed smelled of him; the room and the rooms that adjoined our bedroom all smelled of him. Everything in this place held memories of him. I wanted to drink it in, like the first time I'd seen him. Those eyes had held me prisoner more than he ever had. If I closed my eyes, I could still recall the first time he touched me, the electrical shock that shot through me at his touch. He'd sent a ripple through my tightly controlled world. He'd made me feel things I hadn't wanted to, and at the time, I had hated him and everything about him.

I let my hand slide to my midsection; my fingers splayed across it, and I swallowed guilt. A deep part of me had known what would happen with having such an over-the-top wedding. The Demon tried to warn me about what was surely to come, and he didn't even need to have a vision to call that one for me. We knew what would happen once the announcements were made. The announcements that we had wanted to reach Faolán's ears had done their job.

Pain was a fickle bitch, settling deep into my bones as the reality of what had happened sank in. I'd killed; I'd ripped a man's throat out with my teeth. It wasn't the act of killing that bothered me; it was the emotions that came with it. I'd felt sick the moment the showdown had ended, the nauseating scent of copper still lingering upon my skin. The sour taste of bile clung to the back of my throat and no amount of water or wine could wash it away.

I let what I had done sink in, and thought about what I might have to do to get Ryder back. I'd do anything—anything and everything it took to get my beast back. I knew how the Guild worked; they would cut him to pieces if they thought it would give them any answers about the Horde. I'd seen the dissected remains of the Fae they'd captured before, as well as the Guild's failed science projects as they'd tried to create monsters that could stand against the Fae.

Ryder couldn't be killed, but he could be tortured, much like his brother was, if not worse. He could be in pain right now, and there was nothing I could do. The helpless feeling was making my senses go haywire, and my heart was hurting.

I rolled over on the bed, hating the sick feeling that rushed from my belly, which resulted in me with my face over the toilet, spewing what little I'd managed to eat and drink after ripping the throat out of the Horde's self-appointed spokesperson.

I wiped my mouth with the back of my hand and glamoured my body clean; the taste of fresh mint filled my mouth. I moved back into the bedroom, my mind in total chaos as I considered the Guild's next move.

I was halfway to the bed when my stomach fluttered and turned over, and I rushed back to the bathroom. I emptied my stomach again and gave in to the urge to bathe. I'd been living as Fae, but sometimes I craved the comforts of things like a bath, or just to do things without the magic I was growing accustomed to.

I filled the bath with lavender bath beads and crawled in, inhaling the comforting scent that agreed with my stomach. I ran my hands over my legs, stomach, and breasts as a sob exploded from my throat. I closed my eyes, slid beneath the water, and let out a scream that I'd been holding since I'd discovered he was gone. Tears burned behind my closed eyes, but the scream felt soothing to me, even if no one heard it.

I sat up in the bath and wrapped my arms around my naked legs. Hours had passed since Ryder had been taken, and there was no sign of anything being off in the human world. I'd sent scouts to watch the Guilds, all of them. So far, it was business as usual at the Guilds and not a hint of what was happening to Ryder. If they held him there, they were doing a good job of hiding it.

I took comfort in knowing that there wasn't any weapon that could kill him, other than the one Madisyn had thought would do the job. That tiny toothpick of a knife wouldn't have killed him. We hadn't known that at the time, but what if the Mages had found a way to do it that we didn't know about?

Anything was possible, and that was what terrified me. The Guild had resources that they kept hidden, they had allies hidden in the shadows and, if I was right, they had awoken some pretty bad-assed Witches that were hell bent on destroying their world.

A knock sounded from the door and my eyes moved in that direction, but I didn't answer it. I knew who it was. Zahruk was a constant at my side since Ryder had been taken, willing to do whatever it took to keep me safe. I glanced at him as he came closer and stopped at the bathroom door, only to move just inside the room and pause as his eyes took in the sight of my naked body.

"I've summoned those who you asked me to," he announced, unaffected by the sight of my nakedness. "You should dry off so we can meet with the others in the war room."

I stood up, watching as his eyes slid down my body without a single ounce of heat. Zahruk would fall on his own sword before he touched anything that belonged to Ryder, including me. I accepted the towel he held out as he wrapped it around me.

"I've sent the handmaidens away; however, I am capable of helping you get ready," he offered quietly.

"I do know how to manage without them," I replied as I moved into the bedroom.

"You need to feed," he said offhandedly; his body language seemed awkward as he scratched the back of his neck. "I'm not Ryder, but I know he'd kill anyone else who tried to feed you."

"I don't feed from sex," I smiled weakly at the impassive look on his face.

"I know, but Ryder mentioned that sometimes you grow weak when the world is in pain and with the fractures…he said you take comfort in it. That you can think clearer after it," he said.

"Do you want to fuck?" I asked pointedly.

"No, not particularly, and not with you, no offense," he exhaled deeply. He raised his hands and shook his head a little. "But we need you at your best for this, and I just found you pretending to be a human in a bath. So, if my dick is the key to your brain remembering what is at stake, then yeah, I'll fuck you."

"My brain is fine," I replied sharply. "I took a bath because I kept throwing up pieces of the creature that I tore the throat out of just a little bit ago. So, no—thank you, but no, I don't need your dick to feel smarter. I'm pretty sure it would make me feel anything but smart."

"Was that a compliment?" he smirked.

"Not really, but I guess your dick could make women act foolishly. I've witnessed it enough times," I answered with a smirk. "The only dick I want is attached to your brother, so if you're offering to get me laid, get him back here."

"Thank Gods," he laughed nervously.

"You were seriously offering to have sex with me?" I laughed weakly and shook my head. "Look at you, Z, offering to give it up to be helpful and shit."

"I'm willing to do whatever it takes to get him back. You've known him for a minute compared to us, and he's our King. Before that, he's my brother. He's saved us from shit countless times. So yes, if it took me offering myself as a sacrifice, I'd lay down my life for his."

"Well, let's hope it doesn't come to that, because being stabbed by you once was enough for this girl." I glamoured my version of the Elite Guard armor on and smirked at him. "I'll feed you, though," I offered, and before he could say no, I reached out and touched the side of his face. Power erupted into his system and

I watched his eyes grow wide, then hooded as I fed him with a small taste of my power. He was watching over me, and I had no intention of waiting for him to fuck someone so that he could feel like he was fully capable of being my right arm, aid, and guard all rolled into one. We had too much to do and not enough time for him to indulge in a proper feeding.

"Gods," he moaned as he tried moving, only to fall to his knees as I watched him with a knowing smile. Ryder could reach climax this way, but I had no intention of making this sexual. I did, however, plan on giving him enough power to get him through the next few days. "Stop it, Witch," he grumbled. I pulled back, and swallowed more bile as I started to feel lightheaded. "Are you okay?" He struggled to his feet as the question left his lips. I blinked past some stars that seemed to be obscuring my vision.

"Fine, I'm fine," I murmured as I forced my body to relax, and the spinning in my head stopped. "I think that guy might have eaten something poisonous."

"It's possible," he mumbled as he moved me towards the door. "We should find Eliran."

"No, they're waiting for us in the war room; we go now," I ordered, not waiting to see if he followed as I inhaled deeply of Ryder's scent that lingered in the room before leaving it. "Better not tell him you saw me naked," I smirked.

"It's a body. I've seen thousands of them. I'm Fae. Honestly, I think that human modesty is absurd and oftentimes false," he explained. "Ryder knows my feelings about it; he may have adopted your silly human logic, but I have no place for it."

"Silly human logic?" I repeated thoughtfully,

turning to look at him over my shoulder before I snorted.

We entered the room and I paused, noting that Ristan seemed agitated, while the others seemed anxious. My eyes slid over to Alden, who was poring over papers with Lucian, while Adrian and Vlad whispered about something in the corner.

"Gentlemen," I said as I took my seat and looked around at the faces. "I know most of you have yet to leave or sleep, but there are a few things we need to discuss."

"Such as?" Alden asked as he shuffled the papers aside and gave me his attention.

"The Seattle Guild would anticipate that it would be the first place we would go to look for Ryder. Before we take an army there, we need to be sure they are actually holding him at that Guild. We also have no idea what the Seattle Guild has up their sleeve. They normally do not walk in and take someone, not on this scale. We know they had help, but we don't know for sure who it was. These are things we can't leave to chance. I know the National Guild used to do experiments with the Fae that went far beyond what was done at the local Guilds. Where was it done?" I asked Alden directly.

"There is a lab, deep in the mountains of Alaska. Once they are sure the Fae are harmless, they move them to other locations to be studied in a controlled environment. I don't think they would take him there, not when the Seattle Guild has a similar lab deep beneath their building. The lab was carved out of a large iron pyrite deposit under the Guild, and they added large quantities of powdered iron to the cement mix that they poured into slabs for the walls, so that if someone of the Fae persuasion tried to get in, they wouldn't sense it until they'd become too weak from the iron to fight back."

"That's going to be a problem." Ristan whistled.

"Not for you," I said, turning to look at him. "I'm going to need Sinjinn on this, so I need you to take Olivia and go to the Blood Kingdom and watch over my babies. I also want you to take the children we brought out of the Spokane Guild with you too. In fact, Demon, take any of the young who need shelter. We cannot take chances with the young, not when there are so few of them left."

"I'm needed here with you," he snapped, his eyes narrowing on me as I faced him.

"You are needed to protect my children so that I can focus. You're worried about Olivia, and that worries me. She refused to stay where you took her and came right back here. I need to know they are safe, all of them. You would give your life to save them, and we all know it. I want Liam and Sinjinn with me for this, so that leaves you to protect my babies."

"Flower," he started to protest, and I shook my head. "Fine, but if you get in trouble, you call for me."

"Deal," I acknowledged.

"Now, I need a five-man team to do some recon, and they will need to be able to get in and out without worrying about metal allergies, so to say."

"I can go," Alden said softly, and I shook my head.

"No, you cannot," I argued. "You are needed to

run comms; Zahruk has a bunch of shit that will help us, and so he will be coming with to show us how to use them. I'm thinking of Elijah and his buddies for recon. I want everyone wired with communications, video, and armed to the teeth, but not to the point that they draw unwanted attention. I'll also need someone to help me lure an Enforcer away from the Guild so we can interrogate him and see what he knows. Enforcers are made aware of every threat that could factor in with a target or an asset the Guild has. We catch one and make him tell us what he knows."

"Just like old times," Adam said with a smirk.

"We will need a building to interrogate him in. I know it would be easier to bring him back here, but we will also need to have eyes on the Guild. We need to be aware of every move they make, and being close will accomplish both goals. The building will need to be soundproof, and have power to support comms and video. Adrian, you can find me one, right?"

"I can, easily. There's a huge spike in repossessed buildings in the Fisher's Market area, and it is close enough to the Guild that we can watch it while we handle business."

"Then let's go hunting, gentlemen," I said softly as I stood and watched the men get up to leave. I waited for the room to clear as Ristan remained behind. Once the others had left, he turned angry, swirling eyes on me.

"You know you need me with you," he snapped. "Olivia's fine with the babies, but me, I'm needed with you. Don't ask me to be idle in this. He's my brother."

"I know, but the others didn't need to know that. I want you to watch our backs and I want you to do it from a safe distance until I say otherwise. I do need Sinjinn and Liam with us for this. I want you to give Olivia a reason to stay put and out of harm's way." His angry stance relaxed and his face softened at my words.

"You're pale," he said offhandedly.

"I gave Zahruk some power and I didn't sleep," I murmured.

"Something else is wrong," he probed.

"No, it's not. Let's just say I had a bad Sluagh for dinner. C'mon, let's do this," I said, cutting him off.

Chapter
TWENTY-FOUR

The chosen building was empty except for the belongings of a homeless man, who Zahruk had ousted by paying him generously with enough money to purchase a new home. It overlooked Pike's Place Market, and had a bird's eye view of the Guild. Comms had been set up and everyone had body armor, comms, and a camera, including Zahruk, who refused to let me out of his sight.

Pike's Place Market was a huge farmers market. It was one of the many attractions that brought tourists into Seattle. It was the epicenter of fresh produce, specialty foods, and other ingredients that were unlike any other in the state of Washington, or several others for that matter.

Huge fishing boats came and went from the pier, unloading fresh catches from the Pacific Ocean at all hours of the day and night. The fishmongers throwing fish at the market were always a huge hit with the tourists. Shops lined the pier, from butcher shops to produce stands that sold pretty much anything you could ever want. There were over two hundred unique shops that filled up the rest of the nine acres that comprised the market and drew large crowds, which made it full of bustling people until late into the night.

The noise level itself reminded me of the carnival that Adam, me, and Larissa had once snuck off to when Adrian had been in bed, laid up from an injury. There was the nauseating smell of too many foods being cooked at once as the noise of people droned endlessly on.

I'd once loved this place, and the old Historic area was something to see. It was almost as if you'd stepped back into another time and era. The economy had taken a hit here, and with most of the businesses being in the family and small business categories, it was sad to see.

I diverted my attention to Zahruk as he began talking. "So, the feed from the cameras will fill these screens. Each of your body cams has a pulse reader so we can monitor your vitals from here. If you get in trouble, we will know it and can intervene. We can hear everything being said via the comms. There are five Enforcers on the Pier; one is currently following a Pixie who seems rather harmless, other than her weird obsession with the fish throwing."

I nodded to Zahruk and grinned. "That fish throwing is pretty badass," I commented.

"Game plan?" he questioned, deliberately ignoring my comment.

I felt like shit. My body was working against me, and I refused to listen to it as I nodded in reply. The briny smell of the ocean mixed with the smells of the market had my senses in an uproar.

"Adam and I can lure one of the Enforcers away from his team. I can make myself look human enough to make it appear as if he's feeding from me—that will catch enough attention to make them break protocol. We only want one, so if more follow us, handle them," I said to Adrian and Vlad, who nodded. "By handle, I mean don't kill them."

"Didn't plan on it, sugar," Adrian said softly as he curiously watched me.

"Problem?" I asked, and he shook his head.

"You plan on telling the others?" he enquired carefully, and I blinked at him.

"Telling the others what?"

"Nothing," he said, turning and leaving me standing there, confused.

I watched him as he walked to Vlad and nodded, and those silver eyes of Vlad's moved to mine. Something like worry showed in them before he masked it and left with Adrian to get into position.

I turned to Adam, nodded, and quickly tested my comms and equipment as we made our way to our positions. Within minutes, we were outside and moving down the pier to the place where we had tracked down one of the Enforcers, who seemed younger than the others he was with.

"Just like old times, huh?" Adam said softly as he turned and smiled at me.

"New bodies, better equipment, it's just not quite the same," I mumbled. I wasn't feeling it. There was no rush from the missions we'd gone out on as Enforcers. There was too much riding on this. "There he is," I said as we rounded a corner and found the

Enforcer staring openly at the Pixie. He wasn't even hiding what he was. Weapons reflected the afternoon sunlight, occasionally glinting when he would move as he watched her with his hand on his blades.

"So, how are we going to do this?" Adam asked.

"I'm going to scream, and then you're going to pull me back into that alley," I pointed at one a few feet from us. "You'll go all glowy with the Fae brands, and I'll play hard to get and then seem to fall under your spell."

"Ready?" His smile was mischievous as his hands touched my naked arm.

I wore a sundress; my attire had been planned to look innocent with a touch of sex appeal. I was wearing small heels, and enough knives to take down a small army underneath my skirt. I exhaled past the nausea and nodded.

I walked around Adam to make it easier for him to push me towards the alley. Once there, I let out an ear-piercing shriek that cut through the chatter on the pier, and even made Adam wince. His hands grabbed my waist and he pushed my body towards the alley. I kept up my screams for help as his brands began to glow.

"Damn, been a long time since I've heard you scream like a girl," he laughed, fighting me earnestly to make it appear real enough to get the Enforcer to leave his post.

"It's been a long time since I've had to play victim," I breathed, and then took in another lungful of air before I started yelling over his shoulder. The Enforcer watched, but he wasn't budging. "Try tearing my dress off," I demanded under my breath, and watched Adam's eyes grow as round as saucers. "Do it; he's torn, but he doesn't want to leave his post," I hissed and then winced as Adam did as I instructed, his fingers accidently biting into my skin as he yanked and tore the bodice of the dress I was wearing.

The Enforcer was moving towards us with a look that bothered me. I pretended to succumb to Adam as he pretended to kiss me into silence. The heat of his mouth was nothing new; we'd done this before too. We were masters at pretending to be a couple. I jumped up and wrapped my legs around him as my arms did the same to his neck. I ran my fingers through his hair, and the moment my back touched the wall of the alley, pain shot through my belly.

I winced; tears burned my eyes, but I pushed the pain away and continued to pretend I had been turned FIZ. I made incoherent noises that sounded more like a chicken dying as the pain gnawed through me. I watched the Enforcer round the corner, draw his blade, and rush towards Adam's unprotected back.

A moment before he would have sunk the iron-tipped blade into Adam's back, I moved around Adam, brought my hand up, caught the Enforcer's arm, and flipped him over, his head giving the cement a forceful thump during his downward descent. The moment I did, I looked up as the other Enforcers rushed around the corner.

Vlad, Adrian, and Lucian appeared, grabbing each from behind with an arm locked around their throats. One after another, they went limp in their respective chokeholds. I exhaled and stood up, then glamoured my formfitting armor back on as I watched Adam heft the one we'd captured over his shoulder and looked at the others.

"Hate to point this out, but once they wake up, they'll alert the Guild to our presence by sounding an alarm," he said grimly.

"Bring them, they can be our guests until Ryder is back with us," I ordered begrudgingly. We moved down the alley in silence, no one chancing our luck by talking. Once inside our command outpost, I moved to the larger room, where the rest of our Fae comrades waited, and watched as our little raiding party brought in and bound each Enforcer to the chairs that Zahruk had glamoured. What his imagination could come up with was almost frightening when he was in inquisitor mode.

They resembled something you'd see in a dentist office. The arms had manacles to hold them in place. One chair had been placed strategically so that the others had full view of it. I paced the room, waiting for the men to move the Enforcers into their positions.

As the Enforcers began to wake, I pulled out a knife and ran my fingertip over the sharp edge. I felt their eyes on me, which was why I let the blood run down my finger before I whispered a spell that made the blood rise into the air. As it rose, it stretched and molded itself until it took the shape of a butterfly that fluttered around me for a moment before circling back and landing on my shoulder. I whispered to it and watched as it once again took flight. It landed on the Enforcer who appeared to be the oldest and was strapped to the chair that the others would have an unobstructed view of.

"What is your name?" I inquired, watching him carefully as the others moved closer to me.

"Go to hell," he snapped, fierce green eyes

glowering at me.

"Oh, sugar, I've been to hell, and that shithole couldn't contain me." I watched him from beneath my lashes and repeated my question. "What is your name?"

"Satan's whore," he growled as he struggled against the restraints and moved his shoulder to dislodge the butterfly.

"Mmm, I don't think that's your name, try again." I slowly moved my eyes to the butterfly. "Do you think keeping secrets will protect you?" I watched his eyes narrow as he tried to figure out how I was going to get those secrets. "It won't take me long to find out. Your walls are weak. Your will, however, is strong. You think you're doing what is right, even though you suspect the Guild is tainted."

"Get out of my head, bitch," he demanded, and I swallowed as Zahruk moved faster than any human eye could detect. His dagger sank into the soft leather of the chair as it sliced through the Enforcer's ear.

"Watch your tongue, boy, or I will remove it from your vile mouth," Zahruk cautioned. "I won't warn you again. There are others here she can question; she doesn't need you."

I looked over his head to where the other Enforcers watched in silence. I didn't have time for this shit. I whispered the spell that encouraged the bug to thin out and slip into his ear canal. His screaming ripped through the room, echoing and bouncing off the soundproof walls as it crawled inside his head and the first thought that was right on the surface of his mind that came to me was his name. Andrew.

"Oh God, it's in him," one of the other Enforcers cried in horror.

"Not an it," I murmured, smiling as the room began to fade for me as I became one with the butterfly inside of Andrew's head.

Andrew's childhood was nothing new. Loving parents, but somewhere along the way, something went wrong. He was shipped to the Guild when his father killed his mother. He had trained hard, done his best to impress the Elders, who hadn't even noticed him. That was probably why he had been assigned to the pier. I pushed away from personal memories and dug into the pieces that I wanted, discovering that the surface memories I had passed through were a lie. A very powerful spell, which allowed Andrew to disguise what he really was.

I pushed his thoughts away, using butterfly precision so as to not damage any of his memories. It took time and effort; my power was strong, but to use the magic precisely took a toll. Sweat beaded on my breasts and the back of my neck as I continued to dig until I found his recent assignment.

I became Andrew, watching as the decrepit Elder spoke. The Guild stank of sage, myrrh and other pungent ointments. Runes glowed around the walls from ancient magic. This place was sanctified in spells. I turned his head, taking in the details of his memory.

"I want to see him." Andrew's voice almost shook with barely contained excitement.

"It is not a him, but an it, and if you must address the creature. You played a huge part in helping us obtain the Druid that made all of this possible, so you

deserve to have a peek." The Elder was known to me; he was one that had frequented both the Seattle and Spokane Guilds. He lifted his robe and reached for his cane as he stood and indicated that Andrew should follow him.

"Have we discovered how to kill it?" he asked, staring at the Elder's silver robes, which marked him one of the highest ranking in the Guild.

"Not yet, but soon enough." The Elder coughed and they began to make their way down a hallway that ended at a staircase. "The Witches are sure that every Caste of Fae has a weakness; his weakness is most likely in his blood. They have been drawing it and coating their runes with it to discover what can kill the formidable King of the Horde. They are ancient, and have more power than all of the Guilds combined. If anyone can destroy this monster, it is them."

Once at the staircase, he paused and chanted while his fingers fluttered in a complex pattern to remove a binding ward that must have acted as a sentry, a barrier, or both. Runes on the wall came alive, pulsing as his gnarled fingers worked the ward. My eyes followed his fingers and then moved to the walls, noting the runes that had been set into them. The pungent aroma of myrrh mixed with sage and other herbs was nauseatingly strong as we moved down the stairs once the wards had been removed.

We passed rooms with doors that had been similarly marked with runes, while others had bars in addition to the runes. We passed several larger rooms that held Fae inside of them, ones that had been experimented on and didn't make a sound as we walked by them.

The large cell at the end of the hallway made my heart thud loudly, but once inside, my hope went flat. It was another room, another staircase, and more wards. We passed several more hallways until we reached a room that was like a lead box, and iron surrounded that lead on all but one side, which had a door that had iron inlaid into it. The iron must have been fired, melted down, and poured into the runes that had been etched into the wood.

Cackling sounded as that door was opened and we stepped through. Inside the room, Ryder was immobile. God bolts had been driven into his arms and legs, and other rods had been impaled into his flesh as well.

There were two Witches leaning over him. They both wore ancient robes, and their hair was long and the color of a raven's wing: black with a tint of blue mixed in. Blue-green eyes glowed as power filled the room. They moved around him, chanting as they watched him struggle painfully against the bolts. They looked young, in their early twenties, their smooth porcelain flesh exposed as they pulled their skirts up and danced around him. He was naked, exposed, and unimpressed by them. His powerful, sleek muscles were covered in perspiration from his efforts to get free.

I wanted to scream. I wanted to rail and reach out and touch him. I wanted to tell him to hold on, that I was coming, but I couldn't. Here, I was Andrew.

I watched as golden eyes opened and locked with mine. The harshness in his eyes softened briefly, as if he felt me there in the room with him. It was impossible; this was a memory. It wasn't even my memory. I watched as he struggled against the bolts, an impossible feat. I'd felt the power of them before. Cold, ice cold as they nulled your strength and dulled your senses.

"It's awake," Andrew stated, and the Witch closest to Ryder smiled. "Can I?" he asked as she produced a blade.

"You think you can kill the Horde King? If he escaped, he'll surely want your blood," she whispered throatily, as if the thought excited her.

"I want to," Andrew breathed fervently as he accepted the blade. There was so much darkness in his heart that I choked on it. He moved closer, then jumped back in fear as Ryder growled. Those eyes, though, once again locked with mine. He knew. *He knew I was here, that I was searching for him. The look in his eyes said it all, and it took a lot of strength to remain in this memory.*

The blade Andrew held ripped through skin as he stabbed it into Ryder's chest over and over again. I stumbled back from the memory, pulling myself out of it.

My surroundings snapped into focus for me once more, and I watched the morbid smile that played across Andrew's lips as he relived his actions with relish. I moved closer to him and called back the butterfly, and enjoyed the cry that tore through his lips as he screamed in pain.

Once he was fully back in the present, I glamoured one of my long blades that Zahruk had made me and stabbed Andrew in the chest. His shocked scream gave me comfort. The warlike, bloodthirsty Goddess in me purred for more.

"I should stab you for every time you stabbed him," I whispered as I fought against nausea at what the Guild and those Witches were doing to Ryder. "I should tear you limb from fucking limb as you beg me to stop." I smiled against his ear. "Worse, I should leave you alive for when I retrieve him, and let him skin the flesh from your bones to bandage his wounds. Alas, I'm a selfish bitch. You took pleasure in giving him pain, and so I shall take pleasure in taking your life."

"Synthia?" Alden cautioned as he placed a hand on my shoulder.

"Don't; he can't be saved. None of them can," I spat as I turned to face my mentor. "They're a poison that bleeds into the Guild. Andrew is a Mage, not an Enforcer. His childhood was rough, but the Elders only looked at his surface memories when they brought him into the Guild to be trained. They were a lie. His mother and father were Mages. His mother visited him once a week and she has been feeding Andrew his orders. He was Enforcer in name only; he was born and will always be a Mage in his heart. So no, he can't be saved."

"He was planted?" Alden asked. At my nod, he shook his head. "How many have they planted inside our Guilds that we are unaware of? We trained them to kill the Fae."

"You did." I wasn't going to sugarcoat this and assuage his guilt. "Then you let them loose on the Fae with hidden agendas. It matters little now, and Ryder is inside that Guild. He's being held with God bolts, and some other type of bolt. I've never seen anything like it before. There are other Fae in there being experimented on, as well. The hallways are littered with runes embedded in the walls. The wards are somehow connected to them. My guess is, one mess-up and the entire building locks down."

"So, what do you plan on doing?" he enquired.

"Andrew here had some great memories of where to find a Druid or two. I'm going to need one," I answered.

"For?" Alden asked, which he hated doing. It wasn't easy being on the other end of a mission.

"To wake a Witch, of course. That's how the Guild woke the rest of 'em," I quipped as I caught the glimmer of a shape forming into a woman out of the corner of my eye. The gasping death rattle of the Enforcer didn't bother me; the Goddess who materialized with her eyes locked on him did.

What the fuck was Destiny doing here?

"I'll be right back; dispose of the corpse," I directed.

Chapter
TWENTY~FIVE

"Why are you here?" I demanded once I'd closed the door to the main room behind me and entered the staircase. I didn't ask her to follow me, I knew without asking that she would. I moved down to the next floor and made my way to one of the couches, ignoring the racing of my heart.

"You have no business being here; meddling in human affairs is prohibited," she said haughtily.

"I haven't meddled in any human lives; monsters, yes. I've killed many of them, but no humans. I have always tried to keep my hands clean of them," I snapped.

"You are in the human world, child. These lives, they are all part of a tangled web. They're all connected. You may not see it, but I assure you, they are. There are consequences for being here and harming any who dwell in this world."

"They attacked us, and they took Ryder from me. Am I just supposed to sit on my hands while they torture him?" I protested.

"You cannot interfere!"

"I cannot sit around while they tear him apart!" I shouted back angrily.

"Synthia, there are forces greater than us that make the rules. We are no more than pawns in this world, and by world, I mean universe. You meddle in things you can't even begin to understand," she said softly as she watched me with a wary look.

"They came into my world, ripped Ryder from it, and you're telling me that I can't do anything to get him back?" I demanded, as I struggled with the tears that threatened to betray me.

"Every life here is connected. The Guild protects the humans. You plan to raid it, and you will take a life. That life may be destined to save another, or to take another's life. Humans are like dominos. It's why, after all this time, no God has ever intervened in this world. The human God connected every life with its own purpose, and that purpose has to play out. Say you kill a child in the human world, and his life was supposed to lead him to meet a woman and create a child. That child has a destiny, which you just severed. Whether his destiny was to simply smile at someone who was having the worst possible day, and that simple smile resulted in that one person not committing suicide; that is a destiny. A single gesture of kindness can change a world; they are fickle creatures at best, but each of them has a purpose. You are the Goddess of Faery and you have now taken a life in the human world, and now *they* will demand something from you in return."

"Those assholes took him from my wedding!" I snapped as I pointed my finger in the general direction of the Guild. I understood her logic; it was flawed, but so was this world. "I can't just stand here and not help him, can't you understand that?"

"You are a Goddess," she explained. "Your hands are tied in this world, Synthia Raine. You cannot tamper with the balance."

"Right now, Faery and Tèrra are connected, and that makes this my playground as well. I can feel it, Destiny. I can feel this world because no matter what, all worlds are tied to it. It is the anchor for every world in the universe. Danu made sure I was able to meddle in Faery, since I would become its Goddess."

"It doesn't work like that," she sighed as if she was trying to be patient with me, and failing a bit. "You can lead them, but you can't be hands-on in this world. None can die by your hand. Do you understand me? Lead them, but do not interfere directly. The price will be more than you are willing to pay, I assure you of this," she pleaded.

"He's the love of my life, the father of my children. I will pay whatever *they*," I entreated, making air quotes, "want, but I will get him back!"

"I fear my words fall on deaf ears," she murmured sadly as she waved her hand and the raggedy old couch turned into a beautiful white couch. "Sit with me, child."

"You won't change my mind," I warned as I watched her warily.

"Danu warned me that there wasn't anything that I could tell you that would prevent you from your course, not once you'd set your mind to it," she laughed, but it was hollow and empty.

"I love him," I sighed helplessly as a vise tightened around my heart. "He'd destroy worlds for me."

"No, Synthia. He wouldn't. He didn't. He chose to let you die," she snapped offhandedly.

"Because he knew it was what I wanted," I demurred. "He also didn't have a choice; I was dying either way. He couldn't stop that. No one could, not even Danu."

"That is the truth, and if I am being honest, the situation was shit at best. He would have had to choose between you and his children, and you took that choice away from him. Your last words sealed your fate, but we already knew what would happen. Your mother created you to save the world she loved. She made you for Ryder, but your destiny has always been to replace your mother. Your mother has been aware of it since the moment you were born and I was shown your destiny. I begged her to destroy you. To stop it from happening, to let go of the world she'd created and make a new one. She couldn't, though; after Madisyn bore you, Danu held you in her arms as Madisyn slept, and the moment she did that, she knew a love that she had never known before. She looked into the eyes of her child and she couldn't do what she should to save herself. Instead, she tied me to you. She wrapped a strand of my hair around your finger, and tied your destiny to that of the Gods. She should have allowed you to die and avoided this fate, but she couldn't do it.

"There were many times she watched you as an infant, then later, as a toddler, and throughout your life. The day Faolán killed your parents, she almost interfered for you. I gave her the same warning then that I am giving you now. If she had intervened, who is to say that your life wouldn't have been the payment for interfering in this world?"

"She was there?" I asked as my chest heaved. "She could have helped me."

"And forfeit your life, or hers? The Gods are vicious creatures. They make the Mages look like children at play. They can demand blood, or worse. She knows it; why do you think she sent me? What do you think the cost was for meddling in your life? You were an Enforcer; you were destined to save hundreds of lives. It didn't matter that you were of her blood, or that the Fates blessed it. You were sent to this world and became a part of it. Now, now you're not. Whatever destiny you had here was severed with your mortal life. You are not Fae; you are not a Demi-Goddess. You are a full Goddess now."

"Then take it back! Because I'd give up my immortality for one mortal life with him! He is everything to me," I sobbed as I got to my feet, furious that I was crying, but it wasn't because I was upset. It was because I was pissed.

"My Gods, you're as sweet as she said," she whispered as she stood and looked at me. "It can't be undone, ever. The only way you can lose your life is to make the Gods angry enough to take it, or as payment for meddling where you have no business being."

"What will they demand of me?" I couldn't and wouldn't let him sit in that room to become what the other Fae there were. He had Witches experimenting on ways to kill him. How long before they succeeded? No. Whatever the price was, I'd pay it.

"It's a first offense, so it's hard to say. I do know they cannot touch your children. They have already been given their own destinies, and Danu has an arrangement with the Fates that, no matter what you do, they are protected. She took into account that you are as stubborn as she is. Thankfully. It doesn't mean that they will be kind to you, though."

"My children are safe?" I asked warily, and when she nodded, I grinned. "Then they can have my life if it is the cost. If it is my life for his, so be it."

"Ryder's life could be the price they ask," she whispered carefully.

"If they take his, they better take mine," I warned. "Because the monster I would become would be unlike anything they have ever seen before."

"Synthia, one doesn't threaten the Gods."

"It's not a threat," I stated coldly. "Right now, they have the luxury of sitting around and watching how things unfold, but if it was the love of their lives being tortured, I'm sure they wouldn't mind bending the rules a little. I will try very hard not to kill anyone, but I am not a saint. If they fight, I prefer to think it's because their destiny is to die by my hand. It's a choice, right? Destiny is what you make of it, not some preordained shit. It may tie in with others, but we control where our lives lead us. You just guide us, because you're a Goddess, and this gig isn't all that it's cracked up to be. It's a lot of tied hands, and rules that don't allow you to actually control shit."

She smiled. "I see so much of her in you," she said tightly, her eyes misting with tears. "She won't last much longer; if you hurry and save your King, we might be able to have your mother with us when you walk down the aisle to wed your beast." She swallowed. "How far you've come from that angry little girl who cursed me for my interference in your life, Synthia Raine," she whispered with choked emotion as she expelled a long sigh and smiled softly. "I can't even be angry with Danu for her choices, because I see it; I see that you are worth dying for. You will do everything she couldn't and so much more. You are both mother and warrior; something she could never be."

"She is a warrior, and she is my mother. She will never truly die, not for us or history. We will keep her alive in everything we do."

"So right, but you are needed below. They've taken care of the body and are waiting for you. Go, and hurry. Time is something we don't have."

Chapter
TWENTY~SIX

The sound of boots on cold marble floor was the only noise inside the newly built upper level of the Guild. There was no chatter, no sounds of people moving about as they prepared Enforcers for missions or the sound of children as they were being taught to become great Enforcers. The silence was unnerving, and made a place that used to be familiar to me, feel almost foreign now.

Foul had indeed been hard at work rebuilding it, but so far, only the main floor had been finished. Even so, it was progress. My eyes scanned the cold marble, taking in the emblems of the royal houses of Faery. Four crests for four royal castes of the Fae.

The reception desk, which would be the first point of contact with anyone needing our help, was fortified with wards to protect those who would man it. The walls were covered in similar wards, all invisible to the naked or untrained eye.

"It's a start," Dristan mused softly, noting my interest in the furnishings. "Not very much to look at yet, nor is it posh, but those things can be added in time."

"There's no noise," I commented and frowned. "That will come with time too, I suppose. It's just unnerving to me, that this place could ever be so quiet."

"It's as quiet as what it was supposed to become: a tomb," he agreed as he pushed his brown locks away from his face and smiled. "But you're right. The noise will come once this place is open for business. I'm sure we'll wish for a little peace and quiet when that happens."

"The Demon's here and he's brought us a present," I announced, sensing the wards as they buzzed with a warning of the men just outside the door. Seconds later, a commotion sounded from the doors as the Demon dragged the Druid inside and pushed him towards my feet.

He was younger than I'd expected, or at least he looked younger than I thought he'd be. I didn't try to guess anyone's age anymore, since the Fae didn't exactly make it an easy thing to do. The Druid had shoulder-length brown hair and gentle brown eyes. His neck and arms were covered in runes, along with ancient scrawling that looked similar to wards of protection in magical ink—something I'd once had at the base of my skull. His eyes took me in, slowly, then widening with apprehension as he noted the glow coming from within.

"That's…" He paused, shook his head, and once again continued in disbelief. "That's a Goddess!" He did a double take before he turned to Ristan, who had dragged him into the Guild. "She's a Goddess, Demon."

"Must have slipped my mind," he mumbled as he

turned to look at me. "In all fairness, I never said she wasn't." Ristan's tone was dry and void of emotion.

"I am a Goddess," I confirmed as I inserted myself into the conversation. "I have it on good authority that the only way to awaken the Witch who sleeps beneath this Guild is with the help of a Druid who can break the spell that keeps her in stasis."

"You think I would help you awaken her? Or that I would help the Fae for any reason?" he snapped, and I smiled confidently. Good; at least he had a little backbone.

"You'll help me," I assured him as I looked at my freshly manicured nails.

"No, I will not. I'm going to tell you the same thing I told the Guilds: Those Witches were never meant to be awakened after the Paladins put them in stasis. I, along with the rest of the Druid order, vowed that I would make sure they stayed in that state. You cannot force me to do it, not even with threat of torture," he retorted, his tone firm and a bit forceful. Well, shit. This didn't explain how Andrew the Enforcer/Mage knew about two Druids when these guys were in short supply and notorious about keeping themselves hidden, but it did explain why they had contacted two.

"Somehow, the Guild was able to find a way for the other Druid they dug up to break his oath. I wonder what it was, bribery…torture…or perhaps appealing to similar ideology? I suppose I could peel it out of your mind if you want me to, but I'd really prefer not to ruin my nails." I kept the tone of my voice low and even. "It will hurt like a bitch, and it's rather messy for you."

"And just how would you peel it from my mind?

My mind and body are warded against the Fae and Witches of the Guilds."

"Good, because I'm neither of those; I'm not sure those wards could withstand me. I do, however, love a good challenge," I offered with a dangerous smile. "Shall we put them to the test?" I glamoured a dagger into my hand, wrapped my fingers more securely around the handle, and watched as he stiffened. His pupils dilated as the pulse in his neck accelerated— subtle signs of fear that I'd seen many times when I was an Enforcer.

I pressed the tip of the dagger into my finger, softly repeating the spell to draw forth the magical butterfly. I had been toying with calling it a brain sucker, since that was technically what it did. Perhaps as I got better with this spell, I would come up with a name that was a little more catchy and I wouldn't be afraid to say it around the Fae, as I was pretty sure the Demon would thrive off of the puns he could make with 'brain sucker'.

"This little beauty is about to go inside your head, and I know for a fact that it's going to hurt like hell. I should also warn you: the last time I allowed him out, the mind he entered was…not quite the same when I was done," I purred. It wasn't a lie. The butterfly hadn't killed the Enforcer; I had. Not that the Druid needed the details. "So, here's a little summary of what he can do." I was almost enjoying the way he squirmed as he watched the beautiful butterfly. "Once I release him, he will slip inside your head through your ear. Hint: That's the painful part. Once inside, I will be able to relive every memory you have. I will know everything about you, from the first time you pissed your pants, until the Demon dragged you in here. So, why don't we just skip this thing where I threaten you,

we argue, and, of course, the ugly business of pain—
and, well, the drooling isn't something I'd wish for
anyone, because I'm sadistic enough to take pictures
and send them to you periodically later on. What do
you think, Druid?" I bit my lip as I narrowed my eyes
on his.

"So you can destroy the world as the Guild plans
to do? So you can restart the human race in your
image because you find this world flawed? Fuck you.
Do your worst," he growled. I took pause at his words
and the ugly anger buried deep in his tone.

"That's not what I want." I observed him carefully
as he cocked his head to the side and gave me a look
that clearly showed that he didn't believe me. "I'm
going to guess you know something about what's
going on with the holes that lead from Faery into this
world, correct?" His posture stiffened with the change
in line of questioning. "I'll take that as a yes. Tell
me what you know about them," I demanded, as he
swallowed slowly, considering my questions.

"You first, Goddess," he rasped.

"My name is Synthia," I began softly, wondering
if he'd give me his name in return. Baby steps in trust
were sometimes the smartest move. When he remained
silent, I nodded. "Your name is?" I persisted.

"Does it really matter to you what my name is?"
he enquired, watching me, watching my reaction.
When I remained firm, he relented, giving a stubborn
sigh of rebellion. "Fine, it's Derrick."

"Well, Derrick the Druid, I have no intention of
destroying any world. I am the Goddess of Faery
and soon-to-be Queen of the Horde Fae. I was in the
middle of my wedding when the Guild attacked us and

stole the love of my life from the Horde stronghold," I stated, observing as he swallowed nervously at the mention of the Horde. "The Guild isn't strong enough to accomplish that kind of feat alone. You see, it started with the portals of Faery failing, easy enough to blame on the weakening of the world alone, but that wasn't what made them grow. I think I know what they did, and I don't think they were prepared for what they got. The Guild isn't stupid, but they have a little management issue going on these days. There are Mages hiding in the ranks of the Guild, and it seems as though they have unofficially taken over a few of the Guilds. From what we can tell, they have been in control for a while now. I believe they woke a couple of those Witches and told them we were holding the one sleeping below in Faery. Now, you and I both know they aren't like Guild Witches at all. They are Hecate's children; Demi-Goddesses, which is probably why you are so keen on keeping them in stasis." At his slight nod, I continued. "I think the Mages encouraged those Witches to open the portals, and I'm pretty sure that the Mages wanted us to think it was because Faery is weakening, which at first glance, we may have bought. After all, the Mages have been sneaking into Faery on and off for a while now, poisoning the world." At his stunned look, I had to smile weakly. Clearly, this was news to him.

"What the Mages didn't count on was that when the Witches cast their spells to open the portals, they also weakened them. Once they were weakened, they continued to expand and grow at a rapid rate. I don't think the Mages comprehend how deep the need for revenge runs with these Goddess-like Witches, and in the Mages' blind hatred of the Fae, they gave those Witches the opportunity they needed. You see, the one thing the Mages don't seem to get is that, if Faery dies, its inhabitants will come here. There are too many creatures in Faery that are too dangerous for this world, and what the Horde was charged to do was to keep them in Faery and away from the Humans. The Mages have been doing their best to poison Faery for a long time. Now they have stolen the King of the Horde and opened the portals. Their reckless actions are going to destroy this world, not just Faery, which I am sure is what those Witches are counting on. Right now, Faery is pouring Fae out of those portals and causing Humans to panic. We can't prevent it, not with how large those portals are. They used those portals as a distraction. Another thing you may not know is that the Mages made a pact with a very powerful Fae who had his own agenda and, with his and the Witches' help, they invaded the Horde Kingdom and took its King. I'm sure the Mages thought they could control him and use him to their benefit. The reality was, he was using them, and once his agenda had been fulfilled, he would have killed them. They are very fortunate he is dead now. So, as you can see, we have no intention of destroying this world. We are trying to save Faery and this world too. We're planning to rebuild this place, and create a new Guild, one that can protect this state from the Fae invading, and eventually we will build in other areas, such as New Orleans, where that Guild has also fallen. I am not the bad guy here and neither are they," I said with a sweep of my hand towards the Fae who protected me. "I want to fix what the Mages broke, but to do that, I need my head in the game. I need my Fairy back. He's my anchor, and without him, I don't know if I will even want to save this world."

"And you're sure they have him?" he inquired, finally getting to his feet.

"I know they have him, and I know why they took him. They were sending us a message, one that said they weren't afraid of us. I plan to answer that message with one of my own."

"What you have told me clarified a good deal, and changes things quite a bit," he sighed warily as he looked at me speculatively, then surprised me with a cocky smile. "You have no idea what I really am, do you?" His eyes seemed to smile as they began to glow from within.

"According to a certain Mage's memories, which I hope are reliable, you are supposed to be a Druid," I answered, watching him closely as I let the butterfly dissolve for now.

"Not really; I am a Paladin. There are a few of us who take on the guise of Druids, just in case the Guild has need of us, we can reach out to the rest of the Order. While I understand your plight, you must understand that what you're asking of me is considered blasphemy by the Paladin order."

"But you can wake her, can't you?" I probed. I didn't care if he was a unicorn who farted rainbows if he could wake her up. I'd send in the brain sucker and take the spell from his mind. As much as I preferred him to be forthcoming, I wasn't taking no for an answer.

"I can, because I helped put her into stasis. My line is very old, and we live by a very strict code."

"And does your code state that you can't help the Fae?" I asked carefully.

"The Fae have been a nuisance since the dawn of time," he admitted with a soft snort of amusement.

"And the Gods, are they also on the list of people

you don't help?" At this question, he tilted his head as though he was considering how much he could tell me.

"That is something I am not at liberty to speak of," he muttered as he frowned for a moment. "What you're asking, though, it could cause worse problems. If those Witches are allowed to reunite as a full coven, they will rain down hell upon earth."

"Oh, honey, hell's already here. We have Fae pouring in; we have some pretty nasty Demons hiding in a quaint town nearby, waiting for hell to open its gates, and the Mages have declared war on the Fae. You can't hide your head in the sand. This world? It's on the brink of a war unlike anything that's come before. Help us, so we can help this world," I said with meaning.

"I still can't help you," he answered.

"Why not?" I countered, growing frustrated.

"Because we had help—and a lot of it—when we put them in stasis. The Guild, Druids and Paladins united in the effort to put them under. It's hard to explain, but there might be a way for you to help me, Goddess. You can give me some juice."

"Elaborate on exactly what 'give me some juice' means?" I asked skeptically, waiting and analyzing his every move. This guy was a lot older than I'd originally thought he was, and a lot stronger than he looked. There was no way I was sexing him up to donate juices or powers, though.

"Nah, not like that, little vixen," he laughed, and the sound echoed through me. He snapped his fingers and I stepped back as I felt the immense power that rushed into the large room we stood in. It sizzled, popped, and I felt like my hair stood up from the electrical current that briefly emanated from him. I expelled a breath as I took him in. His hair was now silvery blond, still shoulder-length, which gently dusted his shoulders. Ocean blue eyes met and held mine prisoner as he smiled. His neck and arms were still covered in tattoos, but the designs were different now. He wore an amulet, one that was full of magic. Deadly magic. "Flattered and all, but you are attached, and I don't do attachments. It's messy and I prefer my world the way it is." He gave me a wink as he allowed me to look him over.

"What the fuck just happened?" I glanced at Ristan, who looked as dumbfounded as I currently felt.

"No fucking clue," he murmured. "That's a new one to me. The Paladin Knights that guarded your uncle wore armor, so I never got a good look at them—and they must have been shielding their power."

"We are shadows," Derrick said softly, a cocky grin on his sexy lips. "You have not seen our true selves because we don't want to be seen. My birth name is Callaghan, first born son to Douglas of the Paladin Knights."

"I'm still Synthia." I smiled weakly. "Daughter of Danu, the Goddess and creator of Faery. I was raised in this Guild. I was an Enforcer, and now I'm a Goddess because my recently deceased brother tried to give me a shady C-section in some sort of freaky Mage ritual that was supposed to steal my birthright as the Blood Heir and give it to him. Didn't work out like he thought it would." I shrugged. "Now I am the Goddess of the Fae, and soon to be the Horde

Queen. Now that we got the fun stuff out of the way; time's getting short and I really need you to wake up the Witch sleeping below so we can trade her for the Horde King."

"You best not be yanking my dick unless you plan to get it off, vixen."

"Do I look like I'm yanking your dick?" I asked with a frown. "Ryder is the King of the Horde, first born son of Alazander."

"It's true, then. You must be the one we have heard of. The one who birthed the first set of triplets ever born to Faery—a very dark omen follows you. The part of your story that you don't know is that what had happened to you is all part of an omen that was shared with the Paladins centuries ago."

"I swear to Faery if you say my kids are bad omens, I will cut your tongue out. My kids are not an omen."

"No, they're not. It has nothing to do with your children, and everything to do with what follows their birth. Many things were pushed into motion when you were brought back. Everything in Faery has some sort of myth attached to it, but the omen I spoke of, that's the kind of shit legends are created from. *Only when the Horde and the Gods produce the three, shall the portals let loose and the Fae be free. Worlds will combine, chaos shall reign.*"

I turned and looked at Zahruk, who gave me a nod, as well as Ristan, who followed his lead. I hadn't heard anything about this kind of myth.

"You're saying the birth of my children ruined the portals, and it had nothing to do with the Original

Witches?" I asked.

"On the contrary," he disagreed. "They opened them, but only because you gave them the keys to do it."

"They can't be both. They can't be the key to fixing Faery, and the key to destroying it."

"But they can; it just depends on how you define *fixed*. You said it yourself: Faery is sick because it was poisoned long ago, and the periodic poisoning continues. Faery is a life force of its own and, logically, to keep itself from dying, it needs to heal itself. It needs this world to feed from, just like the Fae need the humans. Hecate's Witches just sped up the process, probably without knowing it. I think you are right to assume that they opened them as a means for revenge. However, that part of it won't happen. We won't allow it to, and this is how I know it. You and I, Synthia, we are destined."

"For?" I asked carefully.

"You have a rather empty Guild, and I have Knights who will want to help you succeed in policing the Fae, if what you said is true. There's more, though; if I agree to help you, you'd need to help me hunt down a few baddies too," he stated carefully. "Ones who are also hell-bent on destroying this world. And don't worry about the rules and laws of the Gods, for even they will agree that these creatures need to be put down." I looked at him sharply, and then quickly looked at my Fae protectors so I wouldn't give anything away. How did he know about the rules and laws of the Gods that Destiny had been lecturing me on?

"How bad are we talking?" I asked, checking my nails, which were painted *I Can Never Hut Up* OPI.

"Are you afraid you're not up for the task, *Goddess*?" he mocked.

"No, I'm wondering if I can accomplish it before lunch," I answered with a smile. "It's a deal, Callaghan, but only if you wake her up."

"Deal, but you have to shake on it." A dagger materialized into his hand and he nodded at me with a smile. "I'm sure you heard there was a blood cost to put them in and keep them in. It was a lot of blood. I'm hoping that the blood of a Goddess will be enough to get her out." He sliced his palm and held the dagger out to me.

I stared at his hand and hesitated. I looked up to find his eyes glowing with an eerie flame from within. I had a feeling that once I did this there would be no backing out. I was already putting everything on the line…I took the dagger and sliced my own palm. I reached out and shook his hand, wincing as his hand clasped mine and power flared between us, sealing the deal.

"Welcome to the new Guild," I smirked. "Now, let's go wake up that sleeping Witch, shall we?"

We started down into the maze of new hallways, through the winding staircases, and into the library of the Guild that had yet to be fixed. Once inside, Callaghan gave a loud whistle at the destruction that was next on the list of renovations. We continued on until we entered the sacrificial chamber and made our way down the staircase, to the chamber where the ghosts had gathered. They were no longer needed, and they deserved eternal rest for their sacrifice. I paused and looked at Ristan, who nodded, and I smiled.

"It's time to sleep, ladies," I announced, wiggling

my fingers as I lit the flames and carefully wrote runes that would release them from this place on the walls. Ghosts needed to be able to complete whatever unfinished business they had. "Are all of you ready to get out of here, or is there anyone who needs a bit of closure? I'll help, if any of you do."

"We just wish to finally rest," one stated softly. I nodded and closed my eyes, whispering the spell to release them from this tomb.

"You're free," I stated, feeling the eyes of the Paladin and the others on me. A bright light momentarily blinded everyone in the chamber. I rubbed my eyes, trying to clear the black blotchy spots away and was able to focus enough to see that the ghosts were no longer bound here.

Callaghan sighed and made his way to the glass box that held who we knew to be one of Hecate's daughters. He touched the glass and smiled faintly, as if he recognized her.

"Did you know that not all of the Witches we put into stasis were evil?" He shook his head sadly. "It was all or none. If we spared the ones that weren't evil, they would have done everything in their power to revive their sisters. Hannah is this one's name; her only crime was supporting her sisters. Your plan is to give her back to them; it could make her evil."

I stared at Callaghan and wondered if it changed my position. Nope. They were her sisters, so it wasn't like I was handing Sleepy Beauty over to strangers. If she wasn't evil, it would make hunting her sisters down easier if we had an insider. I smiled at the Paladin weakly. "Let's wake her up."

Callaghan glanced around the room and noticed

the wards etched there. He moved to one of the walls and laid his hands on the cold stone surface. Blue flames lit up the walls of the chamber. The Leylines hummed with untold power, and the earthy scent was overwhelming to my heightened senses.

"Whoever placed these wards sure didn't want them to come down," Callaghan grumbled as he began to work the wards. He'd removed his shirt, and thick coils of muscles flexed with every move he made. He had thick runes tatted on his flesh; each one moved with the spell he worked, and as he chanted the spell, the runes fed more power into him.

"It will take a little while, but…" He hesitated as he seemed to consider something else. "No, it's layered. I can do this," he muttered as he moved his hands around.

I couldn't remove them; I couldn't even make out their structure, as they weren't like anything I had seen before. The one thing I could sense for sure was that these wards were ten times more powerful than the ones the Guild Elders typically placed. These ones were triggered to bring the ceiling down, should anyone attempt to remove them. I also noticed a few traps that I hadn't seen the last time I'd been in this chamber. We'd been lucky that the wards we placed hadn't triggered alarms inside the room.

"They're down," Callaghan announced as we watched the blue flames shoot higher. "Now to wake her up; she's not going to be happy. You will need to hold her or she will probably teleport."

"We brought something to prevent that," Zahruk interrupted, and glamoured a golden cuff around her wrist. He looked at me and then Callaghan grimly.

"It was a gift Danu gave to the Fae a long time ago to protect them, should Hecate ever meddle in their affairs. It won't hurt her, but will contain her magic and most likely piss her off," he said, stepping back, giving Callaghan room to work.

He whispered words in another language and the flames moved higher, licking the walls and causing the entire room to sway with the words as he reached a crescendo. My body buzzed with raw power, as if the spell was reaching for it and trying to tap the energy.

His ocean eyes lifted to mine and he smiled as he felt the huge surge of my power. I wasn't sure I liked him knowing I held so much power. I moved closer, taking his hand and pushing a little more power into him. I watched as his eyes glowed, and something dark moved inside his eyes.

"You have secrets." I wondered if I should push to see what they were.

"Of course I do. We all carry secrets with us, vixen. It isn't share or care day, girl. Focus; I need your…juice."

"You irritate me," I blurted, and heard Ristan laugh from behind me.

"Are you always so blunt?" Callaghan countered distractedly.

"No, sometimes I'm sarcastic, but you have to catch me on a good day for that."

"Hmm, you sure you're attached?" He gave me a roguish grin as sweat dripped and ran down his massive chest.

"I'm positive I am," I quipped back. "Can you wake her or not?"

"She's awake." He pulled a soft cloth out of one of his pockets and wiped the sweat from his neck as my eyes narrowed and I looked down at the Witch, who was observing me warily.

"Good morning, beautiful. Welcome to the twenty-first century. You're safe, Hannah, for now. I'm going to need you to get up and help me out a little," I said softly as I stared down into her beautiful eyes and grinned. "Let's get you some coffee, hmm?"

Chapter
TWENTY~SEVEN

Ristan stood beside me as we waited in silence while Hannah explored the room and its contents. She wasn't speaking to us yet, but her curiosity about us was in full swing. She'd pick up one thing, only to get distracted by something else that caught her fancy. Callaghan waited by the door in case he was needed, and Hannah gave him a wide berth.

"You bathed her?" Ristan asked, giving me a sideways glance.

"She's been asleep down there for a long time. For most of us of the female persuasion, a bath is always a good idea if you want to ensure better spirits. She's not my enemy, not yet," I mused, knowing she was listening to us.

Darynda and I had bathed her in a tub, since so much had changed since she and her sisters had been placed into stasis, and glamouring her clean might just freak her out. She marveled quietly at the huge claw-footed tub, but that wasn't what had shocked her the most. I had to refrain from smiling as she'd searched beneath the tub for flames or coal as to why it was heated. Instead of the hauling in buckets of hot water as she'd been used to back then, I'd placed my fingers into the water and heated it to a comfortable temperature. The bubbles had changed colors, giving the water a rich, heady fragrance of lavender.

After her bath, I'd glamoured some undergarments and clothing for her, including an ivy colored skirt that reached her ankles comfortably. Last was a soft white silk camisole top with wide straps and lace edging. She'd hugged her chest, probably wishing she'd had something more to cover up with, but it was the twenty-first century and she'd need to fit in. Darynda had done her hair and clipped midnight barrettes in it to keep the long dark mass out of her face.

I had taken a chance bringing her here. Faery was a maze of powerful Leylines, more powerful than the ones she'd been plugged into. Tapping the lines would be child's play to her, but I was willing to bet she was disoriented and a little confused about her abrupt awakening. Until she knew why she was here, she wouldn't chance showing her cards. Neither would I, though, not until I knew everything she did.

"I'm still not sure why you brought her here," Ristan commented, his mouth slipping into a slight frown. His eyes left mine and moved to the woman, examining her as an unknown factor just as Ryder would have. "It's dangerous showing her any part of our world, considering her sisters are behind the portals," he finished in a soft tone, not chiding or rebuking my decision.

"They opened them, but maybe she can tell us how to close them," I offered.

"You're in pain," Ristan pointed out offhandedly, which caused me to wince at his astute ability to read me like a book.

"Faery is in pain, and so am I. We're attached," I grumbled. "It's the drawback of being connected to the people. We feel what the land around us does. Imagine what Danu must feel as it crumbles to become one with Tèrra?" I turned to him, ignoring the Witch who listened keenly to everything we said.

"I can't say what she is feeling, but you can drop the hard-ass act, Flower. It's me you're talking to. Tell me how to help you. You need to rest as well." The concerned look on his face made me smile weakly.

"I'm exhausted." I laughed but it was as hollow as I felt. "I killed Faolán, and I felt nothing. No regret or remorse. I know I shouldn't feel anything for him because he was a monster, but what about my father? My mother? They have to bury a child that I killed. That weighs on me, because I should feel something, anything for them. There's nothing there, and the worst part was, I'd do it again. I'd do it a million times over and make them have to bury him, just so that my children could live without him hiding in the shadows as a threat. Danu is dying because she saved my life, mine, and there's nothing I can do to save her. Ryder is in the hands of the Guild and you more than anyone else knows what they are probably doing to him. There are so many what ifs, and I know partly what is playing out because of the Enforcer's memories. I mean, I could go in there balls to the walls and get him, but there are too many unknowns in the way. Then to top it all off, Destiny shows up and tells me that if I interfere to get him back, I will have to pay a price but she can't tell me what it is, because she doesn't know what it will be. I can't leave him there; it's not an option. So, I'll have to live with whatever it is they will demand of me. If you can fix any of those problems, Demon, feel free to."

"What do you mean by a price to pay?" he inquired sharply as his eyes narrowed, and I realized I may have said too much. His recent behavior with Danu told me he knew more about how the Gods worked than I did.

"I honestly don't know," I replied, turning to find the Witch observing us closely.

"We will get him back, and we'll make it a safe place so that we can bring the others back as well," he mused softly. I wasn't sure if he was trying to reassure me, or himself.

"I know we will," I agreed with a tight frown. "I would think that since they threw the first punch, I'd at least get to hit back without having to pay for it. I didn't ask for this, nor do I enjoy playing games with the Guild. I'd allow them to live if they handed him back; well, most of them anyway."

"Gods are fickle fuckers, to be sure," he agreed. "They seldom make any sense. They meddle and call it destiny or holy intervention, but when it comes to the humans, it's all a touchy subject."

"That's not something I will argue with." I expelled a shaky breath and rolled my neck. "Hannah, it's time to talk." I watched as her eyes rose with open curiosity she couldn't conceal.

"You are a Goddess. Were you born as a Goddess, or made?" she asked; her accent was thick with a brogue I couldn't place.

"Made, I guess. It's rather complicated." I couldn't find a better way to explain how I came to be.

"And you woke me because you think my sisters took something from you, or did something to this world?" she continued carefully; her eyes spoke of mistrust as she watched me for any sign of lies.

"They did take something from me. Someone, to be exact, someone I love very much. But you knew that already." I watched as heat flushed in her cheeks.

"Matilda and Bettina have him, yes. Inside the Seattle Guild—and you plan to hand me over in exchange for him?"

"That's the plan," I agreed. "How is it you know that? Do you communicate with them?"

"No; stasis does not mean we were asleep. Not exactly; it means you lay there unable to do naught but listen and wait for the day that you are brought out of stasis." She cast an accusatory glare at Callaghan.

"What else did you hear inside the Guild?"

"Everything you said, and you said a lot of things over the years. I slept, but I was not exactly asleep. I have heard everything inside of that place. Every word whispered, every lie ever told, every love affair that transpired behind closed doors. Then there was you; you were one of my favorite beings that lived there. You were such a sad child, with what you endured and what the Guild put you through. Even before you left, it was changing. Over the past twenty or so years, the whispers became different, no longer the innocent hushed tones of lovers, the training of the Enforcers, or the chatter of the children at their lessons; but the conniving Mages who slinked in the shadows. You assume we do not know what we are helping, that we are using them for revenge. We are aware that those who wronged us have long been gone from this earth, but their children are not. Most of our children did not get that choice, to breed, to multiply. They were murdered, slaughtered in horrid ways as if they were naught but animals."

"And Callaghan over there said you were not like your sisters." I waved a hand at the silent but watchful Paladin, who cursed under his breath as I tried to weigh my options for how to handle her.

"I am the nice one." She smirked a little saucily. "And I am also the one who does not wish the humans dead, even though some of them deserved something more than death. Revenge is not something I enjoy. We were good once, but it did little to help us or those who we gave birth to, now did it?"

"Life's a bitch," I muttered softly. "What happened to them shouldn't have ever transpired. However, it's ancient history, literally. You and your sisters will see that. But killing humans who had nothing to do with what their ancestors did isn't the answer. People are flawed, just as we all are. No one is perfect, but they do learn from their mistakes, and the world has changed since the trials."

"Some fates are worse than death," she spat, eyeing me. "I would have preferred death over being made into a lifeless being that could see and hear everything that happened, but could not interact. I felt each sacrifice, each girl's death which was used to secure the state of stasis. I knew each of them after they had been murdered. They deserve justice, but this world did not even weep for those women," she choked out and shook her head. Her eyes misted with tears as she smiled sadly. "I admit, I wanted to wipe out the human race, but unlike my sisters, I listened. I learned that the world went on without us; our own children were inside the Guilds. We went on, they went on. I understand that killing the descendants of the humans responsible for the deaths of our children would mean killing our descendants as, in some cases, our remaining children's descendants bred with the children of theirs. Their deaths are something I cannot allow," she said fiercely with determination in her eyes.

"So, you don't want to kill the human race?" I asked, hopefully.

"Not I," she said calmly. "I will always feel the need for revenge against the lines who committed the crimes, but I realize that they were not responsible for the wrongdoing of their forefathers. I have never taken an innocent life to date, but most of my sisters think otherwise. I am not a saint, and I enjoy sinning. Those who committed the trials did so in mock ones, and I knew they would not stop. That was the reason I agreed to join my sisters. It had to stop. To them, we and our children were monsters and yet they were the ones who did the monstrous acts against our sisters, children, and those of our direct lines. You are a mother. You will eventually be like us, having to feel every child of your bloodline as they die. Could you watch them be murdered like animals, and treated as even less?"

"My children are immortal, like you," I corrected.

"Do you think they will mate with immortals, all of them? No, for love is blind when it comes to longevity. They will not consider it when love finds them. How do you think the Witches of old mated with mere mortals? The first of our kind were immortal, like me. Part God or Goddess; then a few took mortals as mates, and they bore children who were weaker until finally, some became so weak that they were akin to mortals. You cannot know who your children will love, or their children for that matter. You will be as helpless as we were in that endeavor. Now imagine those children of your direct line being slaughtered for having abilities they inherited from your blood. Imagine their screams as they curse you and what you passed on to them as they were murdered for it. You would want revenge; you would crave it like the air you breathe. We killed only a few who put our children and their children to death. The humans who stoned them, burned them, or drowned them to prove they were immortal, and when they died, those who doled out their torment received nothing for their acts. I know how history recorded it, saying no Witches were burned alive, but I can still smell the flesh of my great granddaughter as I collected her burned remains to bury her. The humans did that and *we* were called monsters, put into stasis because we wanted revenge against those who would continue to hunt us and our children. That is why my sisters crave an end to the humans, because it's too late to seek revenge against the humans responsible for the deaths of our children, but there will always be new monsters born of the human race who seek to do the same to our remaining descendants, or anyone who might be different or have something they want. Avarice, jealousy, and bigotry are all human traits that caused the death of our children."

"I couldn't imagine what you were put through. But revenge won't change what happened to them, nor will it bring them back or give you solace for their losses. Do you think your sisters still crave revenge?" I asked.

"I will not pretend to know what is in their minds. Not anymore. I was preparing to leave them when we were captured. I had planned to go to the sacred altar to find our mother, to see if she could reason with the monsters. My sisters discovered my plans and so my stasis, my purgatory, has been in silence for the most part. It was only recently that they started to communicate with me again. Even then, I know not of what lies in their hearts."

"Hecate has been absent for a very long time," I agreed.

"We do not think she chose her absence from this world. We believe she was taken, but we do not know who could have enough strength to accomplish it. At first we thought Morgana had taken her, but then, she too has been missing for centuries. We believe someone is collecting very powerful Witches to either cast or break a spell. I had planned that if I couldn't find our mother and obtain her help, then I would ask for the Gods to help us."

"And that is why your sisters are helping the Guild, because they believe they can help them locate your mother?"

"Has Destiny taught you nothing?" she muttered offhandedly, almost as if she was a little exasperated with me. "Taking your fiancé was not an accident. I asked them to play the Guild's game. I needed to be awoken to find our mother. You more than anyone should understand, considering your own plight with Danu. We care not if the Guild on this continent falls, for they are not of our line anymore. Our bloodlines are in England and Scotland, and those who did come here are safe because of people like you who will ensure they survive. That is where we will go. Most assume that my sisters at the Seattle Guild are the strongest of the thirteen, but they are wrong. We are only strong together, and so we shall go wake the others. Once we've accomplished that, I will ensure we only hunt down those who know what happened to our mother."

"Your sisters opened the portals to Faery. Can they fix them?"

"I do not believe the portals can be fixed. Not until this world is healed. If it fails to heal, they may never close entirely. Everything is linked, and everything happens for a reason. Trust that if you cannot trust anything else."

"And what about Ryder? They are torturing him while your sisters help them search for a way to kill him!" I hissed as Ristan stiffened beside me as my tone grew hard and cold.

"He is immortal and the King of the formidable Horde. He cannot be killed by us, nor would we attempt it. Placate and wait was the plan my sisters and I agreed on. Once you take me to them, we will depart. The Guild will be exposed, but they are not without resources. Not with the evil they have sided with."

"You and your sisters set this entire thing up from the beginning?" I questioned and her smile was answer enough.

"Of course we did. From the first moment we heard the Mages agree on their idea to wake a few of us to help them destroy the Fae, we knew that you were the only thing they were scared of. We had to make you want to fight them, to give you a reason to free me from stasis. You have been away from the Guild for some time, so we did not count on you being a Goddess and a mother when we put our plan into play. As I said, your entire time at the Guild, I watched you.

Larissa made sure of it, and I was so happy when it became clear that you would be our path to freedom."

My stomach dropped. "Leave her out of it."

"Why would I? She was of my direct line. Everything is connected, everything. I am sure Destiny told you how everything is connected, like dominos. Something as simple as a push in the right direction, and you found the Fae; the Fae gave you what you were missing. Your heart, which you forsook when your first fiancé, ahem, died. Your heart brought you to me. Larissa knew what her fate was going to be before it happened, and even knowing what was to come, she chose to stay and complete her purpose, knowing that completing her task would be the prelude to her death. She is not alone in her death; her parents are with her. She loved you, though, so much. So much that she did not want to leave you or Adam, the man she loved even knowing her time was short. So here we are, and it matters little how we arrived here. What matters is what you decide to do next. So tread carefully because dominos are always falling, no matter what you do to stop them."

"You went through an awful lot of trouble to get to me," I said carefully.

"You went through an awful lot to become you, Synthia. You are not of my line, pity that. When the Mages come, I will be there for you when called. I owe you that much. We did make a mess of your wedding, after all, but I also brought Faolán to you. Deals with the devil aren't always a bad thing."

"You had the Mages bring him here, to me?" I asked.

"He lost face when you escaped. They weren't

happy with his lack of control and disappearing when so many of their brethren fell to Fae blades. He did brag about your death, only to hear it whispered among the Fae that you had survived."

I shook my head, wondering if she was insane or I was. I wanted to believe her, but she'd hit it on the nose. I wasn't a trust-giving kinda girl.

"If what you say is true, you and your sisters will abandon the Guild come morning."

"We will leave once you are there to take control of it."

"I don't want control of it," I replied as I shook my head in denial. "I just want Ryder back."

"I understand, but there is something I must warn you about," she hesitated, and I frowned.

"What is it?" I questioned.

"My sisters have tried to do things with him."

"With who and what?" I asked, confused.

"With Ryder; they wish to mate with him."

I swallowed as red-hot rage hit me like a truck going 80 miles an hour on concrete. I felt my magic pop as the roaring in my ears intensified. I felt Ristan's hand as he placed it on my shoulder and saw Hannah step back, placing distance between us.

"I swear to the Gods I will skin them alive if they forced him to do anything. Any. Thing. I don't give a shit who they think they are—he is mine."

"They have not shared with me if they have

succeeded…"

"Don't finish that," I snapped, cutting her off. "Don't you fucking dare! If they've hurt him or done anything *else* to him that he didn't want, or that wasn't part of the show for the Mages, there is nowhere they can hide that I won't find them. That's not an idle threat, just so you are aware. You don't want me for an enemy, because I'll enjoy what I do to them."

"I understand," she murmured softly as she looked at me as if I was a snake poised to strike.

"Get some rest; tomorrow we take the Seattle Guild," I gritted out angrily and turned to look at Ristan, who observed me closely, sensing the power I couldn't fully control.

"Save it for the Guild, Flower. We're going to need it."

Chapter
TWENTY-EIGHT

I stood in front of the Seattle Guild, watching the wards as they glowed brilliantly against the cold slate walls. Once upon a time, I'd been in awe of the sheer size of this Guild, so much larger than the one I'd grown up in. The security was ten times that of the Spokane Guild. The prestigious position it held had added to the wonder and amazement the first time I'd been to it. Now, however, the blinders I'd once worn were off, and I could see the neglect. Chips marred the slate, while cracks lined the foundation on which it was built on. I could see the darkness surrounding the building, basking in the shadows of evil of those who now controlled it.

"The wards are unusual," Ristan observed, pointing out several that pulsed.

"That's because they're not ours," I said sadly. "They are not of the Guild's making, and they weren't here the last time we were here," I clarified, as sometimes I had challenges separating myself from the Guild I grew up in and the Guild it had become. I still felt a part of this place deep down, even though they'd thrown me to the wolves as soon as they had discovered I was Fae. This place was still a part of me, no matter what had transpired between us. I had to admit, that even though they'd thrown me to the wolves—now I was here, leading the pack.

"Mages," Alden muttered from my left. His worried eyes tore away from the wards and looked at me. He looked defeated at the knowledge that the wards were indeed of the Mages' magic. "That can't be good."

"No, no it's not. The Guild either fell, or the Elder who is in charge is in fact a Mage," I muttered as I felt anger pulsing to life inside of me as I remembered the Mage from Andrew's memory who was masquerading as an Elder. I hated this shit, hated that the Mages were infiltrating my life from every angle. The one establishment meant to protect the humans from the Fae had fallen into the hands of those who wished to eradicate us from existence. They'd let Hecate's daughters open the portals, fracturing them to a state where they couldn't be closed, and they'd done it knowing it would place humans in harm's way.

I exhaled and released my bottom lip as I turned to fully face Alden. My heart was in my throat, beating rapidly as I saw his eyes fill with unshed tears. He knew what those wards meant; there was no reason to deny it after the proof was staring us in the face.

"I'd like to hear your thoughts on it," I said softly, giving him time to consider his answer. This man was my family. He'd raised most of us, and I loved him no matter what he'd thrown me into, because as Destiny had said, he had only pushed a domino into action. He hadn't controlled the rest of the pieces.

"I don't know, kid," he sighed, his hands tightening against his sides as he struggled against the emotions churning inside of him.

"Do you think they are beyond saving?" I inquired, knowing I was asking him to admit the Guild here had been defeated. I wasn't sure how many of the other Guilds had fallen to the Mages, but the ones in this state were gone.

"This Guild has fallen," he admitted, his face tightening with anger, and I knew it was killing him to admit defeat. We knew that other Guilds would soon be facing the same thing if we didn't get ahead of the Mages.

"What the hell does that mean?" Callaghan asked, finally speaking.

I turned away from Alden to face Callaghan with a grim look. Lucian stood beside him and barely gave the white-armored Paladin a glance, as though having a Paladin in our midst was an everyday occurrence. I closed my eyes against the pain I felt, drawing strength from those around me, and opened my eyes after a moment had passed. I looked out at those who had gathered in front of the Guild. I could see my Fae protectors, dressed in their uniforms of form-fitting armor that was similar to the armor I wore. The Paladin and Lucian's men stood alongside the Sluagh and the rest of the warriors of the Horde, Blood, Dark, and Light Kingdoms. Even Elijah and his misfits stood with them. The Mages inside had to be shitting themselves with the show of force in front of the Guild. I took a deep breath and addressed the crowd.

"The Guilds in Washington State and Louisiana are no longer under the control of the National or Global Guilds. We are not certain how many others have fallen. The Mages have taken control of them, and it means the Fae are at war on two fronts now. Here and in Faery." I swallowed hard as the words on my tongue tasted bitter. "It means they've either taken the other Guild members as prisoners, or murdered them. Spokane and New Orleans were tests, Seattle was their goal and it looks like they've achieved it."

"You can tell that just from the wards?" Lucian glanced at me skeptically.

"Yes." I nodded and looked back to the crowd. "No true Guild Elder would allow a separate faction to place their wards on the Guild. It would be considered a sign of weakness. An Elder is supposed to be the strongest in residence, and if he cannot place the wards, another would have taken his place to do so. An Elder's wards are the strongest in this realm, because he himself can draw power from every coven and Enforcer under his control. My guess is, they killed them once they gained control." I swallowed hard. "Or the Elder in charge is a Mage."

"It could also mean that they've killed any who argued against allowing the Mages control," Alden added. "An Elder cannot cast without those beneath him adding power. I do not believe they would flee either, or argue against an Elder. We instill fear of insubordination from the moment we begin teaching them as children. To abandon a Guild in its hour of need wouldn't be an option either, for failure would result in retirement. Those wards are not the work of Druids, nor the Original Witches." He looked at Callaghan, who shook his head. "Nor are they the work of Paladins. The Mages cannot be allowed to do this to the other Guilds."

"So, it's beyond saving," Zahruk growled.

"I don't think it can be saved," I said without hesitation. "These people are not our friends, nor are they part of the Guild. Any that were loyal to the true Guild are most likely dead, just like what happened in Spokane and New Orleans. The Mages took our King, and they will pay for it with their lives. No Mage is to be spared; we will show them the same mercy they gave to those inside the Spokane and New Orleans Guilds. We take no prisoners. The only ones to be spared are the Fae that we know are being held inside, and any members of the true Guild that might be prisoners. Any Guild member who fights us will die."

"Why kill them?" Alden questioned hesitantly.

"Because if they are in there and are freely moving around, they've chosen the wrong side," I stated with finality. "The Mages want absolute control, and Seattle is a stepping stone to achieve that goal, which will be the National Guild. All orders go through that Guild before being sent to any other one in the United States, sometimes even Europe. Imagine it like this: all of the Embassies around the world get their orders from the White House, where would you attack if you wanted to control them?"

"The White House," Ristan replied as his eyes left mine and moved to the Seattle Guild. "But I'd need help from others familiar with the building."

"You'd also need someone who could help prove that you were chosen to lead, so that means that, the someone from the Guild that helped them, is still alive. That, Alden, is why anyone moving about freely in that Guild can't be saved."

"I'm sorry, Flower," Ristan murmured, but I

shrugged it off.

"It is done; nothing we do can change what has happened here. What we *can* do is avenge those who were lost trying to protect it. We can stop them from poisoning the other Guilds." Movement caught my eye in front of the Guild. "It's show time."

We watched as Mages in the robes of the Elders filed out of the huge double doors. No familiar faces, but they had taken care with their appearances. They looked the part, but seemed to be missing some of the finer details that usually marked an Elder. All except one, a familiar Elder, who I had last seen in the memories of a dead wanna-be Enforcer.

"You have brought war to our door?" the one demanded; his eyes were blue, but dulled in comparison to the color of his robes. "You will pay for this! This is our world; we are the protectors of it!" he sputtered.

"What makes you say that?" I challenged, moving past the others to stand at the head of the army amassed in front of the Guild. "What makes you think you are the protectors?"

"Because I am the Elder of the Seattle Guild. I hold the power of the western seaboard! And you, you have no right to bring these monstrosities into this world. It is an act of aggression against the humans. You will bear the responsibility for this," he laughed quietly, as if we'd played right into his hands. "You stupid girl, you've misjudged us, though, haven't you? You brought lambs to be slaughtered. You cannot control them without their King."

"How do you figure that?" I watched as he smirked and waved his hands, bringing my attention to the humans that cowered in the doorways of the buildings surrounding the Guild, watching the monsters standing in front of it. Phones were lifted, filming our every move. News crews were setting up; no doubt they had been called by the Mages. Yes, they'd wanted an audience, to build strength for their claim for their self-appointed Elder. They wanted the other Guilds watching as they defeated the Horde, but that wasn't what was going to happen here.

"Because I have the Gods on my side; the Guild has always protected the weak!" he shouted, turning to make sure the cameras got his face. "The humans have supported us; they've watched us defeat monsters before to protect them. The Gods have taken note of our work here at this very Guild and have rewarded us for protecting the humans' way of life."

"Gods?" I questioned, wondering if he actually had Gods on his side, or if he thought to pass the Original Witches off as such to the humans.

He clapped his hands and smiled coldly at me as his voice boomed out, carrying to all those around us. "Come forth, my Goddesses."

I watched as Hannah's sisters moved to the front of the Mages. The moment they did, they sent a magical pulse searching through the crowd. They were the same Witches I had seen in Andrew's memory. I took in every detail of them, from the glow of their fingertips to their arms, where runes and magical spells had been written on their flesh.

Their eyes lingered on me before dismissing me as they surveyed the united army in all its glory. I'd painted runes on my skin, ones that concealed the immense power that I hadn't mastered hiding yet.

Their eyes remained on Zahruk and Ristan a little too long for my liking, but then again, they could probably sense the power both held.

"Destroy them all," the Mage leader hissed with something odd in his tone.

The Witches lifted their hands and weaved them in a wide pattern. The Fae behind me grunted in response and started to cover their ears as Hannah's sisters began to chant in sync. It was a spell of death. I brought my own hands up and slammed them down, brought them up again, and then pushed my palms out towards them.

I watched as their eyes widened, just before the small assembly was slammed against the walls of the Guild. The Fae behind me rose with little effort. I stepped forward, past the runes that the Mages had scattered on the ground to contain us. I smiled as the Mage in charge blinked in slow motion as I passed the wards meant to prevent Fae from entering or escaping, and ascended the steps to where they waited.

They'd known we were coming. They'd taken steps to ensnare any Fae who was bold enough to try and breach the Guild.

"Demi-Goddess does not a Goddess make," I said coldly. "Enough with your lies, Mage," I shouted, making sure those cameras heard my side. "Where are the real members of this Guild?"

"You cannot pass the runes!" he shouted, as if by telling me I'd passed them, I'd magically fall to my knees and give up.

I looked behind me, looked at him, and pointed to my feet. "Well I did, so obviously I can," I replied sarcastically as I noticed Callaghan, Ristan, Elijah, Lucian, and his men also walking through the Fae wards, picking up the ones that had been scattered on the ground and throwing them away. "Now, for the last time," I hissed. "Where are the real members of this Guild?" I repeated loudly.

"She's a Witch, she's mortal! Kill her!" he screamed, and I felt the Original Witches as they tried to peel through the layers of protection I wore to reveal what I was.

I turned and looked at them, watching as their eyes grew red with their chants as they tried to fight me off, or debilitate me.

"They can't kill me," I stated offhandedly. I watched as the sweat dripped from their brows as they continued chanting anyway. I dismissed them, turning my attention back to the Mage. I smiled coldly, flipped my hand, pushing outward, and enjoyed the sound of his body breaking as bones gave way inside of him. The moment he fell over, pain shot through my midsection, catching me off guard. My stomach seemed to heave as a sour taste filled my mouth and I glanced at the Original Witches, wondering if they could spell me or something. I caught a glimpse of Destiny as she watched me from the shadows. Her thick curls moved as she shook her head, and then she disappeared into the very shadows in which she had stood.

"Where is he?" I demanded of Hecate's daughters, who watched me with a worried look.

Hannah placed her hand on my shoulder and I turned to look at her. Gentle eyes moved from mine to her sisters, and she nodded in their direction. The

Mages sputtered with rage as the sisters moved to Hannah.

"Where is the King?" she asked them. They looked at her, as if they weren't sure they should answer. She allowed a sliver of power out and I swallowed as I felt it. She'd been holding it back, but the moment it was freed, they closed their eyes and smiled. "Where is the Horde King being held?" she repeated.

"He has been spelled, and they hold him in the bowels of this place. He is weakened, but he is unharmed. They have the building warded and spelled so that once the Fae are inside, they will not be able to escape; bombs filled with iron will detonate throughout the structure. This Guild will become a tomb. It is the Mages' failsafe in case they lost the Guild. Once the Fae are inside, a timer will start to count down."

"What else lies in wait for us?" I questioned, knowing that wasn't everything.

"Nothing that should be a problem for you, Goddess," one of the sisters offered quietly.

Pain was tearing me apart. It felt as if I was being ripped open from the inside out. The Mages were inching their way towards the doors. I raised my hand, flicked my wrist, and pushed down with both hands, hard. The Mages were smashed into the concrete; their bodies looked twisted and warped. More pain; this time I felt something break apart inside of me. As if something was detaching or eroding my organs.

"What else?" I demanded, trying to ignore the intense pain.

"Mages, a lot of them," she continued. "Some of

their strongest are hidden inside. Many are hidden among the corpses of the Guild's residents. They've set it up to look as if the Fae fought the Guild, and at the last minute, they sacrificed themselves to save mankind and the Guild. It's been staged to make the Fae look evil." Her meaning was clear. The Mages had staged several types of traps here. Some to trap and destroy the Fae; other's to woo the court of public opinion. "The King is in a chamber far below."

"Do you know if he is able to walk?" I asked.

"Doubtful; they rather enjoyed hurting him. We did add a spell to keep him awake, but I cannot say that we did not do anything else to him. If we hadn't, the Mages would have noticed. They wrapped chains that had been enchanted around him, and then they positioned quite a few Guild Enforcers that had been drugged in the chamber with him. Their plan was to have the King break free and rip the Enforcers apart. The other Guilds would condemn him for his actions and it would rally the humans to their cause. He was to take the fall for the mess here if the Mages couldn't hold it."

"And the children of this Guild, where are they?" I questioned.

"In the chamber with the King, so that when he grew weak, he would be unable to stop himself from feeding; he would feed off the innocent lives around him."

"You can go," I said with meaning. They didn't move, not even when I turned to the Horde.

"Goddess," Hannah called before I could step away from them.

"What?" I snapped, hating that once again, we'd look like monsters to the humans.

"They've spelled this place to prevent my sisters from leaving. I kept up my end of our agreement, please keep yours."

"I said I would get you to your sisters. I said I would allow you to leave this place, but I never agreed to help you do it." I could leave them here. I'd know right where they were, but I knew how they felt. I understood their anger and reasoning. They couldn't undo what they'd set into motion.

Hannah moved closer to where I stood and leaned close. She whispered into my ear and pulled away from me. I shivered and nodded at what she had said. I swallowed more pain as it tore through me, and turned to her sisters.

"Humans are off-limits; say it," I demanded.

"You don't know the evils they can do," one argued.

"I know exactly what they are capable of. I know who the real monsters are, and what they can do to us. We are not their judge or jury. What happened in the past is to stay in the past. If you bring about a war on their race, I will face you with them. This world has enough wars already, and murdering the descendants of those who wronged you isn't the answer. It won't bring them back, and it won't make you feel any better. It won't assuage the guilt you feel for losing them or being unable to save them. Trust me, nothing you do can bring them back. For every life you take, the Gods will take something from you, or at least that's what I kept being told. It's not worth the cost."

"You've never had to pick up the remains of your children's children when they've been cast into the woods like trash. I hope you never have to. We will not wage war on the entire race; the Fae will wage that war for us. They are drawn to those who hold immense power. That is enough for me, for now," one of the sisters said softly.

"I won't allow them to wage a war against the humans, ever."

"Good luck with that," she laughed with a wide grin.

"You are free, but remember, Hannah, I have eyes everywhere," I replied, ignoring the taunts coming from her sisters. "There is nowhere that you can hide that we cannot reach you."

"We are even," Hannah said softly.

"I'm sure we will meet again soon enough," I grumbled.

"When war comes to Faery, call on us," she said firmly. "You may not be of my line, but, for the love you bear for Larissa, I will forever be indebted to you and yours. Until we meet again, Goddess," she whispered and moved to her sisters as they vanished together as one.

My hands fisted at my sides as I moved back to the Fae, who observed me carefully. The pain had yet to let up, and every step was an effort to take. Once I was back to Ristan and Zahruk, I explained what waited for us inside.

"Ready?" I asked, unwilling to wait any longer to get Ryder back.

"The moment we cross the threshold, the timer starts counting down," Zahruk pointed out.

"Then there's the part about not getting out alive," Ristan added.

"And?" I asked, knowing that somehow, we'd survive this.

"And count me in." Ristan shrugged, watching me. "Sounds like fun times."

The moment we started towards the doors, all hell broke loose.

Chapter
TWENTY~NINE

The sisters hadn't been lying. Mages had been inside, waiting and listening to everything going on outside. The moment we breached the doors, energy balls sailed past us, hitting the walls around us. I erected a wall of magic as more were sent flying in our direction. I turned, catching sight of Zahruk as he beat against an invisible barrier that held him outside. Only Ristan, Lucian, his men, Callaghan, and the misfits had been able to cross the threshold in the initial charge. I scanned the floors until I caught sight of the runes preventing the Fae from entering. I used a pulse of magic to disturb the pattern that created the spell, forcing each rune to move from its perch to disrupt the magic and break the spell.

Once the Fae were inside, the clock started on the bombs. I withdrew my swords, watching as Zahruk and the rest of the Fae followed my lead. Lucian led his men to the other side of the reception chamber and nodded in my direction as his own nightmarish armor materialized; smaller blades that extended into long wicked ones appeared, gripped firmly in his hands.

I could smell death the moment the runes had been moved from their placement. The lifeless bodies of the Enforcers and Guild support staff littered the floor at odd angles, where they'd fought for their lives and lost. The sound of metal striking metal filled the Guild as I stood back, watching the army pour into the Guild and wage war against the Mages. The thick coppery scent of blood filled the evening air as I watched the fight unfolding.

When a Mage lunged at me, I deflected his blow easily, slowly moving him around in a circle until the wall protected my back. I swung my blades without warning, severing flesh from bone as the young Mage moved into an attack position, one that he would never be able to follow through with as his body slid apart, pooling on the floor in an awkward angle.

Ristan and Zahruk closed ranks, guarding me as we forced our way through the crowd that was fighting. Callaghan, Lucian and his men followed us deeper into the darkened Guild. I wasn't afraid of the darkness—I could see as clearly as if it was day—but the deeper we went, the more bodies we found. Some had been torn to pieces with bite marks around their throats.

The sisters hadn't been lying when they'd said Ryder was to be blamed for this. The marks left no other plausible conclusion. I could hear the screams of the Mages as the Horde and the rest of the army continued to infiltrate the Guild. They would feed well tonight on the bodies of our enemies. That was, if we survived the bombs.

"If the bombs go off with us inside," Zahruk started to warn, but I was aware of what it meant. The Fae could live through almost anything, but bombs with iron inside of them would debilitate them.

"I can get the bombs out if I know what we're looking for," Lucian offered and I stopped cold. He wasn't Fae.

"Do it," I ordered. I pointed to a few I'd noted on the way in, and his men moved into action. "Here, in the plants. Some are inside the walls; I can hear them ticking. I turned in time to watch as Zahruk swung his blades at a Mage that lunged at us from the shadows.

Both blades cut through muscle like butter, and Zahruk didn't so much as flinch as he wiped the blood off on the Mage's robes. He turned, his blue eyes scanned the shadows and, faster than my eyes could follow, he'd slid his swords into their sheaths that were harnessed to his back, trading them for daggers. Knives flew without warning, hitting their targets with a sickening thud that sent a shiver rushing through me.

"Have your people comb the planters and any nooks and other hidden areas," I whispered to Lucian as we started back down the long, winding hallways of the Guild.

No sooner had we started our push forward, when more Mages converged on our location with weapons and magic. I slid out of the way, watching as the men fought against them as I held my stomach as more pain ripped through me. Something was wrong with me, but I didn't know what, or how to stop it.

"Synthia," Zahruk growled, forcing me to look up into his electric blue eyes.

"I'm fine, let's keep moving," I lied.

I wondered if it was the cost of meddling; for the lives I'd taken here. We moved through room after room, clearing it in haste as we descended into the

Guild. I could sense Lucian's men, removing the hidden bombs as fast as they could.

Another warded doorway blocked us, and in moments I had it open using Andrew's memories. We moved through it, finding remains of Fae who weren't dead, but they weren't exactly alive either. Some had been dissected, their stomachs cut wide open so that the Mages could watch how their insides worked. Zahruk issued orders in an angry tone, forcing some of the Fae who had followed us to collect those who had been experimented on, and take them to the front of the Guild, where the Fae who waited just outside of the threshold would take them back to Faery.

We were working against a clock, one that we had no idea when it would go off. The grunts of the Fae echoed all around us, and the smell of rotting corpses was pungent down here. The rich scent of the earth around us did little to hide the smell of decaying flesh.

The last room we entered was full of small bodies. I paused, hating the tears that filled my eyes as I stared at their innocent faces. My hands shook with the waste of life, the innocents that had been wiped out for just being in the way of the Mages.

"They're alive," Ristan exclaimed in surprise as he knelt down and touched a little girl's cheek. "They're alive; we need to get them out of here."

"Start moving them, now," I ordered, watching as both Ristan and Zahruk jumped into action. They sifted in and out, scooping up the children and moving them to the front of the Guild, where others would help take the little ones to safety. Once the last child had been moved I turned to Ristan. "There has to be a faster way. The Witches warned us that this was a trap to keep the Fae inside the Guild once they had gotten in. It looks like you guys can sift inside the building, but I'm not sure the Fae can sift out. I need for you to find and destroy whatever is keeping us inside this place."

"On it," the Demon said as he sifted out.

Zahruk, Callaghan, and I moved to the back of the chamber, where we found Ryder. He was chained to a table with thick coils of chain forged from iron. The Mages must have removed the God bolts just before they came out to confront me and the army. The unconscious Enforcers lay on the floor surrounding the table. I swallowed as I took in his unmoving form. Even from where I stood, I could smell the iron that they'd forced inside of him. I rushed forward, unable to stop myself as I touched him.

His skin was ice cold, and yet the moment I touched his face, he thrashed against it. He growled as saliva laced with blood dripped from his mouth. Wild eyes met mine and he calmed a little, and yet, he didn't fully stop fighting to break free from the chains.

"Ryder." I pulled at the chain crisscrossing his chest, managing to tug it free. "It's me, Fairy," I crooned as I lowered my face and kissed his temple.

"Synthia," Zahruk warned, sensing something was wrong.

My eyes looked at the discarded chains and then back to Ryder, who watched me with mistrust in his eyes. He looked wild, untamed…like a true beast bred to kill anything that got too close to him. He was tracking every movement I made as I moved closer, and my heart raced with apprehension.

No God bolts held him here, and yet those chains wouldn't have been able to hold him alone. So why hadn't he escaped? He stood slowly, sleek muscles moving as perspiration beaded on them.

I took a step back, away from him. Zahruk moved in front of him, catching his attention and, before I could do anything, Ryder struck him, sending him sailing across the room without warning. Zahruk hit the wall with a loud thump, and slid down it. I trembled as my eyes moved back to the man before me.

He was trapping me, cutting off any chance of escape as he herded me into a corner. I saw Callaghan moving into position to attack, and shook my head at him to tell them to stand down. I heard the others as they came rushing down the corridor and hallway, but I shook my head as they watched Ryder push me up against the wall.

He growled; the sound was inhuman and heartbreaking as the fingers of one hand extended into claws and ripped at my armor before retracting again. Strong hands found one breast as the other pushed against my throat, stopping my air flow. He wasn't my Ryder, he was a monster, experimented on, tortured, and left for dead with enough iron in him to kill a hundred Fae.

"Ryder," I gasped, using what precious little air I had left to reach him. I felt him loosening his hold, but only enough that I wouldn't pass out. He used his knee to part my legs as he pressed his growing cock against my stomach.

His hand hurt my breast; I could feel his claws sliding across my skin as they extended. The pressure more than I could stand, I cried out, but my eyes gave silent warning for the men across the room to remain where they are. I could get away, but something was forcing me to stay with him. To not give up; telling me that my Ryder was inside the monster that, even then, was licking my neck as if priming it to sample it.

The moment his teeth entered the flesh of my collarbone, I cried out, which made him hesitate and pull away from my neck. I lifted my legs, wrapping them around his waist and using his own body to push his upper torso away from me.

"Ryder, come back to me," I pleaded. His hands rose, capturing my face as his mouth curved into a dangerous smile. His lips touched mine, but it was primal. His teeth scraped my lip, breaking the soft flesh as he kissed me like a starving man who hadn't touched flesh in decades. I moaned against him, tears sliding down my face as he pulled on my hair, tilting my face until he had full access. His tongue delved inside, capturing mine as his teeth scraped me. I felt him growing larger; his cock throbbed against my belly as he rubbed against it, needing to feed.

It hit me then. He was starving. He hadn't fed from the children, so he was just what he looked like: A starving beast! I pulsed with power, forcing it into his system, forcing out the iron, as the men behind us gave warning. I felt his hands as he grabbed my waist, intending to drive that cock deep into my welcoming depths. The moment I thought we'd end up giving his brothers a bird's eye view into our sex life, he paused. His mouth moved slower, deeper, and unforgiving in its conquest to claim ownership.

I felt his claws retract, and his cock slowly deflated as golden flecks returned to his obsidian eyes.

I swallowed a cry as I wrapped my arms around his naked form and cried.

"Synthia, you need to get away, now," Ristan ordered, not understanding what was happening.

"He is in there, I know it," I whispered. "He's coming back."

"He could hurt you," he argued.

He'd handed over the pain to the beast. It was his way of escaping what they had been doing to him, but he was still inside there. He was becoming gentler with me, and yet he was struggling to control whatever it was that was holding him back. The beast was dominant, but so was Ryder. When he pulled his mouth away from me, I reclaimed it hungrily.

I rained kisses over his face as he tried again to pull away from my mouth. I fed him enough power to run a small city, but nothing brought back the burning amber gaze I was searching for in his inky depths.

"I love you," I sobbed as tears slid down my cheeks. I closed my eyes against the denial that maybe I'd lost him. Maybe he was the price I would pay for coming to save him. "I love you so much, Ryder," I whimpered as pain continued to tear me apart. "Come back to me, Fairy. Come home."

"Pet," he growled thickly as he wiped the blood from his mouth, on my shredded armor. I opened my eyes and cried out as golden eyes met my hopeful stare.

"I'm going to kick your fucking ass, Fairy," I cried as I wrapped my arms around him as he held me tightly. "I was so afraid I'd lost you," I whimpered, exhausted from the fight to get him back. We still weren't out of the woods yet.

"I sensed you in this room; tell me I wasn't crazy," he whispered as he kissed my tears away.

"I'll tell you all about it, but right now we have to get out of here." I was sensing the fighting above was dying down. "We have to go, now." As Ryder's armor materialized around his body, I pulled away and stood up, only to double over in agony.

"Synthia?" Zahruk barked, stepping closer as Ryder also struggled to stay upright. "She's hurt." But I wasn't, at least not wounded in the way Zahruk thought I might be. He searched me for blood, and found none. I tried to stand on my own and felt wetness between my legs, slowly saturating the leggings of the armor as it descended. "What the hell?" Zahruk picked me up as he scented the blood that was making its way down my legs.

"I'm fine, help Ryder," I demanded. "We have to get out of here before those bombs go off."

"Bombs?" Ryder asked, and I shook my head.

"Not now, we don't have time." I wrapped my arms around my stomach as Callaghan pulled Ryder's arm around his shoulder, supporting him while Zahruk carried me. We took off, racing through the hallways and back out the way we'd come. Luckily, Ristan had been successful in removing the spells that the Mages had cast to hold the Fae inside the structure of the Guild.

Once outside, the ground shook. The bombs in the lower levels that Lucian and his men hadn't found detonated one by one, until the top floor erupted in deafening noise and explosions. I began to fall as strong hands wrapped around my waist and took me to the ground, covering my body with his.

I stared into Zahruk's unblinking eyes as debris rained down around our bodies. I turned my head, finding golden eyes watching me with worry. Lucian shouted something to Ryder, but I couldn't hear him. I was falling, as if I couldn't stop myself as my eyes watched stars burst behind my eyelids.

I'd done it; he was out and alive. I felt the exhaustion as it slammed against me. I let my heavy eyes close as the pain took me over the edge to oblivion.

Chapter
THIRTY

"How far along was she?" Ryder's voice pulled me from sleep. I blinked, barely aware of where I was.

"Not very far along at all, but with how much she was pushing herself, I'm not surprised she didn't notice it," Eliran answered.

I closed my eyes, listening as they spoke around me. Ryder was in bed with me, his arms wrapped around my body, holding me tightly. Those arms were more comforting than a thousand narcotics. They took the pain away, kept it at arm's length. This man was worth whatever the Gods demanded in price.

"And will she heal?" Ryder's tone was soothing as I drifted between sleep and wakefulness.

"She's already healing at a rapid rate. It's incredible how fast she heals, faster than any of us can."

"Will she be able to have more?" Ryder enquired hesitantly, and I blinked.

"More what?" I asked without meaning to. Exhaustion made my tone more irritable than I'd intended to sound. I'd known I'd pushed my body to its limits. I'd remained alert and awake the entire time he'd been away from me. I was still exhausted, tired to the point that I couldn't keep my eyes open.

"Children," murmured said with a hint of anger in his tone.

"Huh?" I was confused as to why it would matter at this moment in time. "Why are you even asking that? Of course we can, but not right now." I opened my eyes to find him leaning over me, studying me.

"You miscarried, Pet," he explained softly. "You were pregnant." He squeezed me for comfort as I closed my eyes and swallowed.

"I wasn't pregnant; I couldn't be."

"You were; you were at least a few weeks along, judging by the size of the child. Remember, Fae pregnancies are shorter than human ones, and who knows how fast gestation will be now that you are a Goddess. That's why you lost so much blood and blacked out. We had to wait for your body to heal itself, because nothing I did helped; in fact, it made it worse. You lost a lot of blood, and you've been out for days." Eliran's voice, as always, was gentle and calming.

"How many days?" I asked woodenly.

"Three," Ryder answered as he lightly kissed my forehead. "I called for Danu, but she didn't respond. We had done everything we could think of to wake you up, and Eliran tried to stop the miscarriage but nothing worked. I'm sorry, Synthia."

I blinked back tears as I heard the pain in his tone. I struggled to sit up, but I was still exhausted. "It's the price the Gods demanded," I whispered. "To get you back, I had to meddle with the human world. I interfered directly with that world. I killed in it. I was warned that there would be a price if I did it." A sob ripped from my chest as I turned to look at him. "I didn't know; I didn't have any idea that I was pregnant. I was so stressed out, and I couldn't think past getting you back."

"You had no idea that you were pregnant?" Eliran blurted, his eyes filled with disbelief. "You were a few weeks along. Haven't you had a cycle since the triplets were born? There should have at least been some symptoms."

"I haven't had one since I got pregnant with the triplets." I blushed as I looked at Ryder. "You knocked me up again?" I glared. "I thought we had a talk about that?" I'd lost a baby, one I hadn't even known existed. "I don't…I don't feel anything," I cried as guilt washed over me. I didn't feel sorry for the loss, or that I'd sacrificed it for Ryder. "How…why don't I feel anything?"

"Because I blocked the pain *they* wanted you to feel," Destiny commented from the doorway, forcing all eyes to her. "You didn't do this for a selfish reason. What you did, you did out of blind love, and Danu asked me to protect you because you have a bigger purpose to serve, should you agree to it. I can't have you messing up my plans."

"Your plans?" I repeated, noting how Ryder's arms pulled me closer.

"I need you to come with me, please. There's someone who wants to say goodbye," she sniffed softly, tears shining in her eyes.

"She's leaving, isn't she?" I tried to force the heaviness in my heart to remain out of my voice.

"Yes, she is. We don't have time to waste if you wish to see her," Destiny explained softly. "You will have lifetimes to cherish your beast, but I'm afraid it's time to say goodbye to your mother."

I rose up enough to sit, leaned over, and kissed Ryder on his forehead. "I'll be right back," I assured him as I started to get out of bed, not caring that I was naked. I felt soft cashmere covering my body as I struggled to stand and gave Ryder a smile of thanks as I accepted Destiny's hand and we vanished.

~~*

Danu lay on a chaise in a brilliantly lit garden that was filled with rare, exotic flowers that I'd never seen before. The buds covered the lush greenery, creating a glow effect for each rare flower. To the left of the garden was a sparkling pool, lotus blossoms and lilies floated on its surface, and without asking, I knew she'd created Faery to mirror her own lush, magical garden. The buds of the flowers opened, released an intoxicating fragrance into the air, and closed.

"Beautiful, are they not?" she asked, and I noticed the sun shining on her beautiful face.

"I don't care about your damn flowers," I growled without managing to hide the fear in my tone. "I can't lose you; I just got you. I don't accept that there's no way to save you."

"You're not losing me." She shifted to get a better

look at me. She looked just like me. Platinum curls fell below her shoulders, and azure blue eyes locked with mine. "You're my daughter." She laughed, but it sounded forced. "Where do you think your beauty came from?"

"This is the real you, no magic?" I questioned, taken aback by how much we looked alike. I moved to a large rock that had a smooth surface and sat beside her.

"Over the years, there have been a handful of beings who have known my true form. You are now one of them. I can no longer use glamour," she explained, waving it off as if she'd just said there would be no rain tomorrow or something mundane. "I've lost the ability to use magic as well. Destiny said I have only a short time left, so I sent for you. I was told of the loss you suffered for interfering to save your intended mate, and I am sorry for that. No mother should lose a babe, but we knew telling you of the child wouldn't have made much difference. You are my daughter, after all."

"Destiny told me she stopped me from feeling the loss," I replied.

"She is still blocking the emotion you should be feeling with the miscarriage," she confessed. "I asked her to do it, but then again, I have something to ask of you. Something that is selfish, but facing mortality is something I'm finding is worse than death."

"You and your riddles," I mused. "You knew this would happen, so why do it? Why pick me over yourself?"

"I'm a Goddess, yes, but I am your mother," she said, as if it made sense. "I would do it again in a heartbeat. You're my creation, and my most treasured one, at that. I sacrificed my life for you, but also Faery by loving you enough to save your children. They were the key to fixing it, yes, but also the key to undoing it. The prophecy didn't show us exactly what could happen, or why it would. They are tied to both lands, therefore the key to fracturing the portals. They triggered it the moment they drew breath into their lungs, but it's not the end of Faery. You are Faery, Synthia. It will live as long as you do, even if it is unstable right now."

"Can't they be closed?"

"No, but Faery won't merge with Tèrra, not as you think it will. Faery has been opened to Tèrra, but as it draws from their world to heal itself, it is also healing the damage they have done to their own world in return. Eventually, a solution will present itself; speak to the Stag, he will guide you. Enough about that," she crooned, switching direction and interrupting my train of thought. "My time is near, and I must ask you something of great importance."

She leaned over and whispered into my ear. I closed my eyes as tears rushed to them, burning them as what she asked sent my world spiraling around me. I nodded and pulled away.

"Yes," I agreed without having to consider it.

"I love you, Synthia. I will always love you. I'll always be with you. I promise you that. In everything you do, and everything you are," she assured me as she nodded at Destiny. I looked at Destiny as she nodded and smiled at me.

"We must hurry; say your goodbyes, ladies," she ordered.

Chapter
THIRTY~ONE

I made my way through the lush grasses of the glen, as the sound of one of the streams that fed the Fairy Pools became louder. It was calm here, and so beautiful; the memories of this place were ingrained in my head. This was where Ryder took me after the Wild Hunt, where we were first together. This was where we made love, if you could call it that. Our first time had been savage, but then everything with Ryder was. He was alpha male to his core, and I loved that about him. I'd wanted it, even though I'd been terrified of accepting what he made me feel.

He'd made me face my feelings, made me accept what I'd been terrified to admit. Our relationship had started out turbulent; the most hair-raising rollercoaster ride imaginable. Although this path hadn't been an easy one, I couldn't imagine life without him.

When I'd lost him, I hadn't been able to breathe. He was my air, the very stuff I needed to live. We'd faced losses, battles, and so much more together. Death had tried, and lost against us. The price for being together hadn't been easy to pay, but it had been worth every hardship we'd faced to be together.

"I hate to disappoint you, but this won't work. Not like this." Ristan shook his head as he surveyed the landscape surrounding the Faery Pools. "It will leave us exposed. We can't guarantee that it wouldn't be attacked. I have a different location in mind for the ceremony. As far as the reception goes, your idea does have some merit."

"Just some?" I shot him an offended look as he shrugged. "The honeymoon. Now that's what I'm looking forward to." I grinned as I gave him an exaggerated wink, which made him snort.

"I'm just glad you planned to have your honeymoon away from the castle," he replied as he smirked knowingly. "Gods know when you two go at it, the entire power grid and magical field around the castle is high voltage."

"You can feel it?" I gasped.

"What did you expect, Flower? You're a Goddess of Faery; your mother is a fertility Goddess. When you two fuck, even the flowers feel it. Last night, they bloomed. You know, the ones that only open once a year were awakened by the power you two gave off. The willows wept, and the animals—don't even get me started on what they did together. When you're happy, the land feels it, but when you mate, so too does the land around you. You're a part of it." He pushed some of his hair away from his face and looked back at the glen. "Have you heard from her lately?" he asked uncomfortably.

"Yes. I saw her briefly yesterday," I said softly. I watched a line in his brow crease, as if my words touched a nerve. "Will you ever tell me what you had with her?"

"It's complicated," he muttered, turning away from me.

"I got that much figured out, Demon. You love her, though," I said, watching him. His shoulders tensed and I smiled. He had loved her, at least he did until whatever it was between them had come to a boil. I had no doubt that he loved Olivia with everything he had to give, but at one time or another, he had been in love with Danu.

"She gave me a child," he shrugged offhandedly. "One I will spend the rest of eternity wondering if it is really mine or hers."

"It is yours, and I can tell you what it is if you'd like," I offered. More often than not, I was discovering my new powers by accident. How I knew what the sex was, I wasn't sure. Perhaps it was because their child was tied to our land, and I was tied to the baby through it.

"You know what we're having?" He turned around and stared at me with a closed-off expression. "How can you know for sure it's ours and not another seed she planted?"

"Because the baby is part Demon and part Angel," I explained. "Oh, I'm pretty sure she could have shaken up a Dangel cocktail, but why would she? It doesn't make any sense why she would do something like that rather than to give you back what was taken from you. Your baby is tied to the land, as you are. By the way, the baby doesn't like the pickles Olivia keeps eating. I can't blame it, though. She's been dipping them in hot sauce and peanut butter."

He smirked and nodded. "She's had some wild cravings."

"Pickles in hot sauce and peanut butter are mild in comparison to her craving for a human heart. I'm going to guess, and say that the little Demon is growing with a hankering for blood. Although, her reaction to having such a craving was fucking awesome," I laughed as I caught the grimace on his face. "It's yours; Danu wouldn't do that to you. She told me she fixed it because she owed you some debt."

"A debt," he snorted. "That is sort of a mild way of simplifying it, and I am not quite sure you understand what Danu would and would not do," he growled as his eyes turned hard. "I was her lover. Well, one of them."

"I figured that out a while ago, but what I don't know is why you hate her so much." I dipped my toes into the soothing pools.

"I don't hate her." He tilted his head back, as though he was taking comfort from the warmth of the sun, and sighed. "I may be angry with her and resent what she has done to me, but I can't hate her. I was bound to her, and yes, I loved her. For almost eight hundred years, she put me through hell. Any female I cared for, or could have possibly even loved, she killed," he gritted out, and my blood turned to ice.

"I'm sorry," I murmured, carefully watching him. "I can't understand why she would do that to you. The only thing I know is that she isn't like we are. I'm just beginning to understand the things that she was responsible for and the choices she had to make. Most of what I have seen so far is pretty fucked up. She also let you go, Ristan. She let you find love with Olivia, and if you had loved another, you wouldn't be where you are today. Maybe Destiny is right; maybe everything we go through is so that when the pieces fall into place, we are ready for them. Look at me and Ryder: I wanted to punch him in the throat when I first met him. Now, I can't imagine my world without him."

"Flower, she didn't *let* me find love with Olivia, she was trying to kill her, Cyrus just succeeded in the act. I demanded for Danu to release me from her service. I was at my limit as to what I could take from her, and honestly, I think she feared what I would do if she didn't release me. I know a good deal of what was going on, yet there was a lot that I was never allowed to see. She wouldn't let me help her. I would have, had she asked. Instead she used me as a tool; albeit a very useful tool. Loyal, so fucking loyal," he said as he shook his head grimly. "But she wouldn't, or couldn't reciprocate that sense of loyalty. She knew how I felt, and I must admit, my centuries with her had many good times. But the bad moments were horrific. She would disappear for long periods of time, sometimes years, then suddenly appear and demand attention. That was when I would see the other side of her. Imagine making love with someone," he snorted. "One minute they would be with me, and the next their body would be taken over by an irate Goddess who decided that I was paying too much attention to that someone. That I cared too much for someone other than her, and then watch her cut their body to ribbons as I begged her to stop. That is just one of the things she would do to me. Another favorite trick of hers was taking over a body and using it to fuck me, only to have the consciousness of that person wake up when I'm buried inside of her, and she's begging me to stop as if I raped her. It happened more times than I care to admit, and forgiving her for that isn't easy," he chuckled darkly. "Alden and I being captured was just fallout from her fucking with me. Bilé also had a hand in the fun and games with my balls at the Guild because I *'smelled of her'* and I was disinclined to tell him why."

"You must have felt like you were taking a big chance helping me," I murmured, and my throat tightened at his stiff nod.

"Oftentimes I would get a warning before she struck. It seemed odd that she was almost encouraging me to look out for you, and I figured it was because you were meant for my brother." He shook his head sadly. "When I found out you were her daughter, it all made sense."

"Why didn't you say anything to me?"

"To what end? What good would have come from it? You're still so new to this world and learning to navigate it." He breathed out heavily. "You were so happy having not one, but two mothers all of a sudden. I didn't want to taint anything for you by trying to explain how benevolent your mother could be and at the same time, how malevolent she could be. Two extreme faces of the same coin," he explained.

I swallowed the lump in my throat as I looked at him. Danu and Ristan had a rocky relationship, but I knew she had to have loved him back, because she'd used her limited power to right her wrong the only way she knew how.

"I guess giving you back what you lost was the only way she thought she could even begin to make things right," I sighed. Danu certainly wasn't the easiest of beings, that was for sure. "Thank you for telling me; I know it couldn't have been easy," I said softly. "Have you told Olivia about Danu?"

"No, she knows something is off when others ask

me about Danu or my visions. It's not something that is easy to talk about, but eventually she is going to have to know."

"Yeah, that's sort of a big thing. Keeping secrets or withholding something like that is a time bomb. You better tell her; sooner rather than later." I watched the fairies dance across the glen, pop up, and then dive bomb the Fairy Pools. Iridescent wings touched the water, skimming the serene surface and creating a brilliant glow as fairy dust settled across the water.

"Tonight is your wedding; we shouldn't be stuck in the past. I'd like you to keep the sex of my child to yourself for now. Olivia is old-fashioned; she prefers to remain unaware until the birth. Unless there's some secret," he said, giving me a sharp glance. "Like quadruplets or something, I'd like to give her a heads up about something like that."

"There's only one in there," I laughed.

"How are you feeling about your loss?" His hand slipped into mine as we walked through the glen.

"I don't feel anything," I admitted. "Destiny numbed my emotions regarding it, and so far I haven't been able to mourn for it, even though I know I should. I wasn't even aware that I was pregnant, so I'm sort of having trouble wrapping my head around it. I know we'll have more children when the time is right. Sooner or later, we will face the Mages. I hope to be a part of that fight, and not have it be seen as interfering or meddling."

"Synthia, if you have to pay a price each time you interfere…" he warned.

"I don't, not when they are here, in this world.

Destiny was clear about that. If they threaten Faery, it is my fight. The Guild will be a challenge, but with the Guilds falling, it's needed more than ever. There has to be a balance kept. I can lead, but I cannot be hands-on. We will need to start recruiting as well. Speaking of which, you heard Callaghan has other Paladins who might be interested in helping. I think it a wise step to bring them on board with us."

"Hmm, I have also heard rumor that Foul has gone missing." He smiled. "You wouldn't know where he is, would you?"

"Of course not," I smirked. "Did you know some Fae eat other Fae?" I asked innocently as I watched his lips twitch into a blinding smile.

"You don't say," he drawled with mock surprise, then laughed. "You're evil, Flower." He released my hand and turned towards me. "Let's get back to the castle so we can get you ready to marry my brother. Lucky fucker probably doesn't deserve something like you. I knew you'd be good for both Faery and Ryder the day I let you escape—not to mention—I got to kiss the bride before she even knew there'd be a wedding. Even though I saw parts of what would happen in Ryder's future, I wish I could have been shown things that I could have prevented."

"Like cutting me open?" I teased, and watched an evil grin spread across his face.

"No…no, that part I wouldn't change," he laughed as I slapped his arm.

"Asshole," I giggled.

"Okay, maybe that part. I'd like to think we could have prevented that, then again, we wouldn't have a

Goddess in our midst. I think you're right; sometimes the pieces have to be allowed to fall where they land so that we can get to where we need to be."

"You know something, Demon?" I asked and waited for him to look at me before I continued. "You talk too fucking much. Get my ass home; I need to paint my nails so I can marry my beast."

"Oh yeah, what color?" he smirked.

"*Getting Nadi On My Honeymoon*." I chuckled when he made a face.

"And what color is that?"

"Pink; it's pretty, and your brother will ask me what color it is too, because he's been learning to judge my moods from my nails."

"Smart man," he said.

"I agree; that's why I'm planning to keep him forever."

"Forever is a very long time."

"Forever with that man will never be long enough."

Chapter
THIRTY~TWO

I was a fucking mess. I was bouncing from foot to foot as my nerves flared. I was worried, ticking off a list inside my head of what could go wrong tonight. Ristan kept frowning at me, certain I would ruin his plans with the wild look in my eyes.

"Calm down," he chuckled softly. "You have nothing to fear tonight, Flower; your Fairy God-Brother has this shit handled."

"What if he changes his mind?" I snapped, my palms sweating from a nasty combination of nerves mixed with fear. I had a lead ball in my stomach, and my heart seemed to be stuck in my throat.

"He would never change his mind about you," he replied softly. "He's as much of a mess as you are." He absently raised Olivia's hand and kissed it. The gesture was so sweet; it had me freaking out all over again.

"She looks like she is going to throw up," Olivia worried aloud. "Do something, Ristan."

"I'm trying, minx." He patted her hand

reassuringly. "Talk to me, Flower," he urged.

"Madisyn isn't out there," I whispered as I worried my bottom lip. "They didn't come because I killed their son."

"He was an evil fucker; they knew that," he offered.

"They're my parents; I have no one here for me. No one, just Adam," I whispered, as if someone would overhear it.

"I think you're going to be surprised if that is your worry," Olivia worried with a gentle smile. "I'm going to go take my place, Demon. My feet are killing me."

"Kiss me," he demanded softly, and I watched as he kissed her gently, as if he was afraid she'd break if he touched her too hard.

When she was gone, he turned and looked at me pointedly. "It is time to get you into the dress."

"Fine, but I swear to the Gods I will rip someone's throat out if he isn't at the end of that aisle when I walk out of this room."

He laughed and shook his head. He'd created a little pavilion with cloth walls. It awarded us privacy as I dealt with my panic attack. I'd never been so nervous in my entire life. Fighting Mages I could handle with my eyes closed, but this? This was ridiculous. I felt as if I was going to implode.

He startled me when his hand touched my shoulder and he turned me to face him. The makeshift tent smelled of fresh peaches, which Ristan had decided would be my perfume. He smiled when I frowned at him.

"I can't create a masterpiece if you can't hold still," he growled, stepping back and releasing me. "I'm thinking something not so elaborate and poufy, because you're you. Something pretty, but not too long," he mumbled as he tilted his head from one side to the other. "That's it. Beautiful." He nodded approvingly when he'd picked whatever design he'd settled on inside his head. I placed my hands on my hips and was about to speak, when the air snapped with magic and wrapped around me as the soft fabric skimmed across my flesh.

I looked down, finding myself dressed in a beautiful Grecian style wedding gown. It was a stunning dress; vintage and white, with a V-neckline and lace flowers at the midsection and shoulders. It was backless, and had an A-line waist with a gauzy chiffon skirt that fell in soft folds and swirled when I moved. Delicate ruffles edged the hem of it. It wasn't extravagant, but it was amazing and everything I wanted.

I smiled and looked up at the Demon. It was perfect, and the length was something I could deal with. I was barefoot; instead of shoes, delicate silver anklets glittered around my ankles. I grinned, thankful that he understood how I wanted to marry my beast. Just as I am. I really didn't want some over-the-top wedding; it just wasn't me.

I wanted to be at the glen, in my bare feet, without any makeup on my face. I wanted it to be basic, no fuss or fanfare. Barebones, as Ryder called it. Just the bare essentials.

I tilted my head, feeling the cool breeze as it touched my ass. I frowned and stared at Ristan, who grinned a little naughtier than I liked.

I felt smooth fabric covering my ass, and I frowned at Ristan as he smirked, although it didn't seem as if he was looking at me. He was concentrating on whatever I now wore beneath the dress. I felt chains as they wrapped around the lower edge of my tummy, delicate ones that made a soft chiming noise as I moved. The panties felt like they were barely there, hardly enough to cover much up.

"Demon," I warned, wondering what it was that he'd done.

"The man deserves that ass wrapped in a bow. After everything you two have been through? You are being served up as a very enticing, pretty present. Besides, it's my reputation as a Fairy God-Brother on the line here, Flower. Can't have them not talking about it, right?" he laughed.

"My hair?" I asked, and he grinned.

"All in good time." He patted my shoulder. "First, jewelry," he said, and started to wave his magic fingers. I felt pressure on my arms as the silver bands of royalty wrapped around my upper biceps, silver bangle bands with the Dragons of Ryder's crest engraved on them. Small, thin silver bracelets that made music when I moved my arms encircled my wrist. I smiled, liking the direction he was moving in. If his Demon gig didn't work out, he could always be a stylist.

He dragged two fingers along my collarbone in a 'V' motion and around my neck, and trailed them down my back, leaving behind a necklace that was simple, yet beautiful. The design was very art deco and probably worn around 1912 or so. It was made up of cushion and oval shaped aquamarines that were joined together with tiny diamonds and silver wing-like shapes that comprised the chain of the necklace. Trailing from the clasp of the necklace in the back was a string of diamonds, which trailed down to the arch of my ass.

"Move on to the crown and hair; I want to see Ryder," I laughed when he stared a little bit too long at the jewels. Any more and I'd never make it down the aisle. His fingers moved, curling my hair as he tied it up and piled it atop my head with tiny flowers mixed into the curls. The crown was a simple platinum band, and in the center was the Blood Kingdom's mark carved from a ruby.

He tilted his head and then wiggled his fingers again, and when I looked down to see what he'd changed, the aquamarines in the necklace matched the ruby on my crown.

"Do you think they will come?" I blurted anxiously.

"I think they don't blame you for your brother. He was evil long before you were born. They've been quiet, and I have a feeling that they mourn him no matter what he was, or what he became. They were his parents," he said softly, his frown increasing as he wiggled his fingers again, and my ears were weighed down slightly. I brought my hand up, touching the chandelier earrings that I was sure matched the necklace and crown. "Done; it's time, Flower. Adam is waiting to walk you down the aisle."

"Tell him I am ready," I replied, turning to look in the mirror. "Oh wow," I whispered as I took in the beautiful bride who looked back at me. "You really rock at being a Fairy God-Brother."

"Thanks, remember that," he chuckled as he

blurred and sifted from the tent-like structure and Adam entered it a few moments later.

"I was waiting outside…oh wow," Adam stammered, as he took in my reflection. "This makes three times now that you've gotten ready for a wedding," he said. "I think you get prettier with each one, but this, this is perfection at its best."

"You look pretty good too." I smiled as I took in his kilt and sash. "Same outfit as you wore for our wedding."

"Couldn't let it go to waste, after all; my glamour isn't spot-on yet. So, let's do this, baby girl." He grinned with a mischievous wink and offered me his arm.

I slipped my arm through his and swallowed as I fought to calm the nerves and butterflies that assaulted me. I stepped from the tent and gasped. The forest was alive with the glitter of a thousand pixies. Small jars hung from the trees, tiny pixies inside of them dancing as their dust lit the jar, giving it a colorful glow.

The lush green forest was carpeted with flowers of every color. The ground that I walked on was covered in blood red roses. Kahleena giggled and tears filled my eyes as I took in her red dress, which was more ruffle and fluff than any girl should ever have to wear.

I knelt down, held my arms out, and caught her as she rushed into them. I hadn't seen her for days, and each moment had been torture.

"Oh, my sweet baby," I whispered as I pulled back and looked into the golden eyes that were so much like her father's. "You're beautiful." I swallowed, trying not to cry. I stood up, looking for the boys.

"They're with your father and Ryder," Adam offered. I smiled and held out my arm, only to watch as Adam froze in place, along with Kahleena. I searched the area and my blood ran cold as I felt myself falling.

Chapter
THIRTY-THREE

I landed on my feet in a room that had huge fires burning at different locations within it. Flames leapt from the giant cauldrons, and men and women walked around, talking and drinking and in a subdued way, almost looked like they were enjoying a party, until they noticed me decked out in my wedding finery.

"Oh, come on!" I growled as I stomped forward, sensing Destiny before I saw her at the front of the rather large crowd. "I was getting married!" I snapped, and then paused as I noticed the blood that was spattered across her robes. Her nose dripped with blood, as if she'd been in a fight recently.

"Synthia," Destiny said in a meek tone I'd never heard her use before. She turned to stare at a man who watched me as I slowly walked forward. My every move was accompanied by a faint chiming sound. The delicate jewelry I wore announced every move I made. "It is time for you to meet our King," she murmured softly as she nodded towards a beautiful man, who watched me with chocolate brown eyes. There was a radiant glow that emanated from him that almost hurt my eyes. "He has been known by many names. Some have known him as Atum, others have worshipped him as Chaos…he was there in the beginning. The first of us."

His hair was a white-blonde shade, reminiscent of the color of the sandy shores of the Caribbean. He was bronzed, as if he spent entire days upon those beaches, and the ozone that wafted from him spoke of immense, electrical power. I wasn't sure if I should curtsy or get on my knees.

"Why am I here?" I inquired, and winced as the people in the room erupted in chatter about me and my lack of manners.

"You will be silent until I allow it to be otherwise," Chaos or Atum, or whatever his name was, snapped. I decided his looks could cause chaos wherever he went but it sounded weird in my head to call him that. "She is very new, and definitely not Fae pretending to be one of us. Interesting; you look just like her. Danu has chosen to sacrifice her life for yours. In doing so, she has given you her life," he murmured, forcing me to strain my ears to hear him. "I thought you were like the others; Fae pretending to be a God to collect followers, and fast food."

"I have heard of Fae doing so, yes. I'm not one of them," I admitted.

"What do you intend to do with her sacrifice?" he asked, ignoring the Goddesses and Gods who snickered behind me.

"I plan to continue what she started. I want the Fae to stay where they belong: in Faery. I will do my best to keep her alive, no matter what the cost is. I understand that the Fae flooding the humans' realm is something that none of you want, and I intend to ensure that they don't stay there."

"You did not let them out; it should not be your problem," he responded, as though what I intended to do puzzled him. "Why do anything about it?"

"Because she is my mother, and they are her people. Because I was raised as a human and care about them too? Why wouldn't I try to keep the Fae in check?"

"Because it is Danu's problem, and easily fixed." A deep, sensuous voice called out behind me. I turned and looked at the speaker, and found the most beautiful blue eyes I'd ever seen in my entire life observing me.

"Easily fixed?" I asked.

"Who do you think neutralized her first race? She created Dragons and other creatures that were not bound to any one world, and they threatened many of the world's we Gods have created."

"Zeus, introduce yourself to our visitor," Atum admonished.

"Zeus," he said briskly.

"Synthia," I greeted with a firm nod. "I am aware of the first race, but I wasn't aware that you helped her put them down. The Fae think she made them turn on each other." He gave me a condescending look, as though he pitied me.

"Most of them were put down, but not all of them. Then she created the High Fae and the rest of the castes and creatures and bound them to Faery. She failed to bring it to us, or to disclose what she had done. Those ancient beings share a world with you," he said softly with a wicked smile as he took in the look of confusion in my eyes.

"And you're sure of it?" I asked.

"Do you think I lie?"

"I don't pretend to know you, or if you would lie. What I do know is that I have been told by multiple beings that if Faery dies, all of the creatures of that world will try and jump to the world that is intended for humans. If that happens, both worlds will be destroyed. I grew up in that world and I think she wanted me there so I could care about the humans too. She wanted me to appreciate both worlds, so I intend to do my best to stop the destruction of Faery and look for a way to heal that world. I will, to the best of my ability, try and police the Fae who have escaped and have them comply with the laws of the Horde, as well as try to keep the remaining Fae in Faery."

"Do you intend to keep your mother alive as well?" Atum interrupted.

I stared at him and considered why he was entertaining this line of questioning. Was it some kind of test? I chewed my lip and tilted my head.

"If I could, I would," I admitted. "Frankly, I think the reason she is dying is bullshit."

I heard the other Gods begin to argue that I should be punished or banished, but Atum remained silent, staring at me with curiosity.

"It is a rare girl who would stand in front of a King and speak what is on her mind, even when she knows it could end her very existence."

"Yeah, I tend to not have a filter for my mouth, and sometimes I word-vomit. That's something most people tend to learn about me rather quickly," I admitted and watched as he threw his head back and laughed.

"With all due respect, Atum," I started, hoping I didn't end up a pile of ash. "Destiny and Danu have, in not so many words, told me that this is your doing. That this was the price she had to pay for interfering with me, and there isn't anything I can do about it. So, at the end of the day, this is sort of a moot conversation. One thing I know in my heart about death, and I have experienced enough of it, is that just because a body dies, doesn't mean the memory fades. You can keep someone alive until the end of time as long as you remember them. They live inside of you. They alter who you are with their presence; they become a part of you. She's my mother, but she was also my protector. In the little time I knew her, she changed me more than those I lived with every day of my life. So, respectfully, I will keep Danu alive in my memories—she *is* Faery. She's inside of everything that is Faery, and therefore, she will always be a part of me and what I will protect."

I wiped at a tear that had made its way down my cheek and swallowed against the tightness of my throat.

"You love her," he murmured; his eyes softened and he sat back and stared at me, causing me to fidget under the intensity. "You look just like her, so beautiful and full of fire. I do not believe she made her decision hastily. She saw herself when she looked into your eyes, as I do."

I wondered if Danu had gotten busy with Atum at any point in time. I could have sworn in the mythologies I had read at the Guild that he had a consort or wife or something, so I wondered if he had gotten horizontal with Danu. Atum didn't strike me as living up to the same randy reputation Zeus had. Zeus was chronicled in most every story as getting it on with just about anyone, Goddesses and humans alike. Atum's eyes smiled as if he could read my thoughts.

Oh, please don't let him be able to have heard that. Please?

"I'll pretend I didn't hear your thoughts, child," he teased, and the crowd laughed.

Well. Shit.

"You were given several warnings about meddling with the humans, and yet you persisted. I need to know that if you walk out of here, you will not interfere with their affairs again. The next life that will be taken will be one that you know and love."

"Mages came into Faery and took something from me. I simply took it back. I intended no harm or disrespect, but I won't be made to look weak, and neither would you. They weren't human either; they were creatures of both races, ones who intend to do harm to the Fae, and the humans are just collateral damage for them."

"There are rules, ones you must adhere to. I need your word that you understand me. Destiny has informed me of your plans for a new Guild on Tèrra and while I cannot give permission, I cannot say no either. It is my duty to warn you that should you follow this course, your every step and move will be monitored. Tread carefully, and make sure that if you give an order, it must be received with free will. You cannot demand they do it, or force the outcome. You order and watch. You do not participate while on that soil."

"Noted and agreed," I answered. "I intend to run it, but I do not intend to force anyone to be there, or become employed without their own free will deciding it. Unlike the Guild. I will be the one in control, but I will be in the shadows as others are the face of it."

"You smell of her," he commented offhandedly. "Out of all of my women, she was my favorite."

Oh, holy farting fairy buckets.

"Rest assured that my consort is in the room and I no longer 'caveman' it up, as you would call it. Return to your wedding, but do so with care, for I will give you no more warnings, no matter how much I cared for your mother. Go," he ordered, flicking his hand, and I was right back where I'd been.

I stared at Adam and looked down at Kahleena with a worried look as they were still frozen in time. Oh shit. What the fuck had just happened?

"Synthia," Destiny called softly from beside me. Her hands held a delicate chain with a blue crystal the size of my pinkie nail dangling from it. "When you're ready, swallow it," she said softly. "It will take root, and the rest will play out the way it was meant to be. I will be here if you have need of me. Your mother is…" Pain shot through me and a huge wind gust shook the giant trees. Faery cried, screaming in pain. I swayed on my feet as tears filled my eyes. "Gone, she's gone," Destiny cried softly, deep sadness etched in her eyes.

The necklace lit from within and I stared at it briefly before ripping the delicate chain of the necklace Ristan had created away from my neck, and replacing it with the one Destiny had given me. My hand wrapped, around it and I closed my eyes as I said a prayer that everything would work out.

"Marry him, Synthia. He's waited this long for you. Your mother approved; she created the perfect mate for him with her own essence. Be blessed and, again, if you need me, all you have to do is whisper my name on the wind," she said and then vanished.

"What the fuck just happened?" Adam demanded, his tricolored green eyes looked at me as if he was hallucinating. "The land is crying," he mumbled, feeling what every living thing inside Faery was.

"Danu is dead," I murmured, slipping my arm through his as I straightened my spine and looked at Kahleena, who couldn't understand what she felt. "Stand up straight, daughter mine."

"Momma," she whispered sadly, and I wondered if even the innocent of the land understood the severity of what had just happened. "Momma," she whimpered as she rushed to me and grasped the folds of my dress, burying her face into the soft fabric. I bent down, picking her up, and hefted her onto my hip.

"We will be okay, Kahleena, no matter where we are," I whispered.

I nodded to Adam, who started towards the willow limbs that blocked the others from seeing us. Adam nodded to a woman who gave us a wary look, and she wiped at her eyes as she started the music.

All of Me by John Legend played, and I smiled. I'd forced Ryder to choose a song; it had been the only thing he'd been asked to do. The limbs of the willow moved and I stared at my King. He was dressed in his armor, which was traditional for the Horde.

This entire wedding I had asked to be a tribute to his people, and they'd been allowed in to watch it. My eyes drifted to the side of the aisle that I'd assumed would be empty, but it wasn't. Madisyn was there, my father, and my entire family of Blood Fae. Alden was beside them, along with Lucian and his men. Adrian nodded and mouthed 'wow' which caused a growl from the end of the aisle. I smiled through the tears and blew him a kiss, even though it forced me to bend closer to my palm since Adam had my arm.

I leaned down to let Kahleena go as she was handed a basket, and I smiled as she grinned mischievously and threw a handful at me before she took her place in front of me. The little imp. My eyes lifted from her bouncing curls to the matching gold eyes and I was a goner.

I started to move towards Ryder, which caught Adam off guard, as he'd been waiting for a cue. I didn't wait for him, because right now I was marrying my man, and I was doing it before anything else could happen.

I released Adam's arm and sifted, slamming against Ryder with a smile as I reached up and pulled his mouth to mine.

"I fucking do," I whispered.

Laughter erupted from the rows of people.

"You skipped the vows," the High Priest admonished with a wry smirk.

I smiled against Ryder's mouth and laughed as he lifted me up and fisted my hair, growling as his lips found mine in a soul-crushing kiss. Coughing erupted behind us and I pulled away and smiled at him, but his eyes searched mine. He knew she was dead, he'd felt it. They all had.

"I'm so sorry, Pet," he whispered.

"It's okay, I know how to fix it," I replied as I pulled away and slid down his body. "Let's get hitched, Fairy. Quickly, before something else happens."

"Hurry," he said as he turned to the High Priest. It took ten minutes for us to get through repeating our vows, and five to get away from the crowds of onlookers. I changed for the party and smiled when I realized he wasn't changing.

"Armor?" I asked. "How are you planning on dancing with me?"

"I may need this armor to protect my feet from your clumsy dancing, Witch," he teased.

"We're married," I mused as I chewed my lip. "Fuck me, Fairy. The first time I met you, I was pretty sure I was going to kill you."

"And I was pretty sure I was going to fuck you," he laughed. "I had never wanted anything so bad in my entire life. I wanted to fuck you until you begged me to stop, and then I intended to bend you over and keep going until the only thing you knew how to say was my name as you screamed it to the Gods."

"You and that mouth, Fairy," I grinned. "You better hold that thought and save that shit for the honeymoon."

"You think we should still go?" he asked. His hands pulled me close and he wrapped his arms around me.

"I think we should go more than ever. There's always going to be something trying to kill us, and that's okay. We will face whatever comes at us together.

We can't live in fear anymore. It almost destroyed us. So yes, we're going on the damn honeymoon, and there will be beaches and we will be naked on them. I plan to ride that cock in all sorts of different positions, and do really bad things to you."

"Fuck the party. Let's go, Pet; let's go now."

"No way," I laughed. "I want to see our children before we go. I've missed them so much."

"Fine, we'll go see them and then we sneak out."

Chapter
THIRTY~FOUR

I'd thought we were going to skip the human traditions at the reception, but it wasn't to be. There was the obligatory cake cutting and I was able to swipe a bit of frosting on Ryder's face before he painted a smear on my lips and then licked it off. Although he wasn't used to public speaking that had nothing to do with battle or training for battle, Zahruk did his very best to do the toast before Ristan interrupted and took the toast down a far raunchier path. Adam glamoured a bouquet for me to throw, and Darynda caught it, then anxiously asked Adrian what she was supposed to do with it.

Then came the dance of the father and bride. I danced awkwardly with my father to Rascal Flatts *My Wish* as he'd told me that he was glad Faolán was dead and couldn't touch us anymore. He'd explained that, while they had needed space after his death, having the babies there had helped them to heal and see the reason why it had to happen.

Alden had danced with me next, and the old man could cut a rug for his age, which he assured me wasn't as old as I had always made him out to be. I'd danced with my brothers, and laughed at their expense with the women who had come with them. Even Liam had asked me to dance.

Adrian took a turn with me as well, and when I danced with him, Ryder managed not to pull his spine out through his mouth as he'd threatened to do many times before.

"You look so beautiful tonight," Adrian commented as he watched me. "I think it has little to do with the outfit, and everything to do with that smile in your eyes. I almost hate you because you're so fucking happy without me."

"I was happy with you at one time, but we were kids," I replied gently as I wrapped my arms around his neck and smiled as we danced. "That kind of love, it wouldn't have lasted. We weren't in love as much as we loved the idea of being in love."

"I know I loved you," he affirmed. "I still love you, and I will always love you. You will always love him, though, and it's okay. I'm happy because you're happy. Plus, you guys make really cute kids. You'll have others, eventually."

"You knew I was pregnant." All of his and Vlad's worried looks made sense now. His turquoise eyes roamed around the room before finally returning to mine.

"I heard the heartbeat, but you didn't seem to know. It wasn't the time to bring it up. We were in the field, and I knew you'd ignore it no matter what I said. Besides, I don't think it would have lived much longer. The heartbeat was slow, weak. Probably because its mother was exhausted and had no idea it needed her to rest. It wasn't your fault; sometimes, these things just happen."

"They took it from me, for interfering in the human world." I replied as I watched him frown with the news. "I didn't know I was pregnant, but I killed an Enforcer, and it didn't matter that he was really a Mage. I'm winging this Goddess shit, and I didn't understand what they meant when they said a sacrifice was going to be demanded of me if I didn't stop interfering with human affairs. So, lesson learned. I can give orders there, but I can't be an active participant or they will demand another sacrifice. I know I'm going to need a lot of help running the new Guild, and I have to find people that will man it and follow my orders without feeling like they are being forced or coerced."

"Talking war at your own wedding?" Adam interrupted as he cut in and twirled me around. "Tsk, what are we going to do with you?"

"Love me," I smirked. "You're coming with me to the Guild when we start recruiting, right?" I asked and Adam frowned.

"Keir is sending me to the Dark Towers because it's time I find my missing bride," he said with a pained look. ""I'm supposed to divide my time between there and the stewardship of the Light Kingdom, but I'll still be close to you. If you need me, you can tell him that I have to put aside my duties to serve the newly-crowned Queen of the Horde."

I looked over to where Keir was speaking with Ryder, whose eyes searched for me on the dance floor. I was about to move towards him when the sound of giggling caught my attention.

I turned, finding the men with the babies, playing what looked like leapfrog over each other as the women around them ogled them.

"Excuse me; I think my little beasties are being used to catch pussy," I groaned as I moved towards the men, finding Sinjinn watching me as I approached.

"You look stunning, sister," he remarked. "Hardly the time to get married when our flesh and blood sister is missing, wouldn't you agree, Synthia?"

I was taken aback at his words, and shook my head in denial. Sinjinn was one of those people who could be a lot of fun, but you never knew when they were teasing or serious. "Ciara is handling her situation. There's always a threat hanging over our heads. Should we stop life every time it happens? Do you think we'd be living if we stopped to deal with every threat that comes to our door?"

He swallowed and I felt the electrical hum of Ryder as he stood at my back. He didn't say anything, nor did the others. He was quietly supporting me, he just wasn't taking control.

"I heard you ripped the throat out of the leader of the Sluagh?" Sinjinn asked after he'd considered my words.

"Indeed; I've been told that to lead the Horde you have to become them, but that is neither here nor there. We will get Ciara back; she asked for me to leave her there. There is something she wants to do and I have to give her that chance. She's earned it. If she isn't home soon, I will bring her back. She asked me to trust her, and that's what family does. They have your back, but they also trust you. Ciara isn't weak; she's the Princess of the Horde. I'm sure if she is in danger, more throats will be torn apart. Give her a chance; she just might surprise you."

"I believe this dance is mine, Pet," Ryder

interrupted as he slipped his fingers through mine and pulled me out onto the dance floor as the others looked on. Ed Sheeran's *Thinking Out Loud* started to play. "You have exactly one last song and one last dance before I rip this dress off of you and take you in front of everyone here."

"One song?" I smirked.

"One, because the moment I saw you at the other end of the aisle, I've wanted to do nothing else besides rip this dress off and slide into you slowly."

"Slowly?" I asked softly, my eyes locked on his lips as he moved us around the floor. "That's a new one," I whispered. "I don't think you can take me slowly."

"Is that a challenge?" he teased, his reverent gaze warmed me as he moved us—and by move us, I mean my feet were on his, and he effortlessly danced without missing a step.

"You bet your ass it is." I laughed, and then we were gone.

I was tossed on a bed; the gentle sound of the waves lapping the shore made me sit up and look around the moonlit beach that the gigantic bed was situated on. Not quite the idea I had in mind to begin our honeymoon, but I liked it.

"We didn't even say goodbye," I quipped.

"You challenged me; you should know by now that I take challenges seriously."

"Did I challenge you?" I gave him a wicked smile. "I don't recall it happening like that." I giggled as he shook his head. His eyes sparkled with a million stars trapped in their amber depths.

"Slowly was the challenge? I can make you beg for me, working this body…slowly, for hours."

"Shit," I smiled. "I fear I'm going to like this as much as you, Fairy."

"Doubt it," he growled as he leaned over and claimed my lips.

Chapter
THIRTY~FIVE

I smiled at him, feeling shy, which didn't make sense considering I'd watched him strip naked a million times before. I watched as he removed each piece of armor slowly. I was certain he did it for show, but I wanted him now. That beautiful masculine body undid me; it made me feel like every time was the first time. This beast, this mythical creature who I loved, undid me. This man was my life. Somewhere in the midst of fighting him, I'd fallen in love with him so deeply that I no longer cared if there was a bottom to the depths for which I fell for him.

"You're so beautiful," he growled, and tears filled my eyes. "What's wrong?" he hesitated, sensing my unease.

"I love you," I whispered through the tightening of my throat. "I love you so much that I bit into a nasty, smelly neck and killed a bunch of creatures just to get you back."

"And that scares you?" he guessed.

"No; I'd do it again in a heartbeat. I'd even drink his icky blood for you," I winced as I repeated it inside my head.

"Then why the tears?" he asked.

"Because I love you," I whispered and leaned back against the pillows and looked at him sadly. "You are my world, Ryder. I wanted to kill you and now...now I can't imagine a world where you don't exist." His eyes lit from within. "I thought I lost you and I wanted to destroy everything to get you back. That scares me, because I imagine if I had to, I would have. I don't think I could have stopped myself, had I wanted to."

"You did what you had to do," he said softly, with no blame or chastisement in his tone. "You are fierce, and I couldn't imagine a world without you in it either. I'm not sure how I did it before I met you. I don't even want to remember who I was before you. My world was black and white, and then you entered it with those fierce blue eyes that challenged me at every turn, and added color to my world. You are my weakness, but you're also my greatest strength." He glanced down and he spread my legs and shifted to sit between them.

He smiled as he took me in, still dressed in my elegant wedding reception attire. I smiled as he pulled me up, forcing me into a sitting position. His mouth lowered, kissing my neck before he stood up and brought me with him. He slowly turned my body until my back was against his chest. His arms wrapped around me, one hand finding my waist as the other slowly explored the curve of my neck. His mouth fanned the back of my shoulder, kissing it gently as he pushed the straps down until my shoulder was naked for his leisurely exploration.

Shivers raced down my spine as the heat of his

mouth collided with the chilled evening air. His tongue touched me, but it was his lips that drove me to the brink of crazed anticipation. The dress slowly slid down and pooled at my feet. He slowly moved around me and stood back, looking at the skimpy, almost diaphanous panties and thin, delicate chains with the tiny bells that chimed as I moved.

"Ristan's gift to you," I explained, once again feeling shy when I knew I shouldn't. I couldn't help it; he made me nervous. His eyes leisurely exploring my exposed curves made me nervous. He went to his knees and did the last thing I expected. He kissed my tummy, and looked up at me with a look of concern.

"We will have more. When you are ready, we can have as many as you want to," he whispered before he continued kissing my belly as my hands rested in his hair.

"I know I lost it, but it's like it was taken from us before it was ours, if that makes sense," I replied thickly, fighting off the unshed tears that threatened to fall.

"I know, but we did," he whispered as he stood up and looked down at me.

"We can't have another baby with the Mages out there," I replied, wondering if I could ever do it again. Having a child wasn't planned, but we had three already. They were beautiful and growing faster than we could predict.

"So, we will wait until we eliminate them," he announced.

"Okay," I agreed.

"I mean, next week should be open for creating our next batch of children, considering my bloodthirsty vixen just goes around ripping out throats and severing knees from giants. Sound good to you?" he asked, sounding more human than ever before.

"You ass," I laughed. "Never going to live that one down, am I?"

"Never; a woman who would rip throats out and take down members of the Horde like they were mere children, is a keeper," he said. "My men couldn't stop telling me about what you did in my absence; I was almost afraid they'd ask me to crown *you* King," he laughed playfully, backing me up as he smiled down at me. "When I met you, I knew you were something special," he admitted. "I couldn't have ever guessed that you'd be what you have become. I don't think Destiny played a huge part in bringing me to you, or you to me. I think we were fated in the stars and that no matter what road we took, they would have brought us together."

"Look at you, being all sweet and shit," I laughed.

"Now get the fuck on the bed, I have to prove you wrong," he ordered and pushed me over, catching me off guard.

I landed on the bed and smiled as I felt the thin scrap of fabric disappear with a brief, happy chiming sound. He leaned over my naked body, trapping my chin with his fingers as his mouth descended on mine. He didn't rush the kiss; instead he let the heat of his mouth comfort me as he nudged my legs apart, and his tongue delved deeper, claiming mine in a gentle kiss.

I moaned as I felt his cock against my flesh,

rubbing against it as he moved his hips in the same seductive dance that his tongue was playing in my mouth. I felt his magic as it washed over me, sending a thousand kisses over my exposed skin. I wanted to demand that he enter me. Now. No more waiting; instead, he teased, slowly forcing me to rock against his massive cock for friction.

Each time my body came close to release; he would pull away; only to start again once the edge was pushed away from me. He nipped my lip, pulling it with his teeth and releasing it each time he pulled away from me.

"Slow and easy, Pet," he warned, and I growled deep in my chest. He slowly lowered his mouth to one breast, suckling it and letting his teeth graze the delicate flesh before he moved to the next one to do the same.

"Ryder, are you trying to kill me?" I asked, only to be answered with a laugh against my tummy as he slowly kissed his way to my heated core. His mouth hovered momentarily, but didn't touch me where I needed him. Instead, he traced the inside of my thighs with his fingertips, letting his mouth follow their lead. I was wet, so fucking wet—dripping with need.

"I'm making love to you," he whispered huskily, his eyes glowing with naked hunger as his brands pulsed, and his wings exploded from his back. Ethereal beauty, terrifyingly so, and yet I wasn't afraid of any of his forms. I loved them all because I accepted everything he was, and even everything he wasn't. This man was my best friend. He was my other half, even the bad stuff.

Fingers slid through my apex, finding it wet with

desire. He moved closer, letting his hot breath fan it until I was writhing against the silk sheets with need as perspiration beaded on the base of my spine.

His mouth inched closer until his tongue darted out, slowly working it from the back to the front, pushing into the heated depths of my pussy until I was crying out for more. Fingers pushed inside, crooking in a come here motion as he found the spot and worked it until I was begging him to finish it. Tears rolled from my eyes as I exploded into a million tiny pieces.

He moved up until he was looking down at me, kissing away the salty tears with his lips before he claimed my mouth as he finally entered me.

"I am discovering that slow may not be something I'm capable of," he mused as he leaned back, spreading my legs to give him better depth. He rocked his hips and I lifted to meet his every thrust. I exploded around him, milking his cock with every orgasm that tore through me. "I take it you don't mind?" He rolled us until I was on top of him.

"Not at all, Fairy," I giggled, filled with the euphoria only he could give me. I rocked my hips in a circular pattern, adjusting to him as he grew until I had all that I could take.

He surprising me as he lifted me, uncaring that we rocked the little island we were on. The candles flickered; the gentle wind that caressed our bodies did little to cool my ardor. He smiled and I found myself slammed against the bed my legs were held apart and he had full control. I let my head fall back against the pillows, and watched the stars as they shot across the sky as he hammered into my body with a determined need that floored me.

"Hecate's daughters," he murmured breathlessly. "They tried to seduce me, they drove me to the brink of release, but I never let them have me. They wanted a child from me," he admitted and I lifted my head. The noises leaving me were too much; I couldn't speak, couldn't think past anything other than the rage that shot through me. I should have killed them, slit their fucking throats. Instead, I'd let them leave. "My child would have created a line they wanted, but my children are yours. Only yours. I withstood their spells, their antics, and even their mirror image of you. They pretended to be you, but I knew it wasn't you, just as I knew when that Enforcer came in the room; I could feel you, somehow you were there, I could sense you looking at me through his eyes. I sensed you, my Queen. I sense you every time you are near, because I am inside of you and you are inside of me. There's no one else I want, not now, not ever. It's only you, it's always been you," he murmured as he exploded inside of me. "You are my Queen."

"And you are my King, forever," I whispered as my body climaxed, and I dropped my head to his shoulder. I nipped his flesh. "I should have killed those Witches."

"No, you did the right thing. We will need them; we will need all the help we can get."

"I know, that's why I let them live. But I didn't know then what I know now. I will kill them; you are mine."

"You won't, because they can bring Larissa back from the void."

"What?" I said, pulling my head from his shoulder.

"I heard them talking; they can bring souls back

and place them into vessels. I had planned to escape and bring them here. I had hoped to find a vessel for them to bring Larissa's soul back."

"We have to tell Adam," I whispered.

"No, not until we know if it is true."

"He loves her," I murmured.

"That won't change from now until then; a love like that doesn't die. It is why he is having a difficult time moving on."

"Opening the void is dangerous," I mused. "She used everything she had to help us. When we said goodbye, she said something about being reborn. How could we ever be certain it was Larissa we are bringing back?"

"Because you'll know her; she was your best friend."

"But what if she doesn't want to come back?" I pressed, a thousand different questions entering my mind.

"It's Larissa; I listen to everything you tell me, and from what you told me about her, she wanted to have her own happy ending. She was obsessed with it; shit, if anyone deserves to be saved, to be happy, it's her."

"Hannah told me that Larissa was of her line. If any of them would be happy to help us, it would be Hannah. But what about the Light Heir? Adam is supposed to find and marry the Light Heir." My voice trailed off sadly. It would kill Adam if he had to marry the Light Heir if he even had a remote chance to have the woman he considered his soul mate back.

"If the Gods could find a way to join us, with all the obstacles we faced, who are we to say that fate or destiny won't find a way for them as well?" Ryder pulled me close and kissed the top of my head.

"Fairy, as much as I want her back, I really want to forget, for at least for a little while, all the problems that are piling up. Just me and you. No wars at the gates, no one trying to kill us, just us acting like two teenagers who discovered that sex is fucking delicious. So bend me over and make me scream."

"That is one thing I can do, wife." He flashed a blinding grin as he rolled the word wife around on his tongue.

"Mate—I am your mate. Wife sounds domesticated and shit."

"And here my brothers said to call you wife to make sure you knew you were mine," he laughed. "They have you all wrong."

"Of course they do, because only one of them *really* knows me," I admitted as I smiled at him.

"Inside and out, Witch."

"Inside and out, Fairy."

Chapter
THIRTY~SIX

Ryder's arms were wrapped around me, holding me against him as we watched the waves rush back out to sea. The crystal blue water rushed back in, hitting us and rocking our bodies as we braced ourselves against the tide. It was calming, the chaos of the ocean that surrounded us. The gentle breeze ruffled my hair, and I let out a happy sigh of contentment as I held on to the man I loved.

We didn't need words to tell each other our thoughts; somehow, even without the mental connection we'd lost, we knew what each other was thinking without needing words. I felt his turmoil at the impending war, as he felt my turmoil over the loss of Danu, but neither of us spoke.

After some time had passed, I pulled away from him and looked into his golden eyes.

"We need to talk," I whispered, knowing I had to tell him something about what I was doing, even though I couldn't tell him everything.

"I know," he admitted, and I tensed, unsure of what he had to tell me. He sifted us to the sandy white beach and glamoured us into bathing suits; mine was a tiny white bikini that left little to the imagination, while he wore black Bermuda shorts, which made me smirk. Seeing Ryder in them was something to behold, but his cock was already pressing against them as he took in the suit I wore.

"You first," I said, wondering what he had to say.

"I don't want you fighting in the war with the Mages," he admitted. I started to argue, but he held up his hand. "I know you will be there, and I know we need you. It doesn't change the fact that it scares me. I know you can fight, and I know of no other warrior Goddess who can handle herself as well as you can, but we have to consider our children."

"They are children," I whispered, taken aback by what he was saying. "That would make them a target for our enemies."

"Yes, which is why one of us needs to stay behind the castle walls with them when the war comes," he whispered against my ear.

"I'm a Goddess; I am needed on the field."

"I know that too," he laughed. "And I'm the King of the Horde, and you and I know that the Horde King can die only at the hands of the Heir of the Horde. I am expected to be on the field. It has to be you or I who stays behind to protect them, unless we can appoint someone guardian of the children, as the humans do, to watch over them in our absence."

"This sucks," I whispered as I chewed on my lip.

"What did you want to talk to me about?" he asked and I paused, wondering if and what I should tell him.

I waved one hand over the other and the necklace Destiny gave me materialized in my hand. The little blue crystal dangling from the chain seemed to glow a little.

"You found a crystal?"

I laughed nervously as I lifted my eyes to hold his. "I found a cure for Faery."

"How can one little bauble be the cure for anything?" he teased, and I frowned.

"I can't tell you everything. I don't even know all of it, or if it will work. What I do know is that Danu thought it would work. Though, she also said I would have to do a few things before it would work as Destiny foretold it. Hannah, the Witch we found under the Guild, whispered in my ear before she left and told me to trust that Danu and Destiny knew what they were doing. She told me that before I entered the Guild to save you. She knew what would happen before it did. So tell me, Ryder, do I go with what could set this world on a path to healing, do I take the leap and trust that they are correct, or do I wait to see if the stars align and then try it?"

"I don't know what you are trying," he whispered, swallowing hard as he watched me.

"I will tell you what I can, but I can't tell you everything."

"Will it affect us?" he asked.

"Absolutely," I murmured as I looked up at him. "Not in a bad way, but it will change our lives. If I don't, Faery will continue to weaken until it is nothing but an extension of earth. If I do, Faery could start to heal itself at a rapid pace, like how I heal." I pulled my hair to the side and clasped the necklace around my neck.

"If it can fix Faery." He watched me as I closed the distance between us and stood on my tiptoes as he leaned down to meet me. My voice barely carried to his ears and my hands trembled as I whispered part of my secrets to him, feeling him tense as I told him what I intended to do. Once I finished, I pulled away and stepped back, giving him room to absorb what I'd told him.

"Gods," he muttered, staring at me. His hands trembled, and I smiled.

"The Gods have nothing to do with this," I replied coldly.

"Synthia," he exhaled as he shook his head watching me.

"Bilé is out there. He was freed when my mother died. He has already found his way back to the Mages and is leading them here. I'm done losing. It's time we stopped waiting around for them to find us. No more waiting for them to come to our gates. It's time we went out to find them. I may not be able to fight them outside of Faery, but that doesn't mean we can't take the fight to them. Just because I cannot fight them outside of this world doesn't mean I will sit around on my hands while you do it. I am Synthia, Daughter of Danu, Goddess of Faery, and the Queen of the Horde. I am a queen by choice *and* birthright. I am not a sit-around-and-wait kind of girl either. It's time we bring the war to them. I say we level the playing field and use their tactics on them. Danu told me to look for loopholes in the rules that the Gods made so that they can't intervene. We find them and we use them. We take back our world and make them tremble in fear of our names. We are the King and Queen of the Horde, and I am ready to hunt."

"That's my girl," he said proudly as he smiled and pulled me to him. "Let's sound the war horns. My Queen wishes to hunt."

"We will ride together and take back what is ours."

"And this?" he asked, touching the crystal.

"We'll wait until the war has been won and we are ready for it."

"I love you, Witch."

"And I love you, Fairy. Now, let's go make some noise, shall we?" I asked, as a smile played on my lips.

The End, For Now

ABOUT

the Author

Amelia lives in the great Pacific Northwest with her family. When she isn't drinking too much coffee, or indulging in a paranormal romance book, she can be found hanging out in her fan group on Facebook, with her amazingly tightknit fans. She loves everything Paranormal, except horror, because she's a wuss when it comes to that type of things. For all new updates, please join the group below and come hang out with her, and others who love hanging out and talking everything books!

Facebook Page: https://www.facebook.com/authorameliahutchins

Website: http://amelia-hutchins.com

Fan group: https://goo.gl/BqpCVK

85567584R00213